MONCADA

A Cuban Story

Paul Webster Hare

iUniverse, Inc.
New York Bloomington

MONCADA
A Cuban Story

iUniverse books may be ordered through booksellers or by contacting:

iUniverse

1663 Liberty Drive

Bloomington, IN 47403

www.iuniverse.com

1-800-Authors (1-800-288-4677)

ISBN: 978-1-4502-0366-1 (sc)

ISBN: 978-1-4502-0364-7 (dj)

ISBN: 978-1-4502-0365-4 (ebk)

Printed in the United States of America

iUniverse rev. date: 4/19/2010

To my parents, Maurice and Dorothy Hare, my wife, Lynda, and our six children, Antonia, Victoria, Andrew, Matthew, Alexander, and Marina, all of whom have treasured memories of their time in Cuba

Acknowledgments

I would like to acknowledge the encouragement and assistance of family and friends, the camaraderie of the Brookings Institution Cuba group, and the gracious permission of Carlos Varela to quote the titles of some of his inspiring songs and his "pequeños sueños."

CHAPTER 1

Tuesday July 20

FELIPE

Moncada will mean nothing to you. That is, unless you're Cuban, and if you're on our island I know you won't be reading this story. So I should explain to the rest of you that Moncada is one of the first words I learned. It was not like the words "Mama" or "Papa," which I could say from the start. When I say learned, I mean I was taught to say the word "Moncada." I was told that Moncada was not just for me but for everyone. That is maybe why I feel uncomfortable when I write "I." It's not I or me that Moncada has to be learned for. You see that compañero Humberto taught me well.

But no one in Cuba will care now about my schooling. This story? Well, maybe. I should explain that I have written only part of it. Like Moncada, the story is not supposed to be about me. There are, I know, too many "I"s in it, and my Cuban friends have added more. They wanted to write so you might understand a little of the story of Cuba and Moncada. It is only about one week in our lives, but we all wanted to tell it. It is about us and our home.

Mateo—who has written some of this as well—asked me to include everything. So I am starting with the mundane. I assumed it would always be that way. It's slow for most stories to start with pieces of ordinary life, but that is the truth. It is what I did for years before the days around Moncada that year, before somehow things began to move more quickly. I should say that July is Moncada time, when all Cubans have to celebrate, and we were never to forget the actions of all who took part in 1953.

It was not every day that I went to the *agromercado*, but that was not because it was hard to get there. It was not one of those interminable Havana journeys. I had plenty of time to stroll over from work. But the prices at the *agro* were really beyond what I liked to pay. Mama was afraid whenever I said I was going to shop there, so I never told her. "Felipe, it's dangerous for you to go over there; you know that these markets are not for people like us." But I went anyway, just to give myself a choice. I liked to plan what I would buy, but you never knew what the market would have. The fruit and vegetables moved quickly even though the prices were high, because money always materialized for the right guava. The stall owners had their favorite customers, and so they held their stuff back. Some of the private restaurant owners with their tourist currencies came early just in case the red peppers had arrived. The music also annoyed me at the agromercado—all they ever played was rap or hip-hop. It was something that took away Cuba and made the world seem closer.

The steps leading to the market were littered with cigarette butts and the debris from a day of Cuban feet looking to buy. In fact that's not true, because many of them just came to look and to see what was left on the ground. I don't know who ever swept it. Armando said he gave a peso to one of the muchachos from the barrio every week to give it a brush. But I didn't believe him. Dogs ran across the shafts of sharp sunlight. One was barking at the owner of the first stall where you could buy used plastic bags for one peso each. The dog had chewed one and was looking for the next. Flowers were droopily nodding to the earth. Armando's was one stall I always looked for. Armando used to be a doctor, a physician who specialized in blood diseases at the institute near where I worked.

"Armando, how can you see that pig's blood and not think you should be using a microscope, not an axe?"

"Felipe, I'm old enough to know that microscopes don't fill bellies in this country. And by the way, I've got just the pork belly for you and your mama." But today I saw that his cut meat was all gone. He had some bony legs hung up behind him and was down to his last three yuccas. Armando was offering them with a few brown limes. Yes, I really remember those details, because you see I am a scientist. Rotting vegetables were thrown onto the floor by the better off. Others who knew their means were busy going through the piles of soft yucca. The flies were startled as someone pulled out an edible piece to carry away.

Bobby, an old black man with no teeth, squatted on a stool with his gray weasel-like dog, George, slumped at his feet. Bobby's boxing hero was George Foreman, but the dog's ribs protruded as George's never did. The man dropped his cigar ash on it without seeing. A kitten skulked around cautiously sniffing some rotting meat.

Bobby had plenty to say. "There's some good mutton that just arrived. Don't buy Armando's pig. Even by his standards, it stinks. That porker, boy, served at the bahía—get my joke, hombre?—you know, pigs, as the Yanquis say."

It was the twentieth of July, and that was always the end of our CUCs for the month. We have lots of coins and notes in Cuba, but the CUC notes are the ones that matter; certainly the ones that matter at the agromercado. I carried my bag of yucca, rice, and pork back to the CBM where I worked. That's the Molecular Biology Center, a part of the "polo" center of Cuban biotechnology in Havana.

The real reason I went to the market was because it was Tuesday and I knew I could get a lift home on Yoel's bike. Yoel delivered bread to the CBM; you know, the free stuff we all got from the government. It had been like that for at least a couple of years now. Yoel, the kid from our block in Cerro, loved to ride that bike. He said he could use the van, but that wasn't cool. Filling the sidecar of the bike with bread was cool, and that was what made delivering worthwhile.

It was 4:30, and Yoel would be around, so I went to pick up the stuff I'd bought in the market from the fridge in the cryogenics lab. I waited in the parking lot where the drivers with nothing to do were washing the official Ladas. The rest were chatting and smoking under a *palma real*. I remember that the director, Carlitos, had just got a new blue Peugeot that week. It had been a day like 1,565 others since I had gone to work there, and the grass outside still needed cutting. Yoel came out of the lobby, brushing his long hair out of his eyes, with a quick step and a clipboard like one of those bicycle courier riders I had seen in the movies in New York City.

"You're the only one in Havana who's in a hurry, amigo," I said.

"Not true, Felipe. Just you tell them they've got eggs at the bodega. I'd have been trampled in the rush."

The sidecar of the bike was never empty. The bike wasn't Yoel's; it "belonged" to Mauricio of the bakery in Marianao. Yoel had already picked up four others, and the sidecar was groaning under their weight.

"We have a great evening planned," said Yoel.

"Oh, yeah? So what's planned?" I asked, forgetting his old joke.

"Exactly nothing, amigo. That's the point. Havana's always best when you don't arrange anything. Before that we have a little business to attend to. I've got to stop by Margarita's to drop off this sandwich. And there are some new pens that just arrived from that tourist clinic in Siboney and new shampoo for Mirta."

Yoel climbed on the bike and revved up the engine. He started chatting to his passengers. "Okay, Fernando, how many fillings is this ride worth? My dad's been offered liposuction by a doctor whose car he fixed," said Yoel, turning to the dentist crouching in the sidecar.

Fernando, the dentist, looked gloomy. "It's been a bad day." Everyone knew not to ask why, because that would have been the end of any conversation. Yoel, his eyes darting to the front and the sidecar, his hair tied back for the ride, made the stops in the same order he had done for months. Fernando was taken to a bar where I guess he found someone who would listen; Hugo, the carpenter, to his game of dominoes. Zilda was taken back home to her aunt's or niece's or grandmother's; whatever she called them. "How many times did she say 'mi amor' today?" I asked Yoel when she had left us in Marianao.

"Sixteen. Is that a record?"

My backpack contained my vegetables, rice, and pork, my plastic lunch box, and several pieces of bread I had taken from colleagues at the CBM in return for a few old pesos, the notes I was paid in and I pretended were money.

Yoel parked the bike down the alleyway behind Calle Jalisco. He left the key under the stone, and Mauricio would pick it up in half an hour. It was protected by a wooden gate with chains and two large dogs kept by our neighbor. The bike hadn't been stolen for over three months, but I put that down to Mama sitting at the window most of the day where she could see the wooden gate. She didn't miss anything, and I think most people knew that. Yoel kissed the saddle and headed off. His kids were calling for him down Jalisco.

I walked up the stairs. Doctor Águila on the first floor was polishing an old brass plate that showed him as an MD cum laude from the University of Havana. He had qualified at Havana University Medical School in 1956 but now spent his time fixing video recorders and TVs. "Hey, Doctor Águila. How's the reconstructive surgery?"

Águila knew the joke. "I had the latest Nintendo in yesterday. Took me twenty minutes, Felipe. They can't fool me, these Orientals. How's your love life, young man?"

"When I know half as much as you do about that, Doctor, I'll figure it out."

As usual Mama was sitting at the window. As usual her face lit up and she greeted me with a kiss.

"Mi amor, just wait until I tell you what happened to me. You'll never believe it. But what's new? How much bread did you get today? I know Rafa was disappointed yesterday. That boy could eat two loaves a day. Just like you were, Felipito." It had been a good day for bread but not exceptional.

"I think Rafa will be okay with it. He might even give some to Tico." Rafa and Tico are my brothers. Rafa is my real brother. Ernesto is much younger and is called Quartico, or Tico, because he was only something like a quarter brother.

So there you have the family and Jalisco, our home. The television programming hadn't started, but the box was turned on, making it the usual center of attention. Celia, our *mestizo*, looked up and whined expectantly as she sensed that bread might be appearing. Mama was just about to tell me about her day when Pepe, my uncle, his vest hanging loosely over his jeans, got up from lounging on the bench by the wall. Pepe's muscles were well covered, but his arms were as wide as his smile. He shoved the beer crate back under the bench where it served as the fourth leg. The shaking of his body threw beads of sweat to the floor. "Hey, Felipe, What's up?"

"Night shift again, huh?" I said to Pepe. "Does that mean you don't have the police bike now?"

"Afraid not, but I guess when I sign in they'll produce one. They've found this Russian guy here who stayed on and knows how to mend those old clutches. He's a genius if you ask me. Anyway, compared to the events of the rest of the day, that's no big deal. Donna's gone back to her mother in Sancti Spíritus. Took Luis too. So I guess I don't have a wife any longer," said Pepe. Then another thought seemed to make him really concerned. "Don't know what I'll do about my tattoo now. Cost me forty CUCs; my two loves, Donna and Harley D, together."

"The tattoo may be a problem, Pepe, but she'll come back, just like she did in May," I said hopefully. I knew this meant another family row.

Pepe seemed more serious than usual. "Donna's losing it, Felipe. I think she misses that girlfriend who's gone off to Mexico. Did a teaching conference visit or something. Isn't that what your outfit at CBM is up to? Anyway, Donna talks no sense anymore. The next thing she'll claim is that there was another woman."

"More like plenty of other women, if you ask me," I said, not caring if Pepe heard. I went inside to find the sitting areas of the apartment empty.

Once I was home Mama would take a nap. It was always like that. I asked her what was unbelievable about her day. She said she saw a dog give birth in the street to six puppies. It was a nice event because it took a long time and attracted a crowd. "My life gives me so much just sitting here," she said.

I was never sure what Cuba gave me. I'm sorry, I mean the Revolution. I know what I was expected to give the Revolution. But I'd long ago given up talking about it. Mama wasn't one for great philosophy. Neither was I but I've tried to put together my way of looking at life, and I like to write a bit about it. You don't want to start yawning somewhere reading this. I can understand that, because I really would like this story to be read. Thinking, of course, is free, but some thinking can get you into trouble. Because once the thoughts are there, they breathe out and so others can read you. That's what I had done, and with it came the trouble I got into. I'll come to that. It will help you understand how I felt those days before Moncada.

The Revolution is not something Cubans think about all the time. The Revolution is our life after all, and in those days it was no different for me. I don't want to sound ungrateful. But the Revolution didn't give me anything because I was part of it. It was inside me, not outside. It was part of me like my genes, like the buildings I saw from the window every day. That is the way we are, and I cannot imagine being without a revolution. Since the triumph, everything changed. I didn't see anything beyond all that. I don't mean I didn't see the rice, the sugar, or the bits of chicken. Cuba gave me a rule book, a past. It gave me a route map for my life. But there was no destination. I received my education, but it was a debt and not a gift. It created an obligation. I was trained to read and study what the Revolution did for me. I was chosen to be a biologist. I did okay at the university. It was fine, you know. Food for us all during the studies, girls, free time. I never thought that would be the best time of my life. It was supposed to get better, but no one told me that, so maybe I shouldn't have believed it. They told me they were building up biotech as the next big thing for the Revolution. I was excited by plants and animals, and my professor, called Tavarez, had written that in one experiment I had shown maturity beyond my years. Tavarez knew Carlitos. You remember Carlitos with the new Peugeot. Well, he said he would give me a chance to shine if I worked hard. I was so excited, coming to CBM as a hand-picked star.

My first day at CBM Carlitos asked me to come for a chat, "Havana is beautiful because of the Revolution. It is the best place to live in the whole world, and the only place where the people's brains are being used to the good of the Revolution. And the Comandante wants science to be used for everyone's benefit. It is an enormous privilege for you to be at the Centro. And remember, Felipe, stay out of the sun, it's not just bad for your skin." I noticed that his face was very pale for a Cuban, but I think he was giving me another message.

After a month Carlitos told me something else and made me feel special.

"Felipe, you have been chosen for your scientific skills but also for your revolutionary firmness. You will be trained to be grateful every minute for what the Revolution is giving you. You will not betray the Revolution because you have been tested."

Then Carlitos shut the door of his office, and there was a silence while he wiped his glasses. "Felipe, what happened to your father will not be held against you. There are many outstanding servants of the Revolution whose families are *gusanos*." I said nothing. I think that is what Carlitos expected. "Felipe, you will never be complete. You will need to prove yourself every day to the Revolution. It will be a lifelong learning process, and revolutionaries must be prepared every day to face down the enemy. Threats are all around us, and you can take nothing for granted. Our science is highly valued by our enemies." Carlitos examined his lenses again and opened the door.

At Jalisco it was now just my normal routine. I knew my bed, or the bed I shared with Rafa, would be free for thirty minutes. The night before Rafa had one nightmare after another. I guess I got barely an hour's sleep. This was my chance to have the good side of the mattress. I laid my yucca, pork, and supplies in the corner of the room where Pepe had tried to create a kitchen. The coffee was permanently on the stove bubbling its thick aroma. The fridge door was staying shut because Rafa had put pieces of old gum on the top and bottom. It was only the second day since Pepe had gotten the damn thing fixed, so the pork would still be fresh tomorrow. There was a Moncada sticker taped to the outside of the fridge. "Moncada Siempre Con Nosotros," it said. I asked Mama why she wanted it. She said she liked the colors and the breaking waves over the Malecón.

I had twenty-five minutes left, but the wind meant there was one more job to attend to. The shutters of the bedroom window creaked back and forth from the breeze, but I found an old *Granma* newspaper to jam in them. Good old *Granma*. It would let me sleep. Now it was quiet and I sprawled on the side of the mattress that Rafa usually took. It had fewer springs that had burst through—it was three against five in my side. I picked up a pen thinking it was new, but it hadn't worked for weeks. Why on earth do we keep these bits of empty plastic?

The silence lasted a couple of minutes. It was the afternoon of July 20, and Havana was hot. It was the time for rain, and it seldom disappointed. The leaden clouds burst like balloons and bombarded our cobblestones. The water raced away to the lower-lying parts of Cerro where the flooding would sweep away yesterday's protective boarding. It was not a good afternoon for sleeping. Why was it that Cubans liked to work in a downpour? The shutters were quiet, but in the street below was a cacophony of metal bashing, Cuban obscenities, and truck engines. The corrugated iron portable toilet cabins were being rolled into place alongside the free bars that were provided for our big revolutionary party—the Moncada celebration. After a while I gave up trying to sleep and looked out on Jalisco. A truck had just reversed into the street, and a dozen guys had jumped off with a load of flags and banners. They were laughing and joking. Everyone knew that an official party meant a good time. "Oh man, let's get all those bars out tonight. The liquid's already arrived. The CDR's hiding the beers they've got until the twenty-sixth. Let's pay Víctor a visit. Old Víctor can lose a few cervezas. Tomorrow I've promised to take my *abuela* to the beach. Moncada, Moncada, I love it."

I watched as they put the toilet cabin in the same place as always. It wasn't really a cabin of any real structure—just a cast iron cubicle placed over a drain. The kids would start to use it now that it was up. The novelty never wore off, so the smells would begin. After a couple of days, the heat would produce a warm stench of urine like a tarpaulin over the street. I remembered the games of baseball with the iron walls as backstop. I would snatch a kiss inside the cabin when Mama disapproved of the girl I was with. I would lie awake listening to the rain clattering on the cabin's roof. There was one thing I always noticed: the same gangs would always remove the cabins by the morning of July 27. Moncada was a party, but our own bigger party always wanted to impress with the efficiency of the Revolution.

The children were now arriving back from school. The first were usually the three children of Víctor, the president of the CDR—the Committee for the Defense of the Revolution. This was the guy whose beer the street gangs were hoping to get their hands on. They were picked up in their dad's van. I walked over to the window and looked upward toward the end of our block; sure enough they were splashing in the blocked drain. They were filling their buckets and throwing them against the cabin. I had seen them all born. Víctor's sons were all called names beginning with F for the Comandante, Freddy, Frank, and Félix. They all seemed pretty much the same age and had different mothers. The boys were polite and a little better dressed than we were, but Víctor had done a good job with raising them. Mama said they would go to the Lenin School just as long as their dad held down his job. Mama had seen the Lenin vetting people arriving to talk to the kids. That's what she said in any case. "It shows the system's fair, Felipe. Even kids of presidents of CDRs are not automatic choices."

Old Víctor was my favorite Communist. He was not particularly friendly; he kept his distance. He was Cuban first, and it was enough for him to talk with you that you were Cuban too. He was always playing the all-knowing official, whatever the question. His mind worked like a Cuban's, always looking to be creative in the system. People came to him because he could fix things. I loved to tell him that he only had a job because so much needed fixing. He said he didn't have time to joke. But he tried to make things work, finding a solution, or "squaring the circle," he loved to say.

Víctor said everything is about labels. "I think the capitalists learned from us, Felipe. You brand yourself—like Nike, Adidas, and Coke. You know who has loyalty to a brand and you sell that brand. My brand is revolutionary servant, and that's why I have a job. That's why I know how people's minds work." Víctor knew what it took to get Yoel to sign his petition calling for Cuban socialism forever—I'm sure it was that Nike t-shirt. Víctor is still around, so I will use the present tense. Víctor is a modern leader. He has friends everywhere, and he seems to say what he thinks. But how can he really think for himself when he names all his sons after one man?

"Felipe, you are always welcome at the CDR. You are a Cuban and we work for you. I have a good career, and I am grateful. All this technology, the Internet, the DVDs, I get them to serve the Revolution." And it's true that everyone loved being invited to see his DVDs, coming into the CDR past the crumbling stairs, past the stinking bathroom with the faded pages of a thousand speeches by El Comandante. All Víctor's apparatus was there and his documents, which seemed to hold up the walls. As kids, we marveled at the heaped shelves with evidence of how the elections to the *municipio* were fair and free and that 98.92 percent voted for the winning candidate. The bright computer screen full of photos from party visits to places that I knew I'd never see: Ukraine, Sudan, and Vietnam. Files and files of opinions expressed at CDR meetings. Víctor knew he could never show these to his bosses and let them see what people really wrote about them. But Víctor is the king of my street in Cerro. No one is able to contradict him. "One day, Felipe, you will understand how Cuba works and I will tell you more about it." Víctor has tried to make me one of them, but he never did. Sometimes he got close. No one else ever did that except Tania.

I should mention Tania now before the story of those days begins. She was someone I can still see as clearly as those three kids throwing water in the street. She was a math teacher I remember from the fourth grade who had spent a lot of time studying in Moscow. It seemed like she was with us forever, but Mama has said she was only in my life for a year. Tania talked to us as though she wanted us to become something big. "Look at these fur hats and beautiful painted boxes. They come from a true socialist country, a country that is Cuba's most loyal ally. The Soviet Union has more math geniuses than anywhere else. Look at the chess grandmasters; they are all Russian. Thanks to the Soviet Union, you Cuban nine-year-olds are learning math that sixteen-year-olds in Miami are doing. We are years ahead of capitalism." Tania made me feel great to be Cuban, and great to be young. I wanted to live my life just as Tania said I should.

Tania was beautiful too, but I'm sure she was in love only with Russia. "People take notice of anything Russian. They win wars. They defend their homeland. No one can boss Russia, because they have tanks and oil to do their talking. Cuba is also noticed now because we have joined the world revolution and we are all socialists together." I remember, though I disagreed with Tania about one thing.

"Compañera Tania. I love Russia but I prefer the baseball and the sun, sand, and ocean of Cuba."

"Felipe, you will learn one day. Cuba needs more than that in the world." She smiled, and I loved that. Our other teachers didn't smile. Then one day Tania did not come to the school. All the other teachers refused to say where she had gone.

At university, an old lady, one of Tania's math professors, told me how she left. She made me promise not to tell anyone she had told me. Tania had planned it for a long time and is now working in Canada. Apparently she is teaching Russian, not math. When she went, I had no dreams of doing something different anymore. The dream I had of perfect life ended. Tania believed what she said; I am absolutely sure of that. But every Cuban knows someone like Tania.

Sometime about four years ago I started writing a diary. That was why I was looking for a pen that day. It was something I wanted to do after all that happened with Papa, his jail, and then the end, you know. It was another routine for the day. I knew I could break it if I wanted. No one would know or get upset, and that made me really happy. That gave me a challenge about how to use the time. I decided I needed a project as a human being, not a Cuban. It was building something that was mine. But then you also forget so much if you don't write something down. What I wrote sounds pretty stupid. But it's there still, so it must have meant something for me. "I will not walk away from another chance. I must look at myself from the outside. Strength, strength, strength, please give me. I must be decisive again. As Papa said, never look back ..."

I have talked of some people, but there is a special place in Cuba I love to think of. I cannot describe the Malecón in a way that brings me satisfaction. So the diary did not help with that. Anything that is set down on paper is of one dimension, and any Cuban knows that the Malecón is not just beautiful to the eye. It's about sounds and smells as well. Beauty is often that way. The Malecón was never the same any day I saw it, but it was always beautiful. I borrowed a tape recorder from the CBM and made my tape of the Malecón sounds. It's in a drawer at Jalisco, but I never played it. I never told anyone that I had this tape, because how could you keep the Malecón on a tape? There was no way I could preserve the smell of wonderment when I arrived there after the stench you passed in the gutters of Jalisco. I remember thinking that every street in Havana was the same until I went to the Malecón. When I visited this temple of special thoughts I would never take the *guagua* as it made the journey too short. I liked to look forward to the surprise and excitement. Every step was worth the wait, and then I felt it—the smell of winds and sea that made the diesel and filth go away. It seemed that the world was looking in on Cuba and was reaching out to us. Cuba was open to the ocean, and the ocean treated us all the same. The Malecón was there without billboards or propaganda, with nothing on the horizon except what you imagined. We could make up our own minds.

CHAPTER 2

Felipe

I may have dozed off. I remember that the noise from below had dropped. The construction gangs had moved on. There was one thought that got to me now. I cannot tell you the number of times I had walked on the Malecón with Father Mateo. But I know the thought was with me that Mateo was leaving and I would be losing something. We did not meet many people from outside, and I know you will find that strange. Of course Mateo had traveled to other places. His mother was Cuban, but I think he was from Galicia or somewhere in Spain. We used to talk more in those days than now. "Why did you become a priest, Mateo?" I assumed, like a fool, that it was to travel, like Víctor did. After all he had been in Spain, Argentina, and I don't know where else. I could tell that Mateo saw my question as serious, because when he said something serious his brows came together and his face seemed stronger.

"Why, Felipe, did I do this? It has given me a plan for my life, I suppose. We must all make plans for our lives. That is what being human means. We have to plan to do good. We can't drift from day to day waiting for something to turn up. We have to be ready to decide. Every day is a gift. Christians believe in the power of good to change things, and that means everyday life, every minute." And Mateo had said all he would ever say to me, because now he was leaving Cuba.

Then I thought about how Mateo used his walks on the Malecón. He noticed everything. He noticed every person, and I realized that I never bothered with the people. I assumed that they thought just like me. Just like every Cuban they had no plans, and there was never much that was new. But Mateo had his plans, and he wanted to talk to them. He knew the CD sellers by name, the bubble *taxistas*. And all the policemen outside the U.S. Interests section, that big building on the Malecón, they knew Mateo so well that they told me they looked forward to his walks.

Mama would end her nap in thirty minutes. She always slept in the chair, her white hair parted on the right, her head lying away from the parting. As a kid, I used to love playing with her metal clip, which was then white against her black hair. It was now rusty and tarnished. Soon Tico would bring his friends up to watch TV, wanting the mattress to lie on. And then Rafa would be home and would begin playing his rap. The mosquitoes would start arriving at dusk, and the power cuts were most likely by eight. Pepe always joked that this was a planned economy and all the power cuts were planned so that party officials and military didn't have them. Or at least not during those speech times on TV.

The fan was on but would probably be cut off before darkness. I checked the phone that Pepe's friend on the police force had installed years ago. Sure enough it didn't make a sound. Pepe had been calling for weeks to get it repaired. Once again there would be no calls, so sleep was now a possibility. But the flies were arriving early. A very bad sign, but maybe they thought that some of the food I had bought would be unprotected. At least the mosquitoes left me alone. Yoel said the mosquitoes were the biggest sector of the Cuban economy. The government needed technology to make all mosquitoes informers for the state; that was why they started the biotech center. Mosquitoes were always busy, and they knew what we were doing. Places to go, people to eat.

Mama liked me to leave the meat in the fridge even when it wasn't working. But the sight of that rusty metal with mold on the inside somehow didn't seem right. I asked Yoel on the ride to Jalisco, "Is there a fridge that works in our street?"

"Felipe, I'll get back to you on that, but in any case the fridge is smart to stay broken. Why would anyone want to get near such terrible meat?"

I may have dozed off for a few more seconds. It was enough, because I felt better. The noise on the staircase grew from below; the kids from upstairs were back from school. I knew there had to be eleven sets of footsteps before they had all passed. A clap of thunder made the kids more excited. They knew that would mean plenty of water to jump in and plenty of old rum bottles to make their own *cócteles*.

I thought of the good times and why they didn't seem to be coming back. "Yoel, forget about the bread. Let's take the bike for the day and we'll go out to find some prawns in Puerto Esperanza. Take some of Pepe's beers to trade. Just like we used to do as kids, free on the *carretera*. I'll bet the police will leave us alone in return for a dozen prawns."

"Felipe, I have my own kids now. I can't just take days off." I don't know how all that happened for Yoel, my buddy, who was now providing for a family when he was only my age. Carlitos would grumble, of course, if I went to Esperanza, but I think Carlitos saw in me the rebel he never was, or never could be. Carlitos would love to hit the carretera. I think he was kind of jealous of me. And in any case, Carlitos would accept my excuse—that I got a fever from the damp in the apartment. I knew Mateo would say taking time off was not going to help. "Felipe, look, you have done it too often before."

I closed my eyes again, but it was no good. I felt on edge. I couldn't just waste another day. A guy of twenty-seven with no plans except skipping work. Just look at yourself; just look at this room. I looked at the picture of the sugar cane. Mama said it was the picture that held our family together. I used to think family pictures were the only ones that every house had. I think the photo had been taken by the local collective—it had some official stamp in the bottom right-hand corner—to show the sugar crop rather than the group of men in the upper left-hand corner. Smiling at the top of the group was Papa. It was the only picture we had of him. I had made a photocopy of it many times at the CBM, but there was only about a half of Papa's face. I think someone tried to tear it once, because the picture wasn't straight. In any case you could see that Papa was smiling, and he was surrounded by friends. I wished someone had borrowed a camera and taken some more of him, but they never did. I knew what the rest of his face looked like, but no one else ever would. I sometimes thought about the children I would have one day. A diary was a photo album that no one opened. Eyes were not just for reading.

I remember the day when I first saw photos in other people's homes. I knew the cinema, the newspapers, but I never saw a camera being used in families. It was the first birthday party I was invited to—and it was held for a beautiful girl, Patricia, our doctor's daughter. She was seven, I think, and her mother took pity on us because of Papa. They had some clowns and balloons, I remember. Patricia loved to talk. "My abuelo is the best fighter in Cuba." Patricia's grandfather had been with the band in the Sierra. And in their house there was a blurred picture of a group of five of them carrying weapons. El Comandante was certainly there in those thick eyeglasses, and Patricia never stopped bragging about the photo. "No one at this party has a photo like ours. My mama says so."

I hated that party and told Mama it was the last I would go to. But soon I didn't care when I learned that there were photos of El Comandante everywhere. In any case I liked the cane one we had. It was special. In Havana we never saw any cane, and there wasn't much that was green around us. Come to think of it, in the picture the cane was now yellow and the sky gray. One day Mama said she didn't like to see it so she would put it behind the other family pictures. She said it was because the others were brighter and sharper, but I knew that wasn't the reason. The others I had taken on the digital camera I borrowed from work. I know Mama loved the one of Laurita laughing as she sat on the Malecón. The wave had caught her by surprise. But I think there was some sadness in her face, the more I looked at it. "Felipe, you are so pessimistic," Laurita had said.

Oh yes, I'll never forget that day of the picture of Laurita. I had told Mama I loved Laurita. "Then you must put the picture in front of Papa's," said Mama. So I did that, but I felt ashamed as well to see Papa's photo not in front. It was the time Laurita came out with those words where she saw me as someone she might be able love. Maybe even as much as she loved Cuba, she said. I opened my heart to Mama about Laurita.

"Mama, why would Laurita pick me? She has a life that is as good as you can have in Cuba. For her every day is different. She has tourism. Why would she pick me?"

Mama was reassuring. "Don't always be doubting, Felipe. Laura knows Cuba is beautiful, and Laura knows about beauty. You are part of the beauty she finds in Cuba. She does not need to explain anymore."

"Mama, Laurita has so much more than the rest of us. Look at the tourists; they need her. The visitors look up to her. They stay in touch with her by e-mail after their vacations." Yes, Laura had e-mail in her office just like the senior people at CBM. And it wasn't just the male tourists who had fallen in love with her. Laura was selling the country and showing that Cuba was somewhere that counted. Warm, efficient, caring. "I will sell Cuba to anyone I meet. I believe in it. So should we all. They must think well of us and not just think of Cuba as somewhere that is cut off from the world."

Laurita was not a saint. She used the perks of tourism like everyone else, collecting carefully the soaps and food and making contacts. But there was something else. Laurita built herself images of the world outside. She fantasized about travel. She knew that one day we would all have the Internet, and she never tired of checking on the best deals to the places of her dreams. She said they all did it at the office and the director knew it was good for his guides to tell the tourists they knew the world.

"Tourists are sophisticated, Felipe. They want to think they are visiting a sophisticated place and not one run by people from the campo." It annoyed me that Laurita would see Cubans like that. But Laurita said it was the truth. She loved to take photos of the fashion the ladies wore from Italy, France, and Germany. She changed her hair because of some Italian movie star or something. Laura knew Rafa wanted to go to England because he said he wanted to see the Beatles and the Queen. Don't know where he got that from. I remember him crying when Laurita told him that John Lennon had died years ago. Laurita spoke of things with certainty. "I never doubt that I will see the world and live in it. I will see new people with new dreams, new eyes on Cuba. I know how they behave. I have seen them at lunch, in the buses, at the *fincas* we visit. They talk freely, they show me photos of their last vacations, they ask questions, they have no fear. And they do all this here in Cuba. Felipe, it will come to us as well. We will visit their countries as well."

I think Laurita told the tourists she had seen those places too. So what? They trusted her; the visitors depended on her, and she could choose what she told them of what a magical place

Cuba was. "You know, Felipe, we have so much compared to other countries. I know that. Who could want for more? "

I wondered why Laurita didn't just join the tourists; you know, take up with some Frenchman, some Italian. I never said it, but every day she had the chance of meeting someone. I think it was over this that we first tasted bitterness between us. She was lucky, I said, to have what she had. But it shouldn't depend on luck. Then I said something like this. "Cuba is all I have known, and it has brought me so much. It has brought me you. Thank you, Cuba, for what I find in you. But what I feel for you was my free will and I made a choice to give everything I have to our friendship. That was what I did. But every day Cuba forces us to make choices we shouldn't have to make." I knew straight away I shouldn't have said that out loud. It was stupid. I repeated some other words to her that Papa had told me. Those were when he sat me on the tractor, one of the last times. I remember that he had started to look old, with wrinkles around his eyes. He looked across the fields and then kissed me. "I have never seen any other country. But I know there is no better."

It wasn't what I wanted to recall when looking at that picture. For that was a perfect day with Laurita. It always would be, but today wasn't the same. The staircase was suddenly full of more noise. More children. The noise of relieved kids after a day over at school.

The youngest voice was that of Tico. He was the smallest, so he was the last up the stairs. He only seemed to have around a quarter of the teeth he was supposed to, but his smile was white and gleaming. With Tico there were no hidden messages.

"Hey Tico," I said, hugging him.

Tico did not say my name. He was bursting too much to tell me about his day. "The guagua broke down. The bus driver said it was only the eleventh time this month. Now he believes he's lucky." I knew I must have slept for at least a minute because I felt good and positive.

"Your turn on the mattress, Tico," I said. "No way," he said. "I'm going to play in the rain. I've learned this new move for the sliders. You wait. I'm going to show them all now."

I headed for the gym, about a forty-minute walk. But I knew it was quicker than waiting for the guagua. In any case I thought it better than fighting for space with my fellow habaneros. I was told the gym was negotiated as a bonus for those of us who worked in the *polo científico*. We called it "el perk" because it was the way of introducing us to global business. Carlitos said we were the only institute to have it, but I know that the gym owner played soccer with his son. All of us Cubans had been educated at school to exercise, to wrestle, box, and work out. It was a practice that died hard, especially when this was a good social club for gossip. I told Mama that the gym was one of my two extravagances. The second was Laurita, who I knew was more than I could really afford. She knew it too, so there was no point in pretending. As usual the gym manager apologized for the lack of air conditioning. "Fully air-conditioned," flickered the neon sign outside. "I know, Felipe, but it's been with maintenance since April. But I did get the water pump fixed, so you can shower. The rest I blame on the embargo," he said proudly.

Of the four exercise bikes, two had paper signs on them saying "No funciona." As usual I saw that Vladimir had bagged one of the working ones. He called to me on my way to the punchbag. "How's life in Frankenstein's castle, Felipe Triana?" said Vladimir, former student president and pioneer at the Lenin Academy. "Found any new spooky potions lately?" Vladimir was tying his new white sneakers, and he brushed his ponytail from across his face. He was about to take his turn on the treadmill but then thought better of it. I knew he expected me to hit back.

"At least we don't rip off the Revolution like the computer compañeros! I wish I had my sparkling new laptop to take home. Our whole laboratory only has two between us," I said. Vlado always liked a fight.

"You wait, Feli. When you're telling your grandchildren how you were close to a Nobel Prize they'll be selling all that DNA junk you worked on. Just think, the revolutionary new man will then be a reality and we won't have to attend any rallies. We will have achieved perfection."

I punched another bag and stayed silent. Whatever I thought about Vladimir, he had a good line in insults, but I knew he could not be heard talking about an end to the Revolution. "At least we're looking to the future," I said. "Maybe biotech will bring something for everyone, even some Cubans who didn't go to Comrade Lenin's academy. We surely have the same brains as the Yanquis. Ninety miles does not change human nature. They look at what we do and marvel. They have billions of dollars and all the equipment that's needed. And they screw up plenty of things as well. You should know. How's your sister doing in Miami?"

"She's fine, I guess, you know. Says there's too many Hernandezes everywhere. Everyone's so sentimental about why they left. Even the Cadillac dealers in Florida fly the Cuban flag. She can't stand the way the Cubans behave. Wants to go to Oregon or somewhere. Feli, you need to lighten up and enjoy life as it is. We can get a good drink together. That's what people do everywhere, you know. No guilt or anything stupid like philosophizing about the meaning of what we're doing. Better beer, better life. That's what I say. Cristal beer will do nicely, not the normal stuff."

Vlado knew that I could not offer to pay. That was a very Cuban thing. Everyone knows everyone else's salary. It's only when you have family "fuera" that the guessing game starts. He would know that 240 pesos did not buy Cristal beer. Vladimir wouldn't mention that, even with his big mouth. He made a hundred times that, mostly illegally. Vlado, quick and slick like he was, would know that by July 20 I wasn't even drawing on my 240 pesos that had probably gone. What did I have to lose with Vlado? Certainly not my pride.

"Okay, Vlado, you could twist my arm. I'll have one of your capitalist beers anytime you like." I took advantage of the cold shower, which was fixed just like the manager said, and then we wandered off to a small café off Calle Obispo. I thought Vlado probably chose it to show off to the tourists. But no, I was wrong; it was the barman. Of course Vladimir knew the barman.

"He'll give us a good deal, that guy. I gave him some computer parts last week. They were obsolete anyway, but he'll sell them on. You'll see, Feli. I feel lucky; we can do better even than Cristal."

We sat down. "What's up, Vlado?" I asked, still surprised at the invitation.

"Oh, nothing much." Vlado looked in the window of the café to make sure his ponytail was in place. He then seemed to rethink. "Well, actually quite a lot, Feli. Who would ever think we had to worry about change here? I'm not exactly quivering with nerves but things are … well a little edgy in Havana. You know, things are difficult for these companies like mine. The official line is that we are traitors and that we've all abused our trust. They say we are seduced by power, by the nectar of good living. They say they want to give power back to the ministries or the military. They say we are too decentralized; too much of a risk. We are corrupt and selfish. Stamp on them. Get back control. Can you believe that? In Cuba you need two ministerial orders each time you breathe. One to breathe in and one to breathe out. I guess maybe I'll be called in for reeducation. Anyway, Feli, you and me, we are no longer the young guys. New guys are sharpening their knives. This new generation out of the schools is pretty ambitious, and they make me feel kind of old."

Here he was, Vlado, always in the loop, trying to impress his poor student buddy. "Bad luck," I said without really knowing what I was supposed to say. "Vlado, if you want me to feel sorry for you ... come on, why should I bother? The old guys here usually win, so if you're old that's good news. There will always be space for the survivors like you. You produce the results they want. They don't really trust anyone new. Your family is five-star revolutionary. No one I know can touch you. In the end they always come back to people who can fix things without a fuss. Maybe you don't score any knockout blows, but you know how to box inside, huh?" I thought that would go down pretty well with Vlado. Maybe he would buy me two drinks.

Vlado stopped looking in the window, suggesting that he was satisfied with his hair. "Felipe, it's more serious now. I am yesterday's man. I've been supported by a different crowd. Nothing like that counts for much. They are making big changes. This time all the openings are being closed."

Vladimir returned with the drinks. "Told you," he said proudly. "Told you we'd do better than Cristal. He gave us free whiskies. This is the best from Scotland, Famous Grouse; you know, what all those big-shot tourists have. I love the way this country has its own rules. You understand when you are a winner. Just think, those computer parts I gave that guy cost me nothing. If you learn how to play the game then no one can touch you and you live like a ..."

"A king, you mean, don't you, Vlado? Where else but here? How many kings can Cuba take? I thought we got rid of the Spanish a few years ago to take care of that."

Vladimir drank a huge gulp before sitting down. He seemed cheered by the whisky. "I guess that's what our Revolution has led to. A new royalty. Maybe the Brits should have stayed in 1762!!"

I had only tasted real Scotch whisky once before—at a party at the CBM. It was worth the wait.

Vlado changed his expression. "Feli, don't underestimate yourself. You're feisty too. But take my word; I'm worried. What's happening here? Has the comandante dropped the baton? Why is he playing with pieces on the chess board? I'm not military, party, or a spy. All I am is a Cuban of thirty-odd years who thought the Revolution would look after him. Look what's happened in Russia and China. No one knows what the rules of the game are anymore. If you haven't bought a new Mercedes yet you can go to hell. Twenty years ago they were all like us."

Even for Vlado this was going on a bit. Normally I would have yawned and looked around for some pretty girls. But the whisky was good. "Vlado, this is really serious, isn't it? I guess I'd never see the signs of change here until it bit me on the nose. Hombre, I'm worried for you. You even sound quite humble. If you go on like that, I'll begin to feel sorry for you. Everyone knows what I think. Forget the government. They're out for themselves, like everyone else. So you have to get real and take a shot at life. Make some plans that depend on you, not the party. The first time you get fired will be the last. Then what else do you have? The sister in Oregon or wherever?" I was surprised at myself. Was that Felipe speaking?

CHAPTER 3

Later on July 20

Mateo

I went on one of my last visits to the Malecón with Felipe the weekend just before Moncada. I stopped by to see if he wanted to join me. I got used to walking when I was in Argentina, in Patagonia. It's perhaps a strange thing for a churchman to do, but sometimes you know you need to be alone. It's what monks do, but I could never find that in the stones of a monastery. I wanted wilderness, wildness, the rawness of what hasn't changed. And the wildest place I could get to in Havana was the Malecón. If you don't know Havana, I owe it to you to tell you something of the boulevard. One side was the majestic, often snarling ocean, an ocean that always challenged the city to forget it was there. Havana started fifty meters away—always too close to repel the furies of nature. Across these fifty meters was the paved walkway and wall top, which was the defining symbol of the city; a city that Cubans loved but did not realize what a jewel they had. Havana is one of the world's great cities, built with determination and elegance by man. But the sweep and curve of the Malecón was a gift from nature, a holy gift of beauty to inspire. Man could not spoil it even with his potholes and spiky, broken slices of concrete.

No Cuban I knew came close to Felipe in his love for the Malecón. It took me a while to find this out, because Felipe was shy about his passion. He talked little about it, and I know as well that he wouldn't claim any special knowledge. "Discover it yourself, Mateo. It's not for me to tell you the secrets. How lucky we are that it is there, forever Cuban. There are no opening or closing hours, and no one has to pay any dues. Mateo, I know every broken stone and I have learned that those missing are never replaced. It is a mark of respect to the battles they have seen and the history of brokenness that is respected." I noticed that the wall had to be patched up sometimes, but the ocean always won. It seemed crazy to build a road so close to an angry onrushing tide, but it connected Cuba with something eternal—it had a history before 1959.

When we did these walks, Felipe often seemed lost in thought until we arrived at the Malecón. I said that was good. We all need space to think and pray, I would say. Felipe did not react, and he never once asked about the seminary. I think he didn't pray; in fact he told me he didn't. He said he couldn't see what good it would do when the reality never changed. "Mateo, prayer is useless in the face of reality."

Felipe

When we got to the shoreline, Mateo's mood changed. He said he had now arrived at his parish. He came to life. He would walk in the fronts of buildings to shout a hello or bang on a door. He told his parishioners they should go there too and would give them a few pesos for the bus ride to encourage them. I remember that I realized what a great job Mama did with our clothes. Mateo's were grimy and stained. The seminary laundry had lost its dry cleaning long ago, and the washing machine had broken. Mama had never had any machines. Mateo was a formal guy, never in t-shirts. He would pull out a gray handkerchief to wipe the beads of sweat collecting on his chin, but he was unaware of how he looked.

There were two men he recognized, and he walked over to them. "Hello, my Malecón brothers. I am so lucky. Only priests and night shifters have time to enjoy the Malecón." Hugo and Pedrito were night workers at the William Soler hospital, and they always came to lie on the wall to get some sleep. It was far too hot at home.

One thing I had never seen in priests before was how tough a man Mateo was—a tough man who spoke his mind. People did not do that in Cuba. We avoided upsetting others. And one thing that shocked me was how rude Mateo was about Cuban coffee. "Felipe, this stuff is terrible compared to Algiers or Buenos Aires. I hope I don't offend you. Life is like that. The beauties of the earth are divided. You see neither Algiers nor Buenos Aires has the Malecón." And this last time we were there, Mateo seemed to want to justify the time he spent on the Malecón. "You know, this place, it's not right to spend every day here. It's like eating chocolate or drinking wine all the time. I thank God the seminary classes are over by two and do not start again until six. There is nothing in this whole world like the five o'clock light on the Morro castle. Just imagine if I had to teach every day at four o'clock."

Mateo had other plans today. "Today I will not have that treat, Felipe. I have to pass by Galiano to see Eusebio. Come with me. Your company will help me avoid my sadness. You see, I am leaving Cuba soon, probably just after Moncada. There is so much I want to do here, but I have to accept my next calling."

I knew this already. Mateo had said he would leave after five years. But I surprised myself. I didn't say I was sorry, that we'd miss him. "Mateo, you may feel you have a lot to achieve, but what we have to do must be done by Cubans. You come and go and live among us. But we can't just wait and listen to you.

Cubans have been sitting and listening for too long." Mateo nodded with apparent approval. I think he was surprised too, but I also think he liked it.

We reached Calle Galiano. I never understood how houses for one family could be built so big. Who had ever needed that amount of space? Now they were all teeming with people. The doorway on Galiano was blocked with bags of rubbish overturned and punctured by dogs. The washing from the window of each floor showed who was home. Down on the street, people were already in line outside the cinema, which opened in the evening. This was a working day, but there were hundreds on the street—a stream of people moving in all directions. Everyone with lots of time to hang around. The walkway was blocked outside the pizza store as the cooks were handing out "free pizzas" to their families at the back. Alongside the cinema was a newspaper seller. He had his display stands with some glossy Spanish publications of kings, queens, and movie stars. Mama said she always used to put on her best clothes to go to Galiano. It was the place to be seen. The children were on the streets after school in their maroon and white uniforms, looking pleased to be free of lessons and checking to see who had enough money to spend on ice cream. As a kid this was a magical time to be alive. "You'd never think they would give up ice cream for Mass. But they do," said Mateo. "Some of these will be stopping by the church later."

We turned off down the Calle Urrutia, an alley much narrower than Galiano. The shops extended a few meters down the street, and Mateo entered a lower-level building. There was nothing on the outside to show it was a furniture store. All that was visible was a sign in wood: "Eusebio Peña, podólogo." I knew Eusebio a bit from church. I guess he went about as often as I did, on big festival days or when they offered some sandwiches or allowed us to use computers. Anyway, everyone around Eusebio knew he hadn't touched chiropody for years. Peña kept a few bottles of lotion around and many dusty medical journals from 1950s Cuba. He said he owed his life to an aunt who had died in San Juan de Padrón with a house full of furniture. In the last twenty years he had learned all there was to know about restored furniture and sold it to tourists and diplomats. They liked him in Urrutia, so no one ever asked why he did not have a display sign about his activities.

Eusebio wiped his hands on a dirty apron and stubbed out his cigar. "Hey, Padre, we thought you'd gone off to Santiago or somewhere. We need your spiritual guidance on Calle Galiano. Where have you been, compañero Mateo? " Eusebio knew that Mateo was always amused by that form of address.

"My dear Eusebio, they have perfectly good priests in Santiago. My parish is here among the wonderful people of Havana. How is chiropody? Still paying as well as ever? That mahogany dresser over there looks fabulous."

"You bet," said Eusebio. "It's one of the best I've seen in years. An Italian will pay six hundred dollars for it. I imagine in Milan he'll sell it for five thousand Euros. Pays for his holidays and all his girlfriends in Havana a few times over."

"Never mind, amigo Eusebio. You'll earn more than that in heaven. There's this sweet little girl from Cienfuegos at the hospital who's got terrible asthma. I know the pilot in the airlines who can get the drops she needs in Canada tonight. But they'll cost a hundred bucks. Is there any way you could help me out?"

Eusebio frowned. "You know I'll help you when it's really needed. A couple of Germans bought this ugly chest yesterday for three hundred dollars, so you can have it. Just help yourself; you know where I keep it," said Eusebio. "But I'm not sure where the next pieces are coming from. I would do anything for those kids, but things are changing here. You know, the money in all this is no secret. The ministry has set up a rival store now in the tourist areas. It looks wonderful, and they offer coffee, accept credit cards, have a Web site—the lot. Everyone's telling me they have the best stuff at better prices. They are clearing out lots of old houses around Santa Fe. It's like a treasure chest of furniture, and some of it is going to the military to fit out some of the new hotels. The government always knew how to undercut the mercenaries! Can you believe it? All that fantastic furniture from the 1920s and 30s, and I could have sold crates of it to the Italian gigolos for five thousand bucks. Makes me weep to think of it, Mateo."

"Don't worry," said Mateo. "There's some wonderful stuff still in the hands of good Catholic families. We have really good taste, despite my less-than-elegant suit. The church built some of the best buildings in Cuba, and some of the bishops' residences have more furniture than they need. I'm sure I can persuade them to 'loan' you a few. How else are these people going to make some bucks? It breaks their hearts sometimes, but I tell them one day they'll be able to buy much better furniture from China."

So that was Mateo, our Spanish priest, doing his deals in Cuba. He'd never bought whisky like Vlado, but the aftertaste of meeting him was better. I shouldn't complain, because I felt good after those drinks. I remember that night really because of the whisky. But I felt good as well, because it made me feel special and privileged. It was a secret from everyone else in Havana just like something I had that tourists had all the time in Cuba. And everywhere I looked Havana looked great. Maybe that was how it looked if you were Spanish or Canadian.

I had never felt sympathy for Vladimir before. But if the whisky was strange so was he. If Vladimir couldn't see the way out, where did that leave everyone else? Vladimir had worked it all out. He had kept his mouth shut, he did all the marches, and knew all the slogans. He had even been a writer for the Rebelde. Yet after all the years he was like me. We waited. We weren't even sure what we waited for, because we knew we'd never be asked.

So I felt I could understand Vlado. But who knows? Maybe next time he would have worked it out again, how to keep one step ahead of everyone and everything else. Yes, that was frightening. Vladimir is something I fear. Something, not someone. He is a nonbeliever. A nonbeliever in anything. He doesn't believe in himself. He has a way of life that is not his own. But he prefers it because it makes life easy when everything is either forbidden or compulsory. We're all done with thinking. When someone told Vlado, "You are free," would he take the chance?

I noticed that I was running. The strollers turned and watched, as Cubans never run. The salsa means minimum movement; you know, the swaying, never that stupid waving and kicking I've seen in discos. So when I started running I knew it was what robbers did after they grabbed a tourist's necklace. But no police were running after me. I splashed through the puddles on the cobblestones and smelled the fresh night air. Could I really stay up all night? The feeling would not last, I knew, but this was a night that shouldn't end.

It would be another four hours before the apartment would be quiet enough to sleep. Pepe was on night shift, so he would leave at midnight. Everyone in Havana seemed like a friend, and no one was standing in my way. Felipe, you have a happy feeling and you are in Cuba. So there was only one place I had to be, and that was with Laurita. "You shouldn't be so pessimistic," she had said. Maybe this night would go on forever. "You shouldn't always be analyzing what's happening. It's complicated. Things will be better tomorrow. The tourists who come here know it's a sham to have smiling singers, palm trees, and endless mojitos. But it's part of life to smile at shams. They do that all over the world. The next four hours will always be the best," Laurita had said.

Sometimes in Havana you knew when you were in luck. That happened when a ride came along when you wanted it. But right away I hitched a ride with a young sports coach who was heading back from the baseball stadium. His car smelled of pain-relieving ointment and sweat. He said he was preparing for a wrestling training camp in Nicaragua. He dropped me at the bridge over the Miramar tunnel, and I started walking down Fifth Avenue, passing the skateboarders and dog walkers. The stars were like car headlights in the sky. The chauffeured limousines were heading into the clubs of Vedado, and the *jineteras* were beginning to sidle along the grass way, dodging into the side streets or parks when a police motorcyclist appeared.

I knew you saw the money of Havana at night because communism seemed a better idea during the daytime. And at night most of the people couldn't see. In Miramar I saw the people looking after themselves, and I didn't care about that. I had had a taste of it as well that night. The guards were smoking outside a large diplomatic residence. I think it was the Belgian or Russian. There was a party for hundreds going on, and a salsa band was struggling to be heard above the talking. They were joined by a group of chauffeurs, awaiting their ambassadors or Cuban officials. They had parked their Mercedes in lines down the side streets. This was the best part of their job, to exchange gossip and pick up a spare drink. I asked them what they were celebrating. I knew they wouldn't invite me in. Oh, and I think I spotted Carlitos's Peugeot. He would be there to represent CBM—he liked the whisky too.

Laura's house was about five minutes walk from these embassies. It had the most rooms of any house I knew, and they didn't ever use half of them. Laura said they were waiting for the family to return one day. Everyone knew about the home and that it had always been with the Regueiro family. They had never left Cuba after the Revolution. Old man Salvador had a school friend at the Central Bank. I wasn't surprised that even in the Revolution some Cubans looked after their friends. The Regueiro family had managed to get their money out to a Swiss bank. The friend—Laura never called him by name—did it for more than one person, but not for long. He was shot by firing squad in 1961.

Laurita's house was on a special street. There were some party people around, and Laurita said the Politburo people used one at the end. The street was blocked off to the public, and there was nowhere to go except the houses on the street. The owners gave plenty of "donations" to the police, so they were always looking for suspicious visitors. Most of the police who roamed around the area were familiar to me since I met Laura. But the guy on duty tonight was new. I could tell by the shades he was wearing, which said Oakley on them. I'd never seen him before. He nodded to me to come over. I knew the routine. The police were there to show they were there. Most of the time they were too lazy to act. Sometimes they would be forced to take people in, but the paperwork was such a bore that they hardly ever bothered. They had the guns and radio if the people got difficult. In any case I trusted in the goodwill of every Cuban that night.

"So, amigo. You've been drinking a little. Of course you have. I can smell, you know, as well as see. Why would a drunk come up here to Miramar?"

I was sure of myself. "It's no crime, compañero, to walk in Havana. Actually I have some friends here. You know I have good family too. We work hard and obey the law. You know Pepe Ávila."

"You mean the traffic cop, Pepe. Sure, I did some fast-driving training with that SOB a couple of years back. Always had some good frozen chicken for sale. I guess someone's caught on to that by now. Anyway you take care. Havana is a dangerous place at night."

Laura's house had not been painted since 1958, and the garden was overgrown. I knew that was deliberate. Paint could be bought on the black market or for barter for twenty CUCs a can, and Laura's stepfather had plenty of money. But what he bought he used on the inside. Money was used for other things. Laura was her mother's only child; her father had long left and had an art gallery in Madrid. Laura said that her mother married her stepfather because of his networks—his *socios*. He supplied the fittings for a German hotel chain, part of the army's empire in tourism. So Laura's mom went to work. She knew that tourism jobs took years of preparation, and her stepfather tried hard for Laura. He had no kids of his own. He had had to arrange several special import orders of laptops and flat-screen TVs for some officials in hotel catering before the opening came about. Laura failed her first interview and was told that the assistant manager was still waiting for his "propina." That was solved the next time around.

The guard outside the house, Edy, knew me well. Laura said he was paid a hundred dollars a month, five times as much as anyone at the CBM except Carlitos. Edy was paid enough to be discreet.

I took a close look at the house with its floodlights recently installed. Edy was bathed in bright light, but that didn't prevent him sleeping. A quick rattle of the railings woke him. "Hi, Felipe. I must have dozed off. Never done that before! Sorry, it's been a hard day. You're up late. Laura's just got back."

Laurita's house was like the whisky. Expensive and something I knew was unusual. Yes, I'd been in it before, but every time you entered it was fresh. In Cuba you watched the Brazilian telenovelas they showed on TV. But that was in another land, on another planet. Fantasy. But here at Laura's it all turned real. The beautiful Spanish tiles in the lobby, the leather settees, the fresh flowers, and the massive TV. The red lights of the alarm system winked at the visitors in the hallway. There were padlocked bars on the windows. All the neighbors knew what lay behind the shabby walls. Laurita told me they had a big Christmas party for the street, and she said her stepfather made sure all the party officials and police got a bottle of vodka. Laurita was smart too.

She still attended the marches she had to, and she had a special set of clothes for all that. She was told that the tourism job made no difference. She had to keep proving that she was worthy of it. I liked her stepfather—better than Laura did, I think. He got what he wanted and never whined, not like Vlado. Laura despised him. She said he treated her as his trophy. "Feli, that guy is so cynical; all he talks about is paying people off. You never know who might be paying the neighbors these days."

Laura was on her cell phone when she opened the door. She put her hand over the receiver and kissed me. I looked at her and smiled. "Wow! My perfect end to a perfect day. You look gorgeous even after charming all those Italians."

She knew I intended to stay. "Feli, I'm sick of being asked if I want a Campari soda. They're all over fifty-five and already have the run of Cuban girls. But there was one from Catania ..."

"Okay, okay. I'm jealous as hell. Let me make you jealous too."

She smiled. "You can always try. How was your day?"

"Kind of strange, actually. I feel pretty good. Unlike you I don't often get taken out for a drink. Well, I did today. Don't worry; it's not some beauty from Andalusia. I'm afraid it's only Vladimir; you know, the Lenin Academy guy. He bought me this Famous Grouse Scotch tonight after the gym. It's what all the tourists drink, he said. I guess that's how life should be. But it all seemed so strange. Maybe it was only because Vlado was different."

"You and Scotch, Felipe. You'd better not get used to it. You might as well dream of owning a beach condo. But what's so strange?" She swept her hair back. It was more Cuban now; she had grown it since her Italian movie star period.

"Vlado seems real upset. Never seen him like that. He's always so confident; you know, an arrogant bastard."

Laurita switched back to her cell phone. "Okay, okay. I'll get back to you." Laura could hear the voice on her phone asking where she had gone. I looked at Laura and was speechless for a moment. Why didn't I say to her there was nothing else that mattered? Why couldn't we start our planning of our lives together?

I knew that when I told Mama I had been seeing Laura, Mama would ask when I would get around to proposing to her. Mama knew that a girl like Laura was not going to wait for me to sort out my life.

"Mama, what would I propose for our lives together? What can I even propose for tomorrow? That I get some frozen chicken in exchange for pens I stole from work? What can I propose when neither of us knows what sort of life we will have? Mama, I propose that no one should live in a couple of rooms in Havana where there are fourteen other people in our house. But who will listen to that?"

I knew Laura would take me to the place she called the twenty-first-century room. We walked through the sitting room that she called the nineteenth century. It was set back from the front lobby and was furnished with heavy chipped furniture with fading family photos and pre-1950s glassware. I expected always to see cobwebs, but Laura's mom had too much pride for that. The pictures were dusted every day by the maid, but they had not been moved from their places for decades. A portrait of Laura's grandfather in his robes as a judge before the Revolution was on the left. A family group at the DuPont residence in Varadero in 1958 was on the right. Laura had once explained where everyone was now, but I couldn't say I was really bothered. My family members were still with me in Cuba, so that was all there was.

We arrived in the room I knew Laura loved. There was a large flat-screen TV, speakers mounted on the walls, beige leather chairs, a settee, and glass tables. Through an archway was the dining area, which could easily seat twenty people. It was also part of the twenty-first century. "I guess you've already had your drinks. But help yourself. You know that Papa Two (that was what she called her stepfather) has pretty good taste in whisky."

Laura's phone rang again. "Okay, okay. I'll be at the Riviera at four. Make sure we have an Italian speaker too. I can't understand those accents from Napoli. Those damn tourists expect everything."

She turned off the phone. She finally had time to talk. "Mi amor. A rough day, I'm afraid. How was yours?"

"Not much better until now, Laurita. Last thing you want to hear is about Vlado. But it does seem that his setup is all collapsing. All his plans he claims are in flames. Vlado's always a moaner, but this time maybe he's trying to tell us something."

"Not sure I know or care very much." Laurita laughed. "I'm kind of tired with complex plotting. Vlado loves all the politics. But politics bores me, especially now. Just shut up and cuddle, Señor Biotech."

I looked around to see where she had in mind and glanced through the archway. I expected to see a glass table, the bowl of fresh fruit, maybe some flowers. The table had all those things, and one place was set. At the near end there was a person dining with his back to us. There was a squat, balding man with Tommy Hilfiger written on the back of his t-shirt and bright white sneakers.

I beckoned Laura into a corner. "Who's that man over there?"

We returned to the old sitting room. "That's Gerardo," said Laura. "He's in the people business."

"What do you mean he's in the people business? He's some guy who hires people for tourism?"

"No, stupid, he's down from Dade County. He's getting some fast boats ready."

So that was the jolt back to reality. Here we were at the end of a great day where we both wanted to be, and someone who wanted to make a fast buck out of Cuba was dining in luxury in Havana. "So Papa Two is now spreading his business. I get it. Fast boats again, and how much is it this time?"

"It's gone down a bit this week. They say it's getting more difficult. Eight thousand CUCs, with a money-back guarantee for up to eight trips." smiled Laura. "That's easy for Calle Ocho. Isn't that why we have all the number eights in this? It's a great deal to see your family again. Felipe, don't look so worried. It's a win-win."

"Don't laugh at me, Laurita. One day you'll go too. You're too smart and pretty to waste your life waiting for biological events. Go now and come back. Then come back to a place that works. I have Mama, Rafa, and Tico. But this old house, it'll still be waiting for you after you have made your fortune. How often does Tommy Hilfiger come over?"

"When there's business, which is most of the time. He's a tourism rep too for a Spanish company."

"Laurita, why is he in your house? I know these things happen, but people traffickers are not my favorite people."

The guy left the table nodding to Laura and went upstairs saying he had to get up early for business meetings. At least he was tactful. Laura and I returned to the same wavelength, and I left at 1:30.

There were still plenty of vans heading into Havana. One thing about official vehicles in Cuba was they all worked around the clock. They were always in demand.

CHAPTER 4

Wednesday July 21

Felipe

I got home at 2:00 AM, and the place was settled for the night. Oh how I love that girl! She is so unspoiled and full of hope. So fresh. Sweet as a mango in July. She lives for the day—every day. Can you be unselfish and dishonest at the same time? Can I tell her the truth later? It's easier sometimes to say nothing, but my mind is unclear. The whisky had gone, but I was very tired. I needed a clear mind to decide.

Mama had saved me some rice and some pizza from a party the police had. Pepe had left for the night shift. Rafa never woke when I got alongside him on the mattress. And that night he didn't shout out. I guess he wasn't hungry after the pizza. As Mama used to say, if you can eat well, you sleep well. I knew I could shower early at the office, so I went back out to the CBM at six. It was barely light, but El Chino Dago was as usual sitting on his stool. A guitar with a broken string and covered in beer stickers was at his side. He was shelling his bowl of *mani* and brushing the debris off a box of CDs, preparing for a day's work.

It was a while since I had taken time for a chat with the old man. He rose off his stool to hug me. There was no white around his eyes, which were raw and red due to tiredness. His face stank of tobacco and rum. "Hola, Felipito, I want to dance I'm so pleased for having seen you. An old man like me needs all the young faces he can find."

"Chino, how can you hope to sell your mani and CDs to the guys at CBM? You know we have no money for that. You need to get down to the Old Town. Catch the tourists. Besides, no one rolls out of bed here until 9:30. You should get some more sleep. I'll wake you up, I promise."

As Chino smiled his eyes became black slits. "No, Felipito, the guitar is only for company now. You know I talk to it every few minutes, but these days I play crap. I wish it could play itself. You bet your life it would be a lot easier. And I never could sing like your dad. Sang like an angel he did. He loved that Varela stuff as well. On good days I can play this damned guitar, but my voice is like a frog's."

"You wrote the songs he sang, Chino. He always said you were the best. I knew a few of the Varela songs, but everyone in Pinar knew yours. They last forever; you are the soul of Cuba. You and Papa cut cane together in Pinar. You wrote a new song every month; every month you wanted to celebrate life."

Chino took out his cigar from behind his ear and started looking for matches in his box. "That's true, *jovencito*, that's certainly true," laughed Chino. "Even the party people sang them when they'd slept with all the girls. I wish I had recorded some of that. It would be worth reminding them one day."

"You could still do all that writing, Chino. Look at all the time you have here sitting on your stool. You're worth more than mani selling. Even in Cuba. You should be selling your own CDs."

"I'm afraid, Felipito. There's no money in music. You pay thousands to record something. The fat cats in the studio take it all. There's nothing in that for an old pensioner like me with a few black marks from El Comandante. In a good month I get 170 pesos; seven bucks, you know, in real money. But as for real 'money,' there is much more 'money,' amigo, in 'mani'!" Chino used his broken English joke for the millionth time. "With the mani I know I can make ten pesos a day. It always sells. It's enough to give my old mum a little chicken on Sunday. And I make as much as a doctor most months."

I lay on the grass by Chino's side. I closed my eyes and sucked in the fresh morning air. The first trucks carrying the construction workers swung by outside the CBM. A couple of guys shouted at us to stop lazing around and get to work. The sun was projecting fingers of light through the row of royal palms.

I tried to help him find the matches. "Do you know something, Chino? This time of day reminds me of getting up in the campo and sharpening the machetes for the *zafra*, how we would begin preparing the pig for roasting so it would be ready for lunch when we came back from the fields. I can smell the pig now. We kids were so excited, you know. It was a party and a feast." I looked up at Chino, but he had dropped his grin.

"They were good days, Felipe. We always had pig or chicken as kids. It seemed so natural in the farms. I feel safe knowing that. Maybe that's why my mamita is ninety-three and I was her second boy. You think I'm old. But she shows how good country living can make you strong. She says she remembers the Spanish here. But that's a lie. But she never saw a doctor, you know, back then. Come to think of it we never knew any doctors. That happened after the July 26 people brought civilization to us. Fidel called it Revolution, but it was really just civilization. The countryside became part of Cuba, and I'll always be grateful for it. You know there was hardly anyone around us who wasn't with the Revolution. Now Mamita is in the hospital half the time, you know. And she says the food is terrible. I know that all her friends complain, because it's something to get over the boredom. But I've seen it, and she's right. My dog would look the other way. Maybe they'll let her home at the weekend. That reminds me. I must save up for the taxi to visit her."

I pulled out a dollar from the packet Laura had given me. "Here, Chino. Have this—a tourist gave it to me."

"What do you take me for, Felipito? Tourists only give dollars to young girls. You're good looking, but not that good looking. Maybe one day in Cuba, but not yet."

When I returned to the office, I felt tired. I had had three hours sleep and needed food. After showering I laid my head on the desk and thought of mani and sugar cane. Chino is the best of the old Cuba. I felt good to have seen him. Like Papa, Chino grew up in the sugar fields. The campo had simple values. No questions. One product. No markets. Papa and Chino on those shiny Russian tractors. They would always give me rides on a Sunday. Proud to cut cane for the Revolution. They said they gave their sweat so Cuba could have its schools and hospitals. One thing exchanged for another. No money. No possessions. Lennon was not the only dreamer.

Moncada was the time for the cane cutters to have their parties. The harvest was long done. They all got drunk, but for Papa Moncada showed him a world beyond Pinar. He felt he was coming together for something bigger, for all of Cuba and the dream of Revolution. He knew that the cane he cut every day was not all there was. Every Moncada he said Cuba was getting closer to the "New Man" that Che wanted. Papa knew the guys got drunk before the Revolution. Now they got drunk differently. Papa said it was now all of us Cubans that mattered. "The Revolution was made for our children, Felipito. Before it we were cowshit. Felipito, whatever you might hear, Cuba is a better place in the year of your birth than it was in 1959. I am forty-one now, but you will see the job finished. Fidel and Raúl did what we needed." Papa was always proud. Proud of his record for cane cutting. Proud of Moncada ... always.

I was more tired than I thought. I remembered that Mama hated the campo; open to the powers of nature, no walls, no limits, and the record sugar zafra they always boasted about. It wasn't real for Mama, because deep down she never believed. Mama never believed in the big dream, so she was left to suffer the pain of disappointment, the boredom of waiting. But we all are told that boredom is what it's supposed to be. Building something proud and something to endure will not always be exciting. It's better that Mama stays lost in her spirit, by the window ... Thy kingdom come, thy will be done. What is the point of thy kingdom coming if there is no control? We are in a random world. They pretend to plan here, but the unexpected always wins.

"Hey Felipe, good to see you at work early." Carlitos looked in my office with an expression that was a mixture of scorn and kindness. "But it's hard to work with your eyes closed."

Mateo
July 21, 8:00

My days were soon running out in Cuba. It was part of the job; I had to move on. I have to confess that I felt good about myself in Cuba, as the time for me had been like no other in any country. I didn't feel Cuban, but we had learned about Cuba in foreign history, a country overseas, how the Spanish brought civilization, how it became the jewel in our empire. My mother never talked about Cuba, her grandparents, and all that. She said, "Mateo, they are all Spanish anyway. They are just like us. Cuba is really Spain with more palm trees." In any case we knew that the church was universal. In Cuba we worked alongside Cubans, but most of the time we were treated as outsiders. The bishops did not want us to develop too close relations with Cuban organizations or to involve ourselves in issues that were called political. This was because the church had received a "space" for its operations that it was supposed to protect and value. The church would make progress, but not through politics. The bishop warned us not to take sides. He argued that the prize that had been won was to run the seminary with the promise of new priests being trained. Those Cuban priests would do the work in society, and the greatest prize of a church role in education would be in reach.

You see yourself in some plan when you get to a certain age. Suddenly you reach a time in life when you feel you should make a difference. I couldn't accept that what I did was random. It was something that took hold of me. I couldn't have continued without that. Those days before that Moncada were dramatic for me, because I realized that I had little time left with the people I loved. I tried to keep focused but knew that at some point my emotions would show through.

That morning I remember receiving the children as they arrived for early Mass. They were on their way to school, but the parents wanted to get them to church first for a few minutes. After school was too chaotic. The children were lively but impatient, and it was not the best time to get them to concentrate.

They would swarm up to me as they arrived. That is when I tried to get them apart. After Mass they lost interest in what was happening as they left the church and returned to Cuba. Of course we gave them food; that was expected.

"Mateo, Mateo, do you have some chocolate cookies for me? Please, just like last week."

"Maybe after Mass, if you have shown good attention. We all deserve a cookie and the nice things, okay. But tell me, what was the best and the worst thing that had happened at school yesterday?"

"The teacher said God was a Communist," joked Guile.

"Well, I'm sure he is," I said, "and a capitalist and a Jew, and Arab ... everything. So don't worry."

The boy was not convinced. "Mateo, Mateo, it's not just that. He said all priests were paid by the Yanquis in secret bank accounts. He said you were mercenaries and not real Cubans. Mateo, is that true as well? Are you just like the baseball stars? All they want is money and big TVs."

"Guile, it's true that I'm not an ordinary Cuban. I was born in Spain just like a lot of your grandfathers and great-grandfathers. I get paid by the church, not the Yanquis. Maybe not much, but it's not in dollars when I spend it. I wish I was paid one one-thousandth of what those guys in baseball make. Did you know I was once a good shortstop? But my name is Mateo, just simple Mateo, not whatever label people want to give me. As for the Yanquis, I haven't been in the United States since I was your age."

Most of the kids were in uniforms ready for school. Some parents put them in t-shirts because the teachers had told them they would lose their uniforms if they wore them to church. One girl was older and dressed in a hugging dress that was not available in Havana shops. She told me it had been delivered in June along with other special gifts by an aunt who visited from Coral Gables.

Carolina looked nervous and waited until the other kids had gone into Mass. "Excuse me, Father Mateo. I want to talk to you about something that is a problem for me. I'm really nervous about what I have to do. And I'm afraid."

"What is it, my dear?"

"It's after the summer, when I have to leave home for the preuniversity. You know, here they call it the campo. I've heard the stories about what happens, and I know they don't like people who have been going to church."

I held her hand and said that wherever she was Jesus Christ would let her know of his presence. She would not be alone.

"But Father Mateo, here I feel that, in this church. Here we feel safe and we can say anything. But if I speak my mind, if I tell the truth there, it will not be good for me. I know I have to go, but what should I do??"

I gave Carolina a hug while I was thinking what to say. This was something I felt a non-Cuban could not understand. These years in the campo were compulsory for all Cuban adolescents. They went to the countryside to learn many things about the revolution and some of the not-very-pleasant things teenagers learn about themselves and adults as well. The church was not allowed to visit them because this was when the state took over.

"Carolina, I can say that our heavenly father faced many difficult times when he was attacked and abused. But his strength of spirit will be always with you. He died for us because he went through the worst times anyone could face on earth. He does not know any barriers. Nothing can separate you from him. Jesus is a man of peace, and anyone will see that in you. They will not be aggressive and hostile if you show his love in your own life."

I knew I would not be around to help Carolina anymore, and it made me sad.

July 21, 9:00
Víctor

My name is Víctor Sánchez Céspedes. Moncada that year was important for me as well. I was born near Artemisa, west of Havana, and have been a member of the Cuban Communist Party since I was eighteen. All the others are giving their side of this story, so now I'll begin mine. There was no softness in what I had done. Cubans, we were tough in those days. They needed people like me. I am as hard as the caoba. So I showed the military I was the toughest of everyone, running longer than anyone in the trials, shouting louder at the drills. I was picked to be regional coordinator for recruitment in the party's youth movement. Don't pick the soft bourgeois because it's the country kids that have balls. At that Moncada I had been president of the Committee for the Defense of the Revolution in Cerro for ten years. My name was visible on a plaque on a wall, and I was proud that I had such a position in the Revolution. Everyone in Cerro knew it was my office. It's nothing really in the top leadership of the Revolution, as there are thousands of CDRs. But my grandfather, who was murdered by Baptista's thugs in Artemisa, would have been proud, I think. I have done good here. The Yanquis would go for me and all the CDRs if they invaded. Let them try, because that is fine with me. I know I have done my job.

What's my job? The job of a CDR president is to organize and defend the Revolution. Okay, I know that sounds like a big job, but it's really about knowing the streets, the houses, the people. Nothing happens in my part of Cerro without me knowing. The system depends on me, and I depend on the system. Moncada was, of course, one of my biggest tests of the year, but the CDR was tested every day. Grumbling was what I received, and intelligence from watching and listening was what I gave. I think I was rather good, but I've already told you that.

It was five days before Moncada—just another Moncada, it should have been. I remember thinking things were not going well. That was nothing new. The leaflets were arriving, and the bus schedules for the march had to be agreed to. One of my problems was that the people did not meet my standards. They were loyal but, well, not the sharpest minds you could imagine. I had to take them because as you know we have no unemployment and all that. There was little for them to do most of the year, so that was fine. But Moncada was different. So I had to start shouting at them. You know, simple things like, "Three cups of coffee will not get the job done," and, "The Revolution will not be held together by paper clips." They'd seen it all before, but what else can you do? They knew I couldn't fire them. But at least they knew that if our CDR didn't deliver we would all lose some perks, like the extra rice and beer that arrived from MININT. What did it all come down to for me? I had twenty-four buses to organize, and thirteen cattle trucks had been promised from a local sugar cooperative in the campo.

As usual I took it out on Hilde. "Who do you think these kids think they are? We used to volunteer to jump under a bus for the *patria*. Now they won't even show up to get on one. And we need hundreds more to give out these damn pieces of paper."

Hilde had stopped reacting to my shouts a long time ago. She had seen it all before in the army. She was a sergeant in logistics, great at organizing distribution of rations. Moncada was, I think, the highlight of her year. She would wear a different t-shirt each day in the week leading up to it. That day I'm sure it was Frank País's face she was displaying. "You know, Hilde, these kids think they can use their bargaining power. They won't even show up to clean the buses without promises of t-shirts. Just try me. I'll get them out of their sociology seminars and back to real work. The buses I get smell like a pig farm. I don't know what parents teach them these days. My dad would have ... I need to get seventeen hundred compañeros to that square by 5:53 AM. Last year Ramiro frowned at me, but we escaped because we weren't the only ones late."

Hilde was reassuring, "Víctor, you know we have some of the best revolutionaries in Havana. Moncada is always a test to keep us ready and fit, so that's why we are set these challenges. It's how our heroes were born," she said, pointing to the Frank País t-shirt. "We will do it just like we did every other year. Viva Fidel. Viva Frank País."

Good old Hilde. Brave for the Revolution. I lit another cigarette, took a long draw, and smiled at her. "Hilde, the Revolution doesn't deserve people as good as you. But don't tell anyone I ever said that."

Hilde glowed with pride. "I ask for nothing but to serve, Compañero Víctor."

I was reassured that Hilde would crack the whip. Everything would be as usual; we would have our shouting matches and then we'd settle back until the next big event. But that morning it was a phone call that made the difference.

I answered the phone, expecting that the call would be about another truck that had broken down. But it wasn't "Hilde, would you mind leaving me? These questions are for the party only." Hilde shrugged but as always obeyed without question. She calmly left the room.

The voice on the line was far from calm. It wasn't what we were taught, and that was a bad sign. Control and calm went together. "Víctor, there's something bad. You have to come over to Calle 13."

The worst part of being head of the CDR was that you were public property and a public spectacle. Any private matters, well, they were very difficult, but there was no alternative. I had to leave for what this telephone call meant. I put on the guayabera I kept in the office—the party people didn't like Nike t-shirts. I padlocked the office and took the keys. No one from outside the CDR was allowed into my office. I remember that I was in such a hurry that I forgot what I had worked out as a security measure. I would arrange the papers in patterns, usually a "V" shape, so I would know if they had been disturbed. Everyone was suspected of plotting in Cuba, and the CDR was always liable to have surprise searches. MININT were supposed to have people watching the CDRs. They wanted us to believe the rumors, but no one knew for sure. Anyway I knew I had been reported many times to superiors in the municipio. They told me. Like a lot of people they were simply too busy with other complaints that mattered more. Some got attended to, but they couldn't do everything.

I picked my way down the staircase of the building. The windows were small, and we kept them closed to keep out the flies. We had one light bulb three floors higher, but like a lot of bulbs in Cuba it did the work of a dozen. Why have more when one will do? It looked good when the party secretary came around—I made a point of showing them. "Frugality is socialism," I remember he said, "Making resources go further is what it's all about." In any case I knew the way down the stairs well enough never to stumble. But no matter for how many years you used that staircase, it did not prepare you for the sunlight. I squinted into the searing heat and light of a summer Havana morning. The caoba trees provided a little shade. I pulled my baseball cap over my face. Baseball cap or not, I was always recognized. There was nowhere to hide in Cerro, but many times I wished there was.

The first group I saw was some kids who had skipped school, I guess telling their teacher they were due at a Moncada practice. Three were trying to fit on the same skateboard. Of course they saw me, as young people are curious about everything. And then it was always ask, ask, ask. They saw me as the guy who could fix their lives. "Hey Víctor, when do I get my place at university? That's where I really want to go; you know, build the Revolution and all that. Muñoz got his for history after only two marches. Computers, Víctor, that's where I want to study. I'd love to get to carry the flag at Moncada. That would be cool."

I had to play the diplomat; you know, Víctor, the guy who stays calm. Try to say something positive. "Don't worry; I've known you since you got your first powdered milk. Why would the Revolution desert you now? You might even be of some use to us one day. I think there may be some other candidates who deserve to carry our flag at Moncada. But one year, you never know. So stay away from the beers."

So that went okay. They would think it was nothing strange to see me. I looked away to try to hide my face from the walkers on the street. But it was the same as always. Madre Ana Maria of the Sisters of Mercy saw me.

"Víctor, I know it's you. That hat will never cover your big head of hair. I can recommend a good barber, compañero. It's the one we sisters use. You see, he takes plenty off. It's great to see you, Víctor. You're going for a stroll to check on your flock, yes? Don't worry; we are all friends, Compañero Víctor. We are all Cubans; let's agree about that. There are no secrets from God—I'm sure he enjoys Moncada as well. Whatever is said at the rally, there will always be a mass every day."

"Ana, I always love to see you. It's good to think that God will be praying for us Communists. I wish I had time to go Mass, but you know the CDR never sleeps."

"We don't exactly sleep at Mass, you know. Come along some time, Víctor; the wine is rather good at the moment. Some friends from Chile have given us some of their best Cabernet." I smiled and I meant it. Ana was a good Cuban.

"I know there are no secrets from God. But someone pays me to do my best to keep some for reasons of national security! You know that those mad guys in Miami would destroy us all. I guess we are doing something right, because so far they are still paying me. But not enough to buy a place in your cemetery." I hurried on.

Manuel, who had made the phone call, was waiting inside the entrance of a dark brown building in Calle 13. It was the regional headquarters of some health group that sent doctors and nurses all over the world. Manuel got to travel around the island talking about what Cuban medicine was bringing to the world. His t-shirt clung to his beer belly and had large circles of sweat under each arm. Manuel used the loose part to wipe his brow.

Manuel checked his cell phone anxiously and carefully stayed out of the direct sunlight. He beckoned me to the back yard of the building, lit a cigarette, and waved dismissively at the notice board outside. It carried transport details of how the organic food experts were to report for the July 26 march.

Manuel thought he was tough and also seemed to enjoy being the most humorless guy in the barrio. He was not interested in small talk. "Look, Víctor. The colonel we have been dealing with has been fired. He's taken a nothing job near Manzanillo while they investigate. His wife is furious as he loses the use of the club in Tarara. She planned to have their daughter's wedding party there. I guess he was too greedy."

I was just mad at the incompetence. Manuel looked helpless. I couldn't stand someone who would drink another beer rather than find a solution.

"So we have to deal with him. What are you waiting for?"

"Víctor, that's not so easy. The colonel is not exactly able to meet us for a *cafecito*. They know when he picks his nose, and they're enjoying watching him stew. The *consejo* is nervous about the image issue. They think the whole story is negative for Cuba, so there'll never be a show trial. Our people are telling everyone to lie low and wait. It could be months, maybe years. What we planned is not going to happen, Víctor, and they will start looking for scapegoats."

On top of Moncada that was not a good start to the day. Manuel always overreacted, but he was right: the colonel was a vital piece in our work. I wanted to encourage Manuel to get off his backside and do something about it.

"There are some folks going to be real angry, Manuel, and that includes me. Part of our world is falling apart."

"You bet your life, Víctor. The world *is* falling apart. And it will fall on us. Why did you trust that SOB? I always said he was nuts. We need to get someone to Manzanillo … I might just go myself," said Manuel, "before they come over to Havana and find this place."

Let him blame me. That was good for his anger.

CHAPTER 5

Mateo

After Mass I had the rendezvous with the Air Canada pilot who had said he would get the asthma inhaler. It had to be at the Hotel Nacional, he said. Anyway, as Eusebio had come up with some money it meant a good excuse for another look at the Malecón. You know, I was really counting the chances I had left. I hadn't been to the Nacional for a month, so there would be no suspicion about the meeting.

The grand entrance lobby was blocked by tourist buses and by uniformed bellboys eager to be the first to greet the new arrivals to Cuba. Impeccable manners meant large tips. A black-suited supervisor checked that the fraternizing did not go too far. There were to be no tips taken in the lobby. I walked up the main driveway, crossing with some young jineteras who were being escorted off by hotel security. I climbed the steps and was greeted by the deputy manager who was explaining currency exchange to an elderly German lady.

I went straight through the lobby and headed for the barbecue grill in the garden at the back. I saw a group of tourists sitting in the wicker chairs examining their purchases from the craft market. As usual the enchantment was overwhelming.

"Oh sweetie, I really like this car made of beer cans. It's like nothing else I've ever seen. I'm going to go back tomorrow to get one of those long truck things. You know, they're called elephants or something like that."

"Actually it's camels, Doris."

"Oh and did you get the ballet tickets? My goodness, how long those mojitos take? Señora, por favor."

I moved on, narrowly avoiding two peacocks fighting over scraps from the barbecue. My priest's uniform attracted no attention—there were plenty of churchmen who came down to Cuba and used the Nacional. I saw the Canadian pilot sitting on a bench with a group of tourists paying close attention.

"Hey Albert," I said, "how's the snow in Winnipeg?"

"Come on, Mateo, even in Winnipeg it doesn't snow in July."

He got up and walked over with his coffee to the stone circle overlooking the steep backdrop to the hotel. "Look, it's better if we talk over here. This is difficult to say." I sat down. "Mateo, this time it didn't work. I was stopped and searched coming in at José Martí. It was all very embarrassing. Anyway they took the inhaler and some drugs I'd brought for an old lady who works in the kitchen here. I'm really sorry."

"Albert, I know sometimes our best plans don't work. But why would they start searching now?"

"Well, Mateo, your guess is a hell of a lot better than mine. You live in this place. I'm sorry more than I can say. But Canadian geese might have more chance of getting in this stuff right now. I'm just grateful they don't take away the mojitos. They are rather good."

July 21, 11:00
Laura

Normally I didn't get to go to the old Havana terminal. Tourists didn't use it because it was kind of shabby. I think the government was ashamed to show it off. So it was the backdoor entrance to Cuba. Nothing fancy. Just the gates, a few boring shops, plenty of police. It was only for the Cuban Americans and some diplomats coming direct in from Miami and New York. José Martí, a couple of miles away, was the showpiece, or at least that was what the Canadians had in mind when they paid for it. No, that's unfair. We Cubans are repaying Canada for it. But the main use of the old terminal was for internal flights.

That day I was meeting a group flying back from Santiago. I was to take them on their next trip; I think it was to the Bellas Artes gallery. But the Russian planes rarely made it on time. So sure enough the "technical problems" meant an extra hour's wait. Felipe would have been shouting and complaining. For him waiting was torture. But one day he would work it out. You know, my father and stepfather are men who waited and waited. They became pretty successful in Cuba. They built a good life. So I didn't mind waiting. But I have to admit I think impatience in a young man is nice. After all, could you imagine Felipe being a night watchman?

In any case, I liked looking at people at airports. The first plane in was from Miami. There was no proper arrivals area, so the crowds waiting were roped back, spilling over into the car park. I mean a cord was all there was to hold back hundreds of people. The kids who could walk were running around, swinging on the ropes and asking any foreigner for money. Their families held firmly to their positions, fearing that they would miss the big moment. I asked a gray-haired guy with a gold necklace how long he'd been there.

"We got up at five, took a guagua. Here at eight. The plane's due at two. But it's worth it. This is our adventure. Happens once every three years to see the *tio* from Yuma."

The woman next to him held a baby high on her shoulders. The man wanted to talk. "Señorita, I can tell you are from Havana; you dress differently. For us, this is what we want. To wait here. This is our greatest day when they come back to Cuba. When they went … Why could anyone go and not come back?" His voice cracked. "We can't waste a second. You know I can hardly bear it. All we have is family."

The police in brown uniforms stood bored and unsmiling. Someone made an announcement about the Miami flight due in thirty minutes. There was another cheer as pilot and crew from an earlier flight came out. It wasn't the flight the necklace man wanted. Waiting, waiting … When the first passengers came out, the police colonel walked up to a tanned man with a bulging belly and a Marlins baseball cap. "Hey, amigo, the tax on that stuff just went up. Sorry, but you have to go back to the kiosk." The man swore and looked back at the queue inside the terminal with the Miami pilot doling out fifty-dollar bills to some official. Then two uniformed women stopped a teenage girl with bulging suitcases and cardboard boxes bound tight with rope. Each case was checked rigorously by the two women as the girl made her way out. I thought they would sting her too, but I was wrong. They let her go with a smile. Not everyone's at this game of blackmail before the final exit. There were tears and shouts. A group of twenty from Artemisa pushed forward. I got kicked on my leg and called out. I moved back from the crowd and decided to get some air in the car park. I found a bench and decided to call the office. The plane was still an hour late.

A large blue van pulled into the parking space behind me. The radio was playing loudly, I couldn't hear my phone conversation, so I was about to tell him to turn it down. I saw a guy get out and immediately open up his cell phone and start talking quickly. I took a close look and realized that it was Felipe's friend Vladimir. He was in a hurry and headed off to a side office, which was the customs headquarters. I finished my call and got up. The van was the strange part. I remember Felipe telling me that Vladimir worked for a computer company. It was definitely him. I'd know that ponytail anywhere. Why would he be using a catering van called "Comida Playa"?

Felipe

I finished my work early—just needed to confirm some results for the laboratory. Nothing new, but that was good. What would we do if we ever found out anything new? I had also done my half-yearly report for the meeting of the Coordinating Committee on Moncada that afternoon. I wasn't invited to attend, so the understanding was that I could leave early. We would all get our orders tomorrow.

Mama knew that Moncada meant there would be new arrivals of food at the bodega; you know, the places where the family's rights to rations were handed out. Mama didn't like going to the bodega. She said she liked to sit and wait for me or Rafa to come back so it would be a surprise. And she would wait in her chair, counting the swings in her chair. Would she get through three hundred before I came back? Mama is the least cynical person I know, but she worked these things out. The government would always try to get good stocks of new rations just before our great patriotic festival. Early afternoon was a good time to shop, because the new supplies, if there were any, would arrive by two. Mama told me we were due some frozen chicken from last month, but they were offering chickpeas instead. Mama had said I should remind them that half of the eggs they had given us last week were bad.

The bodega was open, but there was nothing there that Mama had expected. The posters from the May 1 rally were still stuck on the window. There was an old Christmas tree with a few ornaments stuck at the end of a shelf. Paula, the server, was the most optimistic person in the barrio. I never heard anyone spin a tale better. She was a Cuban in the right job. "Oh Felipe, you should see this new rice we have. It smells so great. The eggs I've been promised tomorrow. He's never let me down that Leonardo, Felipe. You can count on it. Tell your mama she can have a dozen tomorrow." I smiled. I never saw anyone with an angry word for Paula. She was right. There was at least some rice, which had not been in for weeks. But the frozen chicken would have to wait, maybe for a couple of days when the boat came in from Louisiana. It was not a good day, but not as bad as some.

One of Mama's friends, Maria Antonia, called Tita, was sobbing quietly in a corner. "There are no eggs again. I wanted to bake a cake for Kathy's birthday. Just once a year, I needed some eggs. What can I do, Felipe? I can't stand it here anymore. I'm off to Trinidad."

I walked back from the bodega. I hated disappointing Mama. But our situation was not that desperate. It was no better or worse than June. The last of the rations were already spent for the month, and it was only the twenty-first, but I had ninety-five old pesos left. It did not look so bad. There might be a Moncada bonus paid at CBM as there had been once in three years. We never could count on it, but Carlitos would know we expected something. Last year I got forty U.S. dollars, so that would be good, no, very good news. And Pepe would probably get something special in food from the police. There were a lot worse off than us. But it was sad about Kathy's cake. Maybe Mama knew who had some eggs.

I turned the corner to arrive at Calle Jalisco. Yoel was standing by his van, smoking. "Hey Felipe. Didn't expect to see you this early. Have you blown up all the labs at CBM or something? You really must be more careful."

"Yoel, I guess we could always try. But they'd still get us into work. I thought your bread business was still busy though. What's happened—nothing more for the workers to eat?"

"The bread deliveries ran out today. Not sure why. So here I am. There's plenty I can do with my other job. I was going to mention something to you, but it has to wait now. Got to rush, amigo—daughter of the Cameroon ambassador needs another French lesson. She's almost got her head around the subjunctive. But I think they'll be impressed with the new van. My new business partner."

"Yoel, you're a genius. You've never set foot in France and you're teaching the daughter of an ambassador."

"That's why we Cubans will one day rule the world. Or at least those who speak French."

"Yoel, don't give up the day job. That brings in the real bread. I don't think your fancy degrees in French will ever pay for your extravagant lifestyle. Maybe in Paris you'd do better, but I don't think they have fast boats to there. Not yet."

Yoel smiled. I moved on with my bags of rice and a few aging yucca. Mama was sitting by the window waiting for me to return. "Felipito, mi amor, it was 248 swings. And that boy Yoel was looking for you. Didn't come up, though. Never trusted him, Felipito. Don't like the way he treats his family. I bet he took all the stuff from the bodega."

"Mama, there were no eggs. But there was some rice. We need to go again tomorrow for the eggs. Paula will keep you some aside, I'm sure. Poor Tita. She was there. She'd been waiting for two hours. Tita is going back to Trinidad after Moncada. Maybe she won't come back. Says she has more family there and everything is better out there—the men, food, the weather. I think she's losing it, but maybe she just needs a break. Anyway Kathy won't be getting a birthday cake. Not in time for the birthday she won't."

Mama hugged me. "Okay, Felipito, we'll survive. Pepe has promised some more food, as one of the police chiefs had a First Communion party for his daughter; you know, that pretty girl Pepe's always talking about. I must go to see Tita. Without her at home, I guess Jorge and Ricky will be causing a riot. Tita can't cope with them. They're always in and out of jail. Real bad guys. Everyone's tried with them. Mateo tried to get them to work at the seminary just to give them something to do. Jorge might have but not Ricky. Old Víctor of the CDR told Tita they had to be taken out of society. Now Jorge's signed on to the Rapid Reaction Force or something. Pays two hundred pesos a month for sitting in a barracks and doing push-ups. Goodness knows what Ricky will do."

Normally Mama would rush to bring the shopping in to examine everything so she could work out what to cook for dinner. But this time I noticed that Mama turned serious. She moved her fingers behind her neck as if to begin a massage.

"That's sad about Tita. I thought about moving away once a few years ago," she said. "The first time was when I couldn't visit Papa in jail. It was more than three hundred kilometers each way to get there, you know. Hours and hours on the guagua. I could never afford those fares even every six months."

"Mama, you couldn't move then. You know they put these people in jail way away from their pueblos. That's part of the sentence. In any case, I remember you traveling as often as you could. Papa always knew you would do your best. When I went to the campo—that was even further away—you always came to see me every month. Lots of kids from Havana were left alone. Every time you came out you said that cutting cane was not good enough for me. You said I had to use my brains. And the preuniversity thing would all be worth it. So I guess that's why I studied. Yoel and me, there was nobody who put in the hours that we did. I just saw him on the street. He's easy to read, that Yoel, so don't worry. We've been kids together; I know he changes his ideas every minute."

"I don't like him, not from what he said; you know the stuff he used to say about your shoes being like an African's. Pushy and a big head, that's Yoel. Just because they used to have that cousin in New York who bought them shoes. But the travelling. You remember so much, Felipito. You know how much it meant to me going to see Papa. Not just seeing him and being with him.

Over time I grew to like the journey, the planning, the collecting of things I could take; you know, food and some official t-shirts. Pepe always had some of those. The days went so quickly before I was going to travel; when I got news of the date of the visit. And then buying the tickets, standing in line for permissions, chatting to compañeros for hours. The feeling, the thrill when I had everything in my hands. Then the journey, finding a seat and hoping it would be by a window. Deciding when to eat the food, wondering how many breakdowns we would have. I met so many incredible people, you know. Everyone wanted to talk. Even one of Fidel's old schoolmates … I talked all the time I could."

I sat down beside her on her window ledge. We looked out together. The afternoon was still, and the barrio was quiet. I think Mama liked more activity below.

"Mama, there were tough days in the campo too. I always longed for you to come to visit. I hated leaving Havana. Our letters took forever to arrive. I hated the boredom in the campo, no electricity, the blisters, the dormitories. The heavy discussions in the evenings. Some of the kids were, you know, brought very low. They thought it was smart to call their families shit. But really, there was nothing but boredom after the first weeks. The teachers loved their power over us and over the girls. They wanted to show the party how tough they were. No sentiment, no fun. They were the worst I saw. They loved to see the worried parents come and try to love us again. Then the party officials would come and try to pick the stars of the future. The teachers wanted to show us off. We were there in a straitjacket. We learned a language to talk the truth, hiding the meaning of words. We learned to deceive; to play the roles we were supposed to. Never ever say what you really think."

Mama looked at me. "You've been through that, Felipe. I don't think it changed you, thank goodness. It hurt you though,

I know. Your papa thought it would do you good, but he was wrong about so many things."

"Wrong? No, Mama. Papa was a believer. It was part of what he believed in those years. So I trusted him. It hurt so much when something that your father tells you doesn't make sense. It was then that I heard that song. One of the girls had smuggled in a tape player, and one night we listened. She said she felt like the girl in Varela's 'Graffiti' song; you know, that slow beautiful melody when the girl isn't allowed to paint pictures about her sorrow anywhere in the street because the authorities were afraid it would disturb the order and calm. So she paints them in tattoos on her body. That was how I felt. But my world changed when I saw you coming down the road always with so many bags and a big smile on your face. Mama, it was just the greatest feeling."

Mama looked for a cloth but didn't find one. So she used a finger to wipe a tear away from her eye. "Now I don't get to travel much, Felipe. But my family is with me. That is all that counts for me. I guess life is a kind of promise to yourself that one day you will be settled and content. You won't need to make big plans anymore. You realize that someone after all has been watching over you and everything you do. You want to look out, but you don't want to move to what you see. You see, Felipe, I am happy with my life. I wouldn't want to go anywhere else like Tita. Your dada gave me one thing that I have kept. It's this small wooden chair. I think he wanted to make it as a necklace, but he never did. But I like it like this. I put it beside my chair when I'm sitting. I think he meant to say just sit and wait and feel the comfort of what you know. For Tita, it's an escape for her; that's all. She'll find that things are no different there. Havana has everything I want."

I had heard all about the chair before, but Mama saw it as a thing of love and one of those things she wanted beside her. Sometimes she brought it inside and into her bed; it was like that. I knew I had to say something that would cheer Mama. With the stuff about the campo I started well, but I then drifted off into a mood that now did not seem right.

"Mama, it makes me happy to hear that. And sad as well. Why does life always mix up our emotions? We never win everything. There's always a downside. I had a great day yesterday, seeing Vlado, Laurita; even Chino this morning. But I've promised myself something too. It's a little dream that I keep having. I guess it's my way to have a window on the world. I look and I want to see, to put my head further out of the window."

Henry

That Moncada it was forty-five years since the last time I had set foot in Cuba. A lot of people who came from Matanzas were named Enrique, so I changed my name a long time ago to Henry. Few people of my group changed anything else about their lives. We may have had Florida zip codes for our homes and businesses, but we looked across to the island from which my parents had organized my escape. We continued our lives just as we had lived in Cuba.

In Miami that Moncada, we followed Cuba as closely as we did the games of the Marlins. In July they were still in the pennant race. That was a rare thing. In any case I used to tell my kids that one day the Marlins would play MLB games in Havana. Never mind the ninety miles to Cuba from the Keys; the distance to Havana from Miami was more than a hundred miles closer than to Jacksonville. My kids could never understand that.

My business with my partner Sergio was selling cars, and the evening was the best time for doing that. Cubans and Floridians liked the cooler time of day when they were thinking of what they would eat for the evening meal. So we stayed open late. The line of national flags wriggled in the light breeze outside our car lot. The flag of Cuba was next to the Stars and Stripes and the flag of Puerto Rico. Most of them on the strip had the same flags. But every other one we had was Cuban. I liked that. Sergio was drinking his twentieth cafecito of the day.

My Blackberry rang. "Hi Henry, did you ever think we'd be running two trips today? Are you going to dominoes tonight?"

I watched as the clients meandered along the lines of cars. Most of them were there for social reasons. Floridians just liked looking at the gleaming beasts. And some foreigners wonder why Cubans would never give up their Chevys and Pontiacs. Polish them, caress them. They will repay you like a good lover. The punters would come back and back. We knew that, but there was no law against it and better to bring them in—moms, dads, kids, dogs, anything. There were only another fifty dealers within two miles. Sometimes Sergio advertised special "saldos de noche." Today was the ninety-miles day. Five dollars off for every mile from Cuba.

I moved away from Sergio to talk in the midst of the special row of used SUVs. "Not sure about the dominoes, amigo. Dominoes depend on the weather."

The voice remained flat and calm. "But you know we never give up our games. There were eight players from two months ago who want to play again. That is a good earner."

I needed to call Havana. As usual the telephone was answered by a voice without the "have a nice day" sincerity of Miami retailers. "Federación Cubana de Béisbol."

"Abel está?"

I heard a shuffling and a dropping of things on the floor.

"Hola, Federación Cubana de Béisbol"

"How are the games of dominoes?"

This voice was not calm and business like. "It's not good. I don't like it. We have to make some quick moves. The rules of the games are changing."

CHAPTER 6

Thursday July 22

Felipe

It was Thursday morning, very early. Already we were only a few days from Moncada and life was still at its usual pulse, like a steady monitor with no sign the patient's condition was changing. No different. Thursday morning at the CBM. You will now know what my home meant to me. You know what I found there. CBM was like another family. I had moved beyond the excitement, the nerves of the first job, and I was comfortable there. Perhaps too comfortable. You know, I believed I could make whatever impact I wanted. It was what a microbiologist like me should be doing. Every day research, interaction, working for results. I was doing what I had dreamed of and I guess doing what Cuba wanted me to do as well. We had a modern building, and I even had my own office. It sounds good, so why was I confused?

You have seen how my family lived. But we weren't any different. That was it, because most of the time we thought it was the same for everyone. I didn't really mind. The trouble was that when you moved on with your life like I did at the CBM you began to think that you were something else as well. You didn't need to be like everyone else because you had worked out your own life.

I had only just been awarded my office. That was really something, because most of the office was open—everyone together, pressure to conform. We could watch over each other. My office was one that was often shown to visitors as it was close to the fermentation center for monoclonal antibodies. There were photos of past visitors put up on walls as trophies for others to see: the members of the Council of State with the Chinese president and Nobel Prize winners with Carlitos. I was not allowed to lock it, but the section also included a laboratory where there was a safe.

The thing that surprised me about work at the CBM was how slow everything was. We had been told at the university how exciting bio applications were and how the government was determined to make Cuba a world leader in what we did. It was going to produce medicines that would change everything about disease and agriculture. The pace of work was slow, with no deadlines. It was the steady march of research. We were given months longer than we needed and filled up the time with new meetings, teaching interns, and going out to local schools to tell them what a pioneering group we were. We were never allowed to contact the companies outside of Cuba; you know, the ones who invested in new stuff. I mentioned this to Carlitos. He told me to wait. There were other things going on at CBM, and if I waited I would get something better. After two years I was allowed to receive copies of new U.S. and international academic journals. They gave me English lessons as well. They liked me. That was another signal that things were going well. There was plenty of time to browse all the journals and compare what was going on outside Cuba. I was even allowed to e-mail occasionally a researcher at MIT and one at Imperial College London. That was when it got exciting, so exciting to get my first replies from outside Cuba. Carlitos congratulated me on getting the messages. I hadn't told him. He was just reminding me that everything I sent and received was also read by him!

So my work gradually took off. That was good. In fact it had been going in a new direction for the last two years. One day a couple of us at CBM produced some unusual results in the testing of animal vaccines. Carlitos saw them and asked me to write a paper. He said American journals liked to show they were open to receive results from Cuba. They liked to give their readers the forbidden fruit. What we had done could have had big implications for the agriculture industry—the world capitalist market. That was what I was doing. It was a strange feeling thinking that my results would be sent to a U.S. academic journal. For a CBM researcher this was like playing in the World Series.

I worked on this for weeks, months. It went back many times to our official English translator, who told me that no one had ever taken such trouble. We produced the same results time after time, and there was no doubt as to how important it was. Carlitos was excited. I had seen him for long enough to know that. But he was smart and kept insisting that we had to behave like the best in America. So that meant in the article we should not reveal everything we knew. It was business tactics that you whet the appetite for more. So that was what we did. Or rather what I did. We went through three drafts that Carlitos commented on. He kept insisting that we had to meet the journal's deadline for the April edition. So after a late-night session I sent Carlitos the final draft. He said he liked it, and we sent it by DHL to the *American Journal of Virology*. He said we would hear in three months whether it had been accepted.

Those were exciting days in the CBM. We had so many visitors from international labs. The Cuban newspapers were putting out stories every day about breakthroughs from our *polo científico*. Carlitos loved to show off his team, and the visitors poured in. You could tell when Carlitos was in a good mood. It meant he had another delegation of American scientists around who were visiting for congresses organized by the government. Who would turn down a chance to visit Havana in February? The CBM seemed to have money for everything to impress. The PowerPoint slides Carlitos prepared were the best there was. We got the latest software and graphics. Carlitos used his connections with the Council of State to get some bigger entertainment budgets. We loved it too. There was always spare food left over. I saw how those American jaws dropped when Carlitos would give his summary presentation of work at the CBM and how amazed they were that we talked the same language of research. How could this be in a poor communist country? The propaganda was true after all.

I remember the visit of the delegation from the Iowa biotech institute. They joked that they had come into Cuba along with a group of guys selling frozen corn. They were near the end of their tour of the CBM, and they'd seen our vaccines presentation. I'd seen them before at a reception in the convention center. Just before they were leaving, the director came to my office on his own. He made the excuse that he thought he had left something behind. But he pulled out some articles from his briefcase he had photocopied, just saying they might interest me. He put them down quickly and said maybe I hadn't seen these articles. Then he wished me luck and left.

That was a turning point. It sounds weird, I know, but those articles were like discovering a new continent. I knew from the Iowa articles that what I had found in my work was original. The American journals I had seen were nowhere near the full output, and though that shouldn't have surprised me, it did. I suddenly realized that I was part of what was going on in the world outside. Until those articles, I had no idea how many other researchers were looking at the same problems. I had suspected that Carlitos knew more about this than I did. Carlitos found ways of reading most of the international Web sites that were mentioned in the Iowa article. The material gave me other ideas, and I even believed I was ahead of what was going on in the United States. I also knew from the jealousy of the others at CBM that there was little happening that was important in other parts of the organization. The research just moved too slowly, and there was too much checking. It was all produced for the state to show off. Our results should have led to a push to market some products. Even I could see that. Who cared about dusty journals that a handful of people read? But no one had any motivation to push things strongly. The CBM was the front office for visitors, and the staff was supposed to play the game.

One day, May 2—I know the day precisely because we had just had another big rally—Carlitos called me in and said he wanted to offer me a drink.

"Felipe, the article has been published. It is only the third ever from a Cuban Institute accepted by a U.S. journal. As you will see, it has come out at four pages and is prominently featured on the cover of the magazine. It couldn't be better, Felipe, and I and everyone at the CBM are very pleased."

Carlitos had printed off a copy for me to keep, and he said he would pay for a frame to put on my wall. I was excited, more excited than I had ever felt at work. I saw the cover feature and knew Carlitos would see my face was glowing with pride. "New results for animal vaccines from Cuban Research" was the title. The article was on page thirty-six. There it was, signed by Dr. Carlos Istúriz Fernández, Director CBM.

I know I held the magazine for a long time before looking up at Carlitos. I knew that my face showed total dejection. I looked back at the article. Maybe my name would be in a footnote or at the end. No, nothing, nothing at all. Dr. Istúriz Fernández would like to acknowledge the research and dedication of all his colleagues at CBM.

I think Carlitos genuinely thought I would be delighted. "So you see, Felipe, how important our work has become. The Council of State is pleased. We all deserve a drink. This will make news in the American media to show them that the Revolution has a triumphant biotech sector. There is nothing the imperialists can teach us. The minister has promised some recognition of this achievement later this month."

I said nothing, but Carlitos knew what I was thinking. I left the drink. On May 31 I received a brown envelope with fifty dollars in it. There was a note saying, "In recognition of the work of CBM under the direction of Compañero Carlos Istúriz Fernández. This payment is a one-time payment and will not result in any salary increase."

I guess my utter dejection did make its mark. Carlitos knew there had to be a payback. Two months after the journal article appeared, Carlitos called me in again and said there was a delegation being assembled for a visit to Spain. I would be one of the twenty researchers who would visit a Spanish biotech convention and hold two seminars with the University of Salamanca and then on for a couple of days in Madrid. Carlitos did not mention it, but I knew this was intended as a reward. That was how things worked. I had kept my mouth shut, and Carlitos had noticed and was grateful. I was given only two days' warning of the trip, but I knew that this was normal. It was supposed to be like this so that I would have little time to plan any contacts over there. My visa had only been arranged at the Spanish embassy the day before I left. I heard that they had been working on them for three weeks. I knew how these delegations were put together. Of the twenty in the delegation, eight were security minders or party members, and I had been given a nonscientist as a roommate. Fine, I thought; if that's the price, I'll take it.

I had never left Cuba before. None of my family had, except Pepe on his police trips. They called them study visits. So getting on the plane was a big event. I should be sounding cool, but that would not be truthful. It was beyond belief for us Cubans to see those airline magazines with pictures of wonderful hotels and faraway places. And then the excitement of not knowing what would be served as the food. Carlitos had chosen carefully, and I was told that I was the youngest in the delegation, which came from different parts of the polo. The others had been all over the place, including international conventions on every continent, one arrogant oncologist told me.

The plane conversation was artificial. The others were so formal that I doubted they were really Cubans. My roommate was from security and seated next to me on the plane. He only talked about the regulations of the visits. I don't remember a lot, but I had to be back at the hotel every night by midnight. In fact there was little to enjoy about the visit apart from the twenty dollar per diem rates and the reception at the Cuban embassy. Aldo, the leader of the group, was part of the force that had repelled the Playa Girón invasion. He had captured an entire platoon of CIA-trained Cuban exiles and was given regular trips as a reward. Everyone outside Cuba loved to talk to a real revolutionary who had fired a gun. He knew it and played the celebrity whenever he could. Aldo was kind to me as well and said I should make the most of the dollar allowance.

I saw that when the group landed in Spain they began to relax a little. Even my security guard roommate began to talk to me and to drink. I've never seen anyone drink like he did. Aldo and some other members of the group found some cheap tapas bars where they said they were able to save almost twelve dollars a day of their per diems. "If you're careful, young man, you could take back maybe a hundred greenbacks. That will get you that DVD player your girlfriend has asked for!"

So I took that as a signal that I could be myself and enjoy the trip before it was all over. Who knows, it might be the last I ever made. After Salamanca, Madrid was the reward, and I loved it.

I found one bar at the back of the Teatro de Zarzuela, and after the official events were over on the last day I decided to make a final visit. There was this beautiful girl with the short dark hair I had never seen in Cuba. She was with a group of student friends, and she was studying marine biology. She was a *gallega*, and the group was all joking about other provinces that they said were better. Pretty racial stuff as well, but I never heard such lack of respect for politicians everywhere. They talked of corruption and how they would be sent to jail. They started asking me about Cuba, El Comandante, and everything. It was 11:30, and I told them I was leaving for home. They said the night was just starting and not to be so dumb. The girl's name was Blanca, and she insisted she show me the sights of Madrid. Of course she had a car.

"Hey, Cubano, what would you like to see? How about Real Madrid? Did I know Real Madrid? Does Cuban TV ever get around to turning off the baseball and show some real sports?"

Of course I knew Real Madrid. Yes, there was football on Cuban television. I was amazed at the size of their stadium.

In any case we saw it all, and Blanca promised to e-mail me the pictures. I gave her my e-mail address just to impress her, because I knew it would be blocked. It was a great evening, and when we got back at after two Madrid seemed to be only just starting up for the night. I couldn't have cared less about sleeping. I would sleep on the plane. When I arrived at the hotel, the lobby was deserted except for Aldo.

He got up, beckoned me over to him, and said simply, "You're late. You've broken the rules. That is bad."

I started by trying to humor him. "Come on, amigo, you were telling me how to get the DVD player." Aldo's mood had changed. The playfulness had gone and he became the party boss. I knew it would be my last foreign trip. Aldo had a file with him. He glanced down it.

"Compañero Triana, you knew the rules and have broken them. There are no excuses, and I will have to put this in my report here."

It took me two years to recover from the Madrid visit. Carlitos said he had pulled a lot of strings to keep me at CBM. He was disappointed in me, and I should realize that the Revolution demanded total trust. I had been the only member of the group to break the curfew, and I had brought disgrace on the institution. Everyone at CBM knew what had happened. There was a standard way of spreading such gossip. Carlitos would mention it in a phone call, which would be overheard by his private secretary. He knew that within minutes it would be spread around the office. The purpose was served to discourage others.

I had now served my probation. I didn't regret my night in Madrid. I still kept a copy of the menu from the tapas bar—a small souvenir—and the Real Madrid key ring the girl had bought for me. Of course I told Mama about Madrid. I told her about the young people, their fun and the money they had. She just shrugged and said she didn't envy them, but Pepe couldn't believe how stupid I'd been. He never let me forget it.

"Felipe, you behaved like an infant who doesn't know how to use the toilet. You are a selfish bastard, so don't blame the system. You had it made. Me, I paid my dues. I've been sent on these visits, and I saw it as a privilege. Mexico, Nicaragua, I knew how to behave. And you were the one they said had brains." Pepe rarely gave me advice as an uncle, but this time he really meant it.

It was 6:15. Sometimes I couldn't concentrate at the start of the day. I don't know why, but I had a flashback about the drama of the *Journal of Virology* article. I smiled as I thought how exciting that had all been. Today didn't seem half as exciting. I wanted to check my notes on the animal vaccine work. Carlitos claimed he had reassigned others onto it. He was right about never revealing all the details of your research, and I had followed his advice. Never give the full story. Keep more for later. So that's what I had done. I had placed my personal notes in the safe, which was the only one in the lab with a combination. It was supposed to be with my private stuff; you know, some of things Papa had left. Mama had asked me to keep them there after there was a fire near Jalisco. Anyway I was busy checking in the safe when there was a knock on the door. It was Rebecca Fonseca. I couldn't find the documents, and as on most days Rebecca was the last person I wanted to talk to. But I knew you didn't ignore Rebecca, because after Carlitos she mattered most at the CBM.

"Hey, Rebecca, you're in early. What are we doing for Moncada? Is Carlitos having a party?"

Rebecca had been at the top of her biology class at the University of Havana, and she never let her colleagues forget it. She encouraged rumors that Carlitos had chosen her as his successor. Rebecca peered through my door as if there must be something I was hiding. Rebecca had that effect on people.

"Oh, I was just preparing my papers for the day," I lied.

"Okay, Felipe, you can't fool me. But forget about Moncada. All the compañeros who matter here are far too busy, mi amor. Carlitos will be going to all the party stuff; you know, at the very top. But there's no time for those drinking contests here. Don't you know we've got those big presentations on the fungi for the Indians from Bangalore next week? It's a big new opening for CBM. They're even talking of opening a Cuban factory out there. Great for us all. We're the first department to follow through on the comandante's promise to take the biotech benefits overseas; you know, spreading socialism to those less fortunate than Cubans. The comandante said he'll personally meet all the big shots when they come over. It's all on the Web at the *Times* of India."

I knew what I was supposed to say. "Sounds very impressive, Rebecca. Carlitos must be delighted with what you've done." I noticed a wan smile on Rebecca's face. "I wish we could get the same out of the Spanish. But they seem kind of suspicious. I guess it's all political. The EU is pretty much against everything Cuban these days. Kicking us when we're down. Sucking up to the Yanquis. Don't know what happened. I remember when things were going well."

"That's right, Felipe. The EU has become part of the evil empire. We must only trust our friends who are here to do business. Not those who try to get involved with Cuba only to blackmail us later."

Rebecca strode on to finish her PowerPoint presentation for the Indians. I checked again in the safe, but there was no doubt they had disappeared. Those documents meant a lot to me. I didn't understand business but knew that there was money one day in what I had found in my research. But the thing that really annoyed me was that what had gone was mine. Nothing was safe even behind a combination lock.

Víctor

There were some things in Cuba that were controlled in ways we didn't understand, and it was better not to ask. You got on with what you knew. One thing I think I was good at was to know my limits. I know I'm good at fixing some things in Cerro and keeping people in line—all that stuff. But as CDR president you realize you're never going to become a member of the Politburo. What you have to do to survive is to look below and look above. No further. Don't try to pull out the rungs in the ladder, because it doesn't work in Cuba. But there are some people we knew who walked up and down the ladder. They were not supposed to move around the system. But you knew they did and that they knew how to read the signs. Max Pérez was one.

Max Pérez and Pinar del Río. The Vuelta Abajo. That's what you always thought of. July was a busy month in Pinar, and not because of Moncada. It meant preparation time for seeding and planting of new crops in October. Crops, of course, meant tobacco, so I knew Max and his son would be up before dawn. Max worked for himself—and for the Revolution, he told his family. But it wasn't Pinar that made Max. It was Angola. He had grown up with farm machines, vehicles, gearboxes, mechanics, measuring and cutting metal, and knowing the basics of the Willy jeep his abuelo had built in 1953. He knew how to keep jeeps and tanks running. Didn't need the parts, he boasted. Max was our support in the Fiftieth Brigade in the South-Lubango and all around there in '83. He kept us going.

Why did Max ever leave the finca? That was the deal that Max had with the Pinar brigades army commander in Lubango. He knew Max's reputation and said he could offer something useful. Africa was tough, and you couldn't phone for help. It was make it up as you went along. They needed some good engineers to defend the Revolution in Angola, and they put an idea to Max. If he came and ran the engineering of the Pinar brigades, then there would be no ownership issues on his tobacco finca. It would be run by the family, just like over the last seventy years. Lubango, those were the times. It was Cuban boys in battle, so everyone talked about the fighters. But it was Max whom everyone turned to. That was our base, and Max and I kind of lost our youth together.

The army kept their bargain, and Max settled into his business after Africa. Max always said he was lucky that the Revolution had recognized the skill of the tobacco farmer. Stick with a winner, of course was what they saw. Those *barbudos* were practical as well. He didn't brag but would say quietly that in the last ten years he could make far more than the cooperatives he grew up on. He gave his slice to the Revolution. He was so thin that I used to tell him he was giving Raúl and the army more than an arm and a leg. He should think about himself and keep some more, and I'm sure he took my advice. Max was making money, I knew. He tripped off to Spain and places. He told me to look into getting a Spanish passport like him. If your grandfather was born there, then you qualified, he said.

Anyway, Max and I survived the hellhole of Cabinda. Max made sure we always had the best Cohibas in the evening. A few boxes labeled brake pads had different sorts of boxes—*humedores*—in them. Max said you should run your life with nature. Respect it and it would respect you. Your hands were the key to tobacco, because the plants were frail, flimsy. They dreaded the hurricanes of October or November. Powerless to resist. But the leaves could become strong and leathery with a gentle caressing touch.

"Víctor," he said, "look at my hands. The leaves know I love them. I can forget about everything else here. No one, no business can come between me and the leaves. There is something that only Pinar can teach you. The year 1959 changed a lot, but did not change nature."

I had only had the Lada fixed in Cerro that week. You knew everyone would be off work or drunk during Moncada, and without the Lada I was lost. But it began spluttering on the carretera just past Soroa. The tourist buses headed off to Las Terrazas for breakfast. No one could ever say the road to Pinar was beautiful. I told Max that God gave the rest of Cuba beauty but he gave tobacco to Pinar. Okay, Viñales is pretty. But the rest you can keep. Max didn't argue. "Pinar is the soul of Cuba; it will never be a beauty queen. It's this soil that is our gift, you know. Whoever owns Cuba knows that this soil is special. We have the twelve-year malt of tobacco. It's okay right now, just until the next lot who tries to run this place takes their slice."

Thank goodness the Lada made it to Max's house. It would have been a bit difficult explaining to MININT why I was heading out to Pinar a few days before Moncada. You couldn't see anything from the road except this dilapidated barn. It was clever. Behind the barn was the neat wooden house, with a flower garden he said was his wife's pride and joy. It showed a real burst of color all around the front veranda. The tile work was from Andalusia. Max had been making good use of his Spanish passport. To the side of the house was a large white canopied area of cheesecloth covers. Underneath were the seedlings carefully protected for the planting season. Max was stooped over, checking for tears. He looked up at the sight of a Lada churning up the red soil, and I knew his gaze would be first on the green MININT plates.

I parked the car behind the back of the house. When I walked back Max had already left his cheesecloth and was ambling toward me with a big smile. His dogs appeared from behind the barn just to make sure I was a real friend.

"Sorry to interrupt the dogs' breakfast. Amigo Max, it's great to see you, but I would kill for a *refresco*. Do you have a cold one?"

Max came close and looked straight at me. The swept-back gray hair made him look taller than he was. He didn't speak right away, as if assessing why I had come. He put one hand on each of my shoulders, taking a chance to reinspect my face. "Take your time, Víctor. I'm never inconvenienced by a visitor. I assume you didn't drive over just to test the speed of the Lada. Anyway, it's good to see you. I hope you can stay for more than a cola. We don't have the pace of life in the capital out here. Relax. The planting will work just as well in an hour."

Max beckoned me inside, "No dogs in here, but compañeros from Lubango are always welcome." He opened the fridge and pulled out a cola and looked at the can to admire it.

"Thanks Max. I forgot how good that is. Almost as good as the real thing. I feel ready to talk."

I looked around the house. It's an automatic reaction I think most people in government have. Was this the sort of house where someone paid the builders to put in a listening device? I pointed outside to Max, and we headed into the barn.

"It's better to talk in here, Max. The meetings have gone well, but there is a problem with the links out in Santiago. The colonel over there has been removed. Now he's offloaded to a nothing job in Manzanillo. There's a new team in place, and they're inviting the colonel to tell his story. I expect he will."

Max appreciated the humor. Cuban interrogators did not need an invitation to do anything. He wiped his hands on a cloth and walked over to the bench at the back of the barn. He was silent for at least a minute. One of those big hands gripped the edge of the bench tightly.

"This is serious, Víctor. We have only ever worked with trusted people. This has never happened to me before. It comes with new people coming in from outside the province. It is one of the oldest techniques of the Revolution. Bring in the guys who are not cozy with everyone. The important thing for us now is to lie low for a few days."

Max was still thinking. "There was a separate cell, Víctor; you know, a back-up strategy. If the colonel breaks before Moncada we'll know. So maybe he'll talk enough about the fast boat stuff and that will satisfy them. They'll not even wonder what the rest is about. Did you say Manzanillo? I'll get a message to him. I've never worked with anyone who betrayed me," said Max.

Max brushed down his shirt and lit up a stub of a cigar from behind his ear.

"I'll think about things, Víctor. You know me; never make a hasty decision. I'm traveling to Spain in a couple of days, on a cigar marketing trip. Don't do anything until I get back."

He went over to a deep wooden chest at the top of a short staircase leading to a second floor of the barn. He took out a box and gave it to me.

"Here, take a few of these back for the muchachos. They're the ones I saved—revolutionary heroes, I call them. The quality's actually back to the seventies now. I'm really pleased about it. It's too bad the Yanquis can't buy them."

I thought I would tell Max something he didn't know.

"Don't you believe it, Max. All the bankers in London and Tokyo stuff their pockets with these. They know how to get them through the customs. I guarantee that some of the biggest deals on Wall Street are celebrated with Cohibas—just like before. You're sitting on a gold mine." Max smiled. Of course he knew this already.

I walked back to the Lada. I looked back to the finca. Max's gray hair glistened white against the red earth and the green leaves. I noticed that Max didn't return to the cheese cloths but went inside. I think he was worried.

CHAPTER 7

Yoel

You must understand that having a motorbike was the best thing that could happen to anyone in Havana. It gave you transport, it gave you contacts, and it meant you could break free. Felipe was the one who never seemed to break free. He was stuck in this hopeless dream of biology, stuck in that terrible laboratory where he believed something exciting was possible. We were good students, Felipe and I. In fact we were very good. That was great. We thought we would be the leaders of something in Cuba reserved for those who were successful. Then it dawned on us. We didn't study for ourselves. At least it dawned on me. I had worked it out, but Felipe had a long way to go.

My brother Abel worked out something else. Baseball would always mean something in Cuba. The Revolution had no choice, because baseball was always too big in Cuba. Baseball couldn't be changed, because it was successful. And a strikeout was just the same to imperialists as to true socialists. So baseball people would always be royalty in Cuba. Baseball, the game that won Cuban hearts and minds long before Karl Marx. And they knew how good they were at that.

Abel worked and lived at the palace of Cuban baseball, called the Latinoamericano stadium. I'm not saying Abel didn't like baseball. Of course he did, but he liked the system more. He didn't propose anything different until he was told it should be different. He had followed the same routine for twenty years; a very cautious guy, Abel. I guess you know everything in baseball can change with one hit at the bottom of the ninth. You were never the winner until the lights were turned off. So Abel never took anything for granted. Everything was done in handwritten files because Abel could not count on the photocopier being in working order. And it was easier to burn in a hurry than smash a hard disk from a Chinese computer.

Abel was proud of his organization. It took him eight years into the job before he would loan me one of the stadium bikes. Then he discovered anyone could do it. Abel made himself irreplaceable. I don't know what it was, but working with all those baseball heroes made him lose his sense of fun. Abel used to be the joker. No more. I used to try to catch him by checking the dates of his files. All files were kept for five years and not a day more. One day I found one that was sixteen days overdue. He hit the roof. Abel gradually started to show off. His big statistical charts were pinned to his wall. He was so proud of them, and the president of the federation used to bring around visitors to show them. One of them left a highlighter pen on his desk, and Abel became obsessed. From then on Abel used to ask visitors to send him colored highlighters, which I guess are unavailable in Cuba. I can't be sure, because I never looked, but I can tell you that Abel's charts became covered in pink, yellow, and green.

Abel had wanted to be a player or a coach. Most of the guys around the stadium had been big shot players. There was a picture in his office of Julio, a pitcher who'd been with the Washington Senators in the 1950s. Julio had told Abel that he could make it, but I think he was too nervous as a player. He would tell Dad he got itchy skin before going to bat. Used it as an excuse, I think. So baseball for him was more about organization, the statistics, the watching and waiting, the calculating of what had changed. In other words, not a lot.

At least Abel had a home in that stadium. He was like mayor of the village. Abel lived at that stadium, keeping all his clothes there, thinking that if he left someone might take his job! I mean he was a crazy man. They offered him foreign trips, to the Olympics and all that, but Abel said no. He couldn't leave his family. Abel would say it had shown what Cuba could achieve against the biggest powers in the world. There was always the next international championship to plan, and Cuba usually won. No surprises there, either. Abel said that was nothing but he was Cuba's leading fighter against complacency. Sounds pretty pompous, doesn't it? But that was not Abel.

For Abel baseball kept its dignity by not changing. That's a big difference between us. It's pretty boring to stick to the same. The Revolution had it right somehow. If you are going to change things you have to build the new man. Nothing less. And baseball simply built the old one. They say everything in the Havana stadium is modeled on the 1950s. The distances are in feet, the speed guns in miles per hour. Abel was always immaculately turned out—the national track suit, the proud red cap with the C on the front. Effort, preparation, repetition, neatness. His offices were always open as coaches, players, and their families were in and out all day. Who knows, maybe Abel was right. The Revolution will be gone and all we will have left will be baseball. Cuba will always count in baseball.

I went in to see Abel when we needed to talk business. The phone was no good for that. One thing I could never understand about Abel was how he had so many girlfriends. What did they see in him? Maybe it was the uniform; maybe everyone in Cuba thought baseball was cool. I came in that Thursday. A tall lady with bleached hair dressed in yellow spandex walked into his office.

"You never cease to amaze me, Abel. How can you work in here? There's no photocopier, no e-mail, not even any decent pens. You should see how a proper business is run. I thought you were supposed to be world champions." It took me a while to realize the change in hair. I had become used to the different females, but this was Yamelis, Abel's wife, who had stopped by with the boys. The kids were also wearing the Cuban national team shirts.

Abel never saw the joke against the baseball system, even from his wife. Without looking up from his highlighters, he muttered, "Okay, okay, I know. It's what happens on the field that matters. And everyone knows Cuba's still the greatest."

"Anyway, I can see you are busy as usual," said Yamelis. "Can I take the Lada? The boys need to get out to Santa Fe to play their soccer. You know how they love to arrive in a car."

"Wait, chica. Yoel here may need to leave for Santa Clara later. Big job on over there. Can you call your tia? Here, use the phone."

Yamelis was about to throw a book at him. Abel was always the conciliator. "Don't worry. Yoel will take the bike."

Felipe

I should have remembered that it was a special day. Mama had said she used extra washing powder to get Rafa's uniforms looking white. The rest of us would have to wear dark clothes. Appearance is half the battle, and it was a big sports day for Rafa. Volleyball, his passion. Nothing mattered more to a thirteen-year-old. In Cerro the schools were closed anyway, getting ready for the Moncada marches, so instead they had sports that led to some big finals on the day before Moncada.

Rafa's dreams were all in volleyball. I wasn't sure he would be tall enough, but you never knew at thirteen.

"Feli, this is when they pick all the talent. I have to be there and do well. I promise you a week on my side of the

mattress—anything if you can help me with some new moves."
He didn't have to tell me. I knew already. I was woken up by
Rafa's dreams, lived with his disappointments, and celebrated
the triumphs. Rafa was right; sports did matter. At street level it
came just below food in importance. The Comandante loved to
see Cubans compete among themselves and then beat the world.
Everyone wanted their kids to go to the elite sports schools.
There were perks and jobs for everyone. The parents wanted that
more than A grades. I'm not sure Mama had fully realized that
yet. I don't think she ever expected her sons to succeed.

And I think I had been a good brother to Rafa too. For
thirteen years I had held him in my arms, told him about Papa,
and answered his questions about girls. All those long sticky
nights counting the mosquitoes we could hit. I think it helped
make our shoulders strong. So I had some rights to feel good
about it. Most brothers can teach something that is worthwhile,
and I wanted to give him ideas not just for dreams but to stop
the mistakes. I hope he will remember one day that I had been
the one to show him how to time his jumps in volleyball. That's
the small thing. I used to tell him how he should accept defeats
as well. Congratulate the other guys. It was easy to rush around
screaming when you won.

The phone rang in my office. Rafa had just left home to go
to use the phone at the bodega. "Feli, did you forget we have our
game today? Why are you at the office?"

"Of course not, hermano. How could I forget? Your game,
it's what I'm looking forward to; it's the greatest thing about
this Moncada."

"This is serious, Feli. You know that I have a shot at getting to
the regional squad if the coach sees me today. It's all or nothing
today. I need to see you there, Feli. Promise me you won't miss
it. This is our big, big game when we have to smash Playa. Then
we can try Los Baños."

"Okay, okay, Rafa. Take one step at a time. The coach may be there. It's a big day for the whole family. We'll be cheering you every step of the way." I needed to get out and think. A volleyball game would be as good a place as any. No one would notice at CBM if I slipped out now.

Mateo

It had to be today. Thursday was the one fixed time. It was the only chance for me to visit the prisons. It was a long journey anyway, but with the right papers you knew there was a chance it would come to something. I can't say that planning to visit the prison, Kilómetro Cinco y Medio in the province of Pinar del Río, filled me with joy. It was not something I had been used to. But everyone talked of prisons here, and they were as familiar to most families as watching speeches or attending rallies. People went to jail, and I know that one reason was that it was useless for the government to fine people with no money. After all, even El Comandante had been in jail, and a priest had been useful to him. Now there were supposed to be over four hundred jails in Cuba, but no one really knew.

Pinar was the jail where some of my parishioners' families were held. It was the only one I could go to, to get there and back in a day. Clara at the seminary told me that Cubans visited jails like going to visit their grandmothers. No one, of course, liked murderers or rapists, but there were plenty of other categories. Most of them had broken rules; that was true. But they were not troublemakers. People who were not in jail were sympathetic; they knew it could be them or their families. So prisoners in Havana, especially those who were there for "antisocial" crimes, were high on the list for gifts of food from restaurants and hotels. I did my rounds late on Wednesday. I pulled an old suitcase that made me look like a tourist who had just arrived. At the Casablanca there was always pasta, and maybe some ham. The Havana Old World hotel offered rice and beans packed in an old Coppelia ice cream tub. I kept as many separate packets as possible so the guards would find it easy to take some themselves, leaving a little for my prisoners. Some of the hotels which didn't have food would throw in soaps and shampoos. This helped with the governor, who said the "ladies in the jail" were always grateful for such pieces of baggage. Since there were no women prisoners I assumed he meant women on the staff or in his family. Gustavo, the governor of the jail, was a hard and unamusing man, but a few pieces of soap, especially from the Spanish hotels, might produce a smile.

So with the suitcase as full as possible I took my place in the line for bus tickets. As always the lines started forming at 5:30 for the 6:30 bus. We had booked our tickets, but no seats were guaranteed. I had learned the transportation rules. A few extra pesos here and there would get you to the front of the line. I took some bottles of water in a black trash bag. By eleven o'clock the heat in the bus would be unbearable. I looked along the line and up into the bus, which was already half full. Many were laughing and chatting, excited at the prospect of a trip outside Havana. Of course most of them were going on happier trips. There were families carrying toys, soap, and clothes from what they had mustered in Havana. They would return with fruit from the market stalls in Pinar and if they were lucky some pork and fish. A group of schoolkids were off to dance a show in some hotel at Maria La Gorda, and they spotted my water.

"Hey, Padre, it's roasting in here. We have to go all the way to La Gorda. Spare us some water, you angel."

I ignored the cheekiness and tossed a couple of bottles.

"God bless you, brother," one said in English.

I looked behind me and saw that people were still arriving, hoping to cram into the earlier bus. The bus driver was anxious to leave, urging the passengers to get on board. I saw three familiar faces among the crowd. I was pleased they had made it. These were three wives of men in the Pinar prison who were serving time for political crimes or collaborating with the enemy, which in other language was called journalism, opening independent libraries, or activities seen as a danger to the state. They stood out from the other bus passengers because their hands carried little, as they knew they were not allowed to deliver anything. They always traveled together: Zelda, Sara, and Haydée. Two of them had already had a three-hour journey from the campo to get to Havana. They hoped to see the same prisoners I did. Sometimes they got in; sometimes they didn't.

Zelda, Sara, and Haydée were now holding hands, sitting on the curbside singing quietly and swaying to imaginary music. They had put an old box to mark their place in the line for the bus, which everyone seemed to respect.

"I'm pleased to see you young ladies. How have you been?" I asked. "Another three months have passed. Are the guys holding up? This time I'm going to ask to see Silvio. They usually allow me to see only one of the mercenaries."

It was a joke, but the women seemed not to hear. I tried another question. "Do the guys ever talk? Are they ever allowed to meet each other?"

Sara, the youngest of the three, spoke quickly. "No señor. They are never allowed any contact. Not even by sight. That's the one thing they insist on. They live fifty meters apart, but they fix things so they never see each other. The punishment is made extra severe."

The bus driver came around to check the papers and made a perfunctory search of the bags of the women. "We make fourteen stops before Pinar, unless I get a better job in the meantime. But you know after forty years that's pretty unlikely, compañeros," he joked.

The last passengers filed on, swatting the flies. It would be six hours before they reached the final destination. The bus pulled out of the parking lot and headed through Revolution Square and out toward the main carretera to Pinar. Zelda got up to chat with me. She was short and strong with skin blotches burned by too many hours of summer. But her voice was pale and wavering like a child's.

"Padre, here we go again. But I get more depressed every time we visit. How am I going to keep this up for twenty-three years? They say the mercenaries never get released early. It's supposed to be an example to the others."

"Things will change here, my dear. It won't be twenty-three years, Zelda. One day all the prisons will be flung open and Cuba will discover all the talent it didn't know it had. I think your husbands know that to wait for something there must be a goal. "

Zelda was not convinced. "We are supposed to have brains. You know, Padre, I studied law, just like El Comandante, and we learned about other international systems. They teach you all this. Trials, verdicts, appeals. The division of powers. They read us the laws; they have seminars on the constitution. Very nice, but no one asked my opinion. We have no right to appeal anything. The judges work for the same people as the police and the jailers, and they work for the same people as the government. The press is all on the same side. The world never sees the conditions, and we don't either. That's it. We are told to wait and things will change."

Zelda looked up at the ceiling of the bus. A small boy leaped off the lap of his mother to grab a rolling ball. Zelda picked it up and passed it to him, patting him on the head. She turned again to me. She seemed relieved that she had spoken her words. "I'm worried, Padre. Twenty-three years may be too long for him to make it. Silvio is tough. You know he was a boxer for his province. But he's not well now. It a gastro problem he said in his letter. No clean water, insects, other prisoners' vomit, spit. It's all too much to describe. They are normally fed just before we see them, but the food is terrible. We're watched all the time, and sometimes if they aren't well we're told they're working. Then we don't get to see them at all. We have no choice on the day. They pick it. If we don't show up it's another ninety days. We don't know how they spend their days. I've heard some people say they have this aluminum burner where they have to work. They get burned as they don't have any protection. If they do, we can't see them. But what choice do we have? We get one letter a month. And every word of that is read by the guards. We know nothing about what they're going through. My children ask me. They know what's going on. The kids at school taunt them: twenty-three, twenty-three. Now they've made a song out of it …"

I heard the tiredness in her voice and saw a fragile spirit in her eyes.

"It's important to keep visiting. It means so much to them. I'll do what I can to talk to the governor about the conditions. At least we in the church can do something. They know that the church has a voice in the world, and we can use that voice to speak louder."

I was troubled that I did these visits for my own satisfaction. What did it achieve? I took them some bars of soap and stale food. That would last a few seconds. Seconds in twenty-three years.

Víctor

I may have wanted to leave Max and the tobacco seedlings, but the Lada had other ideas. It was now mid-morning in Pinar. I tried to start the Lada, but it was dead. Whatever my achievements in fixing the problems of the Revolution, fixing crappy cars from the Soviet Union was not one. Of course Max came to put his head under the hood. He seemed to be enjoying wrestling with the problem. "This will take some time. But nothing Russian ever defeated me." Always deliberate, he carefully wiped his hands of oil and insisted we make some coffee first.

"Max, I think you're losing your touch. I guess when you're used to the BMW, our old friend the Lada is like fixing a steam engine. Anyway just bear in mind that if I miss this volleyball ceremony I'll be steamed alive as well. I have to head back."

"Stay calm, Víctor. This old girl will get you back. They're just some loose connections."

"What will the Comandante say on Monday?" I asked. "I'm wondering where he's taking us all this time. Hilde, you know, the true believer in Cerro, is saying she's never seen the military so jumpy. Don't know why. Can't you read the leaves and tell me? The tobacco must be giving some signs. Maybe the colonel has been picked up because of something else, you know, really big. I don't like the signs. The Comandante may be lining up some surprises about who runs what. I'll nail those bastards who have become way too comfortable, he's saying. Time for a shakeup. Learned that from Stalin, he did. You remember Ochoa after Angola. Last time this happened the mayors and secretaries in Havana and Pinar were all changed. They brought in all their new guys. All the deals were changed."

Max didn't like distractions. He put his coffee down. He had figured out the Lada, started the motor, and slammed down the hood.

"Look, Víctor, you have to expect some changes. The comandante always knows you have to talk about change. He's been the guiding force of all that we know. Without him we would all be nothing. He's the leader. He's always brought in new guys he trusts. New guys, even some chicas, all wanting more responsibility. The Revolution has to be facing new challenges, new threats. You have to show you can shuffle the cards to produce some fresh faces. Those ready to put their lives on the line, twenty-four hours a day. If you're loyal you have nothing to fear."

"Max, I've given my life to this Revolution. I am fifty-eight years old. I would like to think it owes me some loyalty. But I know it doesn't work like that. It's all right for the ruling family and military. They have made enough to live well, to travel, to do what they want. They are protected from change. Max, you are okay whatever happens. Tobacco is gold here. You have this finca, a life after Fidel. But you know me. We have known each other forever. I have nothing to rely on. I know some people who led the CDRs and they are now sweeping parks."

"It's all rumors, Víctor. I'll check with my brother. He's always barbecuing with the army people. It's the beef he gives them, a few cattle here and there. You know, sometimes it's best to wait and be patient. It took me fifteen years to get this patch of land back from the bunch of amateurs in the cooperative. It matters to me what happens. The others just want some money for lying around all day drinking rum. I work harder, make some money, and the stuff is sold to those Spanish to show off in their tapas bars. If you are employed by the state it's just a job, and nobody cares. Now I keep quiet and have a better life. In the future, Víctor, you will have a great ... what is it the Yanquis say? Oh, yes, you will have a great resume."

I had never seen Max so animated. He seemed to expect to enjoy the future. "Max, that's okay for you. If I'm surplus to requirements tomorrow, what do I have to show? I have three sons, and they get kind of expensive. I know I should have married earlier. But you know me. I spent years in the campo, planning pioneering programs, organizing workshops, explaining Havana policy to the guys who could barely read and write. I have done my apprenticeship, waiting for something better. I never took a vacation ... never. I got to where I was by hard work, nothing else. But now they will take it away in a moment—just a sweep of a pen. Probably some of those guys who couldn't even write."

Max smiled. "Víctor, you underestimate yourself. You could come back to Artemisa and do something for yourself."

"Max, like what? I'd screw up a tobacco crop in an hour. I don't have the patience for that. It's waiting and waiting for something. We never know what to plan for because it's not up to us. You are one of the lucky ones. If I wait fifteen years I'll be dead."

Max had had enough of me. "Thanks for the visit. I'm off to Spain for a couple of days, but I'll let you know what my brother has to say. He's the most discreet person I know in Santiago. He's never done anything for himself. So it can't be in the genes."

The visit to Max hadn't reassured me at all.

CHAPTER 8

Vladimir

I had worked it out. In Cuba if you can control the information, then you can survive. I was the versatile end of the Revolution, I told them. Look, everyone wants to know what's happening. Cubans love gossip, and no one can make gossip a crime. Not even the Communists. So you may not like information technology, but you can't ignore it. The Revolution didn't predict that there would be computers, so we needed to adapt and make them work for us. We had to own the technology and make it serve the Revolution. I was one of the pioneers of information. I got ahead of the curve and made it my own. I was not the only one, but I was the best. Everyone said if it's computers let's ask Vladimir. He's a cocky bastard, but anyone else will give you all that bullshit and pretend he's a Cuban Bill Gates. He's the only one who delivers. Of course the Revolution knew you needed controls on computers; otherwise they will destroy you. I told them that as well. Then I knew some of us would make money from them because we were paid to fix the controls. The government decided who needed computers. So I made it my job to buy them.

My home was on Third Avenue in Playa. That was no accident. I didn't choose it; I was given it. The reason for that will become clear. I lived in an area of many diplomatic and business homes. I knew it was the most beautiful part of the city. You may have read about those wonderful tree-lined streets of western Havana. Well, it's true, the wonderful part of it. This area of Havana was always reserved for those who had made it. And people who made it in Cuba made it big. You know, the rewards in Cuba were always enormous: the wealth, beauty, the big fish on a pretty small island. Life didn't get any better than in Playa. It was built in the 1940s and 50s close to the yacht clubs, the Biltmore, and all that. Most of the wealthy families that owned the property had, of course, left years ago. But I'm sure there were many in Coral Gables who still dreamed of these quiet parts, a July mango sucked and chewed by the ocean, childhood memories of days spent at well-equipped beach clubs with nights in the best restaurants and clubs of the world. Okay, you may try to copy it all in Miami, but there's only one Cuba.

Some of the wise old Politburo guys would stroke their beards and pronounce solemnly that they knew about the computer business. Cuba has no need to worry. Price them at over one thousand dollars and even the Cubans with their meal tickets coming from Miami will throw their hands up in horror. In any case we can screw them on Internet access. After all, a computer is an expensive toy for typing. But no, I knew it was wrong to underestimate Cubans. Even if they don't get to own them they'll use them. That was like communism. They'll find a way. The graybeards loved to surf the net, check what was being said about them by *Le Monde*, the BBC, CNN. They're vain like everyone else. Then they'd find out that others would want to do this as well. The Politburo was thinking they could run it like everything else. I could tell they thought their system had won. But a few months back I noticed that they'd changed. Suddenly they were talking worried. How do we get on top of all this? Cubans have come to know too much about computers. The Revolution had to fight back, and I didn't disagree. I said they were damn right. You should be worried, because you never wanted the world to invent computers. So that's when they called me, Vladimir, the Lenin Academy loyalist who was smarter in fighting in cyberspace than on the battlefield.

Moncada was always a spectacular time for the flamboyant trees in Playa. As if the beautiful houses weren't enough, the planners of Havana had made an even more exotic cocktail: trees and vegetation that couldn't be spoiled by men and required no maintenance. They had provided the same blankets of red for decades. Long avenues with their red archways. The white clouds and blue sky, the red, white, and blue of the Cuban flag. Playa was there for me every day as a reminder to keep going. One day I might even get to Miramar and Siboney. Those were the houses to the west of Playa heading to the Convention Center, and they were fantastic mansions by the standards of anywhere in the world.

But I knew what I did came with a price. I was there not because of what I owned but because of what I did. You can't keep secrets in Cuba, and if neighbors want to know they'll find out. You have to respect them for that as well. No one did well in Playa without a story that they would prefer wasn't told. My job was to piece together the stories. My bosses looked after me. The car was nice, but not special. I had plenty of time to deal in a few computer parts, which had given me a nice store of CUCs. The Doberman, Kurt, also was also mine, but he came out of my state security allowance.

It was my idea to put up a sign outside the house that said "Computer repairs. For CUCs only. The dog bites." Why? Because they asked. I told them that some Cubans might get some cheap laptop that crashed on them. They'd come to me because no one else had offered that. They probably wouldn't know what information I could get about them. No one else was offering to repair things that most Cubans were not supposed to have. I had tried to get Felipe involved in that business too, but he said biology was some promise that he had made to his father. Got to admire that boy's loyalty, but what else has he got?

My house was protected by gates on each entrance and bars on the windows. Actually that wasn't unusual in Playa. Looking around, there was wealth and therefore envy everywhere. The government knew that, but with the importance of business and tourism the foreigners had to be protected. Even the criminals knew that jail sentences in Cuba were doubled if the crime was against a foreigner. That gave the message. Anyway, maybe they hadn't taken it in, or they had but they had figured it was worth the risk. Because everyone was building fences with wire and private guards. But that had not stopped the break-ins. So I bought Kurt. Kurt was from a new Doberman breeding program started by one of the big kennels in Santa Fe. The same breeder supplied the military and seemed to have access to some special dog food. Unfortunately no one told me that Kurt would only eat meat or imported dog food. So far the cost was worth it. I had had no break-ins.

At the back of the entrance to my house there were two locked doors. If anyone asked, I said that they were the storerooms of the computer parts. But in reality there was nothing there apart from boxes from the Huawei Corporation. You see, the government had learned a lot about surveillance, and the obvious people who had computers were the foreigners. Anyone who controlled an Internet server was, of course, master of everything. When an "http" address had the magic letters "cu" after it then we were just lapping up the information for free. So this was why I needed to be in Playa. If they didn't like me as much I'd be in Lawton. But no one had computers there, or no one that we'd found, anyway.

All the messages sent from laptops, PCs, etc., within a five-mile radius came through my screens. My monitors were arranged on shelves around the room. Yes, of course I had to file some reports to justify all this equipment, and these were sent to the MINCOM, the Ministry of Communications. The checking normally took only twenty minutes as the software had been programmed for tracking Internet key words by all those private users of the Cuban servers in Playa. I punched in the key words program. Anything that was dangerous was in there. A real juicy pack of control words. I could add to them if some friendly foreign government asked me to check for a bad guy. But we certainly had the names of the opposition, some churchmen, and naturally a lot of government officials. You may wonder why everyone in Playa didn't know about the Vladimirs and their locked closets. Well, I will be honest. There were indeed few e-mail users stupid enough to send open messages on these subjects. If they did, we figured that they were too incompetent to be any threat to the state. But the thing was that it was like a comforter for the government. Information from computers will never beat the capacity of humans to control them.

I cast a bored eye over the screens while checking my personal e-mails. There were the normal raunchy e-mails from Italian and Spanish businessmen to girlfriends at home, which mentioned El Comandante in terms designed to impress the recipient. The embassies in the area were mostly using overseas servers that were encrypted and secure. I realized that most of the diplomats had been warned never to send unencrypted e-mails. Of course we knew that in private they would be rude about the government, and they knew of our ability to monitor everything. And some of the diplomats were lazy or naïve enough to ignore the warnings. But I rarely reported them to MINCOM. They would probably get expelled from their posts. That would reduce the need for my job and would mean less Christmas whisky for Vladimir.

There were some Cubans who used the Internet café at the Comodoro as well. Their e-mails were pretty pathetic, I'm afraid.

Look, these people were the losers in the Cuban system. They spent their time begging for money from family and friends and sending meaningless messages just to show they had an e-mail. Sad, yes, very sad. But what did they ever do about it?

That day the current crop of messages was pretty typical of the garbage I saw. All the businessmen and diplomats were complaining that they couldn't get the satellite TV. You know, this guy who had the "franchise" for the whole of Playa worked at a hotel and for some reason thought it looked cool to give his clients an e-mail address. All this, of course, was illegal for Cubans. To receive satellite TV for unauthorized broadcasts—that is, those not controlled by the state—was a crime. In any case the codes for the TV cards were regularly zapped from Miami to wrong foot the illegals. Fortunately it didn't work, because the Cubans in Miami or somewhere paid off the programmers to get access to the new numbers. Why didn't we simply grab all the satellites and implement the law? That's easy. Because the Council of State, MININT, and the CDRs all had the TV and watched it every day. The man in Playa, who called himself Larry, was paid two hundred dollars up-front by each client per month, so when something went wrong his customers were incandescent. He was the best in the business, so he used his e-mail. It was useful anyway to know who was using him. Very useful.

I was about to log off when one message attracted my attention. It was short and urgent. Larry was concerned about some other business he was running. I couldn't understand why Larry would be so careless to mention it in an e-mail. But it was alongside his TV business. Sometimes you just have to forget the risk, and even the best Cubans made mistakes. I liked Larry, but he was overconfident. I read it again and again. I copied it and logged out.

I closed the door carefully, put Kurt out in the yard, and immediately got back into my car.

Felipe

I was sitting in the bleachers waiting for the volleyball teams to get themselves organized. As always there were more officials than players, all walking around with clipboards, looking important, comparing notes. The seats were crowded with family and friends, all of them like me having made their excuses from work. The two teams of thirteen-year-old volleyball players lined up, one in orange, one in blue. The wall opposite was plastered with posters of the Moncada marches, concerts, and slogans to inspire "Nunca olvidamos los héroes del 26 Julio."

A woman walked up to the podium. She introduced herself as Compañera Hilde López and said she was proud to present Víctor, "our beloved president of the CDR," who had just returned, she said, from party duties outside Havana. She called for silence for Víctor's speech. The kids stood up in line, and a recording of the revolutionary song "Mi querido comandante" was played. As usual the discipline of each team was impressive. They were well trained in the game preliminaries as well, and each boy stood proudly with a hand across the chest.

Víctor shuffled up to the podium with his text. His moustache was bigger than the last time I had seen him. Maybe with Moncada he had been too busy to trim it. I am sure he knew most of the people who were spectators, but this was an official speech. I liked to see the solemn official Víctor. There would be no jokes or nicknames today. He scratched his head and adjusted his spectacles and the microphone.

"Compañeros … today we look for the best of young Cuban volleyball players who will engage in sport to demonstrate the true values of the Revolution. We will play hard, we will compete, and we will prepare ourselves for greater challenges. Not every team will emerge Víctorious, but winning and losing will prepare your team members for greater challenges that lie ahead in life. We must breed a new generation of Cubans who will need to be prepared and trained in the spirit of our forefathers. You are all aware that every day the Revolution is threatened by the imperialist forces of the Yanqui administration and the mafia that sells drugs and arms in Miami. Every day we face new insults, new plots, and murderous intentions. Many comrades have died in the struggle to defeat the mercenaries. You are here today to show how young Cubans are ready and prepared physically and mentally to fight and die to defend the Revolution and socialism. We are ever vigilant, ever planning, and working to perfect the vision of Fidel and his pioneers. Play today for Che, Camilo, and our beloved Fidel."

Víctor then concluded with his three "vivas": "Viva la Revolución, Viva la Patria ..." The players knew that this was the signal. He had not reached "Viva Fidel" before the players began moving to their benches for conferences with the coaches. Their parents were shuffling anxiously in their seats. Rafa looked over at me. I smiled and raised a fist.

That was the last time Rafa looked at me. It was what I had told him. Concentration always. Don't think of the family, because family doesn't come into it; only the game. Rafa was following this now. He loved being captain, and he brought his team together in a huddle. Rafa was launched into the world without me. He was no longer the kid with bad dreams on the mattress, no longer the baby Papa hardly knew. I'm more sad than I can say with this thought. Rafa can't change his life at his age. Mama needs him, and Mama will never leave. But soon he will be on his own. Maybe a few years ago we might all have gone, but now she will stay here. Rafa and Tico will give her reasons to live. It is okay to be in education in Cuba, and they both still have years of education to come. It will give them a purpose in life, and then you can accept a lot, all that control, all the messages of struggle. You feel part of all that is happening to you. After the game and the education are over he'll look up at the bleachers and see that he's on his own in Cuba. Then it's different. Just stay out of trouble and don't dream too much. One day we will all be united in the right country.

Rafa's team won the game. They play again on the eve of Moncada.

CHAPTER 9

Mateo

Our bus had just passed Baños de San Juan and the sign for Soroa. I think there were around five more stops to Pinar. I was reading some essays from the seminary candidates I needed to correct when the third of the wives, Haydée, got up and asked if she could speak. I knew Haydée from the trials, but she looked gaunt and wrinkled compared to the young woman I remembered. She put a bony hand on my arm.

"Mateo, I can see you're busy. I'm sorry to interrupt your work. But this bus is the only time we get to speak. It seems like years since the trial. I can't believe he was with us a few months ago. It's the silence that is terrible—the silence from Héctor. I just miss him so much. Our eldest boy, José Pablo, left on a raft three years ago. He calls sometime from Orlando and sends some money, but I don't know when we'll see him again. I lost another baby, you know, a few years back. Now Héctor is all I have to hang onto. To keep me sane. You may not remember all this, but we spoke just after Héctor was arrested—you tried to get into the trial, but the police stopped you. They said it was only for four members of each family. Even with all that, there were so many being tried that the court was packed."

I got up and asked the young student sitting next to Haydée if he'd mind changing places.

"I remember the day, Haydée. There were others from the church as well. We stayed outside for hours. So many tears, so much shouting from the mob outside. We just stood there waiting for some news about what was going on."

"Mateo, we knew you were all out there. So was the foreign press. That was a great comfort, I can tell you. But inside, I couldn't believe what was happening. They read things out about Héctor that were like a fairy story. How he'd been paid thousands of dollars, how he had computers, printers for documents, and they found money all over the house. I wish we had, but Héctor never had any money. Nothing for the house. He finally found some deal to get our windows fixed. And then the strangest thing happened when the witnesses came up. First there were some police who said they had seen him visit some foreign diplomats who had paid him the money. Then Héctor's so-called friend from the hospital where he worked was called to testify and called Héctor a 'traitor.' He had kept a diary of things Héctor had said. That was what he was reading from. Incredible. But it was all over in twenty minutes, and the next person was led in. So we left—the sentences came later and no one was allowed to be present then. Just Héctor and the others. Twenty-four years. I still can't believe it."

I felt hopeless again. It was true that I had stayed outside all day, but I was safe and so were the diplomats and the European and American journalists. Haydée continued talking.

"I'm sorry to bore you with all this. It seems so long ago. But do you remember that outside the court with you there were all those police and diplomats? You remember the group that was there with the leaflets? They were printed in bright colors to demand human rights, defense rights, free press. They were handing out those 'never forget' bracelets. And some said

'Cambio' on their t-shirts. They looked good, and I was so pleased to have some support."

"Yes, I remember them," I said. "They came to speak to me as well. They offered us an address to meet up later. I had never heard of that organization before. Wasn't it something like Peaceful Change? I didn't accept their invitation. I said I expected that all the families had a lot to attend to. But we would think about it."

"Yes, that's them. Outside the court I just wanted to get away. I hated that place and everyone in it. It was over and I've never seen anyone of them again. Not until last week. Well, a few days ago I heard from them again. In fact they came around to my house and asked to come inside. We never get strangers calling, so I was afraid. My uncle was with me, and he opened the door. But I wouldn't let them in. We spoke outside."

"Well, you were courteous, so nothing wrong with that. What did they say?"

"There were three people, two men and a woman. They said they all had family members in jail as prisoners of conscience. They said they had been outside the court that day. They mentioned some names that didn't mean anything to me. It was important that we were solid with other families when they had lost fathers, brothers, and husbands to jail. These people were innocent. But they kept saying terrible things about Cuba, you know. We lived in a police state. I never heard Héctor say anything like that. They said they were a growing group who were building an opposition and they needed my support."

"But were they the same people we met at the court?"

"I don't think so," said Haydée. "Can't be sure really. Maybe the woman was the same. But they knew all about Héctor. They knew his job and everything and his work with the free press. So I guess they seemed genuine. They even left an address and phone where they wanted me to meet. I have it here in my bag."

I hugged Haydée. "All this sounds strange. Why would they come now? And why would they come to you as a spouse? I think you should be careful. I'll check out the address. If they come back just tell them you need to settle some other things first."

"Padre, thank you. If you hear anything, anything at all about Héctor, please let me know. Maybe there are some guards who are kinder, more human. Please promise to talk to them about that. Even if I see him today, it will be another three months before anything happens and before I see you again. I'm afraid I don't have a telephone. So I'll write my address on this page of yours."

I hadn't told Haydée or the others I was leaving Cuba. It was wrong, I know, but somehow a lot of choices then were difficult.

The bus reached the outskirts of Pinar del Río, and the passengers had started collecting their belongings. Most of them needed to pick up a truck to take them further on. I waited before crossing the street. Security men were in huddles around the bus stop. I knew their smoking and joking was partly boredom, but a plain-clothes man in the background pulled out a radio. They were watching anything unusual, and maybe my clothes attracted attention. Not even in Cuba would they have been told I was on the bus, surely not? Zelda, Sara, and Haydée were asked to produce their documents. Another official inspected their bags, and as usual there was much scratching of heads and periods of consultation. But with a shrug of the shoulders he nodded, and there was nothing confiscated.

The security, their checking done, moved off to a bar down the road. That was the signal that we were free to move. I spotted a driver with a van who was propping up a stack of boxes in the street. I asked him how the Vegueros baseball team was doing in the championship. "Okay, I guess. But they're nothing like the teams of the past. Can't pitch for their lives, those idiots. What brings you to Pinar, Padre?"

"Any chance of a short ride for me and these ladies here?" The driver beckoned me behind his van. Ten dollars was negotiated for the return trip to Cinco y Medio off the Carretera Central. He would wait at the jail. The driver took the women's bags and opened the back.

I looked at my watch and saw that the visiting time was due to begin in thirty minutes. Checking of documents normally took at least fifteen minutes. There was no point in informing Governor Gustavo in advance. He was not interested in alerting the prisoners, but he would probably guess I would be coming to see some of them. He was certainly expecting the wives of those charged with behavior dangerous to society. This was a special day every three months.

I parted from the three women. As a non-family member I was required to report to Gustavo personally. I was escorted in by a female guard. She eyed my suitcases carefully.

"You know, Padre, you will have to have those inspected. We cannot risk any breach of security. Please come this way. We'll do the checks on the bags while you see Governor Gustavo. He's ready to see you."

I followed a guard to Gustavo's office. "My friend, Padre Mateo, how are things in the big city of sin? You know my superiors don't allow me to visit Havana anymore. They know I'm a naughty boy, so they're afraid I might get corrupted."

"Well, Governor, I can tell you that given the choice I'd live in Pinar any day. I just love the trees around here. The mountains are spectacular. The people are close to the earth and respect solid values. But it's quite a trek from Havana. Makes me get up early."

"Have a coffee, Padre. That will help wake you up. Lily, please bring our friend from the church a coffee."

"Governor, that's very kind. I appreciate the hospitality. I have brought up with me a few soaps and similar things that may please some of your female staff."

"I appreciate that, Padre. Lily, do we not have any mango juice as well? In July no one beats the Pinar mangos."

"Governor, how are the three prisoners who were tried for political offences in Havana?" I said, knowing my time was ticking.

"Which precisely do you mean, Padre? Are you enquiring after the health of prisoners? I am not aware of any with health problems. We have several hundred criminals in this correctional facility. I will check the records of everyone you wish except those prohibited by state security."

"Governor, I think you know what I mean. My visit is not to see criminals, though they also need the support of the spirit as well."

"Padre, I have to disagree with what you say. All the people held in this correctional facility are criminals, tried and convicted according to the laws of Cuba. Some have committed the crime of fraud or theft, taking money from fellow Cubans. It is also a crime in Cuba, you know, to take money from foreign imperialists who plot every day the destruction of Cuba."

"Governor, I think we both know the three prisoners I have come to see. They are Nestor Bayamo, Silvio Reinoso, and Héctor Sebastiano."

"I see, Padre, the three American agents. Well, I'm delighted to say that two have now confessed further to their crimes and are cooperating fully with authorities. They are all being treated with the utmost respect, which I have to say in my personal view is totally unmerited."

CHAPTER 10

Laura

Varadero is where most of the tourists visiting Cuba wanted to go—a long stretch of golden sands, turquoise ocean, only two hours from Havana. For me it was the bread and butter of my job. My visits to Varadero were not what you would imagine. They were some of the strangest of times for me in Cuba. Being with tourists in Havana, or Cojimar for the Hemingway stuff, that was fine. We were all together and I was proud to tell them what I knew. There were things that happened in a different world, but they were at least in Cuba.

The first thing about Varadero is that there wasn't much to know about it before the Revolution. And what happened there many years ago had nothing to do with Revolution. But the point of the Revolution was that it was for everyone, for everyone in Cuba and the rest of the world as well. So that was why Varadero was weird for me. I got to see the most beautiful beaches we had in Cuba. But the people who had the best beaches were not Cuban. Don't get me wrong. Felipe and I could go to Varadero and there were a few places to stay on the outside of the town. Of course poor Felipito couldn't afford it, so we had to "share" the cost. They were okay; you know, what Cubans were used to. But these were places that were far different from those you see further along the beach. Not the places the DuPonts had bought up as their dream houses a long time ago before the Revolution.

We all knew Varadero was part of the job, so I kept my mouth shut. In any case I had been there so often there were plenty of Cubans I knew. Like the girl who sold the golf shirts at the Xanadu, the hotel that was once the home of the DuPont family. And I knew the souvenir seller at the drinks stop on the way to Varadero. I even received some pesos from her for bringing in customers. That made it seem even stranger. I was among friends. But we weren't allowed to go to the same party. I remember that day because I was curious to see the newest of the new hotels in Varadero. It was called the Hotel New Vista. A group of Austrians had come as my first group, so my job was to escort them to the dolphin park from the lobby of the hotel. As a Cuban, I was allowed to stand in the hotel lobby and watch as the tourists arrived and the golfing parties moved off for their tee times. The only eighteen-hole golf course in Cuba was close by.

The New Vista certainly looked new. The chandeliers were still being polished, and new furniture was arriving for the lobby. The bar manager looked on, chatting with the concierge.

"I hear two guys were fired at the Riviera. The idiots took some laptop for an evening but then returned it without the charger. That group from Habana Vieja burned so many CDs on the laptop that they were arrested. Lucky for them they have the money to pay in fines so there'll be no prison."

I listened, but knew I shouldn't speak. I enjoyed the gossip, and I guess probably 50 percent was true. But I also knew some of it was supposed to provoke me. They wanted to hear who would complain about the system, so of course anything I said would eventually be reported. My stepdad knew that and tried to catch me out at home just so I would be used to it. The concierge was also expected to provide information to state security, who would pay good money for the right snippets. Every job in tourism was seen as a privilege. I knew well enough that anyone who wanted to keep working needed to follow the rules.

The bar manager came over to me.

"Hey, Laura, how's that brilliant scientist boyfriend of yours? Pity he only makes three hundred pesitos a month. Poor sod. Has he any time to leave the laboratories? I hear there's a waiter's job going in that glitzy new German hotel along the beach here. The a la carte guy over there took the boat on Monday. Pays two hundred bucks a month, normally. Plus a week's vacation in one of those semi-tourist places. But you need to give the manager five hundred greenbacks to get an interview. Tell your little boy ... you never know."

I smiled. "Felipe's fine and happy where he is. There's a bit more brainpower in biotech than in carrying trays and plates. And maybe he'll hit on this big discovery."

"Great. I'm sure the party top guys would be delighted. Good money for them. But what will Felipe get out of it? Not in his lifetime. I'm interested in Number One. Just tell him that I'm only trying to help. Maybe you two could make plans then."

I knew I shouldn't comment. The loudmouth barman was always showing off. Too many conversations with tourists who lapped it all up after three mojitos. I checked my watch and went outside to the front parking lot. The coach from the Austrian Airlines flight was late. Some trouble with the airport baggage delivery. The airport agent called me and insisted that everything was fine with no damage to cases. They were on their way.

Outside a motorbike sputtered into the parking lot. It had two passengers and two children in the side car. The man had a backpack and a bandana around his long hair, and the children were sitting on suitcases. They were shouting and laughing.

I thought they were hotel workers and went inside to make another check on the rooms allocated to the Austrians.

As I was talking to the receptionist, the motorcyclist appeared with a woman and two children. He took off his bandana. His hair fell down on his shoulders. I recognized the man as Yoel. He hadn't seen me. Yoel beckoned his family forward and went to the reception. He produced a bundle of papers. The check-in clerk looked at the documents.

"We have three days reserved for a family room."

"Could you come inside, compañero? We don't do these things out here," said the receptionist.

"Hey Yoel," I said, "what's going on? Don't see you much in Varadero."

"Laura, you're right. But this trip is worth it. I found this scheme where we can get really good rates for the family."

"You're kidding me, Yoel. Good rates? You're talking like a German. Yoel, since when was this hotel for Cubans, at rates Cubans could afford?"

"Laura, it's great to see you, but there isn't time to talk right now. We have to go into the office. We'll meet up in Havana."

The Austrians were arriving. The concierge returned to his formal style of address.

"Compañera Laura. Please come over here. The tour guide is waiting."

Mateo

The prison waiting room was small and rectangular, painted in yellow with crumbling pieces of plaster showing large patches of its previous color, which was a dark blue. It had two small windows with broken fly screens. Across the walkway I could see the watch towers and rows of concrete cells. The room had a couple of wooden benches, and a ceiling fan struggled to keep turning.

It had been fifty minutes since my meeting with Gustavo. The door opened and Silvio Reinoso arrived, shackled and accompanied by two uniformed guards. He was short, with cropped gray hair and a boxer's nose. His eyes were bloodshot, and his arms had sores from insect bites. The taller guard conveyed a message: "The governor of Pinar del Río Correctional Facility has asked me to convey the following information. Because of the serious nature of prisoner Reinoso's offences against the state of Cuba, his visitors can have no longer than fifteen minutes. His wife has just seen him. The other two prisoners you mentioned are unavailable today."

One of the guards took his place at the adjoining bench and pressed the "Record" button on his portable tape recorder and took two digital photos of me with Reinoso.

"Silvio, my name is Mateo. I am a priest from the Roman Catholic Church. I apologize that this is my first visit. I have tried to see you before but was not permitted. I have visited other prisoners who have been charged under the same statute as you. I come from Havana, and my job is to bring you the love of Jesus Christ. I want to let you know that the church in Cuba is concerned about the conditions in which you are held."

The guard looked up. "These visits, Padre Mateo, are not political events. You must not question the authority of the Cuban court or the treatment of prisoners. Compañero Reinoso broke the laws of Cuba and was convicted in accordance with them."

Reinoso shuffled in his seat. "Padre Mateo, it is kind of you to visit me. Zelda said you might be coming in her last letter a few months ago. We have little time, so I will be brief. Zelda is sick with worry. It's our family and the two children. I am concerned. They have no income. This sentence means my children as well will be made to suffer."

"Padre Mateo," said the guard, "this man is delirious. He is just spouting lies. I must warn you again formally. If this goes on the interview is terminated." Silvio looked at the guard impassively, turned back to me, and carried on.

"Padre, my children have been told they might not get promoted into the next class next year. They need to attend all the July 26 marches. My wife has said the neighbors play loud music all night long and scream all that shit, excuse me, about me, which the children can hear. This doesn't happen every day, but the children are afraid they will return. The children now feel frightened all day long. My wife has said their grades at school have become much worse."

I glanced over at the guard, who seemed to have calmed down, waiting for the fifteen minutes to pass.

"I will report all this to the bishop and the governor here. How are the conditions in the cell?"

Reinoso looked over at the guard. He clenched his teeth and frowned. "They are not good, not good at all. If we complain, then they punish us. That has happened a lot."

The guard interrupted. "These are lies, Padre. And I cannot allow a traitor of the country to slander our profession here. I'm afraid that terminates the visit, Padre, Reinoso ..."

I touched Reinoso's shoulder. "It's important that you know, Silvio, that you are not alone in this. We will support you all through this. And there are others here in Pinar. Do you know Bayamo and Sebastiano?"

The guard moved toward Reinoso. "That question is not relevant. No contact with other mercenaries is allowed. I must insist, Padre. You have to leave. This is a serious matter." He took Reinoso's arm, but Reinoso wanted to respond to my question.

"These men are from different towns. Bayamo is not a journalist like me. I think he was more into the church—social work and so on. And Sebastiano is from Las Tunas. I'm not sure why he was sent here. It's like a thousand kilometers from Las Tunas. How does his family get here?"

As he was leaving the door, Reinoso turned and the tiredness looked gone. His eyes sparkled, and he moved with an athletic enthusiasm. "Thank you, Mateo. It has heartened me to meet you; to know someone has not forgotten us. It is just so long to think about, you know. Twenty-three years more doing this, Padre."

Felipe

I returned to the CBM after the volleyball game. Chino was asleep under his favorite tree. It was the hottest part of the day. The staff at the CBM was chatting under the canopy of the arrivals area, smoking and joking about how the other biotech institutes were not performing, as someone had heard on the latest "Mesa Redonda" on the TV. Lunch was pizza and water. Rebecca was reading her papers and checking her cell phone messages. She had just reminded me that only three others at the CBM had personal phones. Carlitos came out with his assistant.

There was a low buzz as conversation dropped and then fell silent. Carlitos blinked in the sunlight and raised his voice.

"Sorry to break up the party. I know it's great to get out in the fresh air even when it is thirty-eight degrees. We need to have an office briefing. There are some things I must tell you. I'd like you all to come inside to the meeting room for a few minutes."

I followed the group and sat near the back. Carlitos rarely called group meetings, so this was something I needed to hear. Maybe he would confirm our fifty-dollar bonuses. I knew Carlitos would want to claim credit for all that.

"Fellow workers, you know that in a few days El Comandante will be making an important speech to commemorate the first attack of the Revolution many years ago on the brutal regime that had terrorized the Cuban people. This epic event at the Moncada barracks prepared the way for the triumph of the Revolution. Moncada is an historic occasion, and our CBM will be playing a major role. I don't know what exactly El Comandante will say. But his speech will give new impetus to the Revolution. He has great ambitions for the *polo científico* and knows how important the work we do is. But we, like the rest of our agencies of socialism, must remain vigilant and look out for new ways of achieving the goals of the Revolution.

"As you know, Compañero Orlando sits on the Council of State, which will be discussing major changes in economic policy consistent with the aims of socialism. We don't know the results of that debate, and what El Comandante says will be therefore even more important. It is essential that we continue to strive for the highest standards in whatever we are required to do. I have pledged to the Council of State that our staff is ready to do whatever we are asked. No one has a career for life. That is all I wanted to say. We want to have an outstanding Moncada day. That is bigger than all of us."

It wasn't clear whether Carlitos would accept questions. He paused slightly, took off his glasses, and drank some of his water. As usual there were no questions. The staff looked at each other. A new entrant, a university PhD, Roberto, was enthusiastic. "Wow, just to hear Carlitos. That's my first time. He is a hero of science. It makes the polo sound like the center of the action here and all that we can do is exciting for the Revolution."

"Sure, we're important," said Rebecca, "but Roberto, you have missed the point. Carlitos is trying to tell us something that will be important for us all. It's nothing to do with the polo. The Revolution is served by us, but it's a global movement. We are small insects in the universe. Only El Comandante knows what the future will bring. We'll have to wait, but the fundamental principles of socialism will not be affected."

I said nothing. I needed to look for those documents. But what would it matter if they were gone? Who would believe a biologist who used to work for a Cuban institute no one had ever heard of? An insignificant junior researcher was now claiming that he had lost the basis on which he had made his discoveries. Bad luck, but you should have made copies, my friend. Never trust anyone in business. It's everyone for himself. What was the point of trying to work out what Carlitos meant? What would happen would happen. The rest of us were spectators looking in just like at Rafa's game. But at least we could cheer for that. The competition was fair, there was a referee, and Rafa could look forward to the next game.

I knew Carlitos was trying to say something. In his own way he was trying to be kind, just like the trip to Spain. He knew something big that he was not saying, and he felt something for us. Maybe he hoped the codes would come through. "No one has a career for life." We only have Cuba and socialism. Maybe there are new plans for all of us.

I spent years studying and experimenting in biotech. I know things that no one else in Cuba knows, and I have ideas that could change medicine and vaccines. My hero was Carlos Finlay. He was not a revolutionary and he was not even interested in politics. My hero was a scientist, a Cuban, and a world leader in what he did. In my naïve and youthful way I thought we could use more of them. That was when I told Papa that because of Carlos Finlay I wanted to be a biologist. Our new Carlos Finlays are servants of the Revolution, not of mankind, so whatever happens they own our ideas. Once we dreamed that mankind and the Revolution were the same thing, but that dream has died. Our scientists are now in the world for the good of the Revolution. Where is there for me to go if the Revolution changes its mind?

I called Laura's cell on the office phone. "Can we meet up earlier tonight? I'd like to talk."

"Suits me. Just getting rid of some Austrians in Varadero."

I could tell that the little session with the director meant the attention of everyone at CBM had dried up. What Carlitos had said seemed to postpone all the meetings; let's wait until after Moncada to send e-mails Everyone knew everything could wait. I cleared my desk. I asked if the CBM messengers were delivering any documents to Miramar so I could hitch a ride to Laurita's house. She was waiting. Her mother tactfully moved into the kitchen.

"Laurita, you look wonderful. I can remember still when I met you with those Malaysian tourists on the Malecón. It was when one of them tried to speak Spanish with that crazy word he thought meant 'year' in Spanish. And you turned your head and laughed."

"Feli, my, my, you are in a romantic mood. You are so sensitive and kind. I am amazed I found you. Did you call because you like to laugh? I like that too."

"We could have used some laughter at CBM today. It's been a strange day. Carlitos spoke to us, and that's a major event. He never does that sort of thing. He gave us some revolutionary-speak, of course. But there was something else. It looked like he was almost saying goodbye. There's something crazy going on at high level. The worst part is he's well-enough placed to know what it is."

"Feli, I'm not so sure. They're all doing pep talks for Moncada. We had the deputy minister at MINTUR the other day. I think they've been told to talk it up. My bet is they are all trying to make it an event, which of course it isn't. Maybe Moncada means something for all of them who were there. But it happened over fifty years ago. They all admit that there's so much apathy they're afraid the students will stay in bed for the speech. Even the square might look not as full as it should. Now that would be terrible. So they want us to expect something new, maybe even interesting. So there might be a point in turning up for Moncada. You know, the 'I was there' stuff you see in the movies. This sort of thing happens all the time."

"You don't know Carlitos, Laurita. He never speaks on policy—never in years to a group like this. He's a scientist, of course, which I kind of admire. First a scientist, then a revolutionary. It's just that I think he's human enough to want to communicate with us. He knows we don't get a chance to discuss the way he would like. It's not like we're expected to blog our reactions or anything. Isn't that how it works in the real world? You know there wasn't a single question after Carlitos spoke. We all know Moncada is for the beating of the Revolution's drums. Plenty of people saying 'Yes, what wisdom, what leadership,' you know. In any case, why do they need to say anything new? They know we'll all wait to see what happens next. The only difference at Moncada is we have to stand up to hear it. Most days we're just sitting and waiting. If there's one person we know in Cuba, it's El Comandante. No surprises. More of the same."

"Feli, I thought scientists were optimists. Always the promise of something new; the longing for discovery even when it takes years. You never know. The Revolution is not dead to ideas. We might even get something new. In any case you say you know Carlitos. I wonder what you know about Yoel."

"What about him?"

"Has he come into a lot of money lately?"

"No idea. He delivers for the old bakery in Marianao, doesn't he? And he teaches some children of diplomats. Speaks pretty good French, I think. Yoel is a survivor, for sure. I've never met his family, but he's like thousands of others here. Doesn't look like they're rich. The motorbike belongs to the bakery, and he shares it with someone else. Czech, I guess it is."

"Have you ever seen him at the bakery?"

"No. Why would I go there? I've better things to do—not much—but sometimes."

"So why would Yoel and his family have the right to stay in an expensive Varadero hotel? That's pretty rare, Feli, even if you're a loyal revolutionary like me. He certainly wasn't on another honeymoon; you know, the famous three nights the government pays for. He had his kids with him. Yoel's a cool guy, but when I saw him he appeared pretty nervous."

I didn't believe Laurita. "Yoel struggles like the rest of us. I think there must have been some mistake. Yoel is an ordinary guy, kind of wild but ordinary. I don't know any of these tourism rules, but some party and military seem to get to these places. Is that right?"

"Feli, there was no mistake. He said he couldn't talk now, so he recognized me. Feli, take care with Yoel. He's well connected, and maybe the bakery stuff is all a sham. Good for Yoel, if he's made a few CUCs. Vladimir is into lots of things as well. I saw him looking for some deals at the airport."

"Laurita, have you been behaving yourself? Maybe Yoel and Vladimir are checking up on you." But I knew she was needling me. Get out and do something. You're the nowhere man.

Yoel

I knew that seeing Laura would lead to something. In Cuba it was okay to move around and keep people guessing. Everyone was involved in something. We had to be. Otherwise you'd sit on your stool and become a night watchman. But while people got to know about me my value was falling fast. So I had to get moving with that meeting I had fixed. The good thing about Abel's motorbike was it looked just normal, beaten up from too many potholes. It could easily have come from a farm or local party. I had to get out that night from Varadero along the coast. The family was more than happy to stay at the hotel. Who cared if the Cameroon ambassador had pulled some strings. Nice man. The salsa dancing show started at 9:30, and there were unlimited drinks before. I headed off the Varadero peninsula and out east.

Abel had given me a baseball coach's phone just in case. It was the first time we had worked with this contact, a man called César. Abel was getting kind of impatient. I knew the contact thought he was meeting Abel. This was our little security move. I wasn't told where the contact worked, but as it was the Santa Clara baseball stadium, it didn't take much figuring out. I called the number. "I'm about forty kilometers away. We have to meet and work this out quickly. I need to be back to Varadero by dawn. That's the bottom line. If I'm not at the Moncada rehearsal I will be fired." That's what Abel would have said.

The streets of Santa Clara were clear. When I arrived at the stadium it was already past midnight. The cleaners were sweeping up the rubbish from the evening's game and shoveling it onto a skip. Dogs were circling for the best scraps. There was one other motorbike, an old Norton, parked outside, but the stadium was dark. Washing hung out of the building overlooking the lot, and sounds of hip-hop blasted into the night.

A small man with a large earring was applying a chain to padlock the stadium entrance. He heard me approaching and took a long swig of his can of beer.

"Come on, Abel, we have to get going. Why did you wait so long?"

"Don't start that again. I've plenty to do in Havana. So much action it's hard to get away. Moncada's a busy time for baseball."

César scoffed and finished the padlocking. His voice was hoarse as if he had been cheering at some sports game. "No need for the sob stories, Abel. Baseball has armies of thousands it can call on in Havana. Why would they miss you? If you didn't show up for a week no one would notice, amigo. You could organize these things with your eyes closed."

César mounted the bike and took a final swig of the beer. He threw the can away, aiming it at the group of shovelers. "Bet they didn't expect that, those losers. I used to be a good outfielder, you know. Could throw 120 meters easily." He laughed and then decided to rest his voice. I got on behind him. We headed out of Santa Clara on the road to Remedios and the northern *cayos* on the coast beyond.

Felipe

Pepe was home when I returned. It was pretty late; I can't say exactly the time. He had his feet on the table and was on the phone. I was pleased because that meant he had found someone to fix it. But then when the phone was working Pepe was never off it.

It was one of those calls with a new girl. Pepe seemed to have met her at the Convention Center when he'd been escorting some foreign delegation. I knew how the talk would go, and Pepe never seemed embarrassed that anyone else should hear. As the descriptions of their likely activities grew more graphic Pepe's voice got louder. It didn't make any difference if Rafa and Tico were around. Pepe seemed to have a different view of marriage from anyone else. Maybe except for Donna. It was months since Donna had been in the place. Even when Luis was born she never seemed to think babies would make any difference to the number of parties she could go to. Mama had given up and raised Luis herself.

Pepe broke off, as if bored with way the conversation was going. "Feli, grab a beer. That little chat has made me thirsty. Throw me one over too. Got the old cooler fixed for a dozen prawns that arrived from Matanzas. In fact it's been a good day. Got a couple of cases of Cristal chilled as well."

"Come on, Pepe, how can you afford Cristal? Surely the Revolution's traffic police are not now its chief criminals. Cristal is not part of the *libreta*, not last time I looked. Oh I'm sorry. Like you say, I should never ask the questions. A cool beer would be great, thank you very much."

Pepe grinned and I tossed him a can. His Harley-Davidson tattoo at the top of his arm showed out from under his vest as he caught it. "No secret at all, Feli. It's part of the 'perks' of diplomatic parties; you know, these guys are always going to the Martí monument for some special ceremony, all dressed up in black, with medals, ribbons, all that. Slow walking, lots of bowing. Seen so many. You know the drill. Well, the traffic cops provide the outriders and a security van for all the other people who attend these things. I guess they expect some terrorist attack or something. Can you imagine that in Havana? Anyway, after the ceremony the new ambassador goes back to his house and gives a party. Invites all the people who he thinks will like him. Funny really. Anyway, that's none of my business. But there's always lots of spare beer we can put in the van afterward. The guys are pretty good about splitting up the proceeds."

Pepe put down the phone. Someone came to the door and shouted for Pepe. "Who's that, Pepe?"

"Oh those kids two floors up. Just sent by their mom. Asking for rice. Offered to fix that bicycle tire in exchange. I said no deal. We're almost out. They could try old grandpa what's his name. He's a real rice hoarder."

I took my beer into the next room. Tico had taken advantage of Rafa being out with a friend and was asleep on the mattress. Mama was watching the last stages of an old episode of a Spanish soap. Overboiled coffee as ever was bubbling on the stove. The windows were open. Mama was in her usual position with the angle of her chair giving her maximum view of Calle Jalisco. The noise of the two arguing lovers in the street was interrupted by a stone thrown against the wall.

"Mama, how's the day gone?"

Mama's eyes narrowed in a smile. She moved her hands behind her neck to wipe away the sweat.

"Feli, this heat is too much. Never known a July like it. Gets worse each day. Those two in the street are really going at it. I'd hate to see that girl get hurt. She never picks the right man. Claudia called and said she is planning to come up to Havana in September. She has a bus ride offered by the church, I think it is. We had four and a half hours without power, so the chicken was beginning to melt. The fridge blew again. But Pepe got it fixed, the phone as well, and we even have some ice. Can you believe we have some ice? Here, take a piece. Rafa pleaded for some, so I split it with Tico. How's Laurita? Busy with all the tourists? I think it's great to have all these people coming to visit Cuba. We have the most beautiful country in the world."

"Mama, sounds like you've had a busy day. Just looking up the street here Cuba doesn't seem that beautiful to me. But I know what you mean. I'm sure we'd appreciate this beautiful country more if we could compare it with somewhere else. You and I never go anywhere … Oh I'm sorry Mama, you are right. You'd have to be an idiot not to see the beauty. I know we have God's gift as a country. I could spend hours just looking at the palmas reales. But maybe we're not God's only gift. And what goes on beyond this window? Across the Malecón?"

"Feli, I am sorry you're stuck here in Havana. Young people dream always. But I am grateful for what I have. Look at Rafa and Tico. They will be with me always. Claudia has a visit every three years from her son and doesn't even know where that girl of hers is. What was her name, Monica? Went off to New Jersey or somewhere. Just read in *Granma* how much the medicine and colleges cost over in America. No one could ever afford those. It's madness. You just die of any sickness you have. Your education cost us nothing, Feli, so we owe nothing to anyone. I've never been envious or anything …"

The phone rang, and we heard Pepe shout, "Big shit," and then begin his usual lexicon of obscenities on the phone. But this was something unusual. I rushed back into the room. "What on earth …"

Pepe had drunk too much but was coherent. "There's a fight down in the Old Town, near the port. All the guys are tied up at the plaza, so we need reinforcements. Got to get down right now, so I need to hitch a ride. The bike's just passed out …" Pepe began pulling on his boots and then realized he was in his underpants. "Damn, damn, damn. Just when I had the Cristal to enjoy."

He then seemed happy again. "Feli, this could be fun. Dozens of louts all shouting the normal garbage. But they're all up from the Oriente. Sooner they go the better. But this time they say they won't go home. We'll see about that. I'm sick of sitting around here all day. Time for some action. That Cristal's done me good."

Pepe finally pulled on his boots and rushed out down the stairs. I patted him on the shoulder as he left. The street was crammed with people trying to get some cool from a burst water main.

I shouted out of the window, "Hey Pepe, sounds like a good riot. A lot livelier than another revolutionary march. Maybe we won't even get to go Moncada this year."

CHAPTER 11

Yoel

César knew the track off the carretera beyond Remedios, even in the pitch dark. Told me it was where he used to play with the *guajiros* and where he learned to ride. The moon was new, which was how he liked it. There would be no excess illumination. The path was stony, but there was a covering of soil most of the way. "This old Norton could find its way on its own. I keep my eyes shut." There was a warm breeze blowing from the ocean. "Feeling good about this one," said César. "You're a lucky guy to be with me, Abel."

We arrived at the causeway, which I knew took hundreds of tourist buses across to the cayos north of the coastline. It was 1:00 AM, and César said it would be another ninety minutes before the last flight in from Amsterdam arrived at Ignacio Agramonte, the airport north of Camaguey.

César whooped with joy and accelerated along the modern paved road. His voice had recovered, and he turned around to shout into the night air. "As a young kid I did some work on this. All illegal, you know, but the Dutch company didn't mind. They were making a fortune in all they did. Just look at what it is now. Those rich bastards come from all over to our cayos and they don't even need to get their feet wet by getting in a boat. These beaches, I tell you Abel, are the most beautiful in the world. It's not just Cubans who say so, but we have at least twenty more islands with nothing on them. You'd be amazed. This miserable Norton is running over a goldmine. How can we be so dumb just to let it all go by us?"

Five kilometers in there was a small cleared area close to the causeway. The scrub vegetation extended beyond as far as we could see. Wading birds were resting in the bushes, tightly knotted together across the water "Is this it?" I said. "Are you sure these guys are worth coming all this way to meet?"

"You're asking me, Mr. Baseball? Abel, you are in the driver's seat on this. Don't you remember? It's your call," said César impatiently.

César got off the bike and turned off the lights. He offered me another beer from his backpack, but I was too nervous to think of beer. César pulled the ring cap and took another swig. I looked at my watch. It showed 1:23 AM. César sat down and propped himself up against a rock. I walked around looking at the horizon. The water lapped gently against the beach. I lit a cigarette, thinking of my kids sleeping in those crisp sheets in Varadero, dreaming of the "all you can eat" breakfast. I had done something right as a father. But the thoughts wouldn't stay. What I was doing tonight could destroy all that. I began pacing up to the water's edge.

"There, I can smell the diesel on the breeze," said César. A boat was approaching from the west with no lights. Its engine was quiet, and it was far bigger than any launch we had used before.

"Wow, I've never seen one this size," whispered César. The captain was dressed in black and wore a black baseball cap low over his face. He spoke in English.

"Hi guys. Comrade Bill reporting for duty to the Cuban Revolution. I assume you're expecting me rather than just spending the night stargazing. Boy, I love these cayos. Reminds me of the Everglades. Pretty spot you've chosen."

I had been waiting for the password, which was "Everglades," and relaxed. Felipe hasn't mentioned in this story that I could speak good English as well. "You have found your comrades, Bill. Thank you for keeping to the timetable."

The boat driver smiled. "Okay, let's cut to the chase. I'm five hours from Key West. This boat could handle four trips every month. But to make this work we must get more on each boat. Lots more. But right now the success rate is only one in eight. We only get through one-eighth of the time. That, my friends, stinks. It's really bad. I deal with three other guys in Cuba, and they're totally on board with all this. So I'm not here to negotiate. That's the deal they've made. But of course I can't tell you who to take. So, gentlemen, the choice is yours."

César looked at me, expecting me to speak. It didn't come easily to me, so he took the lead. I was surprised at how good his English was as well. "Okay, okay," said César. "Have a beer and calm down. We're some of the best in the business. We can live with rivals. But we need security. You know how risky this is. For you it's just the money risk. For us it's totally different. My friend and I could end up somewhere unpleasant for an awfully long time. I would miss this life too much, Señor Bill. We also need to know about good communications. You provide the water and life jackets. We have children lined up. What are the costs for under tens? They need special food, of course."

"Sorry, no reductions. It's eight thousand capitalist notes per deal. Every passenger costs us the same. You bring your own vest if you want them. You bring the water and food. I'm not in the cruise ship business. We're not working for the FDA either. This is rough. Uncle Sam doesn't do socialism. As long as there's a demand for what we do we do it. If there wasn't, I'd spend my time marlin fishing. Trouble is that doesn't pay. All the other punters are happy with this."

I joined in. "We're some of the best around, Bill. Count on us. We will deliver as well as the others." I'm sure that was what Abel would have wanted me to say.

"Okay amigo, then that's just fine. Usual easy payment terms," joked Bill. "Up front four grand, the rest on arrival. Full money refund without results. You have the account details. Business at its best."

César sighed dramatically. "You mean you rip everyone else off, Bill. Just like all the others, hey Bill? And the bank transfers? Usual Western Union. We get 15 percent."

"Sorry amigo; we never give more than 10 percent. You're getting a great return. This boat holds at least forty people. We make two stops. The first date we could do is next week. Say July 27."

Mateo

It's strange; even when you're about to leave a place you still meet people at the same pace as when you arrived. You remember that appetite you had early on to meet anyone and everybody just to talk, to try to fit in. But three years on it was that sort of meeting that happened when I would normally have made my excuses. If I had been staying I would have followed up. But all that should have been in the past.

"A Cuba Libre please," said the diplomat. Being a foreigner based in Cuba, I was fortunate to be asked to many of the diplomatic parties. Being a churchman didn't harm either. It wasn't the real Cuba, of course, but I'm afraid I have to admit that traveling has had its attractions. Good culture, good food, and plenty of good conversation. I sometimes felt guilty attending these parties, but you need a break from challenges to faith. Maybe that day I was led to something that was ordained.

"Como no," said the waiter.

The waiter moved on. I felt at ease there. I knew so many of the diplomats. I think it was Lorenzo, the Italian deputy head of mission, who had come over, eager to get away from a group of diplomats. We shared a love of opera, and he used to come and chat, I think partly to avoid speaking Spanish, which he said he detested. "Padre Mateo? I'm leaving for vacation in Campari-land soon. Longing to see the new Traviata in La Scala!" A Cuban in a beige guayabera brushed past us. Lorenzo for some reason had said enough about opera and called his name.

"Señor Ministro, do you know Padre Mateo? This is Minister Ricardo Contreras, the minister responsible for cooperation with nongovernmental organizations in Cuba."

I shook Contreras's hand. He was tall with muscular arms and smooth skin. The floodlights in the garden reflected off his bald pate. Unlike almost all the guests at the party he was not sweating. Contreras was heading toward the exit, probably on an evening swing through three other drinks parties. For some reason he seemed prepared to have a conversation, and we moved away from the band to another side of the garden, down some steps to find a quiet patio surrounded by caoba trees. The waiter brought us some more drinks. Lorenzo had told me they were trained to make sure ministers were given special attention.

"Padre, I am delighted to meet any member the Catholic Church. I was myself raised in the church in Holguin, but since the Revolution I have not attended Mass. We owe some of our most beautiful buildings in Cuba to the church. And the church's literature and music, there are some things you never forget."

"I am pleased that the Cuban government allows us to minister now to the spiritual needs of the Cuban people, and that the visit of the Holy Father to Cuba a few years ago made the position clearer. But we have a long way to go."

"Well, we in the government want to make progress in these areas as well. We have a special department now to bring through cooperation with the church. There is a lot we can do. But as you know we insist that the activities of the church are never political. As you say you must stay in the spiritual sphere."

I sensed that the minister knew something of what I had been doing in Cuba and wanted to draw me into discussion of my "unspiritual" activities. "Minister Contreras, I look at the people I meet and see only people. They have many needs and problems they face in Cuba. They need spiritual and other types of support just as in any place in the world. We like to work closely with children and the old ..."

'My dear Padre, in Cuba the Revolution does not neglect any needs. We provide for all Cubans without discrimination. The young need the Revolution for spiritual and material support. The old deserve the support for they have built the Revolution. This is what socialism means. As you know we have some Christian ministers represented in our national assembly."

These parties were never places for long conversations. The three-minute rule worked again as we were interrupted. Some diplomats alongside us were joking with the local press corps, and one spotted the minister. "Minister, how are the foreign investment approvals going?"

I also spotted the deputy editor of *Granma*, Fausto Gómez, a large, cheerful man with dark rings under his eyes. Gómez came over to us. "Padre, we need to have another discussion about that interview on the project for the building of the seminary. I'd love to get it into the special Moncada edition. Could I come around in the next couple of days?"

Contreras held his hand up. "One moment please. Padre, I will give you my card so if you need to discuss anything we can talk. I am always open."

Contreras pulled himself away from the diplomats and took out a card from his wallet.

"Padre Mateo, I have enjoyed our conversation today very much. Ministers here are very busy, but you can normally contact us and we don't pay too much attention to protocol.

Please take this card. It would be good to chat again when I have more time." I was about to tell him I was leaving but took the card. Strange that during all my time in Cuba I had never before received a minister's card.

The sirens of the police cars and ambulances over the residence wall split the warm night air, and heads turned at the party. Another sound of the Havana night as something had broken the calm of the Old Town. The diplomats had spotted that the minister was free and converged as if they had received a simultaneous text message. The band played on, and waiters scurried to get the final canapés. I saw Lorenzo on my way out, and he had remembered the names of the singers playing Violeta and Alfredo in the La Scala production.

Vladimir

I knew how the MINTEL people would want to work. They wanted to see results to show to their bosses just before Moncada. Bertie, my supervisor for the eavesdropping operations, had asked for a meeting, and fortunately he seemed to be in a good mood.

"So what's the news on the street in wealthy Playa? I don't know how such a layabout as you gets to spend your life with gusanos and diplomats. We'll have to get you transferred. But maybe if you bring me some of your cast-off whisky that might be avoided."

I knew that Bertie was joking, and I knew I was supposed to laugh at his jokes. "Supervisor" was just a title anyway that meant nothing. Bertie had been at one time a regional director of the telephone company but had been demoted, probably because of some minor corruption. They said he had failed to detect some theft of equipment at an army base. Anyone who was on their way down in Cuba rarely reversed their path. Bertie's job was for serving time. He had been given just enough to stop him switching loyalties. A telephone engineer was a useful man to keep on one's side.

"Okay, Bertie, at least the muchachos in Playa have plenty to do in the evenings; girlfriends, restaurants, travel. You should be happy they get into less trouble than the gangs in Diez de Octubre or Lawton. Drugs are taken at home after the Scotch. People do not misbehave on the street. I know everyone in Playa, and they know me."

Bertie loved to hint at his former good connections. "Vladimir, don't get complacent. Things are changing in Cuba. When I was regional director I learned and saw things that you would never have dreamed of, my boy. We face new threats now, so you must be vigilant, and we need to be aware of what the comandante wants us to do. All these new visitors from overseas business bring new problems. We have to recognize that they are intelligent people. Some have come to work with Cubans who want to cause trouble, and some have come here to engage in politics. In Cuba we are seeing much more aggressive threats. Even I was scared straight by some of the things we heard in the telephones. Things that would make a young ideologue like you run to your Mama. You should know that, Vladimir. They are not all here as tourists or to visit girlfriends and drink rum."

I tried to remain polite. Young ideologue indeed. "Yes, tell me about it, compañero. But let's be rational. At least we know something that's going on. We can tell what's happening as long as they are careless. If we crack down and they know what we want to control, they won't use any communications that we can track and go underground. Even the might of Cuban intelligence can't pick up whispers or crumpled notes. We'll never know what's being planned. Right now, people are kind of relaxed, so they see the good side of Cuba. They let their guard down, and with some luck we can land some knockout blows."

"Vladimir, in all circumstances it is your job to report absolutely anything unusual. It's a long time since you gave me anything worth having. I must review your activities."

"That's because everything is quiet, compañero. Isn't that good news?"

I know I sounded impatient, but Bertie surprised me. I couldn't remember him ever giving me anything specific. "Well, it might be if nothing was happening. But you are naïve to suppose that everyone in our wonderful country is behaving themselves. We need you to investigate something. It's right under your nose. Do you know anything of a company called Compedex? It's a supplier of computer equipment in Seventh Avenue in Miramar, and it has been losing a lot of stuff. The police have no idea where it's all gone, but it seems to be an inside job. The equipment is all from China and brand new but comes via a warehouse operation in Barcelona. The equipment is supposed to be used for advanced computer graphics. It's been disappearing now for over three weeks. At first they thought it was just the normal way of resolving poverty issues. Losing stuff is part of business. But in the last few days it has begun to take off, and so have the computers."

"Okay, but why would my consumers be involved? They have all the computers they need, and more money than you and I could dream of. Why would they need some cheap Chinese computer parts?"

"Vladimir, again you are showing yourself typical of your age group. Always making excuses. We have been asked to investigate, and if you take the lead it will not raise suspicions. Get off your soft rear end. I expect a report back. Vladimir, you may think I am an old pussy cat, but I still have claws."

CHAPTER 12

Friday July 23, 2:00 am

Felipe

The phone rang at Jalisco. Everyone was sleeping. Often these were prank calls from local kids who would be in a bar and dial the number just to show resentment that we had a phone. But not tonight. "This is Doctor Raúl Sotolongo from the hospital Ameijeiras, ciudad de la Habana. We have an officer of the Havana traffic police, Compañero Francisco Ávila, admitted to the police wing of the hospital. I am sorry to say he has had a bad blow to the head and is in a coma. He got hurt in some incidents tonight in Habana Vieja and is showing only slight signs of life. In fact Compañero Ávila is in critical condition. He needs someone to authorize some surgery. We have him listed as having a wife called Donna Manuela. Can I please speak to her?"

They wanted Donna, the angry wife who ran off to Sancti Spíritus. I cleared my throat. "Donna Manuela is not here. She's my aunt. My mother's younger sister. But it's better I come around. There's no one else. How is Pepe? He's strong and fit."

"Just get someone here, please. It's urgent."

I looked around and saw that the phone hadn't woken Rafa next to me and Tico across by the window. Mama was also lying down. She had left the radio on. I stood in the middle of the room looking around. Pepe's beer cans were still on the table. His poster of the Mexican bullfight had been blown off of its pins by the wind. Part of it was flapping loose. I knew he would be devastated if it tore. It's a silly thing I remember, but I pinned it back for him. I went over to Mama and touched her face. There were gleams of sweat along her hair parting, and the gray hair was dark with moisture.

"Mama, there's bad news about Pepe. He's had an accident. Some trouble in Habana Vieja. This time someone hit him over the head. We've got to get over there. They want permission to operate. Do you know where Donna is?"

"She'll be in Sancti Spíritus or maybe Regla. But they don't have a phone. You'd better go, Feli. I can't believe that in her mood right now she'd even be interested. You know, Donna was devastated after their last row. She pulled a knife on Pepe."

I went over to the drawer where Pepe kept his CUCs. He called it his investment bank. I think every family in Cerro had a special place for them. It's always there for any of you, Pepe would say. He was a generous bastard. I had never known the drawer to be empty. I think he watched it carefully, but he never explained how he got them. I called a Coco taxi. There were always plenty returning from the restaurants of Vedado. It took about fifteen minutes to get to Ameijeiras hospital.

An ambulance was parked outside with its lights flashing. The driver was chatting to someone on crutches at the door. "They're three more coming from Obispo," he said. I proceeded to the reception desk, where a young man in a white coat was scribbling details on some registration forms. "We have no more capacity here, amigo," he shouted into a phone. "You need to try at Soler."

"Where do I find my uncle, Pepe Ávila, a traffic cop who was injured in the riot? You know, the one down in the Old Town."

"Try *emergencias*, right down there. Just follow the shouting."

At the emergencias entrance a young black nurse broke off from bandaging the bleeding arm of another guy in uniform.

"Try the eleventh floor, mi amor. We had some spare rooms there when the first police injured came in. We keep them for security staff."

The lifts weren't working, so I had to scramble up the stairs. I passed groups of military and police who were arguing about what had happened and who was to blame. They were talking of trouble in the Marina Hemingway as well as Habana Vieja.

"What happened down in Old Town?" I shouted. "Why were so many hurt?"

"Hombre, this is Havana, not Baghdad. We are all Cubans, not Sunni and Shiites. It was nothing, just some drunks. It's normal here; you know, wanting Moncada to happen too early."

I said something like, "Desperate people do desperate things. Do you know Pepe Ávila?"

A military guy stopped and turned around. "Is he that big guy with the tattoo? New Harley-Davidson on his arm? Good guy. I saw him. Yeah I'm sure it was him—it wasn't good. Up on the eleventh?"

I climbed further. Some crumbling paint on the door said Piso 11. A guy sitting on a stool said he was the security of the ward and asked me for ID. The military guy was right. Pepe was the fifth along in an area curtained off. His head was swathed in bandages, and a monitor had its diodes placed on his temple. A nurse followed me in. "That guy's in bad shape. It's a real shame. I'm afraid we have done all we can for him at the moment. But we'd need you to give permission as a family member for an operation if needed."

"Sure," I said, without thinking. "But what are his chances?"

"We just have to wait," said the nurse. "You can sit here," she said. "There are a lot of people waiting overnight. You know, they come from all over Cuba for treatment here. We are very busy." There was no place alongside Pepe's bed, so I took a chair at the end of the corridor. I closed my eyes; even with the clanking of trolleys and shouting of orders, I dozed off after a few minutes.

Henry

It was Friday morning in Miami, July 23. Sergio always came in early to claim the copy of the *El Nuevo Herald*, the *Miami Herald* in Spanish. "Marlins five games clear," headlined the back page.

"Can you imagine that this team is in Miami? They're doing it without any Cubans," joked Sergio. "Maybe this new boat will bring us a decent pitcher. I'm sick of these Dominicans and Puerto Ricans. The stadium needs some Cubans to get in and show that this is a city built by Cubans. It's all so polite. Even this paper. Everything the *Herald* says these days is so international, so correct, so nice. They're losing their *cojones*."

"Everyone feels good about this city right now. I don't care if the Marlins all come from Kazakhstan as long as they win," I said. "It's good for business. I could show you a graph. Look what happened when those jokers won the World Series. People buy new cars when their team is winning. They don't care about Cubans anymore. If you want to cry through your nostalgia, you could always call a July 26 party. It's Moncada day soon, you know."

Sergio, old Sergio, resented the joke. "Don't talk about things like that, Henry; you're too young. Moncada is not a joke. It started the years of darkness and of violence in Cuba. Tyranny, killings; we lost our damn country. My family lost everything.

We got out by the skin of our frigging teeth. Not everyone made it. The minute you mention Moncada here any Cuban will run as fast as they can to another dealer. Otherwise, you may get a knife in your back. Anyway, when's the meeting with customers? The boat has already made the trial trip. It's time for action."

"Calm down, Sergio. Cubans may hate Moncada. They may have lost their houses, but since when did they lose their humor? The group is coming around tomorrow. Some have already paid. There are some that want to move things quickly. There's also one guy who wants to talk about something else. He says he wants something delivered to Santiago. It's a pretty small package he says, but important."

"As long as he's not from a frigging newspaper." said Sergio. "Those guys who've been to journalism school think they know all the answers. They might as well join the Communist Party. Use what they write as toilet paper, that's what I say. It's a disgrace to all red-blooded Cubans. Fidel must be laughing himself silly in Lagunita. Just Google that *Granma* online. I need to take a look."

Felipe

I woke up in the ward and I remember seeing a copy of the *Granma* on a table. I guess it was brought in by one of the hospital night shift. Hospitals, waiting, it's always like that. Of course the *Granma* was giving the message from the government, and the front-page picture was a historic one of the Moncada barracks. There was a short statement in bold print alongside. "The Revolution prepares new celebrations of Moncada; triumphs and challenges. Moncada is alive and with us today. Moncada was where all the heroism for the triumph of the Revolution started and the building of a socialist utopia. We expect that a record attendance will show the strength of the Revolution. Our leaders will give important new directions to the comrades that must be heard."

I walked along and looked at Pepe. I guess he had moved slightly, because more of the Harley tattoo was visible than before. The heart monitor beside his bed was producing as many signs as when I left. I spotted the nurse who was on his case. "Hey nurse, sorry. I'm dog-tired. Just dozed off. Is there any change in Pepe?"

"Ah, mi hijo! At the moment he's stable. We're just watching him. I know the doctor said he'd be back at nine. But there's nothing to be decided until then. We've done all we can. He's lost a lot of blood. But you know Ameijeiras is the best we have. As a police officer, Comrade Ávila is in special hands here."

More waiting. But at least something would happen in three hours. I left the hospital for some air. I needed to come back to Pepe with something from the outside. I needed to remind myself what he had left behind. I knew I was feeling sorry for myself. How long do I have to be here? How long before I can get on with my life? I'm sorry. I thought of what Mateo might have done, but I didn't pray. I trusted. In hospitals you trust the good nurses because you know they will look after you. They have an interest beyond themselves. That's what's reassuring. I shouldn't have been so selfish and worried about the waiting. In any case Pepe was a strong guy. A knock on the head was nothing. I trudged down the stairs. The morning shift of hospital staff was arriving. It seemed like a fresh start, a new day straight out of the dark, and I was in that light of a Havana morning. My eyes strained, and I headed for the shade of the stall outside the hospital. I had a couple of Pepe's CUCs left. The stall was selling candy, yesterday's sandwiches, and platanos, none of which appealed. I picked up another copy of *Granma*. There might be at least one article to pass the time.

I walked over to the Malecón, just across from Ameijeiras. It wasn't my favorite part of the strip, but it was what I needed.

The boulevard bore the marks of the last night's entertainment. It was littered with papers, soda cans, and discarded shoes. The street sweepers had just arrived and were chatting over their first cigarette. I walked along the boulevard toward the theater of Amadeo Roldán. Down that end there might be some tranquility. The podium with its crumbling gothic pillars was surrounded by bougainvillea. Children were out playing before the walk to school. A broken skateboard was the center of attention, and the air was sweet and fresh with the promise of a new day.

I sat down and opened the *Granma*. It has only a few pages, but sometimes they reprint articles from foreign newspapers. But of course I couldn't concentrate on what was on the pages. Pepe is strong and doesn't deserve this to happen. How he would like to see this Cuban morning! He went to help the Revolution to sort out its mess. Pepe and his Mexican bullfighter. He is one of the true believers, long after the Revolution realized they would never win by arguments. Papa helped the Revolution too. I took a pen one of the kids had dropped and was surprised when it worked. I began to write. Those things Pepe did and Mama hated. Mama never talks about the tough things. That chair he made for her. Papa knew she would sit and wait. How can we tell Donna about all this? Pepe broke up his family. Donna sleeps with someone else now. Luis has us. But only Pepe is his father. I underlined the word father. Pepe and Papa, did you both let us down?

I tried to read some of the *Granma*. Cuba, Cuba, Cuba, I want to read and write about you. This newspaper? A Revolution should challenge us, involve us. What do I learn about Cubans? To *Granma* there is only one Cuban; one that matters. I don't care if no one will read what I write. In a world of gags and straitjackets, my actions will have to speak. On July 26 every line of the newspapers will be occupied by one speech. There will be no comments, no questions, just the speech. My story will never be read.

I looked up and saw a gardener with a plastic bag clipping some dead branches off the bougainvillea. A man carrying a rolled-up piece of carpet, brown as his skin and knotted as his hair, stumbled by, heading nowhere. I forced my eyes to move forward through the newspaper. I had reached the margins of page four, the middle of the *Granma* newspaper. At the bottom there was a ten-line report. "Antisocial elements disrupted the life in Habana Vieja for a few moments last night at 11:30 PM. There were some attacks on shops before the security forces arrived quickly to put an end to the disturbance. Some of the criminals screamed slogans supporting the imperialist Yanquis. They were shouting obscenities, which showed they had been seduced by the agents of consumerism. They attacked and robbed loyal servants of the Revolution. Three of the mercenary criminals have since confessed to having been paid by the government of the United States of America. Other antisocial elements will be put on trial. Some of the state security officers who responded to the incident suffered minor injuries."

I read it again. I underlined the words "minor injuries." Maybe Pepe will read this one day. He would like that. An article about state security officers. Another Cuban hero unnamed. So I drew Pepe's Harley heart tattoo with the word Donna written through the heart. It should be your heart, Pepe. You protected the Revolution and gave *Granma* their story. The Revolution says you were slightly injured.

Víctor

I had been to see a Moncada rehearsal at that old stadium near Casa de las Americas. It started at 6:00 AM to make sure the kids got out of bed. How I hated this extra-special effort, and I'm sure I let my mood show. I couldn't wait to get away, and I walked through the park near Amadeo Roldán, wanting some space too. Normally I was just doing the automatic, and that would have been better. I wished it was like all the other years, but Manuel and Max had removed all the comfort from this tedious routine we do every year. I guess if we thought what we had done was okay, why change it? No one came in with new ideas. For plenty of years it had worked. If it didn't work then that would be different. Change makes you restless; that's why I never liked these foreign companies coming to our country. They have too many that are not Cubans. I didn't understand them, so why should they understand us? They brought in strange people with too many ideas and too much money. It was all too unsettling.

As I walked, a gardener who said he was called Tommy recognized me from some exercise he said we had run on war games in Cerro where his job was to fill the sandbags.

"Hey, comrade. Here's another bag for the revolution. It's good to see you in these parts."

I went over to admire his plants and saw a young man slumped over a copy of the *Granma*. His t-shirt showed some scientific design on the back, I remember. I was never any good at science. Tough night out I guessed he'd had; trying to shake it off. But a strange way to get over a hangover. It could have been the kid from Jalisco, Felipe Triana, but I wasn't sure. In any case, I'm not in the business of starting conversations. People come to me, not the other way around.

I walked on to where I had parked the Lada. I had some important papers to look at in the office, but this was a problem in Cuba. Where do you store what you need? I mean when the papers are important to you and it would be inconvenient if others found them. Obviously the last place would be at home, because there was simply no privacy. Computers were out, of course, as everything was accessible to the state. There are no banks in Cuba, at least none that the government isn't running. That old safe in the office was also likely to be checked. So it had to be in something that was never read; you know, the old racks of speeches, CDR regulations, Article 564, subparagraph D of the municipal sewer access order of 1979. So that was it. I had this backroom where the CDR files dated back to 1960, and it had shelves stretching to the ceiling. Copies of old magazines, proceedings of the municipal assembly, and collected speeches from members of the Politburo were stacked in chronological order.

Sometimes I had used the speeches. There was one volume entitled "International socialism. Themes from the deliberations of the International Committee of the Cuban Communist Party. 1985–92." But another favorite was a study of diabetes patterns in Cerro. I opened the brochure and found the right pages. All diabetic patients served by the Cerro Teaching Polyclinic in Cerro municipality, Havana, were studied. I opened the first page. "This municipality has a population of 35,157 inhabitants. The incidence of diabetes was found to be 39.5 per 1,000 inhabitants. The characteristics, complications, mortality, and lifestyle of these patients were analyzed." There were plenty of statistics in this study by five doctors who managed to publish it on the Internet. Cerro was very proud to be the first municipality to get themselves on the Web like this. Toward the end of the study, I had added some figures that looked like notes I made at the meeting.

The table of statistics was a list of phone numbers with no names written but initials alongside each. I wanted the initials RC and a cell phone number. I called Ricardo Contreras.

Felipe

I left the park. It was still an hour before the doctor was due to see Pepe. It was too early to wake them all at home. I folded the *Granma* and tossed it in a trash basket. I had second thoughts, turned around, and pulled it out. I wanted to show it to Pepe. I decided to take a detour before returning to the hospital. I was used to walking in Havana to kill time, and Vedado was the best place to do it. It was the sort of place that seemed to have its own rhythm. I can see it all now. Vedado was what the best Cuban minds and spirits could build; symmetry, beauty, elegance. Everywhere you looked you felt inferior, inadequate, seeing the meaninglessness of an individual. The giant caoba trees cast their gentle shade on the old chewed-up sidewalks. Fifty years of wanderers had left all those unhealed scars. I walked up Paseo, the climb up from the Malecón, heading to the commanding promise of Revolution Square.

I turned off Paseo into 15, past those mansions that looked on us as stern and dignified grandparents. Grandparents I had never known. I reached the place that I thought would be the right one for now. Somehow this was the place that has always touched me. Who was he? This man called Lennon. This man who has a statue for him, and all this after he was banned by El Comandante. But we loved him. Cubans really loved him. So they apologized. Or did they? They banned him, and now we have a statue. Of a man who never came here. But we heard him secretly, Papa told me, from radio stations up north. His messages of young love, rebellion, vision. They were only songs, but the Cubans built a statue.

I stopped in front of the statue. As usual there were flowers left by young lovers. Lennon seemed to fill a gap in so many lives. It was touching, really touching, but the flowers were dying. A truck with construction materials had stopped near the park, and the men were unloading wooden boards and microphones.

"Sorry, amigo, you'll have to move. This place is going to be churned up today. There's this big concert here; you know, everyone singing Los Beatles, all the Revolution stuff. Can't stand it myself. Heavy metal, hip-hop, rap, that's my style ..."

"Okay. I was just trying to find some peace, so it's not a good place. When's the concert? At Moncada?"

"Sooner, amigo. It's tomorrow, the twenty-fourth. It's called 'Give Peace a Chance.' So maybe tomorrow night would be a good place for you, hermano. Lennon against imperialism. It'll start the big weekend party."

I left the park and walked back to Paseo and then up through Revolution Square and beyond the Latino Americano stadium. The streets were still pretty clear. A few yellow school buses were transporting students from the Latin American medical school. The *camello* buses were beginning to appear but were not yet so crowded that they had people hanging on from the outside. Another convoy of trucks loaded with construction material was headed for the square, ready to begin the work on the platform for Moncada day in Havana.

Walking might fill in time, but it could not make the day go away. It was useless to prolong things. I was needed back at the hospital. As I got to the lobby, a group of African visitors were being escorted in and appeared to be on some sort of official tour. I noticed that the elevator had just acquired a sign saying "fuera de servicio."

"A technician has been called. We expect it to be fixed shortly," said the young Cuban guide. "We will be offering some coffee here in the lobby."

I took the stairs two at a time. I passed the night shift of nurses leaving from the children's ward. On the eleventh floor, I saw one of the nurses I had talked to earlier. She called back to me.

"Señor, señor, we have been looking for you. I didn't know you were gone. I'm sorry. The news is bad. I'm afraid the traffic police officer Compañero Francisco did not make it. His injuries were just too bad. We're all …"

I don't know why, but I was expecting it. His job was done. There was no way he could get up and do any more. Pepe had already gone in my mind.

The nurse stopped and lowered her voice.

"Look, I know this is difficult, mi amor. I can see how much you loved this man, but I think I should tell you a few things. It's better to go into the doctor's office. He doesn't get in for another hour."

She asked me to sit down and continued talking. "I heard some of the other cops talking overnight, so I can tell you something of what happened. Compañero Ávila was in the wrong place at the wrong time, and it isn't easy to piece together what happened. There was a lot of shouting and blaming through the night right here in the hospital. The commander came in and told everyone to shut up and only speak in turn. A lot of them were drunk. The traffic cops arrived to find the trouble; you know, down in the Calle Obispo. It was very late, but there were still lots of tourists around. They had come out of their hotels at the noise of sirens and were walking down the *calle* from the Parque Central. They thought they should get a look. The police all said the violence was flaring up in a small area, and I think there were some other cops from the traffic police there already trying to agree a plan. Some motorbikes had been kicked over and set on fire."

The nurse looked at me, but I didn't say anything. "One of the cops said there was a group of a few kids who were shouting and waving but appeared to have surrendered. There was a big row among the police over what to do with them. Compañero Ávila walked over to one of the burning bikes. All the regular police were really nervous. You know, those guys kind of resent the flashy bikes and boots of the traffic cops."

I started to get impatient. Your mind gets restless and you want to find some solutions.

"I'm not sure I want to wait here with all this happening."

"I'm sorry. But this is my only chance to see you. You see, my dad is a cop in Ciego, so it's out of respect to him. I think you should hear the truth. What's your name?"

"I'm Felipe Triana, and I appreciate it, really. You're right. Pepe deserves people like you. It's just that my mind wanders. But please tell me what you know."

"Then there were these other youths as well coming up from Old Havana who were a sort of second wave. The police had stopped them from stealing some pizza, which they had found around the back of some shop. They refused to give it up. They got really angry. They said they were starving and something like it was the job of the Communists to give them food. The commander said that Ávila must have been confused. He had never handled anything like this. There was no training for traffic cops in riots. They said he had had quite a few beers. Anyway it was no contest as the cops were outnumbered. This group of youths had come up from the docks areas. They had been terrorizing some of the tourists just off the cruise ships. No one had seen it coming. A group of around thirty went storming down the street using broken bottles and stones to smash shop fronts. Three were leading the charge and had stolen some kitchen knives from a restaurant on Obispo.

"None of the other cops seemed to know your friend. There was no one taking charge. I get to see a lot of chaos here in the hospital when we have injuries to police. It's important to organize a command. They said Ávila didn't know any of the other police who'd arrived, and he was trying to take charge. He tried to get someone's phone to call the riot police. That seems to be what he was doing when three of the rioters came up to him.

"Ávila shouted at a side group who were busy kicking in the door of a souvenir shop. He was making threats to them to stop. But they could see he was on his own. He was shouting things, trying to play for time. Anything I guess to scare them. The guys who were here said they heard Ávila say 'I have photos of you. There's no escape. The special forces are on their way. We'll put you away. See how you enjoy prison food.' Then Ávila pulled his gun and said something like 'Remember there's nowhere to hide. No one will ever allow you off this island. You can't escape anywhere.'

"At that point one of youths with his kitchen knife shouted, 'Screw you and this rotting garbage.'

"Apparently it wasn't a knife that killed him. Someone hit him from behind in the neck. At that moment the riot squad arrived. It was Ávila's call that brought them. They rushed in—you know how they operate—beating, clubbing everything. The commander who came here said they needed to get rid of the disturbance quickly before the foreign journalists came. The youths were dragged into a truck by feet, hair, and anything else that came to hand.

"I've nearly finished." The nurse smiled. "But this part is really why I think you should know this. The tourists were still looking on at the end of Obispo. The big thing was to stop them talking about what they saw, all the rumors. A uniformed guy came in to talk to the group of police here—just a few minutes ago. He insisted that none of this should ever be known. He said it made the police looked unprepared. He told the others here to use the same words he had used with the tourists. So the explanation was that a few guys had too much to drink and had been arrested. All tourists should continue to enjoy Havana nightlife safely. The ambulance arrived shortly after. Three traffic police were treated on the spot. Ávila was carried off unconscious. That's it. I'm sorry it's so distressing."

I stared at her. I looked at the copy of *Granma* in my hands and said, "I guess I won't be needing this anymore."

The nurse tapped me on my shoulder. I remember how tired she looked. "My dad would have wanted you to hear all this, but now I have to go. There are a few more like Ávila."

She walked off. I headed out of the ward, rested my head against the wall of the stairwell, and closed my eyes. I saw Pepe with his feet up on the table, no shirt, sweat pouring down his back with a row of empty beer cans. I saw his pride in looking at Luis. I saw him telling Luis when he passed his advanced motorcycle test. "Did you really see a Mexican bullfighter?" asked Luis, wide-eyed.

I asked if I could see Pepe's body, but they had already removed it from the hospital and taken it to the police morgue. I decided that I needed to go home. The family would be waiting and wondering. Everyone thought Pepe could never be destroyed.

I tossed the copy of *Granma* away and began a new day. Mothers and children were already staring out of the tall blocks opposite Ameijeiras to see what events of the day might be of interest, just as Donna used to. Mama would be at her window now too. I used the rest of Pepe's money to get home quickly. It was right that it was spent on him. I returned to Jalisco and the scene I had left eight hours before. Rafa and Tico were still asleep.

CHAPTER 13

Yoel

Chino Dagoberto was part of the Cuba I despised. Every time I delivered bread at the CBM he was lying around outside. Fine, he minded his own business, but what example was he to the future? He had bet on the past and lost. He was left by the side of the road by the Revolution. I despised him, but I liked him; you know, someone who was good to talk to because it made you feel good about yourself. It was late Friday morning and I knew it was Chino's domino day. He would make his long walk from near the CBM with his bag in hand. Sometimes I would see him sleeping halfway there, normally near the Lebanese embassy where he knew one of the guards.

Today Chino was back early. "What's up? Lost all your money at dominoes?"

"The Lebanese muchachos are trying to get me to sing at a gig they're putting on. Maybe one of them heard me wailing outside here. But you know those days are behind me. My voice sounds more and more like a camello in the Morro tunnel these days."

"Well, it's hard to find work these days, Chino. You should grab what they offer. You can't be that bad. Felipe said you used to sing with his dad."

"Oh hombre, this job selling mani pays too well. I don't need the band gigs now, Yoel, even though they offered me a lot of booze too. These Lebanese, of course, don't use that stuff, you know. One of those guards they have is a pretty neat drummer. He could make some, I tell him. Oh and by the way, *joven*, was there any bread left over today?"

"Sorry, Chino. All the bread went to Carlitos today. He came out to check it himself. I heard about one of your old buddies from the band—wasn't he called Arturo? A great bass player? He went over to the other side. Hope he makes some real money there."

Chino looked away. I moved to get back on the bike. "Yoel, thanks for the chat. It's Friday and it should be dominoes all day, but an old friend showed up. Well, he's not really a friend. He knew where I'd be, I guess. I don't move around too much. In fact that's why I asked about the bread, because I have an extra mouth to feed."

"Who's that, Chino? Excuse me for asking, but I have to be honest with you. If I was hungry you wouldn't be top of the list of people I'd call."

"Well, it's a guy I used to know when I worked at the gym; you know, the Kid Chocolate downtown. I could run for miles you know, day after day. So they hired me to work with all those boxers who trained for the Olympics, world championships, right down to the junior regionals. Helped with some fitness stuff. I knew them all, I guess. It is all a long way from playing dominoes with a bunch of pensioners near the Cupet gas station."

"So what about the boxers? What happened to their food supplies? I deliver to INDER pretty often, and they never go short for anything."

"This is a guy who used to be a boxer, Yoel. You must know him—The Black Torpedo, Oscarcito. He was unbeatable."

"Chino, get to the point, old man. I've lost you somewhere between dominoes, bread, and boxing. Yes, I've heard of a boxer called Oscarcito."

"Oscarcito had been fighting overseas. Somewhere like Venezuela. Anyway he thought he'd try to make it to Mexico. You know, he thought he was close and maybe he had some contacts with those sports agents there. They promised him the earth because they loved Olympic champions like Oscarcito. They said he could turn professional and then he could buy up all these damn buildings here. I know he could." Chino's arms waved in the general direction of the CBM.

"So he chose dominoes instead; is that what you're saying, Chino?"

"It's tough, you know, Yoel. I've seen a lot of these young kids go astray. They tell me a lot, even now. They think they know everything about what goes on in the world. You know, I tell them to wait here and learn about life. Oscarcito was a bighead who thought he'd already learned. He came to the dominoes today. You see, he didn't make it to Mexico. The coaches caught him. Never even got to box this time. They sent him home with two minders right away. Now he's nobody, and you'll never read about it in *Granma*. They don't mention what happened. They said he hurt his hand in training or something."

"Chino, this sounds rather sad for the Black Torpedo. But what's it got to do with you?"

"Well, Oscarcito came to ask me if he could stay in my place. He has nowhere else to go, he says. What am I supposed to say? The boy's in a bad state. 'Oscar, my boy,' I said, 'you look terrible. Why aren't you in the gym training? I don't know many boxers who would try their hand at dominoes. We settle our disputes more peacefully around this table.'"

Chino seemed to enjoy telling the tales. "But Oscar wasn't in the mood for jokes. He was like one of these mani shells. Broken and useless. A champion boxer who'll never box again. Oh yes, Oscarcito's slipped on his backside. Let down his guard and took a knockout blow. At least if I play a wrong note, I get another chance."

I suppose I wasn't surprised at Chino, but it still annoyed me.

"If you ask me, Chino, Oscarcito did the right thing. He did it for himself. What if he lost out?"

Chino laughed. "What do we have here, Yoel? Only our pride. If he goes he stops being Cuban. This is what we did here. Outside you become a number for agents to call, a boxer, not a Cuban. You can't get paid here, but you get dignity."

"Well, tell me about it, Chino. I'm a Cuban, but sometimes I wonder why. Dignity is not what my kids ask for. You just wait. Oscarcito will try again."

"Go on, Yoel. You talk like them all. Get on your bike. See where it takes you."

"Chino, I'll remember that advice when I have the money in the bank account; you know, when I've bought the cell phones, the laptops just like we are allowed. I'll remember that it was Chino who told me to forget about it."

I had had enough and got on the bike. Five minutes was way beyond what I could stand with him.

"Okay, Chino. If your friend wants to try again, just let me know."

"I'm not sure I heard that, Yoel. But he's with me now. We could sure use some bread."

"I have a wife and kids, Chino, you know. I got them a day at Varadero. It cost me like fifty French lessons with the Cameroon. That's it. It's about all I have to aim at right now, Chino. But now Oscarcito, he could make real bucks. Las Vegas. Madison Square Garden. You know all about that."

"Why don't you stop by, Yoel? Oscar could do to talk to someone his own age."

Laura

The Havana airport José Martí surprises a lot of people. It is a place that is supposed to be spectacular. It is, I think, a happy place; excitement at arrivals, shops where we Cubans could mix with the tourists, announcements about things happening, a gateway to Cuba. I often thought about what I would see arriving as a stranger in my homeland. My first glimpse of Cuba. Was it what they expected? Was it what they wanted?

Felipe hated coming to Martí. He said if you wanted the real Cuba come to the Malecón. See the cracked stones, the broken bottles, the people lounging all day, the kids diving in the water. I think Felipe was jealous. He had this thing about travel now. Said it was pointless because to travel you had to make choices. We had none of that, so why pretend? If we traveled it was under orders. Just like his visit to Spain. When he first went there, he thought things were changing for him. It's just the start, he said, and he used to talk all the time about his visit. He knew he screwed up, he said, but it would soon be forgotten. They had big plans for him. That was what that Carlos told him all the time. I don't know why he called him Carlitos if he didn't like him. I think he was trying to impress me, to conceal something.

But the Martí terminals were honest; they didn't try to conceal anything. They were supposed to be the same for everyone—Cubans and foreigners. That ceiling covered in flags, I loved counting them during the waiting. It was a meeting place for new arrivals in Cuba. They were always excited. Cuba is different from anywhere else, they said, pointing to tour books and photos in hotel brochures; the visions of palms, dolphins, turquoise ocean, and sand; the information they all wanted on the Comandante and Che. The official books were all there at the airport. They sold well, so why not? Then the same questions. Had I met them all? Where could they take salsa classes? When could we see some baseball?

This group arriving that day would know it all—they were architects and doctors from a Spanish university. For them I knew it would be about statistics, agriculture. Was it true that we had no private farms? What do we export? So the answer would be there for them to see just as we left the airport. We would pass the beautiful greenhouses on the road into town. New vegetables would be glistening in the early morning sun. Oh, and Señorita Laura, what about the health and education services? We'd heard that they are the best in the world. And as we left the airport they would read the billboards, the statistics of road safety, tourist numbers, and the successes in the fight against SIDA (AIDS). I had to agree with Felipe that this was what we wanted them to believe. We were giving our best side. But didn't every country do just that? The sweeping smooth highway. Which international airport would put on a show of their best potholes?

My group was late—I can't remember why, but I think it was some weather problems in Madrid. I went up to the departure area to go for a chat with Miranda, who was an old school friend who worked in customs. Up there I saw a group of Canadians I had taken to the Bellas Artes leaving, checking in at the departure area. Young kids rubbing their eyes from the early start, students lying on the floor with heads resting against suitcases, admiring their tans. The richer middle-aged were laden with rum, cigars, and the Che berets.

"Time for a coffee before we leave? Where do we pay the exit tax?"

I said my goodbyes, and some of them insisted I take from them some spare CUCs. I had an airport pass through to the protocol lounge. This was where the customs officers hung out. They did some interviewing, baggage checks, I guess, secret stuff. Miranda, my friend, never talked about it much. But I knew the guys she worked with. So they were cheerful when I arrived.

"Hey, you guys, is there no work to be done in this airport? Where's Miranda? Funny, I thought today was her day on duty. Guess she's checking some drug runners for the customs. Anyway, if you see her, please say Laura looked in."

I called my boss at Cuba Vacaciones to tell him the Spanish were late. "Alex, can you get Fredy to cover for me later with the Germans? I'm running late here. The Spanish are not expected for another hour. Must sort some things out here."

"Laurita, everything's delayed today. The Germans won't need you. They're off to the Tropicana; you know, girls rather than ballet. You know what suits them."

I walked back to the departure lounge. An elderly Canadian lady was still waiting to check in. The rest of the group seemed to have moved on.

"Señorita Laura, let's have one more picture to take back to Vancouver." I kissed the lady goodbye and headed to the main customs office. I didn't know the people there.

"Miranda who? Oh wait a minute. I know, that pretty mulata. Sorry, I don't know. We had to get a sub this morning as she didn't show. It's really unusual for her. She's the most reliable I've got, apart from my niece Gisela here. I guess she's been reassigned somewhere. No idea why."

"But she called me a couple of days ago. She didn't say anything had changed."

"I know," said the customs leader. "It's very strange. Maybe some family problems. You know these young girls. Some of them never tell us."

The Spanish group came out of the baggage area. Most of them were elderly men with a few women who looked academic as well, carrying their briefcases. They were dressed like the Spanish do, lots of designer clothes, beautiful shoes. Polite and formal. I greeted each one in turn and stepped out to the row of empty buses parked in line waiting to take the tourists to their Cuban adventure. Air-conditioned of course.

I tried Miranda's cell number, but it had been disconnected.

Felipe

Mama was in tears. Another death, another man taken from the family.

"You have to talk to Donna, Felipe. I know she always dreaded this. She may have been a wild one, but she really loved that man. She hated the knives and guns. Pepe was strong, but he trusted people too much. He even thought that all these animals on the streets were basically good and all they needed was some fatherly advice. You know, he went over to the traffic police for Donna—to stop her worrying. Poor, poor Luisito. That boy—with no one to look up to. No Papa, no Pepe? We need to talk to Mateo. He could maybe help Luisito. Oh Mateo, I wish you weren't leaving. No one could talk to Luisito like him. Felipe, you know he'll depend on you too. Anything that he knows and loves we must help him. Mateo never got Pepe into that church. Not since Luisito was baptized."

I hugged Mama. Rafa and Tico had gone to school. They were used to Pepe being away, so they had not asked where he was.

"Luisito is a great kid. He's small but a fighter. We'll tell him Pepe died a hero; he'll like that. In any case, Pepe wouldn't want the fuss. He would want us all to have a beer and move on. He made the most of his life, what he wanted to do. He told Papa he hoped to make a great baseball player; he had those shoulders. But he found out there was never any money in sport. They offered him an Adidas track suit and seven bucks a month. So Pepe went for the police."

Mama sat down and looked across at Pepe's posters of his foreign trips. The bullfighter was still stuck firmly to the wall. "You know it really hurt Pepe that he couldn't help Papa over all those years. He put family first. His own dad died in Africa. They never said what happened. He just didn't come back. Pepe never sucked up to those big guys who just loved the uniform. He loved our family. He loved Jalisco. These guys who leave us.

It's a good thing we have Rafa, Tico, and you, my dear, dear Feli. Now's the time for the family to come together. Pepe knew there was no use whining. Just get on with it, he would say."

I phoned Rebecca at CBM to say I couldn't get into work. I put down the phone, thinking it was only Pepe who kept it for us. Even the phone depended on the government.

Víctor

Friday was always open day at the CDR. It was another part of routine. They used to joke that it gave the people from the barrio hope to get through the weekend. Hilde's job was to prepare the waiting room and sift out the most crazy of complaints from those that might be a real embarrassment; you know, the sort that had the compañeros threatening to go to the party people or the police.

Hilde had her usual gloomy messages "We still have sixteen buses that are good for space in a parking lot. They have four wheels but little else that resembles a vehicle. The colonel of the army engineers has promised that seven will be repaired from the parts they have. But that leaves nine that are, let's say, worse than useless."

Sometimes I wondered how Hilde ever got to be a sergeant in the army. She took orders but never gave them. "Hilde, tell that fancy engineer colonel that he'd better enjoy his last couple of days in that uniform. Because I will personally make sure he's demoted to private if I don't get at least fourteen. We can manage with all the kids packed in. I always knew that. In Cuba you never ask for fourteen if you really need them. Leave some scope for negotiation; then everyone is happy. People like to make problems in Cuba. They know problems are power."

Hilde had opened the door for the first couple of the residents. It was not how Hilde was supposed to work, but they may have slipped her some pesos simply to get to see me. But who cared? Here it goes again, but at least I can promise them some t-shirts for Moncada. It was a familiar couple again. Lucia and Lucas were some of the most regular. Lucas could fix teeth, though it was not clear whether he had ever been to dental school. They had brought their usual crate to sit on, and Lucia was picking at what remained of her teeth. I suspect he refused to treat his wife.

I greeted him in the usual way. "What's the problem today, Lucas? How's the microwave?" Lucas and his wife had been "chosen" by Hilde to receive one of the new Chinese consignments of microwaves we had received under a cooperation agreement.

"The microwave is great for warming the rice. But you must be joking if you think we can pay for it. It'll take at least twenty years. That'll make me 103 years old. Anyway, Víctor, today it's Lucia's problem, so this time she can do the talking. You know those new people from Boyeros? God knows how they got to live here. They're in the room below us; Compañero Julio only died last week. I can tell you Cerro can do without them. They have no respect for their neighbors. We don't like the noise of all this music that the idiots play. They only moved in last week, and I haven't slept a minute since."

Lucia jumped up from her seat, "You're a liar, Lucas. You slept for plenty of time last night if your snoring was anything to go by. I don't know which is worse—the music or your snoring. Whichever way I'm stuck with a headache."

Lucas got up as well. "I'm not sitting here with that woman … or anyone who will call me a liar."

Lucia was as usual enjoying the exchange. "Fine. I've always enjoyed talking to Víctor on my own. Get lost."

I gritted my teeth and knew this wouldn't last forever. The important thing was to keep up normality. My job was to be predictable. I had to sit there. Once you gave that up you counted for nothing. I have to admit that in the moments like these I thought I would rather sweep a park. I knew that both

Lucas and Lucia would stay together and have their public row for a few minutes. Of course the real reason they had come to see me was to play the role of marriage counselor. I didn't take the bait this time.

"Who's behind the music, Lucia? I thought you were a singer yourself. Why don't you talk to the new guys from Boyeros? Maybe you can do some performing down there."

"Tried that," said Lucia, "but they slammed the door in my face."

"In any case, Cuba is one big music club. Give me the names of these guys and I'll send one of the muchachos around later."

"There's something else,' said Lucia. "We don't have any eggs this week. We were given ten on the libreta, but three were cracked. I know that Hilde here had some extra for her niece's party. That's not fair, and we want to complain."

"These are personal issues, compañera. I can't get into these disputes. A few eggs are always going to be bad. You must take that up with the bodega. They look after old people. Hilde here is a servant of the revolution who is the most honest person I know. I'm afraid I must move on to the next citizen. Otherwise, we'll never get around to everyone. Not even if we wait until the next Moncada."

Lucas and Lucia continued arguing, but Lucas picked up their crate. The next person to come was a young woman who was carrying a baby. The baby was staring at her mother. The mother was looking straight ahead and had dark patches on her bare arms.

She sat down, and I said, "I don't think I know you. Have you come from far?"

The woman didn't reply. "I'm sorry, compañera," I said, "but I can't help you without you telling me who you are and why you have come. I am here to sort out problems as far as I can. Every Cuban knows that the CDR will help. Where are you living? Who is living with you?"

The woman started to mumble. "It's all over. I have nothing left. I don't even know why I came here. We had Yipsi's first birthday party last week. I was happy and so was Rolando. We have nothing apart from ourselves."

I leaned back in my chair. "Un refresco, un cafecito?"

Hilde came in. She thought I liked her to do it for effect, I think, but sometimes it got on my nerves. "Víctor, we have big problems with the march. We've just heard the kids at San Joaquin have failed their grades. You know they can't march; it's never allowed—"

I interrupted, "That will have to wait, Hilde. Always problems. We have to sort out the problems of the compañera … I'm sorry, I don't know your name."

"It's not my name that matters. I am nobody. Yipsi here is all I have."

"I'll ask you again. Where do you live? I thought I knew everyone here—even outside the barrio. I've never seen you before."

"You don't know me. That's the point. I moved here a few weeks ago with Rolando."

"Rolando who?"

"Everyone knows Rolando. He's a hero. You know how much the Cuban ballet means here."

It's hard to understand that a rough guy like me would know anything about ballet. But in Cuba that's different. Ballet is a big prestige thing. All I know is that we're supposed to be the best in the world.

"You mean Rolando Sequier? Our dancing hero?"

The woman hissed her contempt. "Of course that's him. I've known him since way before all this garbage started. I've known Rolando since we were thirteen. We only just got permission to come to live here. We're from Las Tunas. Rolando wanted to be here so he could start some studying; you know, for when the dancing is finished."

"So it all sounds okay. I know the Culture Ministry looks after Cuban champions very well."

The woman bent her head, squeezed her child, and dabbed her eyes. "He just got the apartment from the minister or something, while he was preparing for the new season; you know, the big tour. Goes all over Cuba and lots of countries. It's a big deal. Extra money for dancers. It's all over now. I have no one here. And my baby's sick."

I didn't see what she was saying. "But Rolando has no problems. He can get everything fixed. He's a hero. He came up from nothing."

"Señor, that's all in the past. Rolando *se fue*. He was in Venezuela and found a way to get away. He never talked about doing it before. He's gone. Wants us to leave too, but he doesn't know when."

"Compañera, if Rolando has left Cuba, Rolando has made a big mistake … Look, please tell me your name."

"It's Celeste, but no one knows me here. I have no papers for living here. Rolando has everything with him. No one wants to look after a useless woman with a baby. How can we get food now? I need to buy a ticket for Las Tunas. I must go back to start my life again. All Rolando's family is there as well."

I knew exactly how to react. I felt relieved. This was an easy problem because there was an approved response. "Celeste, I have to tell you that Rolando is now a traitor to the Revolution. You as his family are assumed to be part of his conspiracy. We can no longer trust you, and Rolando will no longer qualify for all the benefits that the Revolution brings. I will call my superiors and inform them of what you have told me. Rolando was given everything by the Revolution, and this is how he repays us."

The woman now raised her head and gestured with one arm hitting the table. The baby was startled and began to cry. "I know nothing about what's going on with the Revolution. Rolando has always fought for Cuba and his family." Her striking of the table became impassioned. "My Rolando is a good guy—not a traitor. I met Rolando when he could hardly read. The schools taught him some pride and to believe in himself. Damn you all. He achieved everything they wanted him to. He is all I have. Yipsi ... Why has he gone when he is a hero?"

"*Was* a hero ..." I said. "And please, it is not necessary to be angry. We don't achieve things that way."

Celeste lowered her voice and stroked her baby. "He's not the only one. A bunch of the boxers also left with Rolando. One of them—Oscar "The Black Torpedo"—has come back, I think. God help him. But what about us? I'm Cuban just as much as Rolando ..."

Celeste got up and left without a word. It was a family issue. It was out of my league to deal with Rolando Sequier.

Vladimir

I returned to my house in Playa. It was something in the atmosphere of the meeting with Bertie that made me sense that the heat was coming. Anything to do with computers made the powers nervous. If the parts were leaving who was getting them? I have to say that Bertie was right that I needed to check on the operations of Compedex. Bertie was right to hear alarm bells that a company had lost computer parts that were already in the country. The problem was that I was used to padding the information, but this time I needed something specific. Bertie might be looking for someone to fire, someone like me who had grown too comfortable. That was how things had always worked. One day I would find my house had been "inspected" and all the equipment removed.

The other possibility was that Bertie had been set up to test me. Of course it might be as simple as that. There might be no problem at Compedex at all. Okay, I will show them. Vladimir of the Lenin Academy would do the sharpest report they'd ever seen. I'd solve this mess, and who knows, I might get a nice little bonus. I ordered the phone transcripts of Compedex and the secret establishment report on approved foreign businesses, provided by MINTEL. I examined the computer suppliers' registry, approved by the Ministry of Light Industry. Every company in Cuba operated under a specific agreement that allowed particular items to be traded. This time I had to make it sound convincing.

I had the first reports in an hour. The intelligence files would take twenty-four hours. All the hundreds of e-mails sent since the start of July, which was when the thefts began, came in. The pattern was steady but slow until around July 10. Then there was a surge of sometimes over a hundred a day. The manager became more and more agitated about losing supplies. He was asking the warehouse in Barcelona for urgent new shipments. The Ministry of Agriculture was refusing to pay any more until they received a new server they had been authorized to have in October. On July 17 the manager e-mailed the Ministry of Light Industry to say he suspected that someone was not selling the stuff but was actually building a system somewhere. He listed the complete series of transactions. He was asking for instructions.

I had enough material to write the first report. The idea of someone stealing parts for building a computer system was original. But it hardly created a situation of panic where the security of the state was threatened. I needed to look a bit more at what the parts would be capable of. That would help me play for time. In any case it was not my job to sort out the problem. There were thousands paid to find out what was really going on in Cuba.

I was due to sell some modems from my stock to hotels in Old Havana. They had just come in from the cargo at the Havana airport. Yes, I borrowed a van sometimes so that no one saw me take delivery. That would give me some opportunities for creative accounting. It would be my guaranteed Moncada bonus. The second e-mailer I wanted to check, Larry, had been silent. The guy appeared to be out of town. He had left an automatic reply message with a smiley face saying he would return today, on July 23. These guys who had e-mail all liked using these gadgets. Good to show off. I bet he's got a massive page on Facebook as well.

CHAPTER 14

Mateo

Never get involved. That was what we were told. You have a spiritual mission for all mankind. You cannot have favorites. But I couldn't get Haydée out of my mind. It was the thought of leaving her behind. She had no hope of seeing Héctor again outside the jail. If you crossed the system then you had no support from the government; that was it. You were without protection, and like Haydée you looked around for anything. Haydée just seemed so helpless to deal with these things. I had a couple of hours before the bishop's seminar on the use of computers in churches. I took a taxi to Calle San Joaquin, San Francisco de Paula, where I am sure few people had ever used a computer.

Haydée had told me she had a job at a youth center where they had a video machine. She opened up the place three evenings a week and watched over the teenagers who came to see videos. She had been told she would lose the job when Héctor was sentenced. But the director of the center was married to Haydée's sister and conveniently forgot to fire her. I remember that she told me that Héctor had been working on their apartment at the time he was arrested. It was a two-story building that had the new breeze-block framed windows that Héctor had just got from his brother when the police had called. Haydée told me that Héctor had thought the police were coming to tell him that he didn't have the right permits. But then it was at four o'clock in the morning. The day after the arrest the party "arranged" another visit. I saw the spray-painted evidence on the outside staircase. "Mercenaries and parasites will never destroy the Revolution. Viva el socialismo." Haydée said the painting was all done before his conviction.

I climbed the staircase, passing the first-floor flat where the door was open. A small red-faced woman was seated on the right-hand side of her room bent over her sewing machine. Her glasses were at the end of her nose, her knee jerking the old controls under the table. A cat slept on the table by her, and the constant whirring of the machine blocked out the sound of my footsteps. I carried on up the stairs and arrived at Haydée and Héctor's door. It was shut, but the window that Héctor had been installing was open. The job was half done, and there appeared to be no catch installed. I knocked. I peered through the window. No one was there, so I felt happy that she was probably at the youth center.

I started down the stairs and knocked on the neighbor's door. "Excuse me. My name is Mateo. I was looking for my friend Haydée who I think lives above here. You know Haydée and her husband Héctor."

She looked up. "Yes, of course I know them, Padre. I have known them for thirty years, I guess, ever since Héctor moved out of his place down the road."

"Oh, I didn't realize he was local too. I remember she told me about your sewing. You must be Silvia," I said.

"I am Silvia. Yes indeed. Oh, everyone's local here, Padre. Some people from San Francisco have never been to Havana. It's that kind of place. That's good for my business, you know, sewing. There aren't many shops around here. I can repair anything, make things fit. Keeps me busy."

"Oh, I can see that's a machine that's kept very busy as well. We could do with some new curtains at the seminary. I will pass on your skills. But I was wondering where Haydée could be right now. She told me she had a job at the local youth center."

"She and Héctor broke the rules, Padre. I used to tell her; those are the rules. I've been telling people for years. You are not Cuban, I can tell. This country of ours is not a place for politics. We had to decide at the start of all this all those years ago if we wanted to be part of it. We made our choice, and now it's over. There are no more choices. For most of us, we preferred to stay at our sewing machines; you know, the old reliable. The rest just left. My husband did that too."

I could see she had plenty more to tell me. "But Silvia, Haydée and Héctor believed in what they do, or did. In any case I don't think you could say that Haydée broke the rules. She was Héctor's wife. She supported him. But it was Héctor who did the journalism or whatever got him into trouble with the government."

Silvia laughed. "Is that what she told you? Come and sit down, Padre. What is your name?"

"My name is Mateo."

"Padre Mateo, I have known Haydée and Héctor since they were kids. I made Haydée's wedding dress, and I know she sold it for four hundred pesos. Maybe that paid for that no-good husband's little adventures. Look where all that got him."

"Well, it's been good to meet you, Silvia," I said. "But it appears that I've missed Haydée. I just wanted to say goodbye. You know I'm leaving Cuba soon, so I won't be able to see her again."

"Señor Mateo, I think that Haydée didn't listen to me. She got in with the wrong crowd. Look at this skirt, señor. In Miami it would be used to dry dishes probably, but I'm proud that I can repair it for a while. I can earn three hundred pesos a month. I have no worries, no stress. That is Cuba. But I keep my mouth shut except to sing a little. I know there will never be anything else."

"Anyway, Silvia, I'm sure you will be a good friend to Haydée. I hope she gets to keep her job. That will be very important to her without Héctor."

"Well, señor, I'm not sure we will be seeing Haydée for some time. This group of people came around yesterday. They came up the stairs just like you did. You see, though I'm working I never miss anything. Anyway, I'd never seen them before. They only stayed a few minutes, but there was some talking between them in low voices, you know. Not exactly whispering, but it was like when people don't want to be overheard. And Haydée came down the stairs with them."

"When was this, Silvia?"

"Just last night, señor. I'm sorry, but there was nothing I could do. In any case there have been many years like this here when strange people used to come to the building. If you ask me, Haydée was stupid, as everyone here knows they are being watched. I think they thought they could outwit the police or something."

"So were these people—were they police?"

"I have no idea. 'You need to be careful, Haydée,'" I said. "'Héctor is well known around here. You will follow him to jail.'"

"I don't understand. Haydée was Héctor's wife."

"Haydée was the brains, Padre. She convinced Héctor to do what he did. But the police left Haydée alone until now. Police watch and listen, and then they pounce. Or maybe it was those people she was mixed up with over in Santiago. Now they were the wild ones, if you ask me. There's always more smoke where there's some fire."

Silvia put down her sewing. "You know, this make me very sad to think of them both gone. I never knew Haydée to spend a night away from here. Can't think what got into her to go off

like that. My room here is all I need. There's been trouble in
San Francisco over the years. You know there's not much work
here unless you travel a long way. The teenagers are on edge a
lot. There was this boy around here a few years back who would
come and sweep the stairs, the yard. Said he was a social pioneer.
But he used to hang around doing next to nothing, and then
suddenly he disappeared and a couple of the neighbors were
seeing the police. They never came back either."

Felipe

I was trying to sort out Pepe's possessions. He surprised me
with how tidy he was. Tidy in what he had left in the box under
his bed. There was no lock. "Mama, shouldn't Donna get to see
this first?"

"Feli, I'm afraid of what there might be in there. You know,
the girlfriends; all that. You should check it out for Donna. She's
sent a message with a bus driver. A kid brought it around to tell
us that she's arriving tomorrow."

I knew Pepe had something in this box that he used to joke
about. It's a kind of testament he mentioned. "Don't all rush
at once when I'm gone. I'd like to leave enough to buy a little
Harley in there, but don't count on it."

I opened the box. There was a sealed envelope addressed to
Donna. That was all there was, thank goodness. Maybe that had
the money in it as well. Pepe had done something right.

I tried the phone again. "Laura, please call me back. I need
to talk to you. It's about Pepe."

Mama was strong and proud. She had done her crying.
"Today is not a day for weeping. I'm getting out of my chair
just like we have always done, and we will show Jalisco we are
a family of Cubans. When Pepe started to come over here to
meet Donna, he was a wild kid. You were half his age, Felipe.
But Pepe was like a kid with no manners, no values, I thought.
He used to roam around here with the Cerro gang members.

They were younger than him. They were broken up by the law, and Pepe just missed going to jail. Maybe it was his big smile as well. Donna just couldn't stop herself loving him. She saw him as strong, sure of what he wanted. He proved her right. He said he wanted Donna as much as the Revolution."

I hugged Mama again. "Mama, you're used to dealing with deaths. Papa's, then Tico's Dad. For me, this is new and painful. Pepe, well … I know he didn't like the things I said. Saw me as a selfish SOB who never did a real job. But …" The phone rang; Pepe's phone. It was Vlado.

"Felipe, can we meet today? There are some things I want to talk about—kind of urgent."

"Vlado. It's really difficult today. My uncle—you know, Pepe—has just been killed in a riot downtown. Everything's up in the air. It's terrible for all of us, you know."

"Felipe, I'm sorry, man. But this is really important for everyone here Every little bit of time matters right now. I need to see you." I covered the phone.

"Mama, it's that guy you can't stand from the Lenin, Vladimir. He really wants to see me. Never heard him in a state like that …"

"Felipe, you should go … There's nothing more to be done here. In Cuba you need friends everywhere. Papa said you never know when we Communists will need each other."

"But I need to talk to Rafa and Tico. What have you told them?"

"Just that Pepe has been hurt and he's in hospital. You know how he adored the boys as much as his own. Donna's had a tougher life than any of us. It's good she's coming back to see us. When she left she was numbed with hatred. She never thought the man she loved would turn out that way. I lost my men along the way, but they still loved me. Sometimes you lose your man but they've already left you. But that can wait. Felipe, you go and see Vladimir."

I walked down the stairs. I remembered the noise Pepe's boots would make coming home, pointing at his tattoo. "Another day at work and I'm that much closer to paying for my Harley." Then I realized what Mama had meant. Get on with your life. As always Mama would take care of Jalisco.

It was pouring with rain—the afternoon cloudburst—and the Havana traffic was at a standstill. I thought of Vladimir inside his air-conditioned office van making his way to meet me, listening to his Led Zeppelin CDs. I raised my face to the water and walked by instinct. I kept walking. The rain gave me a caress from nature, washing away the dust of my efforts to make sense of the day. It helped, but not for long. The rain was gone, mocking me for thinking freshness might last so long. I reached Old Havana, and the sun had returned. The horse-drawn trucks in Parque Central were being wiped down by their drivers preparing for the tourists who would soon be coming out for the evening sun. I headed to a café tucked away behind the back of Hotel Telegrafo. It never seemed to close, a place for a refresco for the tourists on their way back to hotels and the sports players leaving the gym Kid Chocolate. A strange choice by Vlado. This time, I knew there would be no whisky on offer.

Vlado, with his carefully folded golfing umbrella that matched the green of his shirt, was waiting for me. "I come here nearly every day. It's important to follow habits. No one will have followed me. Let's go into this corner."

Vlado sounded more confident than he looked. He had a quick look around the café. The table he had targeted was in an area under a loud ceiling fan.

"Felipe, look, I'm sorry about Pepe. I remember him too. There are a lot like him in the police. Good guys, trying their best. How's Donna?"

"Donna left him—she left him for the hundredth time last week. Too many girls. If only he could have stuck to the motorbikes. Anyway, you'll have to excuse me. I have a lot on my mind. It was Mama who thought it would be good for me to have a break."

"Felipe. We're the same age. We're kids of the Revolution. We've made our choices. We understand the rules."

"Vlado, come on. You said this was urgent. I'm not in a beginner's class on revolutionary philosophy. We've had this conversation dozens of times. At least you could buy me a coffee."

"Sure … compañera? Dos cafecitos …"

"Felipe, I promise I'm not wasting your time. I know the clock is ticking here now. The rules will change. Maybe everything will change. You and I need to forget the past."

"Okay, okay. Slow down, Vlado. Nothing's changed here for half a century. Why will it all be different this time? Is someone new arriving from outer space? I don't see it here, amigo. Look at all those who've tried and failed. Nothing changes overnight. Take a look around Old Havana. Look at those horses and carts outside. It's not going to change."

"You don't understand, Felipe. Look, you'll just have to trust me. But there are some things I know. I have been on the inside track for a while here because it helps to know a bit about computers. Take my word for it. We all need to make plans."

"I'm glad you have something to be excited about. But why tell me? I may be on a track at the CBM, but it's certainly not the inside. I guess I'm on the furthest track from the center you can imagine. Right now I count for nothing in the polo. They've made that clear. So no one asks me anything. I never hear anything that a million people haven't heard before me. You know that Rebecca. She's the leader of official thinking, if you really want to know."

Vlado paused as the waitress brought the coffees. "Felipe, I wanted to ask you to find out something as a friend. I know how you despise what I have done and what I seem to you. Everything is wrong for you about how I made my choices. But it's time for another choice now. And I wanted to give you a chance to think again as well; you know, think about what might happen even if we do nothing about it."

"Vlado, I have a lot on my mind. Apart from Pepe, someone's stolen some really important documents. They were my work, and they were what I wanted for my future, so that's gone. It's not been the best of times. And I really don't have a clue what you mean about being part of something. But if it is of any interest for you, I can tell you that Carlitos has been talking in some pretty strange ways. Never really heard him like this before. He seemed kind of nervous yesterday. But what else could I possibly find out? I can't just invite Carlitos for a beer, not even if you gave me the CUCs to pay for it."

"Felipe, there are messages being sent that mean that things could turn nasty here. There are some people getting impatient with things who are …, well prepared to force the issue."

"You mean use guns, Vlado?"

"I don't know what's going on. That's the point. They know they won't get anywhere with guns. They just want a new system that is supported by …"

"Vladimir, look, I've seen the effects of violence today. If you're trying to bring me aboard on some shooting adventure, then count me out. In any case the guys with the good ideas don't usually shoot to kill."

"No, no, it's not that at all, Felipe. I know you'd be useless with a gun. I just want you to ask around a bit, see what's really happening. You know people who think like you, who may know some of them involved. If not you, Feli; your papa might have known someone. One thing I've learned is that you should get the best information before you act on anything. These messages are the only things I have to go on. But before I tell you anything more I need you to promise not to speak any further about this. To anyone."

I laughed sarcastically. This was not what I had expected. "Come on, Vlado. I'm not into secret societies. If I find out anything I'll let you know; for free, or maybe for a little more of that whisky. Vlado, I can't talk to anyone in organized crime or organized anything. I'm just me, trying to survive here. Actually you're right. I have thought about talking to the so-called dissidents. They are brave and intelligent people, but there's a lot of talk, squabbles. It's the government running a lot of it anyway. I'll give it a think—if it makes you feel better and ..."

Vladimir looked around, and his fingers twisted the end of his ponytail. He leaned forward on the table, staring at me. "Felipe, I'm not kidding. There are people who think like you who are planning something big. I don't know what it is, but a lot of people could get hurt. If, and I really have no idea, if they succeed, Carlitos will be a lot more than nervous. Just ask, that's all, and see if there is any lead we can work on."

"Vlado, a lot has happened today. I have to help the family first. But I'll see what I can do in the next couple of days."

"Thanks, Felipe. Sooner rather than later might be better for us both."

Laura

I took the Spanish group to their hotel. They said they wanted some free time. So did I. It didn't happen at one moment, but it was this week when I began to doubt what my family had told me. Seeing Yoel in strange places, and now Miranda, was part of it. But there was more. My family was still doing the usual things. So if things were going well with their lives, why were others changing? My stepdad was in the Masons, never seemed short of money, and went to meetings, and we had great parties at home. I felt guilty about this for my Cuban friends. I knew lots of them were jealous, and so would I be. But it wasn't possible for all of them to come. My parents were suspicious of showing the house because of all the paintings and silver they had. My mom did what she was told.

"Why don't you open up to people in Havana? It's obvious that we live in a fortress. It's a stupid way to live. These people are not violent; they won't rob us. They will accept some differences in wealth. It's impossible to hate the rich so much that you make everyone poor." Of course that was why they were not enthusiastic about Felipe. My stepdad checked these things out. But Felipe's family had always been a mess. I told them that was not his fault.

With Miranda's family it was different. Her father was a manager of the airline Air Cubana and travelled a lot, always in business class. Miranda was a bit of a rebel though and was into all the Che legend stuff. I liked it myself too. You know this brave asthmatic pediatrician who never lost his ideals. It was what young people like, with all that romance, right or wrong. Well, I got into it a bit, telling the tourists Che stories, the Sierra, Santa Clara, the train bulldozer. Every Cuban knew all that, but it really meant a lot to me. In the end I think I grew out of it a little. Che was human, and why worship another human? Miranda never really has grown out of it. She has her room full of berets, photos, his sayings, the family tree, the motorbike. All that. It was so much that we called her Cheranda.

It wasn't like me to get all distracted. An American told me about the word "multitask" in English. He said I was real good at it.

"You'd do well back in Cincinnati, honey. Let me know if you'd like a job with Procter and Gamble."

Anyway, he was right. I have a lot of confidence in myself to concentrate on my business. But that wasn't happening with all that stuff at the airport about Miranda. Cubans did not get reassigned or moved without reason. Miranda had been groomed for the very top. I knew that and she knew that, but we never talked about it. Cubans just knew the ladder of the

Revolution. Miranda's grades were always posted as the best. Customs was a place where the Revolution would perfect her. Good luck to her, I said. I told her that the customs uniform was terrible, but that they would have good parties where she could show off on the dance floor. I could not imagine a time when I could not speak to her. There was nothing she would not tell me. I never asked about the customs business. Miranda would joke, saying it was all form-filling. Next would be an office job in the ministry, and then another promotion. But it didn't interest me.

I started thinking that maybe Miranda had just got involved in something, a new boyfriend. Calm down, Laura; all this stuff from Felipe, Vladimir. These people didn't have enough to think about. Then I thought of Eric. Maybe she had gone back to Eric, this smart guy who was at the top of his English literature class at the university. Eric knew everything there was to know about George Orwell, except that he found that most of his books were banned in Cuba. So he chose W. H. Auden and used to boast that he'd been invited to lecture in London. I didn't believe him, but Miranda did. They dated all through university; he was a pretty good dancer as well.

Eric's professor had left to work for an embassy in the accounts department. So he tipped off Eric about a job at a school where the embassy kids went. They all went to the International School in Siboney, which is only for non-Cuban kids, of course. But the teachers were mostly very smart Cubans, and Eric landed a job teaching eight-year-olds. It wasn't as much fun as discussing W. H. Auden, but it paid three hundred dollars a month. Eric kept track of Miranda's new boyfriends. But I guess for Miranda it would never work. Eric, the maverick who laughed at *Animal Farm*, would never be a match for the star of the customs directorate, Miranda.

"Love will never conquer the Revolution," Eric would say.

I called the school in Siboney. "Señor Eric is busy with the advanced international baccalaureate students," the receptionist said proudly.

"When would he be free?" I asked.

"I'll check his schedule in my computer." I guess I remembered that because no one ever said that in Cuba. International, yes, I thought. Enjoy your computer. "He'll be free in around thirty minutes, but has a lot of meetings with parents."

"Tell him not to worry. I'm not a parent and I only need to see him for two minutes. I'll stop by."

Mateo

After the computer seminar, the bishop's driver was free. I told him I wanted to visit a parishioner in San Francisco. I wanted to check on something at Haydée's apartment. There was a sign I noticed on the walls inside, the design of which I partially remembered. I arrived at the building, and dogs were roaming around the trash bags at the bottom of the stairwell. Opposite there was some union branch for writers and artists. It was bolted up, maybe for the Moncada weekend, but a watchman guardian got up from his stool to warn off the scavenging dogs. I said, "Good afternoon," and walked up the steps. The first floor window was flapping in the breeze. So Héctor had never found a proper catch. The room suggested a quick exit had been made. There were glasses on the table, some clothes on the floor. A small plant was tipped over by the wall, maybe by the wind, and soil had spilled over. There were wires coming out of the walls with some crude antennae over a Chinese TV. Next to the window papers were piled on a shelf. In the far corner I saw what I had remembered.

I climbed in through the window. I guess all that hiking in Patagonia had made me reasonably fit. I walked over to take a better look. It was a picture that had a central scene of Christ on the cross, surrounded by seven smaller images. There was nothing else on the walls, which badly needed plaster. The thing that surprised me was that it was in good condition. It was the Santería picture known as the Seven African Powers. I had seen it a few times in my visits down to Santiago, but never in Havana. I walked over to the papers and rummaged in the top layer. The paper that had been marked in red was near the top. It gave a short description of the meaning of the picture—how the seven orisha powers were mixed up with the teachings of Christianity. "Santería teaches that the seven powerful orishas, the 'siete potencias,' control every aspect of life. Each has different characteristics and plays different roles. The immense power of the orisha is sought by individuals who pay homage to that particular one. At the same time, it is recognized that they act as a group to chart the destiny of each human life." The word seven was underlined in red three times.

I was unsettled with what Silvia had told me. Haydée seemed to me the heartbroken spouse who was desperate to see her man again. Of course Silvia was not her greatest admirer, and she found incomprehensible everyone who didn't accept everything. But I couldn't escape from the fact that Silvia knew Héctor and Haydée. And even if Haydée was a political activist, after all, why should it matter? A child was crying on the second floor, and I folded the paper about the orishas, put it in my pocket, and climbed back out of the room. I walked down the stairs.

Silvia was bent over her sewing machine, but of course she had noticed me, "So, Padre, do you believe me now? I told you she went off with some people, and I don't think she'll come back. I never saw her stay away a night even when Héctor was off in Santiago. I'm sad to think of her in the cárcel."

"Silvia, I'm not interested in what Haydée was doing. In any case, I'm not Cuban, so really it's none of my business. Haydée was distressed yesterday, and I think she would have told me if she was planning to go away. So I will try and find out. I don't have much time, because I'm due to leave Cuba soon. But

Haydée is vulnerable, and there are plenty of people, so it seems, who would be interested in exploiting her."

"Padre, Haydée is a smart girl. But she's impulsive; you know, just like how she married Héctor. She likes everything to happen overnight. Could never sit still as a little girl. She drove her poor mother to despair."

I left Haydée's place. It wasn't the home of a house-proud stay-at-home Cuban. I checked on the card Minister Contreras had given me.

Felipe

Your mind rejects the drama, the difficult parts, when the tragedy hits. It tries to return to normality and to shut out the rest. If Vladimir had come to me with his stuff, then I would usually just forget it. I pretended for a while that I'd done something for Pepe. Now I felt useless. I'd done nothing to help him. He died alone. Vlado made me forget that. Vlado seemed actually to care what I thought, and I felt I needed something new to do.

So that was the reason I went back to the CBM. I was grateful as well to have somewhere to go. The CBM was also where I had no real friends. They did not know my family. Or at least only Carlitos knew Papa's story. It was around four in the afternoon when I arrived, and most of the staff was leaving. But the usual senior managers were still working. I looked in on Carlitos. "Director Carlitos, I am sorry I was not able to come into work today. We have had serious family issues. I have come in now to catch up. I know you have many important projects …"

"Felipe, yes we all have family issues. It is your duty to inform us when these things happen. But we did need you here for the PowerPoint presentation on monoclonal antibodies. Your phone seems to have been disconnected."

"I'm sorry. The phone was working this morning. There were only so many things I could do. Pepe, my uncle is, or was, a traffic cop. He was the guy who got us the phone, and he has been killed in a riot. Maybe someone was quick off the mark and cut us off. It's pretty incredible how efficient some people are in our system."

"Felipe, that's sarcasm, which leads to cynicism, and we don't want any of that here. The Revolution always remembers its loyal servants. You can be sure of that."

I wasn't in the mood for a fight. I had done my duty and put up my hands in apology. "Anyway, Señor Director, I apologize. I am here to pick up some pieces."

I walked around to my office. Rebecca had gone out and had left a note on her door saying "Back at eight. Meeting at Council of State." I smiled. Rebecca was never one to lose an opportunity to impress.

It was good anyway that she was not around. However busy she was, she always had time to snoop into others' affairs. I wanted to look at more than one thing in the safe. The problem was that whoever had taken my documents may have seen what else was in there as well. But I had taken some precautions. What was left looked like useless sentimental albums, childhood memories. There were some student papers from high school and some children's books that Mama had asked me to keep. She liked the idea of them in an official safe. Then I had a beaten-up green folder that was coffee stained and torn. They were random individual pages with the headings of each describing the contents carefully cut off. I checked each one. They were all there. Whoever took the documents knew what they wanted.

In the folder there was a small cardboard notebook. It was covered in some gift-wrapping paper, which I guess Papa must have received from someone. In any case nothing much was left of the flowery design. It had peeled away, and the first page was half torn. But the bottom half contained two words: "Besos, Papa." The rest of the writing was torn off, but some numbers remained. They read 23 10 1. I had never understood what those numbers were.

The rest was well known to me because Papa had asked me to keep it. I checked again that no one was looking through the window of the office. I flicked through the pages. They were all numbered. There were poems that covered pages twelve to thirty-one. The last one was barely three lines long and ended with the words "a seguir."

After came "Palabras del cárcel"—"Words from jail."

I sat down and realized that it was years since I had read them.

"Felipe, you and Mama came to see me today. I don't write well, as I have never been trained in any of that. But I need to set down what I felt today. It was one of those moments when I looked at you and saw everything a father sees. You were strong, you had bright eyes, and you showed respect to me in spite of everything you saw in my failure. You were quiet and listened. You were growing from a boy to a man. You were helping Mama with all those things she brought for me. You were planning for your life; you were excited. I told you I loved you. Maybe you thought that what I said were just easy words. You must have thought I was using words to stop a silence that would be embarrassing within a family. If we were silent, maybe you would think we were strangers. Of course I have a lot of time here to think. We never have much time to speak. That is my worst punishment. My pride was to think I would be able to offer you everything I knew, most of it useless. But every father wants to pass on something. I know it is only by my writing this that you will know what you have meant to me. Keep this writing close to you and read it at special moments. My voice will fade and disappear, but writing is forever."

It moved me again. I wished I could write as well. But I had never written my own letters to him. Mama wrote, and she sent love from everyone else, I know. But I think she felt ashamed, somehow.

"You do your studies, Felipe, and you will be the brightest and best of this family. Your father made some mistakes. I have no doubt you will have a better life. Choose your steps carefully and don't be led astray."

I think she wanted to shield me from Papa. If I wrote, he would write back, and maybe that would take over my mind.

I read on to the last part.

"Felipe, I have not discovered many secrets of life. But for me writing and music are the greatest joys. Life takes away all the moments, but we must try to recreate what we felt when we were moved. I am so pleased that the Revolution taught me to read. I was the first in my family. I owe that debt, even though what I read changed my mind. But never stop learning through reading. Think for yourself, my son. In the end, I didn't. Books can be read over and over again, and you will find new truths. Music is the other great comfort. This was what I learned listening to Chino. Chino expresses his heart, his true beliefs, not just in words but in music. His voice is alive for me today. As I shut my eyes I can hear him. It brings his songs to me. His songs always end with his listeners wanting more.

"So Felipe I will tell you this little piece of truth that I have found useful in my life. Our feelings come and go. Always write down what you feel when you feel it. It may seem stupid at the time, but it will give you and Mama comfort in your life. In this small book I have written all I know because I know I cannot tell you. You might think that as an old man who left school at twelve years old I have already used almost all the words I know. I spend a lot of time imagining what you are doing and what you like to think about. You see, my time here will mean I will never really know, and I will be left to imagine. That is what all these years will mean.

"One day (don't ask me when; there are so many here) I decided it was stupid just to imagine and do something that might actually help you. I can do nothing here. I might as well not exist except for those twenty minutes when you come. But I have written something here that will help you one day. I have written here all the people I can think of in my life who may just be able to do things for you that I couldn't do myself. They are all good people. That's a simple word, 'good,' but it means so much. They are people who believe in acts of good, not just talking. You can call on all of them if you need anything. The reason I know that they are good is that I have seen them here in this cell. I told them I felt I had let you all down with ruining my life in this way. They all promised to help you. They told me themselves."

I made some notes, placed them in my wallet, and left. The PowerPoint presentation on monoclonal antibodies would have to wait.

CHAPTER 15

Mateo

I telephoned Minister Contreras on the way back to the seminary. His assistant—I think she was called Ileana—took the call. I heard her go into the minister's office and ask him if he would see me. Maybe she was new. I thought that because her voice carried so clearly, and that was not good security in such an office. "Señor Ministro, there's this man on the telephone. He says he's a padre or something. Met you a few days ago. He wants to come in and see you. Says it's urgent. He doesn't have a Cuban accent, Señor Ministro. What should I do?"

Contreras's voice was lower; the experience of a minister. I couldn't make out what he said. I'm sure he meant it that way.

Ileana returned to her office.

"Padre Mateo, that is your name, you said. The minister can see you for a few minutes later today. Will six o'clock be okay?"

It was a long shot calling Contreras. If I had only just arrived in Cuba I would have been more cautious. But my friend Padre David, my predecessor in Havana, told me of the "dangerous final phase" when you are in a foreign country. In the final days, after all the exploring, the discovery, you begin to feel that you want to leave having done things. You become frustrated. It's like a self-esteem, which I know is bad for a priest. But we all do it. Impatience can be risky but can be a virtue. I think of our Lord throwing out the merchants from the temple.

There were some things the bishops did not like, and a priest talking to ministers was high on the list. By heading for the Council of State I knew I was taking a risk. The bishop was out of town, and by the time he heard about it I'd be gone.

When you see a building close up you realize what it was meant to do. The Council of State was supposed to look grand. Every Cuban knows that, of course, but it's a building you look at from afar. Even alongside the vast dimensions of Revolution Square it is still a massive building. The little Lada cab was like a lizard crawling up the side of a rock. We stopped at the guard box. The guard asked the cab driver for the identity of his passenger. I produced my foreign resident's ID and watched the guard examine it carefully.

"I can see you're in a church setup here. We don't meet many of you now. But I was baptized out in Guantanamo. Seems like a lifetime ago, but I hope to be buried in a Catholic cemetery one day. That's why I take care to behave. It's a pleasure to meet you, Padre. We have you down to see Minister Contreras. Have a good day, Padre."

The cab driver drove on and looked around at me, "Seems like you have a good effect on people, my friend. Normally the best thing I ever get coming here is a grunt and with luck they'll lift the barrier. Maybe I should wear one of those white collars like you."

"Well, I'm not sure the bishop would approve. In fact he doesn't approve much of me in any case. But you're right. This job has its ups and downs like any other. I'm grateful to you for your patience," I said. I paid the driver and got out. Ileana was waiting for me in the lobby.

"Good evening, Padre. I am the minister's personal assistant. He is waiting for you. May I escort you to the elevator?"

Grand, marble, and empty of people, the lobby of the Council of State was designed to impress on the inside as well.

I was greeted by the minister, now dressed in a white guayabera ready for the evening's receptions. Contreras filled the doorway to his cavernous office, which commanded panoramic views of Revolution Square. As I entered, a small bald man carrying a large holdall walked nervously from the minister's room. The minister turned to me. "Welcome, Padre. Can I introduce my friend Tony here, who's the best barber in Havana? Like me, he's lost most of his hair, but he knows how to help you keep yours. He has come very kindly to make sure I look my best for the evening's events."

I shook the man's hand. "I can see you do an excellent job. I'm sorry I'm leaving Cuba, because I wish I could have had a final haircut."

Tony seemed in no hurry to leave. "I would be delighted to offer you my services, Padre. Here is my card. Or perhaps if you are leaving then your colleagues from the church might be interested. I'm a little busy until Moncada. Everyone, of course, wants to look their best for the TV cameras."

Contreras seemed to be getting impatient. "Okay, Tony, always the businessman. Don't worry; I'll look into what is happening to the telephone you've asked for. I know that these things take time."

"That would be very much appreciated, Señor Ministro. And if there were any of the latest shipment of Chinese televisions that happen to be available, that would also be wonderful. I would of course pay what the asking price is."

"Tony, I will do my best. But I really can't keep the Padre waiting any longer. I'm sure he's got a big mass to preside over. We all have to be patient in Cuba, Tony, but in the end everything will be provided."

Ileana was perhaps not as new as I thought. She came in and supported the minister's message to Tony, the sociable barber.

"Minister, excuse the interruption ... Don't forget the Indonesian reception you have to attend after seeing the Padre."

Tony turned to me. "Thank you, Minister. It's always a privilege and a pleasure to serve. I'll await your call, Padre. I once cut a bishop's hair, so you see I have the right experience. I think he is likely to be a cardinal one day."

Tony checked his holdall and left. Contreras rolled his eyes. He beckoned me into his office and took a quick look in the mirror as he entered. At least he seemed pleased with Tony's work.

"I'm delighted we were able to meet your request for a meeting, Padre. Please come in. I'm afraid I am due to attend a reception at the Indonesian embassy in half an hour. And then there's a seminar at the UN Development Agency. What can I offer you to drink?" Contreras carefully rearranged the papers on his desk. He was a tidy man and checked that there was no hair from the barber's operations on his guayabera.

"Thank you, Minister. It's very kind of you to see me. I know I said it was urgent, so I won't waste your time. I did not come here for a social occasion, Minister. A little water would be fine, thank you."

"Please call me Ricardo, Padre. Ileana, please bring some water for Padre Mateo and a cafecito for me. So Padre, how are you and how is your fine work in, what is it called, the seminary? I hope you are attracting some of the most talented Cuba youth to help the ..."

I kept thinking of the dangerous final phase. This could lead to something you could regret. This is not a job for a priest. "Minister, I'm fine and so is the seminary, all things considered. But I have one pressing matter I need to talk about and that is to ask about what has happened to my friend, Haydée Sebastiano."

"Padre, I'm sorry, but I don't think I know the lady. Does she live in Havana?"

"Yes, she lives not far from here in San Francisco de Paula. Her husband is a journalist called Héctor Sebastiano. He is currently in jail."

With that, Contreras's bland expression changed. He frowned and cleared his throat. "I see," said Contreras. "I assume you mean one of the mercenaries now serving time for their crimes."

"With respect, Minister, Haydée Sebastiano has committed no crime. And, as far as I know, she hasn't been accused of anything."

"Padre, in these cases, the position is clear. The spouse of Sebastiano cannot be seen as entirely innocent. She is a suspect because without her help and support her husband could not have done his treacherous acts. As she knew of his treachery, and taking money from overseas governments, she would be a suspect as an accomplice to a crime."

"So that's why she has disappeared, because she is suspected of being an accomplice?"

"Disappeared ... I don't understand. I think, Padre, you must be mistaken. No one disappears in Cuba. Every person, every child is valued by the Revolution. Some people need to be watched and reeducated in the ways of the Revolution. But we never give up on people as lost to the Revolution."

"I was with her at Cinco y Medio visiting people in Pinar jail. You know, that is where some of the dissidents are held. And it was just a couple of days ago the last time I was there. I called around to see her today and was told by a neighbor that she had been taken away."

"Padre, I am disturbed to hear you have been visiting jails, especially that type of jail. That is no place for a minister of religion. These people are there because they have committed crimes and according to the laws of Cuba need to be punished."

Mateo, I thought, take a deep breath. I paused and I am sure looked nervous to this large, confident man in a large office. But this was my only chance. I would never see Contreras again. "Minister, our religion is a religion of forgiveness. My place is to spread the word of God to all situations where we find God's children, especially for the lonely, the hungry, the vulnerable. There is no place in this country where a minister of religion should not go."

"Well, Padre, that is your position. I think our Revolution has helped the lonely, hungry, and vulnerable rather a lot. Before us Cuba was a divided and violent country. A huge difference from what you see today. That is why we have built such solid support for it. But I will tell you, as a friend and as a Cuban friend, that it will not do those in jail any good to receive your visits. And it will not help Sra. Haydée Sebastiano."

"Minister, Cuba has some strange rules. But a lady who is on her own cannot just be taken away without anyone hearing from her."

"Padre, she will not be alone wherever she is. Cubans help each other."

"Minister, perhaps I could ask a favor of you. You said that no one disappears in Cuba. Well, I suppose you would be well placed to find the whereabouts of someone; would that be true?"

"Well, I could make inquiries, yes."

"I would be very grateful to know where Haydée is. I think she is a very frightened person. She needs to know that there's someone who is concerned for her."

"Padre I will do what I can. Could you write down her address? There are inquiries that can be made."

I checked my watch. I had to return to the church to conduct a mass.

Laura

Eric was waiting at the entrance to the school in Siboney. He wore a tie, which I guessed the embassy kids expected. He waved me to a staff parking place outside the entrance that he had reserved for me. Eric, the former student president, was as organized as ever. I kissed him and asked if there was anywhere we could talk. "Come around the back here to the basketball court. The kids are not due out for twenty minutes."

"Look, it's great to see you again, Eric, but this is no social call. It's something about Miranda. Have you seen her lately? They told me she didn't work at the airport anymore."

"Laura, I know. Something has happened in her life, because Miranda lives by method. She's always in control. That's what makes it all really strange. I speak to her nearly every day, but last night her mother said she didn't know what she was doing. Her mother tried the customs, and they said that Miranda had been reassigned to something in the provinces. But they wouldn't tell her anything else. No contacts or anything."

I knew Eric would have views on what had happened. "So why would that be?"

"Laura, I expect it was the same with you, but Miranda only spoke about what she wanted. There were parts she wouldn't touch, and maybe there were some special operations or something. I know she did some recent training out on the Coast Guard station that she wasn't allowed to discuss. That was her way of life. Sometimes you have to do things out of the routine. Not like here, where everything is predictable." He waved his hand in the direction of the well-kept school.

"What about that guy we used to know in customs? Jimmy, he called himself, didn't he? He always claimed he knew what was going on."

"I'm not sure about Jimmy, Laurita. You know he seemed to live very well. He liked Miranda for sure. But that was below his work in order of loyalty. In any case Miranda can look after herself. She wouldn't want her friends thinking she needed us. She knows the rules of survival."

Yoel

I returned the motorbike to the baseball stadium. I was feeling good. This was going to be a major payday, and I was more sure than ever that Abel had been thinking small for too long. He worked for months on one *balsero* at a time. He brought in a few bucks, but the people business saw Abel as someone who didn't count in the big deals. That was the strange part about Captain Bill and all that. Why would César come to us?

Maybe even Abel was bored. Maybe that was the reason why he was interested in doing this thing. Not so interested, of course, that he wanted to show up himself. No, not our Abel. It was all the same to that damned baseball crowd. Year after year, nothing changed. Their championship. No risks. All nice and orderly. What did it matter who won? At the stadium it was early evening and the fans were arriving for a game against the Industriales. The visitors were from Ciego, and their coaches had just delivered the players. What a pointless exercise it all was! No one made any money. The players were trying to get overseas, the coaches were paid less than a bread delivery driver, and who wanted a load of Chinese baseballs as their perk? The fans, ah yes, the fans. They loved to see the Industriales win, which they usually did. So even that was predictable. Okay, in the long term it might make sense. Maybe they were hoping for an American major league franchise one day. Maybe.

It was good that the fans were there on that day. For me there was safety in numbers. Abel was in the reception area of the stadium, checking on the arrivals. Abel had a certain cunning, so if he thought about it he rarely made a false move. He noticed me in the entrance hall but ignored me. I waited under one of the enormous murals of revolutionary leaders. I felt small, which was fine. Abel was addressing a group of students who were examining the trophies on display. They were volunteers being given their instructions for the evening.

"There's a visiting group from the UN Food and Agriculture. We must keep the first three rows free behind home plate. Hey, have you noticed those kids playing soccer? Can you boot them out right now? No soccer allowed in here. That's definite."

Abel turned to a female assistant. "The president of INDER just called. They want to bring a group of athletes just in from Ethiopia. So you'd better get some refrescos ready. We'll take them into the secretary's office first. Show them all the world champions stuff. You know what to do."

Of course. I shouldn't have forgotten. Abel had done well to impress his masters by his skills at baseball diplomacy.

Abel was done with the game crowd. He nodded at me and we went into his office. He was not in a good mood. "What's up? It's not a great idea to come here right now. We have all sorts of officials in for the game. You know they all love to see a winner."

"Abel, okay, okay, but not everything stops for baseball. Do you want to make a living or what? It's urgent. That's why I came straight back with the bike. We need to come up with these guys for the fast boats. It's eight thousand bucks a time with 10 percent to us. You're sitting on your hands, Abel. If we don't come up with some people quick they'll count us out. What's happened to all the baseball players you said you had?"

Abel was a big brother again. About time. "Yoel, don't come in here acting like Mr. Bighead. Don't you know there are already over fifty Cuban *peloteros* waiting in Santo Domingo to get tryouts? The market is kind of saturated. All these kids from Industriales know the score."

"Then we need to target the families in Miami. They have more money than they know what to do with. You've got to tell them it's charity, helping your Cuban brothers. Anything that sells, Abel; this business is serious. Can't you see? Do something that matters for a change instead of filling in your charts. You have two more days or I'm cutting you out."

Abel looked surprised. It suddenly got through to him. I hadn't seen him that angry since I put a few dents in his precious bike. "Little brother, you listen to me. You were nothing in this until I brought you in. Don't you forget that I was in it before Mariel, all that mass *salida* business. No one knows more than me, Yoel. I've sent you two for sure already this month, so that's my cut. I'm working on the rest. But people think the price is high. These fancy boat captains down from Dade County. They've all got their private planes let alone those damn boats. Personally I'd rather stay in Cuba. Some people are not as greedy as you. And by the way, Yoel, I know enough about all this to keep you in jail well beyond the ninth inning."

That really shook me. Maybe Abel had had a tough day. All those Ethiopian athletes or something. But it was getting to him. "Put me in jail, Abel. And you think you would carry on here in this baseball hell, with all your stupid students and ridiculous uniforms. You need to get into the real world. Baseball coaches are meant to stay calm under fire. That's what you're supposed to be good at; you know, two outs, at the bottom of the ninth. Stay calm and play good baseball. So hang in there, buddy. We have maybe one last chance to make some good bucks. If you bring us down because you failed, the whole team will go down, not just those you choose."

Víctor

Thank goodness there were no more calls from Manuel. I knew he had gone over to Manzanillo and had built up this thing into a personal mission. I told him he could always escape with his doctors to Venezuela, but Manuel had this thing about personal success. I think Max was the same. They always felt that they had been underappreciated. They saw themselves as individuals. Manuel and Max. It was all about the medals and honors they could get. Pride will drive you to some desperate acts. Forget it. Who will ever remember what we did?

Felipe

The only car I could get back from the CBM was heading for downtown, right in the center of Habana Vieja. I felt down because I had run out of things to do. I had the notes, but now I had to go home. I couldn't keep running away. I needed a few minutes, so I sat on the steps outside the Capitolio. The storm had passed over, and the evening light had that inviting glow. The colors were washed clean. There was enough going on to lose myself again. I watched the arrivals of the tour buses, the bicycle rickshaws, the Coco taxis. Those guys in the taxis, what a great idea. Easy to make a motorbike with a covered seat. But the tourists loved it, bright and yellow, great for a photograph, and the fare was "whatever you want." Cubans were pretty bright, smarter than the tourists. Those Cocos tipped over without much trouble. No belts, no safety. Just looked good. Then some other beautifully designed products from Cuba. The beautiful girls, the jineteras. The tourists loved them as well, of course. Pay them in national money or make sure the police get a share. Sad but an everyday story of life in Havana. There were the police too to keep a watch over the muggers, only a few hundred meters from where Pepe died. Life had returned to normal. Another evening of activity was being prepared. Prepared but not just yet. The jineteras knew when to keep their distance. The night had not yet arrived. Patience would be needed.

That was it. I felt I knew. Nothing was changing in Havana. Vladimir must be wrong, because everything was in equilibrium. The police were still allowing the rules to be broken if they got something. A policeman slapped a girl on her backside. That was the signal that she would be okay. All is well in Cuba. A camello was parked just beyond the Kid Chocolate gymnasium. A group of Japanese tourists were flashing their digital cameras in the darkening afternoon, dozens of flashes for the coco taxis and camellos. I saw a friend who worked for the water company coming out of the Hotel Telégrafo. The old system was working. He would take me. That was what he wanted to do.

"Will you help a friend?"

"Yes, hermano, of course," he said.

Cuba, you anger and frustrate me. How much good do we have in us, and how have we learned to help each other? Did we need to do all the rest as well? Or did we only get the good parts because of what we went through? Of course the water company van would take me through Cerro. I had no excuses anymore. Get on with it.

At Jalisco Rafa and Tico were watching TV, their daily intake of cartoons. They weren't sitting in Pepe's drinking chair. Of course they left it empty, but this was not the real Rafa and Tico. Normally they would joke around and offer me high-fives. Today they were gloomy. They weren't even fighting. They just ignored me.

I looked around for Mama, but she had gone out. She never went far. But with the boys in a strange mood it was something that surprised me.

"Hey muchachos, where's Mama?" No reply. "Gone to get some food maybe."

Rafa spoke without looking up from the cartoons. "She said she wanted to find some American cola. You know the type that Pepe used to get us."

"It was so bad about Pepe, Rafa. I know it's not going to be the same. Pepe was very brave, and we are all proud of him. But we can live without cola. Mama should know that."

Mama's place for hiding money was in an old cushion. She said it was one that Donna made. It wasn't very secure, because you just unzipped the back. She only ever did it when Rafa and Tico were asleep. Pepe would sometimes contribute some dollar bills handed out by the police commander as special bonuses. The cushion was empty. The boys were right. You could only get real Coke with real dollars. I tried the phone, but as Carlitos had said it was cut off. The day wasn't getting any better, but with phones you could usually do something. There was always someone who knew someone. We'd get it fixed after all this was over. Just like the water company guy, something would turn up. But that would have to wait.

"Mama will be back soon. I just need to make a phone call."

I knew the bodega had a phone at the corner of Jalisco. Fortunately Gloria, an old girlfriend of Pepe's, was on duty. "Hey Gloria, You've heard, I guess, about Pepe."

Gloria looked blank. "Pepe? You mean that Donna's left him? Sure, I heard that. It's about time. Serves him right. There was quite a fight, I hear. Most people in Jalisco seem to have heard it."

"No, no, Gloria. Pepe was killed yesterday in a riot downtown. You know, he went to help with an emergency response unit. There was a lot of fighting. He didn't make it."

"Mi amor, I'm so sorry. Pepe was a bastard to me, but he had his good points."

"Gloria, could I use the phone? We've lost our line."

Gloria wiped a tear from her eye and nodded, pointing out back. I dialed Laura's cell phone number. She picked up.

"Laurita. I've been trying to call. Pepe has been killed in a riot. A mob attacked him and he didn't run. You know what he meant to Mama and the boys. It's just horrible, so horrible."

"I'm so sorry, Felipe. Bad things really seem to be happening. You know that girl at the airport who's been my friend forever, Miranda? Well, she's disappeared and no one seems to know where she's gone."

"Wasn't she some sort of customs official?"

"Yes, Miranda is on the fast track—committed to her job and the government. But underneath she's a young kid. You know, we had swimming lessons together. We were in the campo preuniversity. Her mother and boyfriend have no idea where she is, or that's what they're saying. She's a big part of my life. I'm really worried."

"Laurita, these things happen—she's a big girl. No one disappears here. Can we see each other tonight? It's been a long day. As soon as Mama gets back, I'll be over." I returned to the apartment, but Mama was still on her Coca Cola mission.

CHAPTER 16

Mateo

It was my favorite time to conduct Mass. Early evening. Those who came were somehow more spiritual. They had come through another day, and they were close to their social period, of meeting with friends, eating something, and they were ready to contemplate and pray. They felt they had time to think about life. That is a productive time for a priest.

I needed to refocus. After all, Haydée was one Cuban, and there were many more who needed my attention. I wanted to be able to trust more. Haydée would be held in safe hands. I turned to the congregation and swung the incense. "And now to God the Father, God the Son ... But remember that those who die in the name of Christ are fulfilling a promise he made to all mankind. Those who live by me shall not perish but have eternal life.

"Before we conclude the service, I have some announcements that form part of our Christian duty. I would like to remind you to keep in your prayers all our friends and family whose concerns have been expressed to us. They are all in the family of Christ in Cuba. Juan Ignacio Fuentes who has been taken to hospital again. And Haydée Sebastiano, wife of Héctor, has not been seen in her neighborhood for two days. We pray that

Haydée feels the presence of the Lord Almighty where she is and that she knows that her friends in Christ are giving her spiritual support. Finally, we pray for all the prisoners in Cuba. We pray that they seek and receive forgiveness and that those who have been punished for holding beliefs in the sanctity of human rights will hold fast to their ideals."

I left the altar with my assistant and returned to my robing quarters. I felt that I had returned to what I should be doing. My life was not climbing through windows, pretending to be a superman. I believed in the power of prayer. I took a last drink of the wine, thanked the staff, and wished them a good evening.

As I was leaving, a tall black man appeared from inside the sanctuary. He was carrying a small child who was asleep. The man smiled and said nervously, "Padre, I only have come here a few times; you know, at Easter, Christmas, and when I feel troubled. You don't know me at all, so I don't feel deserving to take up your time."

I looked into the man's eyes and tried to look sympathetic. Here it goes again—meeting new people when you're leaving. "I'm delighted to meet you. My name is Mateo. Can we sit down? Please come into my room."

As we walked back in the staff were still chatting. It was that evening feeling for them. I asked if they could just give me a few minutes. I wanted to be alone with the visitor.

"Please sit over here. My name is Mateo. Please tell me your name."

"Padre, it's better you don't know my real name. I think you'll understand. Perhaps you could just call me Cubano."

"Fine," I said. "I am ready to listen. How old is your little boy?"

"He's five, I see him on weekends and … His mother is involved in the parades on Moncada. She's gone down to Santiago, which is where we both come from."

"So what will you do this weekend? Will you be taking him to see some of the parks in Havana? I guess he would love the zoo. I wish I could do all the things I wanted to do. I'm feeling a little sad because I'm leaving Cuba soon," I said, trying to raise his spirits.

"Padre, I didn't realize you were not Cuban. But then from your accent, I suppose, I see that now. Moncada will be very busy. I'm afraid I don't have much time for showing my son that sort of thing. I'm not a very good father, you know. I am struggling with the question of what I should be doing, so that is why I have come here to this church. I have heard things that I should not have heard; you know, from people who do not like certain things that are happening in Cuba."

I could see that the man was hoping for and needing more than a few words of comfort. "Cubano, my friend, why don't you start at the beginning."

The man got up, laid the boy on the settee, and checked that he was still asleep.

He continued, "I have to tell you, sir, that I am not a Christian. But I knew some missionaries once who called in Santiago. They said if you turned to the church, then you would get the answers about right or wrong. If you chose wrong, even knowing what was right, then you would be punished, forever. And all those you love would also be punished. Have I learned it correctly, sir?"

"My friend, you have heard some of the messages correctly. But to let Jesus Christ into your heart, we do not think about being punished. If you love him and follow his word, then you let go of these earthly fears."

"I am afraid right now, sir. I found the Mass you gave to be peaceful, full of big ideas. These ideas are so different from what I have heard. What I have heard is from Santiago, you know, way over in the east. There are men there who look like me, and there are problems with how we live our lives. Santiago is not like Havana. We don't have the tourists. We don't have the families in Miami who send the money. We have to live day to day. My black friends and I, we are seen as a social problem. Some of them have decided that there is no hope for them in Cuba and want to take things, you know, into their own hands. One of them is my brother."

"How do you know this? Was this something you are not supposed to know?"

"I have to tell you, sir. No one trusts me. I have been in jail a few times over many years. Sam over there is the only good thing that has ever happened to me. But I used to hang out with some bad guys, so I deserved these punishments. But I was not real bad like some of the guys. They're the sort that would kill their own grandmother; you know, savages. Or more like animals really. But I ask myself what made them like that. Is it really their fault, sir, that they know nothing of right or wrong?"

"We have them in Havana too, I'm afraid," I said. It was one of those conversations where you thought it would be difficult to say anything that was not banal. The man had seen things I never had. Who was I to advise?

Maybe he thought I wasn't listening. "Padre, I am serious, sir. This is not normal fighting or violence. This involves hundreds, thousands ..."

"Cubano, it sounds terrible. But I am a man of the church, and this sounds like something for the police."

"No, no, Padre. It's not like this is criminal. The leaders of these people call themselves politicians. They are looking to change things but realize that along the way people will get hurt. My brother is always telling me. It's always happened like that. If you make an omelet you have to break eggs. You get just one chance to play a part. If we stop them now, how can we explain to our children, like little Sam over there, that we did nothing? We knew what to do, but we didn't do it. We took the bottle of rum and went off to sit under a tree just like before. I ask myself, if we stop them now, there will be no change. And without change nothing will happen."

"I see, Cubano. You are afraid but hope for better things." That sounded terrible I know, and I thought, Mateo, you have to do better than that.

"What should I do, Padre? Those missionaries said something else. I've tried it, pray and you will receive the answer. What God wills will become clear, but that may not be what you think you need. I have come here and prayed. I need guidance from someone who knows how human beings receive their messages from God. But Padre, I am too confused. Should we stop the violence, or should we let it happen? My brother says he's sorry the innocent will die as well. But ..." Cubano looked over at Sam.

"I can see, Cubano, that this is really troubling you. How long has your brother been involved in this planning?"

"Many weeks, I think. Most of the plan I don't know, and you must see that my brother and I are worlds apart. He has been in the party, you know. Never been in jail like me. He has brains, but he is betraying those people he knows. I think he would never have told me because all this is too serious. I found out by chance—it's crazy really. A few weeks ago my mother died in a car accident. We worked at this chicken farm on the road to La Maya, near the Gran Piedra. Me and my mother. She got me the job. Anyway, you know how people travel there in the campo. Sixty or more on the back of a truck. The driver had had maybe five more beers than normal. This pack of stray dogs could smell the chickens and ran up to the truck. It started as a joke as the driver was trying to outdrive the dogs. He was looking back and hit some trees. My mother was one of ten people killed.

"I'm telling you that, Padre, because that is how I found out. You see, my brother has no phone, so I went around to his house to tell him the news, of course. He never invites me; why should he? But I wanted to show him that I could be serious too. Responsible. It was dark at the house. He has one floor only, and it's not far from the railway station in Santiago. I got there on foot; the windows were open and I heard a lot of voices. There was constant talking. At first I thought he was being robbed. But it was the planning that was going on; you know, for the big days in Moncada. I couldn't take it all in, but I stood outside for a few minutes. They were talking in low voices and with nervousness and fear. I had to knock and tell my brother. It was his mother after all. That was when I knew this was for real. The looks on those guys' faces. My brother didn't grieve for her, I'm afraid. His mind was somewhere else. I saw that his eyes were cold; that was frightening. He was prepared to give up everything"

"I am listening carefully, Cubano, but I have lived here for some time in Cuba, and the government here is strong and well informed. I think those people you speak of have very little chance of getting their plans through. The government will be prepared for trouble. So maybe what you speak of will never happen."

"It's not just that, sir. It's the news on the streets. People know who is saying what. You know, there is even a form of words people say to each other: 'We are Cubans too.' That shows that they think something will happen. Big time. Santiago is not like Havana. It's real bad out there. It's the beautiful white kids who get it all from the Revolution; you know, getting food, work. A lot of people are desperate. They need to survive. I can stop it, sir, but I need you to tell me what I should do."

"Cubano, I am not sure I can help. I will pray for you and all the people in your pueblo. But I think the church would always be on the side of peace. I am pleased to know you, but this is politics. It's a dangerous area for a priest. Life is the highest gift we have, and we can never destroy it."

I had said all I could. I had to tell him that killing was wrong, but I didn't do a very good job. I was never a great improviser. It was against my faith, but I wanted the man to leave. I was tired of wrestling with the difficult decisions of others, and there is only so much you can summon up. I stood up to invite him to go. I saw that Sam was stirring.

"I wonder if your boy is hungry. They do reasonable pizza at the end of this street. It should still be open. Here's a bit of money."

The man's face was expressionless. He stared forward and then at Sam. He bent down to pick up his son. His t-shirt crept up his back, and I saw a tattoo. It was pretty normal in Cuba. But then I saw a symbol that seemed similar to the one I had seen at Haydée's apartment. A number seven under the S, which looked as if it was covering a crucifix.

"Sir, thank you. But I don't need money. I think you don't believe me, and that is the problem. I will have to show you that this is the truth. I will bring you proof, and then you will act. I have never done anything like this, but I cannot forget what I know."

With that the man left and Sam continued to sleep. He left the money on the table.

Felipe

Mama was not worried about wasting the money. "I thought Pepe would have liked the boys to have something they enjoyed; you know, a few proper Cokes. I told them to keep the cans somewhere special and think of Pepe."

It seemed stupid to say what I was thinking, but I did anyway. "Mama, that's nice, but we don't have that much money to spend. Pepe really cared for those boys, but he would want them to be prepared for life here in Cuba. And life is not having one-dollar cans of Coke."

"Felipe, who knows what tomorrow will bring? The boys are not stupid. They know it was something special. We must go to the police crematorium tomorrow morning. Pepe's family is coming in from Matanzas. Donna arrives overnight from Sancti. I've told the boys they should come as well. Your father always liked the family to attend funerals. It's a big thing for them, so what else would we do with the dollars?"

"I have to go back to CBM first. I must do some work or maybe they'll try to get rid of me again. You know that Carlitos is always there, and maybe he needs some scalps ..."

"Laurita ..." I looked in surprise as Laura walked through the door.

She kissed me and Mama. "I wanted to come over and say how sorry I was about Pepe. These robberies in Old Havana are getting worse. I hate to take my tourists there late at night."

Mama was delighted. "Laurita, it's sweet of you to come around. I wish we had some drinks to offer you, but the boys just drank all the Coca Cola. You caught us on a bad day." I smiled.

"I didn't come for that. I stopped by the Western Union, and my tio Andrés—you know, the one in Fort Lauderdale—sent some extra this month. He said we could use it for a new air conditioner. But we don't need it. Here, take it. It would be good to send for some flowers for Pepe." Laurita put fifty dollars on the table.

"Oh Laurita, we don't need that, really. In any case we could buy all the flowers in Havana with that."

"Any news of Miranda?" I asked.

"No," said Laura. "She's still not told her mother anything. Just gone quiet. The customs office won't tell the family anything. The police are looking, but they feel there's something they're not saying. Eric, who's one of her boyfriends, doesn't know what's going on. I can't believe there isn't someone we know who will have a lead. I'm going on to see some of the local reps down at the Nacional. They know the customs offices where she might be."

I think Laura was uncomfortable staying in our place. I knew she was kind, but I didn't expect her to come around so quickly. Pepe was nothing to her. But maybe she did see a future for herself as part of our family.

She made her excuses. "You know, I need to get out a little. It's the weekend. There's this film festival for Moncada at the Chaplin cine. Sometimes those German films are kind of fun. I'll check out what's on."

Yoel

I don't want you to get the impression that I spent my life trying to convince Cubans to get on boats. This thing with César was something Abel had cooked up, but I guess Abel realized that he was out of his depth. I think he brought me in as an excuse to call it off. I think he hoped it would all fail. The passengers for boats simply weren't that easy to pull off. Especially if you were like Abel and didn't have that flair for things. Let's face it, money was the key. Dear Felipe, with all his big ideas, liked to lie around and talk. If his friends didn't call him up, he would stay in Jalisco forever. Yes, I saw some signs that he might change and tried to get him to move, but of course he never did anything about paying for it. What use are some boring lab reports to pay for your boat ride? If those Trianas could only find a cousin in New Jersey or something.

I had never had anything to do with boxers. But I knew enough to know that there was big money. Everyone in Cuba knew that Teófilo had turned down millions to become a hero, and everyone in Cuba was proud of Teófilo. Chino's boxer friend might have some rich promoter who could be into getting a boatload of Olympic champions out of Cuba. It was a risk, but I hadn't got that many leads. So off I went to check out this Black Torpedo.

Chino had a room in one of those gifts from Stalin, a high-rise block built for the new workers' paradise in the 1970s. Out by the Giradilla. Near the science institutes, actually just close to one of those tourist hospitals, where the rich guys from outside Cuba got their cut-price plastic surgery. Chino was way up near the top, probably on the tenth or eleventh floor. He opened the door carefully. Three of the hinges had been removed. "Look, Yoel, if ever you find some hinges, you know, down at the bakery, I'd be really grateful. This door is a load of crap."

Chino's room was small, and I saw Oscar sitting behind him. There was a red Adidas bag on the floor with Federacion Cubana de Boxeo written on the side. Beyond the bag was a pool of water by the window leaving a momento of the evening storm.

"Oscarcito, this is my friend Yoel, who says he may be able to help you. In any case, Oscarcito, this place is not made for two guys with no one to clean up the mess. At least he has this part of the room as his own." Chino made a gesture with his hands. "There's this old couch they threw out from the hospital he can sleep on. I'll have to move it away from the window. Don't worry, it'll dry out. I'll mop up the flood. You know Havana. The good news is that we have water through the pipes since yesterday. The CDR fixed it."

I suppose I should have expected Chino to try to steal the show. "Okay, okay, Chino. We live in Havana as well. We feel sorry for you, but you have a roof over your head. And so does Oscar. Let me talk a little to him. How are you feeling, buddy?"

Chino took the hint. "I'm just going out now to play a few songs for the tourists on the Malecón. It's a good time, you know. The light is romantic; everyone's heading for a restaurant. If I get lucky I'll stop by and get some bread, even some soap. Now that would be a good night, wouldn't it?"

Oscar looked around. "This room's okay, Chino. Better than where I started. You know that. A cigarette would be nice, that's all."

Chino frowned. "Not in my house, my boy. You're a boxer, Oscar. You cut out the tobacco when you were knee high. You'll be a boxer again. I'm counting on it. But you need to get back into shape. Yoel here will help you do that."

Chino walked away, checking that his cigar was behind his ear. Of course he knew that the next ration would not be due until after Moncada, and he wanted to make it last.

Oscar was like most boxers, I imagine; a pretty boring guy but with lots of determination. The problem was when he came to making his plans. He wanted to try to leave again, but he had no money. He had no strategy, zero. Just Chino. He did say there was once a German banker he had met who was a boxing fan, but he couldn't remember his name. Poor Oscar. In another country the right people would come to you because you could make them millionaires as well. Unfortunately you were born in the wrong country.

CHAPTER 17

Saturday July 24

VLADIMIR

It was Saturday—I should have been going to Club Habana at Siboney, to play a little tennis followed by lunch by the pool. It was usually a taste of what proper international business people did. But this was not for that Saturday. There were things happening, and I had some urgent business to do. Real business, not black-market computer parts. It was a feeling like I've never had. The dealing in some of the material that got "lost" from the warehouses gave me some sense of control. But all that was nothing compared to reading that stuff on Compedex.

I never really gave them the credit they deserved; I mean our intelligence people. The files they had were pretty impressive. Within twenty-four hours they had responded to MINTEL. I had now received a bundle of encrypted e-mails from telecommunications intelligence. This was a serious operation. It wasn't every day you got material that had been requested under special authority of the minister. It contained everything that the government knew was listed under Compedex. Compedex had been operating in Cuba for five years. It had originally obtained its license to trade in computer parts through a

Slovakian former communist politician who now spent most of the year living with a girl in Cuba. It had been set up as a trade-off for a Cuban solidarity organization that was to be established in Bratislava.

Compedex had won contracts to supply computers and parts for the Ministry of Agriculture, the tourism companies, and the trade unions. It was well regarded by the government, with one large warehouse near the airport, and had recently imported a large consignment of cell phones and laptops from China. Compedex had just been allowed to establish a regional warehouse in the east, near the port of Santiago. Imports came in from Jamaica and Trinidad, which was cheaper than shipping from Mariel and Cárdenas.

I scrolled down the MINTEL report to the profile of the local managing director. He was a Slovakian national with a PhD in information technology from Purdue University in Indiana. He employed three Cuban salesmen and a resident Cuban director who was also an official of the Ministry of Industry.

The pace of information reported had picked up since the beginning of July. Compedex had filed three reports about missing items with local police in the Boyeros area near the airport. The items had been registered at customs, but the truck carrying them from the air cargo bay had disappeared. This had happened on each occasion, and the total value of equipment stolen had been more than six hundred thousand dollars. The police had been unable to locate any of the drivers, and one commentary by an intelligence analyst suggested that the men had been rewarded by a passage out of the country. Their families had been interviewed but said they had no knowledge about why they should have chosen to leave. The computers had included a complete new server installation for the biology department at the University of Santiago and new laptops for senior officials at the Eastern headquarters of the Ministry of Agriculture.

I rechecked the string of information from the first e-mailer, Larry; you know, the guy who had been on vacation. He had returned to his laptop on July 23 and had begun to e-mail frequently a company called Saluki enterprises. Saluki seemed to be consultants and technicians. According to Larry, they were to be installing a computer system in Santiago. They had been travelling a lot down to the Oriente, and the latest e-mail from Saluki mentioned a computer installation at the University of Santiago that was due the day after Moncada. Larry was in touch with some friends in Santiago. The tone of all this was one of organization. The guys were calm and confident, but Larry was just too confident to be doing all this e-mailing. I looked up the registry of foreign companies in Playa. Saluki had two employees who were Colombian and Russian and one Cuban secretary. They were described as IT administrators and had done recent installations for the tobacco growers' federation.

The last e-mail from Larry was in upper-case letters. It called all members of the "Board" to an important meeting at lunchtime on Saturday July 24 at the address of Saluki Enterprises in La Playa. The meeting would be to discuss final planning for the Santiago project.

I sat back and looked at the ceiling. Kurt wanted to go out. After all it was Saturday and the sun was shining. Okay, Kurt, I'll do my duty, but you can help me out a little as well.

Víctor

"The Moncada roundup meeting happens in one hour. Be at Karl Marx promptly." Hilde took the call. It came as a relief as we were finally into the finishing stretch.

That was a good time. I was excited. Víctor, you have come this far. Víctor, you can play a role. Our little scheme, it was ours, and it was still on track. It was like having an empty book and knowing you could write the story. I'd never thought that could be me. And to be in the Karl Marx. We never went there, and I wondered why the bureau had chosen it. Maybe it was simply to show that they could use it, because it was the biggest theater they had. Maybe they were going to do things differently as well and this would be something fresh from what would otherwise be the usual tedious roundabout. Some of us had done over thirty Moncadas. In any case it was better than another Saturday in the CDR. When I arrived, the guys from around Havana were already in the lobby, smoking and carrying clipboards. No one knew how many CDRs there were in total. But someone from the party had once said at least eighty thousand. Anyway it seemed that no one from Havana had missed the chance to show up in the Marx. There was bragging and swearing, and there was a long line at the coffee stall. Beer would be on offer after the meeting. There was no music, just politics and organization, and it was around forty minutes late starting.

I knew they could organize those party people, and that day I had to admit that they were better than me. I took my seat in the section reserved for Cerro. The room was crowded with guys from the police, the emergency services, fire and ambulance, and the local party secretaries. The student bodies and young Communists were set out in groups behind us. All of us were placed in front of a large screen with the first slide showing the area around Revolution Square. The presentation was on arrival times, the parking areas, tables for distribution of Moncada t-shirts, water, bread, and the papers showing the order of proceedings. Everyone needed to be in place by 5:45 AM. Buses would be issued with entry passes, and trucks would bring in the banners and would have precedence.

The slide show moved to the next three hours. I noticed the layout of the podium, and I knew the familiar surrounding entourage with the keynote speakers. As usual there was no discussion of which individuals would appear, only when each group of students, social workers, trade unionists, and representatives of municipios would be arranged. We were told it was particularly important to applaud the foreign visitors who this year would be from Guatemala, Nicaragua, and Canada. There would be different singing and musical groups, a Bolivian band of indigenous people, and a rock band from the new Russian communist party. The president of La Lisa CDR for some reason stood up to remind everyone to sing loudly and look at the podium.

"Moncada is about concentration and vigilance. All those goons who look around when they are on TV. Everyone must be prepared to smile, shout, and sing. The international media will be measuring the decibels compared to last year." A few delegates applauded the smart-ass, which delighted him.

He was ahead of the agenda. The final section of the meeting was devoted to media coverage. We were to hear about the key messages for the most important Moncada in decades. The speaker was Fausto Gómez, the deputy editor of *Granma*.

"Compañeros, I am honored to have this opportunity to address you on this historic occasion. We will be watched by many millions around the world. It is essential that we speak and act like true revolutionaries. Efficiency and resolution are everything. You know the slogan for the CDRs: "En cada barrio Revolución!" I have been authorized to tell you some of the important themes that our leaders will address. This is the first Moncada of the new collective leadership, and the imperialist media will be looking for cracks in our revolutionary solidarity. They have been doing the same for decades, since the first days after Moncada in 1953. We know how to repel such aggression against us, and we will do so again. My friends, the first theme will be that the new aggressions against Cuba mean we must value ever more our socialist friends."

I noticed the CDR president from Regla trying to stifle a yawn. "Sorry," he whispered out of the corner of his mouth, "you didn't see that. I've been up since four."

"The second theme is that Cuba is the most internationalist country in the world. We send doctors, nurses, and sports trainers to every continent and ask for no payment. This is done out of respect for our fellow human beings. We perform medical operations in Cuba at no charge. We train doctors and students from many countries in the world, including the United States of America. We ask for nothing in return. Nothing except the respect we have the right to demand as an independent and proud nation.

"The third theme is that crime and corruption must be uprooted from the core of our society. In recent days we have been reminded of the need for great vigilance. There have been examples of lawlessness with criminal elements in Havana and Santiago. Corruption has been discovered in our party and military, and the government has taken resolute action to defend the principles of the revolution. We must show the world that traitors and mercenaries have no place in our society and will be eliminated.

"There are some further items that our leadership will address that I am not authorized to discuss. These are significant new thoughts about the next stage in perfecting the revolution and what must be done to defend our economic sovereignty. But the terms in which that strategy will be expressed are still being refined."

Fausto invited some questions. There were some eager comments but no questions. A young man in a leather jacket stood up to say he was the producer for Canal 1 TV. So what? I thought. He was interrupted by a gray-haired woman from the government press office who said that a special Moncada website would be launched with a virtual reconstruction of the struggle at the Moncada barracks in Santiago. This would be accessible to overseas users of the Internet and on the normally controlled basis in Cuba itself. All was well. Wait your turn, young man in the leather jacket.

Henry, Miami

Max Pérez walked into my office right on time. Sergio and I were listening to the weather forecast. Everything looked fine, and it was no big deal to see Max. He was proud of his Spanish passport and kept saying he told all his family they should get one too. He loved to provoke us, Max the Cuban, always one step ahead.

"How was the flight, Max? Business class, I hope, for a big shot in the tobacco trade like you."

"Henry, my friend. I wish. Those guys who got on at Nassau are all up there in business. Have you any idea what the ministry guys pay me for my crops? That's the deal with government. I wish I could feed my family with the stuff. But actually they prefer roast beef."

"Anyway, maybe you won't need to take too many of these flights in the future. All that will change," I said.

Max never liked other people to make jokes. "Henry, none of you have your necks on the line in this one. Selling SUVS, that's what you're good at. Some of the people back home are getting nervous, and it is only for that reason that I have come over. I need to assure my group that this time there will be no slipup."

I knew to ignore Max when he was being patronizing. Sergio was keen to speak, but he could blow the whole thing as he detested Max. "The delivery will be made on time, Max. The organization of all this has been run through more times than the State of the Union address. You forget that we are Cubans too in Hialeah, and we know how to organize. From our side, we have planned well. Abel has had those visits from the guy in Marathon—he said that the liaison went well. The only problem is that we haven't heard from Abel for a few days. We understand the guy from the Keys won't go unless we have some full boats. They're getting greedy. So if you want to get the equipment delivered we need to make sure he goes. The cayos are the perfect place."

Max was always the slow burner. Maybe it was Africa or something. He camouflaged himself so he never showed his true feelings

"Yes, yes, Enrique. That is okay. Simple stuff on the cayos. It's at the other end, in Santiago. We may have a weak link."

Sergio saw an opening and dramatically banged the table. "Oh, yes, you wait until now to tell us Max. Who or what is the weak link?"

Max finished his coffee. "You know a lot of the coordination went through the colonel in Manzanillo. Well, he's gone. I've heard he got a little too ambitious with his other projects."

"What do you mean?"

"Well, this colonel has been taken out. Looks like he's been arrested. It was news to me. But the rumors are that he had links with the Cuban wild guys here. Maybe Rayos de Libertad. He'd been passing information for at least two years. That means he's going to be worked on pretty hard so he tells everything. And we should have known earlier. But we didn't. I'm sorry, but not every part of a story is like a fairy tale."

The thin face and immaculate silver hair gave his words a dignity that sucked the rage from Sergio. I asked the next question.

"Well, shouldn't we know more about the colonel before we bet the ranch on this, Max?"

"Don't worry, Henry. We've sent someone over to take care of it. The colonel knows he only has to keep quiet for a few days and he'll be fine. He's got some plan to pretend he's very sick, I think. That should do it."

Sergio had become confident again. "So if it's all okay, why do you bother coming over?"

"Well, Sergio, I didn't come here to shop. As you know, Miami can't rival Havana in that area."

"So let's have a drink and chat about old times. What was the name of the girl who used to live in the Cuchillo in Barrio Chino? I thought you would have followed her to the Keys. Didn't she end up in Islamorada?"

"Sergio, it would be nice to reminisce all day. But we have business to look after. I'm here to give you a market report. I'm afraid it's not all good and we need to be careful."

The message finally dawned on Sergio. As usual he overreacted. "Oh no, I can't believe it. Screwups again in Havana. Everything to do with Cuba goes rotten if you let it."

"Calm down, Sergio. That's why you left and I didn't. I happen to believe that things do get done. Look at the screwups you have here with your hurricanes. We all have a good laugh in Pinar about that. We have some risks, but we can manage them. It's like I was telling Henry; we're still on track. Look, these guys didn't stay in power forever without planning. Everything was pretty much a disaster to start with at Moncada, just as it was in the fighting in the Sierra. They fought their way through it. And they won. Remember that they won. Deal with it."

I saw that this conversation was heading nowhere. I knew that Sergio was into things we preferred not to discuss. He may have had an excuse. A lot had happened to his family before they left. Sergio the bitter was never far away. There had been so many extreme groups, but Rayos de Libertad—RDL, as they were known—contained some of the worst nutters around.

"Max, you say the colonel has been in touch with RDL. They're a pretty weird bunch, Max. Have we really been dealing with such idiots?"

"I'm just as amazed as you are, Henry," said Max. "To tell you the truth, that's why I've come over. I need to get to know what the RDL is up to and see what the beloved colonel has left us with. I guess the bottom line is we're not sure how much they know."

"Max, look, Sergio and I are not into this extremist stuff. Not anymore, are we, Sergio? We're just making a little money; you know, free enterprise. What you guys don't know about. If you want to get into violence count me out. That's what John Lennon said, isn't it—and Fidel likes him."

Max was unimpressed. "Sergio, there must be someone you know who might have a way into this group. The colonel may have been using all of us. Think hard. It may help save our interests, maybe our skins."

I looked over at Sergio. He looked tense and was pretending to be reading some of the male lifestyle magazines we kept in the showroom. As always he shut off when there was an issue. It was his sort of defense mechanism, and I knew that Sergio would be useless when things got tough.

I had to speak or Max would rush off and that would be the last we would know of him. "This whole thing makes me uneasy, Max. You know about the hotheads in Miami. They fight each other as much as everyone else. They see things in black and white. Most of us here have gone beyond that and think it's dumb. What's the point? Every family has some weird people in it, and Miami is no exception. Anyway, it's up to you. Sergio has this nephew called Wily. It should be Guillermo, but he's a big Will Smith fan so he likes to call himself Wily. He's as nuts as anything if you ask me. But he hangs out with the Calle Ocho wild ones. Maybe he knows someone in RDL. I'll give him a call. But it's better that I come along as well."

Mateo, Havana

It was time for the appointment I had set up to talk to Fausto Gómez. He was right on time. He came to the seminary equipped with a tape recorder and copies of past Moncada supplements. We stopped as he admired the crystal chandeliers, Fausto waving his arms in dramatic gestures. I was impressed with his small talk.

"This is all so elegant, Padre. It's really remarkable what skill is involved in all this glass work."

"It's a piece of Old Cuba, Señor Gómez, but it's good to see it coming to life again. There's a real labor of love in all this. Craftsmen who built things to endure. We hope to extend this building with a new one outside the city. It will double the number of priests we are training here."

"That's just the sort of thing I'd like to talk about," said Fausto. "I have my tape recorder here. Before we start, I'll give you an idea of the ground I'd like to cover. It would be good to have a few comments from you about how the Catholic Church sees the future of its work in Cuba."

"Fausto, I'm happy to do that. But you know I'm not used to this sort of thing. We in the church never look out for publicity. It's not really our style. I'd like an idea of what this is all for. And I'll try to tell you how we fit in."

"Padre, it's a special *Granma* supplement on the Moncada Revolution, how we see this date as the start of the revolution down in Santiago, and the first sacrifice of martyrs for the Cuban Revolution. You may know Artemisa, which is not far from Havana. Well over twenty revolutionaries from Artemisa died in that noble attack. There is a permanent memorial there. It's important to remind our young people what has been sacrificed for them to build what we have here. It's a bit like the Christian martyrs and saints, I suppose. They built the church over many years. Wouldn't you agree, Padre?"

"Perhaps," I said, looking at Fausto, who surprisingly looked deadly serious.

"Well, Padre, now we are many years after Moncada, and Cuba has changed and made many successes in our Revolution. Many new organizations now work in Cuba, and one of those is your church. I'd like to hear how the church sees itself in Cuba. You know I am asking the UNDP, UNESCO, and the World

Health Organization and other such bodies to contribute. We would like a complete picture."

The journalist was professional and knew I had an official role as well. I wanted to say what the bishop would want me to say. "Sr Gómez. The church has been in Cuba for several centuries. You only have to look at our cathedral, our churches. We have been growing again in the last few years, especially since the visit of the Holy Father in 1998. But we are still small in Cuba. Nothing like the UN, which you mention."

"How many churches do you now have in Cuba? And how many will you have in ten years time?"

"I am not sure of the exact figure. There are the Protestant as well. But it would be only a few hundred in the whole of Cuba. We don't have any definite plans—it depends on all sorts of factors, local and national. But we feel that there is a need for more churches."

"Why do you say there is a need? As you know we here in Cuba have built a unique socialist revolution. We are a system where everyone is valued and organized to contribute to the good of all. There really is no 'need' for other organizations."

"It's not a material need, Señor Gómez. After all the church in Cuba continued to work even when the government here abolished Christmas. Wherever we are active, we feel that churches can do things that governments can't do. This is not just in Cuba. It works that way all over the world. We receive our inspiration from Jesus Christ to go out to society. We are not looking for votes or political support."

"What would you describe as your greatest achievement over the last ten years?"

"I think it is not so much the building of churches but more what we are able to do within the churches. We are feeding the hungry, helping with social work, getting to make a difference to the real Cuba."

Fausto turned off his recorder. "Padre, I have to explain that there are limits to what we can discuss in this interview. I'm sure you know there are certain areas that are—how shall we say?—out of bounds. I cannot promise to print all you have said."

"Of course; the decision is yours. But I sense that you are a reasonable man, doing a difficult job. Can we talk informally for few minutes? As the press men say, I would like to talk to you off the record."

Fausto looked surprised. "Padre, I am happy to talk with you as a human being, but I'm not sure I understand what you have in mind."

"What I mean is the anxiety of a lot of people here. Those who are good people, ordinary people, if you like. They are not fanatics for anything, even for Jesus Christ. They are afraid of change in Cuba but afraid of what their lives will be if there is no change. They see things happen that they don't understand. They don't feel that they can influence anything here. People disappear, and people feel driven to do extreme things, like risk their lives to leave the country of their birth, their family. There is a song they sometimes play here. One line says 'People die because they want to live so much.' Why should that be?"

Fausto put his papers down and looked up again at the chandelier. "Padre, you raise an interesting point. A Revolution is about collective values. The individual has to accept that he is part of a massive movement. We all have these same big objectives. Growing up in the system we realize that these objectives are all in our constitution. We are building a new society here, and the leadership that has come through we trust to be the architects of the new structure. The individual has to accept all this because it has been a collective decision. The alternative is to leave. Because there is no room for doubters."

"I see that we are both men of faith, Sr Gómez. I also have to trust that my architect is at work. But I have my moments of doubt. Sometimes I wonder what is the massive scheme, the big plan. But then I feel close to ordinary people again and what I have to do seems clear. You see, I believe how we treat others is the basis of our life. And if you think of others, as we believe you should, you realize that not everyone wants to be a revolutionary every day. Not everyone can. Human beings for centuries have wanted something bigger than themselves, but that does not get you through all of life."

"Look, Padre, as I said, Communists are human beings. We think a lot about these things. But people cannot realize their true potential without looking at the bigger picture. We were born into a system that has achieved a lot. It would not have done all it has without being firm, even ruthless. You are Spanish, I believe."

"Well yes, more or less. But my mother is Cuban. Half of me has a stake in the country, I think you'd agree."

"Okay, yes, you can be counted in, Padre. Let me tell you one thing that may help you understand. You know we never claim to have a perfect system. We have what we have. But it's a system that people fought for. Without the fighting it would have been destroyed long ago. I am forty-three years old. I always wanted to be a journalist, and I wanted to live in Cuba. Some of us joke that we work in a circus because we are performing intellectual acrobatics every day. But we Cubans are good at that. Padre, have you ever been to the Tropicana nightclub here in Marianao? No? Oh I don't expect that a priest would go to look at the girls. But there are acrobats as well. It will show you that in Cuba we have some of the best acrobats in the world."

"You're right about priests and nightclubs. But I see what you are saying. The problem I would have working for a government with your constitution is that no one has the monopoly of truth. In most of the countries I know the job of the journalist is to hold governments to account. A journalist wants to write on subjects from an independent viewpoint, questioning, exploring the boundaries of truth. He wants his readers to learn something interesting. He may want to make a name for himself. That's sometimes a problem. Even those people who wrote the Bible were rivals with others whose work didn't get included. And the truths of the Bible are sometimes uncomfortable. But it is a remarkable book. It reminds people of some standards. I hope what is written will make better people, and better people make a better society. I am no expert, but I wonder if *Granma* prints things of interest even for those who disagree with this Revolution."

"We give the official messages, Padre. I won't deny that. But our readers know that we can hint at things. They can read the sign language. It's all been built up over so many years. We don't have big ideology debates in print, but neither does the church debate the Bible. You cannot stand up in Mass and doubt that Jesus Christ rose from the dead, can you, Padre? We have our ideology. Mine is a job like some sort of courtroom lawyer; you know, like in the Yanqui series everyone has seen on the TV. I make the best case I can for my clients—you know, my employers—with the material I have."

"Look, Sr Gómez—" I began.

"Please call me Fausto," he said quickly.

"Okay, Fausto, all this seems pretty harmless, but what about the individual people who the government sees as surplus to their requirements? Those who are not prepared to conform to the Revolution. What rights have they to live here?"

"It's better not to enter into politics here in Cuba. That's all I can say, and the people know that. It's like a traffic regulation. If you attempt to park on a double-yellow line you will be punished. After all these years the government holds the cards. If you don't break the law, you will be fine."

"Fausto, I'm going to talk very honestly. I am concerned for some people I have met recently in Cuba. Some have recently been taken away. I have heard disturbing reports about bigger trouble; trouble that could bring changes here that are not even imaginable."

"Well, El Comandante has always predicted changes. No glory lasts over two thousand years, he has said. But the changes to endure must be built by a government that can govern. Stability is now what we have, Padre. That counts for a lot. But maybe one day I will get to be a real journalist. Now that would be really something, and that is my dream. Perhaps I'm being a little arrogant, but I think I would be rather good at it. In any case right now I have work to do, Mateo. I have to get this section in my paper. The dreams will have to wait because the *Granma* must be published."

CHAPTER 18

Felipe

It was the morning of Pepe's burial. Work was now finished at the CBM for Moncada. The staff was given the long weekend, and Carlitos had said we could expect our bonus at the end of the month. I remember that I was counting on twenty CUCs. But even that wouldn't go far with the new taste at home for expensive Coke. At Moncada time you realized how much money there was in the system. It was somewhere in the system, and we were supposed to look and wonder.

I was at Jalisco. The family was quiet and restless; waiting was a big event for us. But there was nothing else to do apart from choosing what seemed like the right clothes to wear to bury Pepe. That's not what I was used to, because I never chose. I wore what Mama had washed. She wanted me to put on Papa's old white guayabera, but it didn't seem right. Pepe had some old black t-shirts. She had already washed Pepe's clothes. One said Harley-Davidson, York, Pennsylvania. I picked that one out. Nothing to do with churches; Pepe would like that. The boys wanted to wear their sports shirts, and Mama wasn't in the mood for a fight so that was fine. And of course the TV was on that Saturday morning. The coverage was a live broadcast showing what was being prepared for the big day.

Everywhere on the TV there were posters and billboards and Cuban flags. The biggest of all were along the Malecón, especially at the U.S. Interests office. I could tell they were not reprints of previous years, because they showed all the new themes. The Miami Five heroes, their pictures were on every lamppost, plastered on the walls, and it had all been done overnight. A reporter was standing with his back to the U.S. building showing the technicians climbing the flagpoles to put up their new displays. Just on cue, the loudspeakers burst into action. The reporter stood back. "Abajo fascismo; abajo imperialistas; abajo los mercenarios" was booming out periodically as a test broadcast. The reporter signed off with a reminder. "There will be detailed coverage of all this in our live broadcast on Monday. You can read all about the historic importance of this Moncada in your special edition of *Granma* for Moncada."

Laura had the day off as well. I think she had asked for it so she could go to Pepe's burial. She never said so, but she had been brought up a Catholic. The cremation was done. We met up at the Cementerio Colón. I had never been there and had never wanted to. They would not allow Papa to be buried at Colón, but for Pepe it was different. Kind of ironic as Pepe had never been into a church since I had known him. It didn't do for a traffic cop to be seen there. Certainly not when the party were around. But Mama knew Pepe had been baptized a Catholic, and the police gave their permission.

Luis and Donna had arrived from Sancti Spíritus. They went straight to the Colón. I gave Donna Pepe's letter, which she stuffed in her bag. Donna brought out some old photos of Pepe and of her and Luis as a baby. I know she told Mama more than once that she had burned everything. Donna was a tough lady who always wanted to be somewhere she wasn't. I think she found it strange that when Luis arrived he would be with her forever. I noticed again how he held Mama's hand rather than Donna's. Luis was built like Pepe, a strong muscular child. Gentle and shy as well. A boy who had moved so much he probably didn't know where home was.

Luis was looking down, but I caught his eye. I told him he would always be welcome to come back to Havana.

"Don't know," said Luis.

"I bet we could have some fun here. Different from Sancti."

Luis wasn't sure. "Sancti is smaller, and the people there are nice. It's quiet, but we have a field near us. Mama Donna says we'll stay there."

I'd forgotten he called her that. I knew what he meant, but now was not the time to philosophize. "Havana is fun sometimes, Luis," I said. "After all this is over, we will have the times here just like we used to. Your dad wants us to laugh like he did."

I didn't want to remind him of anything we had done with Pepe. What could we do that would be different?

"Do you like rock music? You know the Beatles, the Stones, U2? There's a big party tonight."

I had hit lucky with Luis. He was interested. "I thought all that was for old guys. I like rap and hip-hop; you know, the stuff they show on MTV."

"Since when have you seen MTV, my friend?"

The burial was over quickly. Two of Pepe's colleagues from the police followed next. The guard of honor served for all three. The priest gave Donna his police uniform, which she accepted without a word. Neither Donna nor Luis shed a tear. I guess they had done all their weeping months ago. But Mama did, and I saw this was upsetting Luis. So did Laurita.

"Oh Luis, come walk with us now," said Laurita "We'll walk down to Vedado. Let's go to the Lennon and check out the peace concert setting up. There'll be lots of music even before the concert. Jamming. You'd like that, Luis. After that we'll go on up to the Coppelia and grab an ice cream. Now wouldn't that be a good day in Havana?"

I turned to Donna. "Donna, we'll catch up with you later. We'll return Luis in as good a condition as we found him. Is that okay?"

The three of us walked off. I was trying to remember some of my best jokes.

"Be like Che," Luis was reading from a poster near the Chaplin cinema. "What was he to do with Moncada? We were learning about all that. Why is Che everywhere? I don't understand."

"Oh socio, you ask difficult questions. Laurita, you're the expert. Che was brave, a doctor. He suffered from asthma, but in everything he was a great hero. He died young in Bolivia. I think he was thirty-seven, and he was still trying to spread some revolution."

"Luis, you're a smart guy; so was Che. You will learn much more about him. Just like we did. My friend Miranda is in love with him. But he's been dead for years. And he wasn't at Moncada, not right at the beginning of everything. I guess he hated everything apart from Revolution. Nothing else mattered at all. He was someone who maybe would always die young. People admire that. They dream big things and rush around living their lives just how they want. Trying to change things. Make things better. That's why they say 'Be like Che.'"

Luis was now smiling. "I like Che," said Luis. "He was like my dad. My dad would always tell me about his dreams. He was thirty-seven too."

We passed Calle 12 and headed into the heart of Vedado. Trucks were arriving with billboards and t-shirts to deliver to the CDRs. A van labeled "Ministerio de Cultura" was unloading billboards with "Concierto de Paz—Lennon contra imperialismo." We stepped over the wiring that trailed across the grass. The first planks of the podium were now being nailed together.

The brass statue of John Lennon sat on his bench impassively surveying the scene. The musicians were strumming guitars, smoking and taking turns sitting alongside Lennon. "Hey Yani, where's your camera. How many times do you get to sit next to a rock legend? You should hear my band play 'Hide your love away.' They say I sound just like Lennon."

"My boy, don't count on it.. Don't you remember? I heard that copy. I'd say you do a pretty good impersonation of Lenin-the Russian guy who wasn't known for his singing. So don't give up the day job."

"Luis, we should really come to this concert," said Laura. "I could teach you all the songs. I bet Feli doesn't know half of them, hey Feli? He's too busy with his test tubes."

"Who is the guy on the bench?" said Luis, pointing to the statue.

"That's John Lennon; you know, one of Los Beatles …"

"Weren't there more of them? Why did they put a statue of just one of a big band?"

Laura laughed. "Well, Luis, Havana's a big place. But they can't have room for everyone. This Lennon concert's one of the biggest of the year. Tonight this place will be packed. My dada brought me …"

She remembered soon enough that she shouldn't go down there. "I mean I remember coming here when I was your age. I fell in love with that music."

Her cell phone rang.

"Hi Eric … I can't believe that. That must be another Miranda. She would never …"

Laura stared at the ground without seeing. Tears filled her eyes. She let them fall and began to sob. "Laurita, chicita. What is happening?"

Laura took my hand and walked away from Luis, who was watching a guy unload a drum kit. "I don't want Luis to see all this. He's had enough of a day. Miranda se fue. I cannot think about that now. I need to walk. A long walk. Let's head off to Coppelia."

Henry, Miami

Wily agreed to meet easily enough. These people liked the attention, and they were proud of what they thought. They saw themselves as guardians of the flame, the burning desire to bring back the old Cuba. Wily was waiting outside the Maximo Gómez dominoes park on Calle Ocho, checking his Blackberry and joking with a street seller of prawns. "Camarones 3 lb for $10" said his sign. Wily was a short, wiry man with a shaved head. He wore a grubby guayabera, shades, and two diamond earrings.

He didn't make polite conversation but came straight to the point. Sergio had called him but had not mentioned someone named Max. "Who's that, Enrique?"

Max answered for himself. "My name is Max. I'm a friend of Sergio and Enrique. I'm in need of some advice urgently. Can you help out a friend? "

"It depends on what type of friend you are. You are Cuban I know, without even hearing you speak. But there are many Cubans who appear to be friends who aren't. I know all about that."

"Well, I cannot prove anything, amigo," said Max. "But it would be better if we could meet to talk. I think it may be in both our interests. Cubans can tell by the sweetness of the cane. Isn't that what we say?"

"I have learned never to trust without investigating" said Wily. "The people I work with are only the most secure. We have been infiltrated from the south; you know that."

"Well, I agree totally, Wily. I can tell that you're a professional. It will be a privilege to sit down with you. So let's have a cafecito and we can take it from there."

"You say you know Sergio and Enrique. They say some strange things about Cuba these days. I like these guys, but they are ready to surrender. It's not the way I think. No, there are hundreds of people like that at the Versailles café every day.

Let bygones be whatever, they say. But these are matters of life and death. It's our country we're talking about." I looked serious and statesmanlike. Wily was not trying to be amusing.

Max stepped in and knew what was required. "Wily, that's really good to hear. I shake with rage when I hear these whiners surrendering. You know, that Council of State over the water. They are laughing uncontrollably. Where is the spirit of Maceo and Martí?"

"Well said, Max. Let's go to my apartment. It's just a couple of blocks away, behind Lily's Record store."

Laura

I liked the way Felipe was engaging with Luis. He was smart—of course he was—but smart people have to act and decide without the head office telling you every move to make. I noticed for the first time that Luis had blue eyes, just like Feli. So unusual for a Cuban; they had that bond.

Coppelia ice cream was just what we wanted. The fun was in the unexpected, never knowing what might be different, which flavors were available. The signs at Coppelia said there was no coconut, pineapple, or mango. The scribbled note was above a permanent notice saying, "Two scoops of one ice cream for one customer strictly forbidden."

I gave Luis some money, and we said we would watch him in the line from a table nearby. "Hey Luis, smile at the girls and she might give you two scoops, one on each cone. It's illegal, but they have a sense of humor here."

Luis stood in the line folding and refolding his notes. The boy next to him asked what flavor he was going to ask for and produced an old baseball from his pocket. "Let's try kicking it. This line will last a long time. I'll be Ronaldinho." Luis accepted the challenge and started to kick the ball around while they waited.

Felipe found a couple of empty seats. We moved over and watched Luis playing his game. It was the first time I felt I needed Feli to get through something. The relationship had been fun, and my job was a joy, but I never really had done the commitment thing with boys before. But now my best friend had gone. Didn't I matter to Miranda?

"Feli, she never told me a thing. We were like sisters, Miranda and I, every step of the way, and now she leaves without a word. She must have been planning this for months. How can you keep these things and live a lie?"

I blurted out something to Felipe that surprised me, "Can I rely on you, Feli? Will you be here for me?"

Feli surprised me. When he didn't answer that question he didn't look embarrassed. But he talked about Miranda. I think he was trying to help me.

"Laura, it doesn't surprise me about Miranda. It's often those who never talk about it. They are the strongest. They decide and keep it to themselves. I guess it's the most selfish thing you can ever do, so why tell friends? If you do it, you are doing it against your friends. A friend for a lifetime in Havana can never be a friend like that fuera. All that stuff you said about her and Che; you know, calling her Cheranda. Maybe she did that deliberately. I saw all this at the CBM just like with that group of guys who left for Chile. They behaved like revolutionary fanatics. In any case how could they tell anyone what they really felt? This is too painful to talk about. You keep it bottled up. One of the guys in Chile even sent me an e-mail saying he hated to betray us. To me, of all people. Can you believe that? He'd no idea what I had done. No one is comfortable living the lies, and this is the biggest secret you have to hide. Like a rotten tooth that grinds into your soul. But you can't open your mouth to get it taken out."

"You never told me about the guys who left for Chile. Did you think you might go as well? And not tell me?" I didn't wait for Feli's answer. "But Miranda. Look at her. Work hard and everything is yours. Miranda was a chosen person in Cuba. She was the youngest inspector of customs at the airport. She could have become a big shot in government. Her family gave her no problems. You know, if I envied anyone in Havana it was Miranda."

I expected Feli to start a new conversation, complaining about Carlitos or something. But no.

"Laura. Our life here is not like that kids' card game, you know, 'Happy Families.' Everyone dreads that they will lose one or more of their set. The TV, music stars, they go, don't they? One minute they're official heroes; then the next no one mentions them. Who has a better life than they do? Miranda made up her own mind. That was her first achievement. It may have been the first time in her life. Sure, she had plenty of talent and would have made a great revolutionary. Beautiful, lots of brains, and she proved she had one very important thing as well. When the chance came she was brave and could take risks. That's worth a thousand rallies and pioneer camps. It gives us all hope. Laurita, one day you'll meet her again in the right country."

"For me the right country will always be Cuba," I said.

Luis brought over the ice creams. "That was really quick," he said. "In Sancti we wait twice as long. She gave me two scoops, just like you said. Here, I have one in each hand."

"You had fun with that guy with the ball. Time always passes quickly that way. Luis, we have to take you home now. Mama Donna is waiting."

Vladimir

Kurt got his treat. I was walking him along Third Avenue in Playa. Of course I knew that dog-walking would attract no attention on a Saturday morning. Plenty of the diplomats and the business people did just that, so I took my camera along and took a few pictures of Kurt on the way. The houses were low-level and gated with paved exteriors. Cubans did not go in for tending front gardens. The streets were quiet, with a few cars parked up the driveways. Most of the residents who had cars would have left for the beach. I passed a small restaurant called Asia y Cuba with rattan tables outside advertising exotic chicken dishes and a magician on Fridays. What was this fascination of Cubans with magic, I wondered? Pity he couldn't come in on Saturday and get me into that building.

The headquarters of Saluki enterprises was a hundred meters from the restaurant. It was a small sand-colored building with steps at the side leading up to a second floor, which seemed to be separate. The windows had bars on them, which was unusual in Miramar. Apart from that, it looked like any other residence. I noticed that they made no attempt to conceal the satellite TV aerials on the roof. Not afraid to break the law, but then most of the residents of Playa were foreign. Outside the front entrance there was a picture of the tall slender dog, which was the emblem of the company. I had googled the word saluki and read that it was one of the oldest and fastest dog breeds known to man. It was a hunting dog with exceptional sight, close in and at long distance. The gates were padlocked like my own, and there were no vehicles on the driveway. Kurt sniffed around the entrance. I wasn't sure if there were dogs at the back.

"Hey Kurt, what do you expect from a Saluki?"

I moved on back to the restaurant where the lunchtime eaters were arriving. I took a seat at an outside table and ordered a sandwich and a beer. Some tourists had wandered down from the hotels near the water, and most of the tables were full. A small salsa band had started to play "El Cuarto de Tula," a song I detested. I took out my camera and pretended to be taking pictures of the band. After a quick shot I moved the camera left and zoomed in on the Saluki building. I snapped as many as I could before turning back to the band leader and asking in my best broken English if I could take another shot of the group. The meeting should be starting soon at Saluki. I was curious whether a Colombian and a Russian would keep "Cuban" time.

Felipe

Donna had arranged to meet us at the cinema on La Rampa. We walked down the hill with Luis and said our goodbyes. He is a good boy, who loved his father. "Remember, your dad was a hero, Luis, so make him proud," was all I could think of to say. Donna seemed relieved that the day was nearly over and said she was grateful for what I had done. I never told her the true story of what happened to Pepe. She didn't need to be bitter about anything else. Now the two of them were heading back across the country on the bus. I gave Luis a high-five and said we would come to visit him in Sancti Spíritus.

Laurita had to file a report on her Spanish architects or something and said she would meet up for the concert in the evening. I thought of telling her what Vlado had asked about and the list of names Papa had written. But Papa's papers and all that were too much to go into. I knew how she felt about Papa's last years. I'm sure she had found out about most of it, though I never told her.

"There's this old friend of my dad who's asked to see me, so I said I would look him up. It's down in the Old Town. Laurita, don't be sad about Miranda. We'll hear from her. Cubans always find a way to stay in touch." I kissed her. She looked weak and nervous.

Laura walked off to find a car from work that she had called. It happened to be heading back to Miramar.

There was nothing else to do at Jalisco, and those words I had read from Papa's book had spoken to me in a way that made me uncomfortable. I felt I had a duty now to use what I had been told, to believe in Papa's words about the friends he used.

I had written the three names from Papa's list in my wallet. The first was Isaac Rivas Higuera, Calle Obispo y Compostela. I was halfway to the Old Town and ready to explore.

I walked up La Rampa and spotted a tourist car with white letters on maroon plates parked outside the Habana Libre. The family was studying a map of Havana. I tried some English. I knew that one day the courses at CBM would come in useful. "Hey, my friend, can I give you a hand with that? Where do you want to go in Havana? It's my home so I know most of the places."

A large, very white man opened the door and got out to shake my hand. I noticed that he was wearing socks with his sandals. "That's really, really kind of you. Well, actually maybe you can. Do you know the way to Old Havana? Perhaps you could explain."

It was a harmless trick, and I was only too happy to explain. "If you have some space in your car, I could show you now. I'm heading to Old Havana myself."

I got in and began the small talk that I knew would happen with any tourists. The family had arrived that morning, had never been to Cuba before, and had just picked up their hire car. "You know for us it's very strange just to drive on the right. And these road signs, we're already finding you can't see most of them in any case."

The young children in the back joined in. "You promised us we'd see pictures of Che everywhere, Daddy. Will you buy me a beret? I'm tired of the city. Let's go to the beach."

The man driving was sweating liters. "The hire people said the AC would kick in after ten minutes. Beats me." His wife had moved to the back to make room for me.

"Do you have a family? I'm sorry, what's your name?"

"My name is Felipe. Yes I have a family—a mother, brothers, uncles … all that."

"Anyway you know all about family holidays, or vacations, as the Americans say. They're not all they're cracked up to be. Difficult to get the family to agree on anything about holidays, but we always wanted to come to Cuba. For us Brits—I should have told you we're from England—Cuba has this sort of romantic feel. You know, it's different somehow. My dad was in the unions in the sixties, and for them Cuba was building a new world for workers. I've read about the Cuban beaches. Different from Europe where you reserve a couple of feet and can't move for all the Germans. I just wish I could get to speak some languages. You feel bloody helpless in these places, I can tell you. Where do we go to start, Phillip?"

My English was coming back. The last time I had used it was with the Iowa delegation. "No problem, straight down La Rampa; it's not far. You see, we don't really have many cars here in Havana. There are even less in the rest of Cuba."

"What sort of car do you have, Phillip?" I've seen a few Peugeots, Toyotas. Even an old British Triumph, which was really exciting. Wasn't it, Josh?"

The boy nodded.

"Well, actually I don't have a car. It's kind of difficult here."

"Yes, I guess the bloody Americans are always stopping things getting to places they don't approve of. That would certainly apply to cars. They feel they rule the world, eh? Anyway maybe you'll get to buy one of those old Chevys; they are absolutely awesome. Just like they said in the tour guide."

"Maybe," I said. "We don't get to read tour guidebooks over here. Where did you say you are from? England? Well, I bet you know a lot more about what happens here than we do."

The driver edged slowly down La Rampa. "Looks like a nice place to me. Cinemas, shops, restaurants. Isn't that the Hotel Nacional? I saw pictures of that. We've read about that. Churchill stayed there. Isn't that right?"

"It's a beautiful building," I said, "but I've never been there. You see, we Cubans are not allowed in. It's for tourists only; maybe one day."

"Wow! That's really weird. Imagine that in London. There'd be a riot in five minutes. We'd be in there tearing down the 'Brits not allowed' sign."

The man seemed to be relaxing too much and looked at me to see if I was amused. He took his eye off the road. I shouted, "Hey, just watch that cart with the horses. I can tell he's having problems controlling them. You kind of expect it but if you're not used ..."

"Phew, that was close. Bloody animals shouldn't be allowed on the roads." He looked in the driver's mirror and saw the horse disappearing. "So this is the Malecón. This is awesome. Darling, just look at that. I like the way the waves crash over the side. Bet it's a bit wild in a hurricane. Maybe that's why this road is kind of potholey. No disrespect, but let's say it needs some attention. Know what I mean, Phillip?" said the man, now smiling.

"You're right." I said. "The Malecón is really special. It's the most special place in Cuba. For me it's the most special place in the world. And you know everyone is allowed here to enjoy it. We could go for a walk there."

"That's a relief anyway, mate. How far to Old Havana?"

"It's right along the Malecón. A few kilometers. Havana's a big city. This is really kind of you to give me a ride. You might like to see that big building over there. It's occupied by—how is it you say?—those bloody Americans. Just joking really; we love American things here."

"The Americans are here, are they? That's something I didn't know. Guess they're not the most popular guys in town, hey? What was it called? Bay of ..."

"Oh you mean Play Girón, Bahía de Cocinos. We don't know much about America. We're told a lot in *Granma* and everything. We can't understand why they won't trade with us.

We like American visitors, university students; all that. The sports we all love are American—baseball, basketball. It's kind of the forbidden fruit. When we stand on the Malecón, we look out to the ocean there and it's close."

"What's close, Phillip? Do you mean the wall or what?"

"No, it's just our neighbor; you know, Florida—most of us have never seen it. Just think; it used to be a thirty-minute flight to Miami. All that has happened in between. All those wars, movies, the Beatles. And we've lived like some sort of neighbors who never speak."

The man had stopped at the lights. "Hang on a minute. The Beatles aren't American, mate. Did you really think that?"

"Sorry, mate," I said. They all laughed. I liked the idea of being a tourist guide for a minute. I thought of what Laurita might have said. "You know, in Cuba we have free healthcare and education for everyone. It's one of the achievements of the Revolution."

"Oh yes, Phillip, I had heard that. I'm forty-six and I've never paid to see a doctor in England. And we didn't need a bloody revolution to get all that, did we, dear?" He looked around to his wife. I realized I had some way to go to impress the tourists.

"Mum, look at those windows, Everyone's hanging out and the washing too. Dad, see those kids jumping off the rocks. How cool would that be! Can we do that too?"

"Hang on a minute. That's young people going mad. Depends on the rocks you can't see. Isn't that right, Phillip?"

"There's lots you can't see here. But the kids don't care. They feel they're alive. No one is controlling them there. It's what we all like when we're young."

"My kids need all the bloody control they can get, I can tell you. Oh I meant to ask you. Have you met what's his name?"

"You mean our president?" I ignored the question and changed the subject. I know I was inside a car and there was no way this guy was an informer, but it was just that old habits die hard.

We had reached the square dominated by the Spanish embassy, and the Malecón took a swing to the right, heading to the port of Havana. "If you head on straight, you'll come to Old Havana. It's really beautiful, I will say. But not like the Malecón. Good luck with parking, and long live Los Beatles. I'll get out here."

As I got out the kids in the back waved and the driver blew a long blow on the horn. I crossed the square and saw a team erecting a massive reproduction of Picasso's Guernica right in front of the Spanish embassy. Another theme for Moncada; fascists will be eternal enemies of the Revolution. I entered Zulueta and crossed to Compostela.

I reached the crossway with Obispo. There was no number on the building that I wanted, and in any case it was now a pharmacy specializing in herbal remedies. Jars of spices were in the window, all priced in CUCs, indicating that it was in practice a tourist-only shop. Down the side of the shop there was an alleyway blocked by three rusty bicycles. An empty bottle of Havana Club rum was balanced precariously on the handlebars of the one in the middle.

I looked up the steep wall. The stones were covered in moss from cracked pipes, and a window shutter hung loose, having escaped its hinges. The rich blue sky broke out aggressively from the shadows. Some yellow t-shirts fluttered on a washing line on the top floor balcony. The protective railing was two-thirds gone. An old man with white stubble wearing a baseball cap but no shirt sat on a rocking chair on the balcony. He was looking up, so I shouted.

"Hey amigo. Ever heard of a guy called Isaac? He's about sixty; maybe older. Lived here for a long time. But I'm not sure which place was his."

"Isaac. Yes, sure he lived here. He's a youngster, that man. A rascal as a boy. Always in trouble. Like so many of them now."

"You say he lived here, compañero. What happened to him?"

"No idea. But he was in the cárcel. They said he was being paid by the Americans. Bad stuff that. Used to chant traitor at his family, I think. Maybe that's why they all left."

"But I'd like to know where I can talk to him. Who around here might know that? It's kind of urgent."

A drilling sound started in the street, perhaps another water main being repaired. The man leaned over the balcony and gestured to me. "Joven, come up here. It strains my ear to hear you with all this going on."

I entered the alleyway and walked up the staircase. The only light crept in from under the badly-fitting doors at each floor. I wondered how the old man managed it every day. Sitting at desks and laboratory work did not improve physical conditioning. I was breathing hard when I arrived. The old man had not left the rocking chair. The balcony was on the opposite side of a room that had only partially constructed walls. Pieces of metal sheeting patched up the gap between the walls and the ceiling. Wires hung out from behind a satellite dish, receiving CNN Español. The picture flickered brightly and bounced reflections from the walls.

"Boy, I can't tell you how much I get sick of so much news. Twenty-four damn hours it is." He stroked his stubble, outlining an imaginary beard from his chin. "He knew a thing or two, you know, about how to cut off interest in news."

To get across the room I had to pick my way around several cardboard boxes filled with papers and broken glass.

"Hola, my name is Felipe. I live in Jalisco, and my dad knew Isaac many years ago in Pinar."

"Well, I'm sorry; you have been misinformed, my friend. I have not heard of Isaac for many years. Someone told me he may have become a doctor, but that was so long ago. You said your dad knew him. Why doesn't he call him?"

"My dad died a while ago. You know, he mentioned this man as having a special meaning in his life. When he talked with me near the end of his life he said Isaac was a strong man who would fight for what he believed in. My dad would not say that about many people."

"Well, this Isaac sounds like a great guy. There are not many here in Cuba who would do that. But why would someone waste their Saturday before Moncada trying to find this Isaac?"

"It was something a friend asked me to do; you know, the sort of friend who has something important on his mind."

"You mean a girl or something. Or money. It has to be one of the two with young men these days." The old man scratched under his armpit and picked his teeth with a piece of wire.

"No," I said. "He's kind of worried about something more serious. It's about what's going on in Cuba. He wants to make some quick decisions, big decisions, and he thinks Isaac could help him. That's it, really. But I really don't want to waste your time. I need to think again about who I should call. It's pretty urgent, so I should be going."

"You sound like an interesting young man, Felipe. I used to do things urgently as well. Now I just sit here and hope some friends drop by. Most of them have gone to Santiago for Moncada, so until then I'll rock myself to sleep. Damn that CNN. They never spend any time on Cuba anymore. Maybe at Moncada they'll show some films from Havana in Yuma. It would be good for the Yanquis to give us some attention."

"Hombre, you're lucky to have that TV. I guess you're well covered around here. The police don't bother you with it?"

"The police. Bah! They can't do any more to me. We will all have it one day," said the man. "My name is Manny, by the way. You're welcome anytime. What was your dad's name?"

"His name was Alberto Triana. Everyone knew him as Al."

I left the building and returned to Jalisco.

Mateo

There was something in common between those two meetings with Fausto and the Cubano. Both had come to me and didn't really tell me what they thought. But they were expecting some reaction. Or was I merely a cocktail party priest who would be polite and move on to talk about La Traviata? I couldn't just leave and then later read about something I knew would happen. I wondered why these events were happening when I was ready to say, "Goodbye and God Bless Cuba." In any case, I decided to make one call.

"Could I speak to the chief of staff to the bishop in Santiago please?"

"He's right here, Padre Mateo. I'll pass you through."

"Rodrigo, it's good to hear you. I imagine life is busy for Moncada. They tell me the old barracks is what everyone wants to see in Santiago."

"Well, I wish a few more of them would come to the cathedral, Mateo. We need all the funds we can get. Our tins could do with filling. Two vans we have broke an axle trying to get out to some farms last week. But I'm sure you're not phoning to offer some money."

"You're right, my friend. The church here is about the only outfit in Cuba that is obeying market forces. We get no subsidies from the state. Capitalism is no fun when you are on your own. No, it was more to tell you about a rather strange visit I had here yesterday. The man was Cuban, from Santiago he said."

"Well, it's a big city. I trust he was agreeable company."

"He was a very disturbed man, Rodrigo. Had a young boy with him. But he came to see me because of some confusing information that he seemed to have picked up. He was talking about major unrest in Santiago, which he said was a movement that could affect the whole country. Sounded pretty dramatic."

"We pick up some things like that as well. You never know. There's always trouble around here. People are arrested or harassed; sometimes held and sometimes released. It's constant. In and out they go. But they stop the big things happening. What was this guy's name?"

"He wouldn't tell me, and he looked really scared, so I don't think he was making it up. But he said that his brother was involved and maybe even some of the police and government."

"Mateo, what did this man look like? It's not much to go on."

"He was black, shaved head. His son was called Sam I think—about five years old. And he had a tattoo on his back. Looked like a design with the number seven and SP in it. Never seen it before."

"Mateo, that narrows the field down to about a hundred thousand, I would say. I don't mean to sound unhelpful, and I know you wouldn't have called without being worried. I'll ask around the parish and check on the name Sam. It's not that common. Lots of people here are into Santería. We will keep in touch, you know, discreetly."

"Thanks, Rodrigo. People get into trouble here, but you don't usually hear about it in advance. That's what so unsettling about this. What can the church do?"

Henry

Max and I followed Wily to his apartment. I had seen a lot of the Cuba fanatics and what they collected, but Wily lived on a different planet. The apartment was a replica of his family's home in Lawton that they had left in 1962. It was fine to be sentimental, but the degree of obsession was frightening. There were bus tickets, telephone directories, pet competition ribbons, all from 1958. I noticed that he kept his shades on inside.

"I refuse to have any image or reminder of Cuba after the first of January 1959. So in case you're wondering, I'm not a nutcase. It's just the way I feel. I won't rest until …"

I could see that Max didn't want a guided tour. "Okay, Wily, I know what you're saying. But we have a job to do now and there's no point wasting time explaining how we live. This is about Cuba."

"Max, I met you ten minutes ago, and you're not going to convince me to change. And if you came here to find out what my friends are doing so you can get a medal from the Politburo you must think I was born yesterday. Want an espresso?"

Again I thought this was about to leave the rails. Max had a short fuse, and there was too much at stake. I said quietly. "Wily, we thought you were a serious operator, and that's why we recommended that Max talk to you. If that's not the case … But I want to let you know that Max knows what he's doing. I'll put my head on the block for him."

Max took up the mood. "Wily, we are planning something big in the Oriente in the next few days. But we've hit a problem, and we think you may know something."

"Max, I am a person of action, not words. I think it is highly unlikely that we have moved in the same circles. Cuba will change one day. But there are ways of making it happen."

"Okay, Wily, I will tell you what we know. We are working through some deals with the fast boats stuff. You know that for everyone it's been going well and business is good. But we were planning to extend it to something much bigger that wasn't involved in people trading. Last week we had a bit of a shock. A colonel we had been working with was arrested near Manzanillo. We haven't been able to contact him directly, but we've been told a few things that could happen."

"And what were these few things?" I could see that Wily was paying attention.

"Someone told us he has been linked with the Rayos boys. You may know some of them."

"Oh, the Rayos. Now I know which colonel you mean. Yes, you are absolutely right. It's been a long time since anyone has been picked up in Cuba. But there are plenty more, so don't worry."

"I'm not bothered if you have thousands on the island. For me my worry is the colonel from Manzanillo."

Wily threw his head back in contempt. "Max, calm down. You take me for an idiot. The Rayos people are clever, take my word. They are usually ahead of the game. Their people know the risks of working in Cuba."

Max look puzzled. "What do you mean they know the risks?"

"They act quickly, and I know they've dealt with the colonel. He won't cause any problems."

I could see Max shifting nervously in his seat. "He won't cause any problems? How do you know?"

"Because he will be dead in twenty-four hours. You will know probably that he has been ill. We have found a way to get to him."

I saw that Wily had now used the "we" for the first time. "I see, Wily. You are well informed," said Max.

Wily took off his shades."The colonel was not to be trusted. Rayos do not like it when our agents work for two masters. For us there is only one Cuba."

Vladimir

The waiter brought the sandwich. Fortunately it was not difficult to eat it slowly. Even so, he seemed to be impatient to get rid of me. "Are you done with that, señor?" he asked in English. The camera had convinced him that I was not Cuban, which was good.

"No, not yet," I said in English. I wished I had brought a book or magazine. There was no sign of anything happening at Saluki. The salsa band had restarted their cycle of twenty songs. The tourists were about to return to their swimming pools, and Kurt was beginning to whine.

I sensed that waiting for hours outside of Saluki could just be a blind alley. Something else was needed before I made my decision. I had not committed to anything that made me an enemy of the system. Felipe knew what I thought, but I knew he couldn't be bothered even to think of informing on me. Maybe this thing was going to come to nothing. I would do a good report that would show me working for the state. On the strength of that I would get promoted and I would tell Felipe that it was all just another rumor. Nothing was going to change after all. I was sorry I lost it for a while, but I believed that everything was under control. One day I'd run my own computer business, but that would have to wait. The important thing was to be still standing on the field to play the game.

The waiter brought me the bill. It was fifteen CUCs for a sandwich, beer, and coffee. Nice business. These tourist restaurants knew how to make money; nearly a month's wages for my friend Felipe. What a mess that boy was in. Felipe's problem was that he had never come to terms with his dad. My old man left me on my own. He gave me the Lenin Academy, he said. That was the best he could do for me. After that I could do what I wanted. But Felipe always saw himself somehow continuing his dad's plans. Felt he had been cheated of a father somehow. I guess his dad sowed those seeds of guilt as some old men do; stupid men after screwing up their own lives. Fathers are best at getting out of the way, but for some reason Felipe saw his dad as stronger than he was, thinking that there were answers in his life to everything if he only looked. The problem was that he looked too hard. He watched that old movie again and again instead of writing a new plot.

Then of course it happens. The stillness and order here are deceptive, because there are always people making plays in Cuba. Everyone is waiting, but with different expectations, and waiting always needs to be part of the plan. If you don't move it is because it is risky to do so before the game has changed. You need to wait to see who is trying to shift the rules. The system is held together with pins, so you can't touch one thing without collapsing much more. The government did that on purpose; every little thing depends on everything else. Removing one pin could do so much damage. One day those looking to pull out the pins will have their chance. It was like that with Saluki.

I had just finished examining my wallet and the photos for the third time when three cars drew up outside Saluki's office. The first was a small BMW, foreign owned from the black-on-orange plates. The second was a black Lada, with white-on-blue plates, indicating a government department. The third was a Peugeot. They parked on the same side of the street. The restaurant was largely empty now. One elderly couple was reading their maps at a table on the other side. I took out my camera, zoomed in, and shot as the passengers went in. These were people about to make decisions.

CHAPTER 19

Laura

After the burial and the walk with Luis, I was expecting Felipe to be down for while. I knew how he looked at his family, and anything that went wrong with it he would see as his fault. He was already saying that he wanted to do something for Donna. He kept saying she had lost Pepe's income and what little there was left. That day I saw Felipe's family differently. The children they had were strong, caring, and sensible. They were never going to rise very far, but as children they were happy. Home was home, and they all cared about each other. My parents just got on with their own lives. I wondered if we would pull together like this.

I saw now where Felipe was from, but it was something that seemed to make him extra restless. I thought he was over all the Spanish stuff. I thought he had sorted out what he wanted to do. But the way he rushed off after leaving Donna; that was not like him. I knew he was nervous about something. Saturdays were for unwinding. We always did it the best way we could.

So I went home, where there was not much going on. My stepdad was out at the Masons, and my mom had gone to a dog show. You know, the breeders had never really left Havana, and the Revolution had somehow ignored some of the pastimes that used to amuse the rich. My mom had her circle of friends, and you could say it was all due to dogs. So they were both gone for the day.

I was reading an American newspaper given to me by a Canadian tourist. I remember it because I had never seen another country's newspaper and I had already spent many hours reading it from cover to cover. Anyway I was outside in the yard reading about how Indians in Bangalore were doing remote computer repairs when the guard Edy called me. "Hey Laurita, some guy's just left a letter for you. Says it's urgent."

I took the letter. It was addressed just to Laura at our address, but I didn't recognize the handwriting. The envelope was plain. I opened it and immediately recognized the writing. It was from Miranda.

> Dearest Laura,
>
> I don't know how you can ever forgive me. I have deserted my friends and all that I have known. I have never spoken of this. I have not been able to talk of it even for a minute. My aim in my life was always to be true to myself. Once I had decided on my objective I would not rest until I had achieved it. My plan was working well. I knew what I believed. I had pushed myself into everything to realize the dreams of the young revolutionary. There was everything laid out for me in stepping stones. And I stepped on them all and was told every day that I was chosen to be one of the best.
>
> It meant so much to be told that. I didn't know anything or anybody else that mattered as much. I have to be honest that this included all my friends—Eric, you, even my family. I was made to be a winner. And when you get the perfume

of winning, nothing else matters. You even stop wanting to dance, to go out with friends. I didn't need anything else.

You will see from this if you didn't know before how selfish I am. The Revolution was a process for me, and I was happy with that. There was one thing that was missing. It was what came after. I saw that the Revolution was the system. But if you made it perfect what would be the rewards? What promise did you have that you were building something that would last? I know I became even more *egoista* and obsessed.

Did it all matter? Of course it did. It was historic. We did experiments that no small country has ever done. After a while I could see my friends trading their revolutionary wings for something that kept them on the ground. Maybe that's what kept me going so long—the wings of being a revolutionary. It gave me a feeling of being a part of something bigger. But then gradually I realized they were not my wings. They were someone else's.

My dearest Laura, you see that I have always thought of myself and the Revolution. I now see this has been selfish as well. Do we have to sacrifice everything for this Revolution? One life, somebody else's ideas. So you will have this letter. I made one person promise to deliver this on Saturday after I had addressed the envelope and left it. I told them it was your birthday but I wouldn't have time to call. That was the excuse for sending this letter.

I do not know what I will find in the future. When I do I will be back in touch because I know we can reconnect in our lives again. But I have decided to be part of what happens to me rather than accepting another stepping stone that is put in front of me. All those stones, all those false things I said to you about my plans. I'm sorry, but they seemed true. I know you were always true to yourself, and I know what you believed. You and Felipe are a match because you seem to disagree about almost everything. He's not right about everything, but after all these years Felipe has the human spirit of rebellion and not accepting what he is told. You should encourage him to keep trying. I love you.

I was so shocked to get the letter that it took a few times reading it through to take it in. I didn't cry, because Miranda sounded so decided, and there seemed nothing else for her. I wasn't sorry for her. If I cried I knew it would be for me alone, and that was wrong. Then I realized the full meaning of one sentence. "I made one person promise to deliver it on Saturday after I had addressed the envelope." The envelope had been opened and readdressed. The person who opened it would know that Miranda was leaving.

Víctor

I always said it was stupid for us to come together at Saluki that day. All the materials were in place, and there was nothing to stand in our way. The one delivery was now secure. Max had told me what the madman in Calle Ocho had said. The colonel in Manzanillo would not talk. The equipment was in place, and I couldn't see how it could fail. Something the Revolution taught us was never to celebrate before you had a triumph. But we were so sure things were going our way.

The Saluki deal was a long time in coming, though, because it was only when we got a guy inside Compedex that things began to move. He wouldn't be there forever, though. The important thing was to do what we wanted without violence. That was what we needed and what we could teach others. I had thought about this a lot, and it was the violence that started us on the wrong path we took. It was the violence that had left the sour taste. Max never said anything, but his sons had left Cuba years ago, so what did he have to lose?

Saluki had served its purpose. The Colombian and the Russian were both married to Cubans. They had found the consulting skills we needed to get in and prepare. I admired that. But I doubted that it would work in the way they said it would. The equipment was only part of it, but the rest of the plan was what to do with the equipment. I went along with them because I thought something should be tried. There is something that didn't add up in what we were doing. It was not that I had been loyal to a dumb idea. It worked pretty well for those of us who came in from the country. I came to Havana as a nobody. After I showed I was loyal and not stupid I was taken into the revolutionary family. I think they liked the fact that I was uneducated and I found reading and writing difficult. They liked to have people in Havana who were not from the city. So in all that stuff in Cerro, I was always an outsider. There was nothing else to do but follow the rules. I was tough and healthy and liked to take orders, and they liked me, and they liked to give me orders, the guys in power. Old Víctor, he's no threat to anybody. I had my own family too, called all my sons by special names. They were what I wanted as heroes. I was proud of what I had, but the future was running out on me. Yet, through it all, the Revolution had given me confidence in myself.

Why did a president of a CDR mess about with Saluki? The problem was that we had all become materialist. We were getting all this power, and it seemed that we were in charge as well. I had all the Nike and Adidas stuff you could ever want. We got it to give out to the kids who behaved. I had the DVD player in the office that was supposed to show the revolutionary speeches and all that. But the kids from the barrio came in wanting to play their martial arts, their gangster movies they got from families or burned on some computer. I let them borrow the player, including a group from Jalisco. After all I'm a politician who needs support, and it helps with my little mistakes if the kids in the barrio speak well of you. Votes no, but support yes. I accepted all this, but my problem was seeing other people do better than me. They started boasting about what they had, what they gave their kids. The top people we never saw. They ate food we never saw. They lived in places we never saw. And it wasn't that great in Saluki. They were not people with a new vision, not my new vision anyway. There were times when we were talking about things in Saluki when I doubted the reasons people were doing it. We had pretty much nothing in common. One thing I refused ever to do was go to that ridiculous office Saluki had in Playa. At least the CDR never went in for fancy furniture and all that.

We wanted to show that we counted, that we were doing something and not just taking orders. We had different reasons for doing it. But we all agreed we should do it. We all came from the same background, and we had learned some things. So the discipline of the Revolution works just as well outside a CDR. It was our culture to trust only a few, so only twelve people knew the others in Saluki. We swore solemnly that there would be no violence, but I wondered if we had waited too long.

Felipe

I had not mentioned Papa's name for years. Not in the form of Alberto Triana. Of course I knew he had once been in the newspapers, and I had read it over and over again. It was the time when we were famous, when the neighbors stopped talking to us. Mama never left her window, but at that time she did. She cried so much that she left her chair so she wouldn't be seen. It wasn't just that people were organized to shout at her and threw old fruit at her. There were always plenty of resources the state had to do that. But Mama tried to fight back with the people of the barrio. Pepe told me she wanted to show the neighbors we were good people. It was the Trianas against the Revolution. She would do things so people would think better about us. She walked around the barrio, just asking for anything spare, maybe even stealing what she found. She gave the things to those people who had cut us off. I know because they told me later. It didn't work, the Revolution won and noone talked to Mama for weeks. She stopped talking to me as well. I think she just could not face anything. Then one day some of Papa's friends came around and Mama left Jalisco again. I think she went to talk to Gloria at the bodega. For some reason, she thought they were to blame for Papa and she never forgave them

Mama was worried again now; I could tell she wasn't sure the food would last the month. Donna and Luis had been unexpected and had eaten some of her reserves. "We need to be careful and make the best of what we have got. We have seven more days in the month, and we need to look at some trading." I knew the code of what Mama meant. It was the Saturday before Moncada. It should have been predictable, a nothing day just planning the last days of the month, asking for last-minute favors at the bodega, seeing what we could get for nothing. Money was not the issue in Havana; there never was any. But finding exchanges was always possible. No one lived off what they earned; it wasn't possible. So Pepe being gone opened another way of surviving. We were all looking at Pepe's things to see what could be traded. No one said anything. But we were all thinking that way.

There were steps outside, and Mateo appeared at the door. "Hola Felipe, I have just heard about your uncle. I wanted to express my condolences. It's so hard on the family to lose one of its leaders. It makes me sad to think that I'm leaving at this time, but trust that the Holy Spirit will comfort you."

Mama was crying again now. Mateo could not be leaving. Not now. Mateo knew how to face problems. Mateo would help her deal with the burden of her family. She was the rock for us, she knew, but I could see she needed something else. "Oh Mateo, you have come to mean so much to us. You were one of us, but you are wiser than us."

Mateo seemed embarrassed. "I'm sorry, truly sorry, Sra. Triana. It's like stepping out of a play before I've seen the end of the story. I've never been in a place before where you feel that things could change very quickly, and now I am to go. Well, I should have chosen a different profession, some profession where you never have to leave."

I was angry. Mateo maybe said some things he shouldn't have. But there were sometimes when those who were not Cubans were better off not saying anything. Mateo could never be in our play, and it was arrogant of him to think so.

I said these words quickly and then regretted them. "Mateo, we wish you well. You have been a good friend to us. But we have to write the end of the play ourselves. It just complicates everything to get people offstage involved."

Mateo was quiet. Mama was annoyed with me. She turned to Rafa. "I think you had better say goodbye to Padre Mateo, Rafa. He has been a beacon of light for us here."

Rafa said some quiet words; I don't remember exactly what. Mateo looked at me, and his face seemed sad. His eyebrows came together in that tense and concentrated look. I don't know what it was. Maybe it was that stupid visit in Old Havana. I was not in the mood for some meaningless apology. Later in the day, I wished I had. Mama had been gracious, and my little brother knew what to do. That was all that was required.

Mateo left. It was the last time I saw him at Jalisco. I thought maybe he had blessed us somehow, for the phone was reconnected. None of us ever prayed for it, I know that. But Laura's contact and maybe Pepe's friends had worked okay. You never knew. And with luck they would now forget about it for a while. Mateo had told me once there's no such thing as luck.

I called Laura to ask if she was still interested in going to the Lennon concert. She was, but it wasn't for the music.

"It's been quite an afternoon. Now I know everything about why Miranda se fue." Laura promised to bring the letter. She said she'd come directly to Vedado for the concert.

I called Vlado. "Look Vlado, I'm not having much success with these leads. In fact it's all a total waste of time. I just wanted to say I have tried. But don't count on me."

"Feli, I think it would be good if we talked again. I want to show you some photos I've just taken. Where are you going to be?"

"We're headed for Vedado. At the Lennon park."

"The Lennon park would be good."

Mateo

The Triana family members were not big churchgoers; certainly not Felipe. His mother came from Jamaica, I know, and was a Baptist, but somewhere along the way she tried Catholicism and liked it. She once said it was the repetition she liked, the sense of order. Her husband, Alberto, was from Asturias, and she often told me he had blue eyes, which Felipe had also. I guess it was unusual in Cuba.

Felipe's mother was usually unemotional. She spoke in short sentences. "I have my chair and my window. I have been blessed with a home full of people. Why do I need the outside world? The children around me are my world."

She had learned to read and write after the Revolution. "That opened my windows," she said, "to read about other countries, to learn why Cuba made its revolution."

She is a person who shows that warmth and selflessness are part of a human being. I was sorry to see her weeping so much. "We never want to say goodbyes in Cuba, Mateo. There have been too many goodbyes. We feel we have failed with those who leave; everyone who goes we lose. It is only those who stay who understand our soul."

Felipe worried me. He would never have more ambition than now. But there was nothing that seemed to guide him. He wasn't cynical, but he never spoke of any plans. He said he loved Laura, but there were no plans. He didn't seem that concerned about his friends and never talked much about Cuba. That's what surprised me about what he said. I was pleased when he told me to mind my own business. It showed a little passion, some determination. He was right, because my choice of words was wrong. He apologized and I told him it wasn't necessary. I wouldn't be seeing much more of Felipe. What I could do for him from now on would have to be in my prayers.

I left Calle Jalisco with a feeling of overwhelming sadness. This was a family that had lost the best man they had since the father went away. Felipe needed to grow up some more.

Felipe

We had all been to these Beatles events lots of times before. It was the same bands usually playing the same songs. But it was all about familiarity and participation, because these were the songs people loved, you know. So it made us feel fine. It made us feel better that they had been banned and that our families listened in secret. Papa told me he heard them in crackly stations from Yuma. You know the power of music. I often thought if they, John and Paul, had known this they would have come to Cuba. Then George Martin, el quinto Beatle, came a few years back, but we never got tickets. We just saw it on the TV wondering what he thought of our Cuba that had once banned the Beatles and now loved them.

We met on Calle 12 in Vedado. Laura brought her letter from Miranda. I had never seen Miranda's writing before, but it was written in a controlled precise way with large confident writing. Like a scientist's. Certainly not scribbled in a hurry.

"Look Feli, she's sure of herself. She's been planning this for weeks; she even planned who was going to deliver it. That's what worries me. Someone she knew opened the letter and readdressed it."

I tried to be optimistic. "She's a good friend, Laurita. She says she'll be in touch. It's kind of embarrassing what she says about me, especially because I thought she despised me as a loser."

"You never know here. Miranda didn't have family in Florida, at least not that she told me about. So I guess she's been in touch with someone over here to set all that up."

"Laurita, don't tell me your family doesn't know about the people business. Who was that monster in the Tommy Hilfiger gear I saw in your living room the other night?"

The crowd was still arriving, even though it was well over an hour after nine when the concert was due to have started. I guess as usual most people planned to arrive after the speeches. They were all there—the Havana heavy metal set, the bikers, the ministry of culture, some official guitarists, kids taken out to get some cool evening air. They all knew that even though it was an official concert there would still be things to enjoy.

The speeches were still in progress. One was being given by a student who seemed to see this as his big chance to impress. "The way to Víctory over imperialism is to show the harmony of peoples. Our comrade John Lennon said 'Give Peace a Chance.' He became the enemy of our enemy; he became a friend for our struggle. And he became one of the famous campaigners for peace in the world so that the Yanqui imperialism was powerless against him."

I felt a tap on my back. "Hey, amigo, I thought you never showed up for speeches. You're losing your timing." It was Vladimir. "Can we move away somewhere until this guy runs out of steam?"

Laura and I moved back to the other side of the park away from the stage. "Look, Felipe, I have found out about some things that are being planned around Moncada, and I heard about this meeting that was happening. It didn't tell me anything, but I watched who was arriving and shot these pictures. I took shots of the cars as well. Some of them are 'official.' I'd really like you to see them."

"Come on, Vlado. Does it seem to you as if we're on the verge of a new revolution? Just look around you. So you have some pictures. Wow, that's a nice camera."

"Get serious a minute, Felipe. Use that researcher's brain. If you look around Havana there are lots of things happening that we don't know about and are never told. Now here's a chance to find out something we are not supposed to know. Isn't that what human beings were put on the planet to do? And don't be so damn stubborn."

"Well, there's a nice shot of a salsa band; maybe they are all in this conspiracy. That drumstick could be a lethal weapon," I said. Vladimir needed to be irritated.

"Come on, Felipe. This is our country I'm talking about."

"There's a BMW arriving at a pretty nice house, just like your own. There's a shot of its plates; goodness knows what that means. There's a black Lada arriving. There's one of those official Peugeots. These guys travel in style. Obviously Cuba. But wait a minute. These plates, these numbers, I think I've seen them before, maybe around the polo."

"Well, that's something, Feli."

"I can't tell who it's used by."

"Okay, well what about the drivers?"

"First guy looks well dressed. Obviously a foreigner. Second guy in the Lada—never seen him. But wait—the third guy. I certainly know him. It's Carlitos. So you're telling me that he's a counter-revolutionary? Carlitos? Vlado, you must be joking."

"You're absolutely sure, Feli?"

"Of course. I've worked with him since college. He's always around Playa, has lots of friends."

"And he's the head of where you work."

"Sure," I said, "he's always being invited to these things at the Council of State. Claims to know everybody."

"My friend, you know I'm not the sort of guy to get carried away with these things. Things don't change here. There have been hundreds of false starts, but I would bet my life that this meeting and Carlitos mean something new."

"I don't see what you are saying. Carlitos is meeting some friends. It's a Saturday. He's entitled to a day off."

"Felipe, I can't tell you everything I know. That would not be good for you. But take my word for this."

"So I guess you have used us for what you want. And now you count us out. Are you just saying that Laurita and I are basically not the right people to know about these secret deals?"

"There are no secret deals. It's just that when you have a lead you should follow it. It's plain common sense, Felipe. I think some of your dad's friends would know more about what's going on."

Laura

Felipe and Vladimir, seeing them together that day; there was something that made Vladimir seem real. You see the two together and you wonder how two guys can see the same place in such different ways. I think Feli was jealous of Vlado. He preferred to ignore the issues, comfortable not to make decisions, preferring not to go for it as Vlado did. Vlado was the guy who was rolling the dice. Felipe never thought it was worth the effort. "Feli, you should not be so dependent, so defeatist. Life is not just about being kind, hanging out with the family. I know guys in Cuba who have ambitions here in Cuba. You could be one too. You are a Cuban." Yes, Feli would talk. Vlado would act. Vlado had taken lots of training after the Lenin. There was nothing he felt he could not do.

The trouble was that Vlado could be on the side of everything. Winning was more important than which game you played. Don't worry why; it was just the what and how. The Revolution had always needed people like Vlado. So will the next. I should not have been surprised to see him at the airport driving someone else's van, using others for himself.

Felipe

A Cuban party started after the speeches ended and the music began. "Hey, you've got to hide your love away." They were singing along, and the fathers were raising their kids on their shoulders to see. The Lennon statue was surrounded in flowers cut to honor the legend. People were calling out for their favorite songs, but the bands always played the same ones. A gang of youths passed some liquid around, which looked like rum. Some who had no more rum were playing a game of basketball with bottles as the ball and the trashcan as the basket. The sober guys were from G2 security. They began to move toward them, checking with some black vans with bars in the windows parked along the street. We all knew that more security was inside. A couple of the guys were chanting "All you need is love" over and over again and were pushed to the side.

Then a voice shouted, "Hey, Felipe, I used to treat you and your Mama down at the clinic."

I turned around and saw a tall man with a shaved head and a black beard. He was wearing a Beatles t-shirt, the one with the Sergeant Pepper jackets. It was Doctor Menéndez, who had been our family doctor three blocks away from Calle Jalisco. He use to claim that he had fought at Play Girón, I remember, but always seemed too young for that to be true.

"Long time since I saw you, but maybe that's my fault. I joined the overseas medical profession to make some money." Menéndez hadn't lost his sense of humor.

"Doctor Menéndez. I knew you had left, but it was so long ago. I kind of assumed you wouldn't be back; you know, like the others. How are things?"

"Well, Venezuela was okay. In fact it was more than okay. Could be a bit rough, but I made some money. Look at this fancy cell phone I just bought. It's great to take photos too."

I saw Vladimir look at the phone and begin to take an interest in what Menéndez was saying.

"Downloaded lots of music in Caracas. In fact I only got back last month. It's my first Moncada for five years. Oh, and do you know Isaac over here? He just told me he knew your dad. He's one of the reasons I came back. There's always hope for a place where Isaac lives. Isn't that so, Isaac?"

He called over to a group of guys with their backs to us, and I saw an older man in a yellow t-shirt with white stubble. It was the same man I had met a few hours earlier who had denied being called Isaac.

"Well, I had no idea you knew my dad," I said. "After all, you said this afternoon that you didn't."

Isaac smiled. "This is Cuba, Felipe. If somebody wants something badly enough they have to be patient. They always come back if they really want it."

CHAPTER 20

Yoel

Well, what do you know? I thought the Chino thing was a real long shot, but I didn't know all the answers. Henry called back. I couldn't believe it. We hit the jackpot with the boxing promoter in Orlando. Apparently he had had some of his new recruits get in the way of left hooks, and his cupboard was looking pretty bare of Mexican and Nicaraguan flyweights. So there was a chance. Orlando had made an offer. He would pay ten thousand dollars for each Cuban boxer with an Olympic or world title in the last five years. That would give me two thousand dollars profit from each fighter, or one thousand from each fist. Let no one say that Cuba doesn't have world-class exports when we choose to use them. Henry would be going up to see him.

The bread van would be a great way to transport Oscar to the cayos. There would be a double delivery of bread on Sunday but nothing on Monday. That would be ideal. Abel had asked the director of the sports equipment side of baseball to come up with the money for a trip for his son. Apparently he had the money already in Cuba. That complicated things, but it would be okay. We needed another three to meet the boat on the twenty-seventh. Abel said there would always be some last-minute changes, and putting the word out was how it was always done. But the market was not easy. Prices were steep not because of fuel costs, so the joke went. And some people were waiting until after Moncada. Always the dithering. The undecided. Pathetic really, because for most of the people we were talking to, there was no problem with the money. What was eight thousand dollars for a new life? Of course some in Florida had to get the new pool table first, and Cousin Jaime in Matanzas could wait a little longer in the Miami of the south.

When there were problems, it was good for business. If the people fell out of trees then everyone would be in on it and the prices would crash. I figured I deserved the profits. They went much further than hundreds of French lessons to kids of diplomats. I think Abel was frightened that he had made too much already. Poor Abelito; he felt he didn't deserve it.

Mateo

No one called me after 10:00 p.m. in Cuba. No one who knew me, that was. I set aside Saturday evening for preparing for Mass the next day. It was my final message to my Cuban friends, and there was a lot I wanted to say. I know it was selfish because I wanted to use the occasion to justify what I had learned and done in Cuba. I was determined to stay balanced and leave quietly, with dignity. Fausto Gómez changed my quiet routine. He wanted to come around and said it wasn't about the article. He apologized for the inconvenience but said it was urgent.

Fausto came in a taxi, which I thought was strange. He brought with him a briefcase. "Padre, I thought a lot about this before bothering you, but the matters that concern me are so important that I had to take this considerable risk. Am I right in saying you will be leaving Cuba shortly?"

"That's right. I am leaving next week. I'll probably be gone by the end of July, but it really depends on when my successor arrives."

"We talked a lot last week about my work and what it means to be a real journalist, you remember."

"I do remember and think that conversation was one of the most interesting I have had in Cuba."

"You are both a diplomat and a churchman, Mateo," said Fausto, smiling. "I felt that there was some interest there, and in these quiet moments late in the evening, it is a good time to talk some more. Because if I don't talk now there may be no other opportunity."

I misunderstood him. "Well, that's kind, but it is likely that I will return to Havana some day, and then I will give you a call for old time's sake."

"No, no Mateo. I mean it will be the last chance I have before some events that may be of such importance for Cuba; events like no one has foreseen. It is for someone from outside Cuba to know this because you can look at things afterward with no emotion. If you leave the country you will carry with you what I have to say tonight. I hope you will allow me a few minutes so I can feel I did what I needed to. So my conscience as a Cuban is clear."

I thought back to the Cubano episode and just wondered where this was going. "Of course, Fausto. I am ready to listen. Sometimes I am confused as to whether I am really a non-Cuban at all."

"I know you are a man of confidence, Mateo, because this is rather like a confessional in your professional capacity. I am telling you things I would not tell my mother. Here we have survived for many years with solidarity, waiting, believing that we would reach a unique Cuban way of doing things. We admired the deeds, the legends that had made Cuba a beacon for many around the world. Visitors would always tell me that. We had made the best brand name in history. The ideas we had were good as long as we had the Russians paying the bills. It was easier than we realized to convince everyone that we had found the secret to human happiness. Don't question anything; just trust the system and you would be okay. That plan worked, but the world then changed. It changed in a big way. Other countries found out that there was a life without Russia. And there were better ways of running the economy than thousands of controls preventing anyone from becoming rich."

I began to wonder why he had bothered to come out to tell me things he had said in different words when we spoke about the article.

"Well, I never believed that anyone, or particularly any group of Cubans, would do anything about all of this. We all saw that we were squandering so many resources in controlling ourselves, so many people who were paid in security, informers, an expensive apparatus that prevented other Cubans from doing anything for themselves. After all, we had found Venezuela, and the Americans kept us in a blockade, so that was fine. But nothing was moving, really. The same old slogans, the same promises, a few more DVDs, cell phones, you know. The appearance of progress. We had to look busy." Fausto started to open his briefcase.

"But then a few weeks ago we started hearing things that were new. People who worked for *Granma* picked up leaflets around the country. You know they would be left in bus stations, universities, hospitals. The thing that surprised us was not what they said but that they had a printing process that we did not own. We would find it sooner rather than later, but we soon realized that time was short. There was no CCTV footage of anything being dropped. Nothing to go on. None of our informers could come up with anything accurate. Just to show you I am not inventing this here is some of the material." Fausto took a handful of papers and put them on the desk.

"Fausto, I see all this. I have lived here for a few years and know of these things. There have always been groups who come and go. But I don't see why you have come out to me today to show me this."

"It's because you can be trusted to tell the story, Mateo. You will be there to show those who think we are all the same that we have honestly tried to listen. I am not a good man. I struggle with my conscience to be a journalist. I have a family and the same emotions as someone who tells the truth. Just because we work for the government does not mean we support everything. I am a man as well as a Cuban. A lot of us connected to the frustration you know of people sitting and waiting with nothing they can do about it. You must know the Varela song, 'Guillermo Tell.' You know, the *muchacho* who is tired of his father always firing the arrow at the apple on his head. In the next few days these messages may become more important."

"Next week?"

Fausto rummaged in his briefcase and pulled out a paper. "If you look at the yellow-colored piece of paper at the bottom. This is the one that is difficult not to take seriously."

Víctor

Max called again to give me encouragement. Always the leader of weaker spirits. But he did not have time to meet on Saturday.

I called Contreras to say I had some important things he should know. I hadn't decided what I would say. But I needed to hear more about what he promised.

Felipe

"Maybe it proves you should never lie, even to a stranger," Isaac said. "At first I couldn't believe that you were who you said. Triana's son. You know it seemed too much of a coincidence with all that is going on. Suddenly someone comes trying to get me to talk. They've tried that a few times over the years." He gestured toward the plaza.

"Talk about what?" I said. "You sound like Vladimir here."

Vlado wasn't sure he would get involved and looked away. "Who is this guy?" asked Isaac.

"Well, he works in computers, so I guess that means he's pretty smart."

Isaac commented without hesitation. "We need smart people, young Triana. That's what your dad was trying to find. I've just got myself a computer as well. You know, the science is pretty easy. Goes with medicine. Hey Vladimir, you should come around sometime. Down on Compostela there's no one with the slightest clue about computers. Get them onto cement or rum and they're happy. But Felipe, your dad would have been real happy now. He would have been excited today, and not just for the music."

Laurita looked angry. "Felipe, what's all this? I thought we came for a concert. We need to relax. I'm sure Vlado feels the same. Come on; let's just enjoy ourselves without these damn conspiracies."

Vlado was smoking a Marlboro but had begun to plug in. "Laura, just wait a minute. I think Isaac would be good to talk to. Can't we do that?"

Laurita didn't understand. Maybe she was tired of coming to my rescue. Maybe it was Miranda. But that seemed to snap her. She turned around and left without saying anything more. It took me by surprise, but it had to be dealt with later. I wanted to talk to Isaac about my father. It was time I did, and this might be the last chance.

Menéndez the doctor left to find another drink, and Isaac, Vladimir, and I went over to sit on the grass at the far side of the park. They had just reached "Let it Be," which was the song I liked best. It seemed to be a real sacrifice to miss it. But maybe there was a plan after all. Mateo had said we should wait for the kingfisher, and sometimes the kingfisher would come.

Isaac began by doing five push-ups. "See, I still keep in training, Triana. I noticed that you were out of breath coming up those stairs. Oh and by the way, you were right, I was in medicine. It was when we were in Geneva for a UN meeting on malaria that I first heard the Beatles. In fact a couple of the guys playing here are doctors, my buddies. The drummer over there is a vet. Just shows what we could all do given the chance."

"Isaac, it's nice to meet you—again. I'm glad I didn't have to climb all those stairs. But why would my dad have you on his list? You were not just on it; you were at the top."

"Your papa was an exceptional man, Felipe. He hadn't got the education. But he was a natural leader. I saw plenty of them in the Revolution, but Triana was strong, optimistic; someone who made you admire the human spirit. He had this in his music too. You remember that old guy Chino who wrote the songs? I think your dad gave him all the credit, but he did a lot too. I know that. By the way, Old Chino told me that he's seen you and says you are one of the most brilliant young scientists in Cuba."

"I see Chino up there at the CBM, but he's a sad old man. I know my papa was depressed in his last years. But what was the story at the end? No one has ever told me. Mama won't speak, you know; only that he made some mistakes. He was a broken man and just died in jail."

"Triana broken? Never, never. No, that was the point. They couldn't break him. He got out from Boniato."

"Let It Be" had reached the line about the light shining in the cloudy night, and the crowd lit their cigarette lighters.

Vlado suddenly asked a question. "What are we talking about? The gang in '95 that broke from Boniato? You're not saying Felipe's papa got involved in that."

Isaac and Vlado were suddenly connecting. "Sure, sure that was him. I wasn't sent to Boniato but given reeducation, perhaps because I was a doctor. They thought that one day they might be able to use me again, but as things turned out I never got my job back. As for Triana, they saw what he had done with the students."

I lay down on the grass and looked around. I remember seeing the rubbish on the floor, discarded wrappers, beer bottles. Gazing upward, there was no rubbish, just stars.

Isaac saw me. "Yes, It was a night like this Triana chose for the breakout. He reckoned that the others knew the countryside. But he was from Pinar, a different world for Triana from the Oriente. He shouldn't have taken those hostages ..."

"Hostages? What do you mean?"

"It was a family out by the Cobre. You know he got a ride for twenty kilometers from Boniato. And then he got frightened and went into a family home. And well the rest of it was all a misunderstanding. The guy was a former special forces officer or something and had his weapons in the house."

It was that image of Papa, desperate like a hunted animal, that he should have been the person threatening a family like a criminal.

"I know this must seem hard, Felipe, but you never saw the conditions in Boniato. It was too much for anyone to bear."

I knew that I had to deal with Isaac and not get stuck in the past. "Isaac, you haven't told me yet why Papa put you at the top of the list."

"Well, Felipe, there was a time when ideas for change were getting some attention. The government was creating a new 'conciencia' in the early eighties among the students and workers. And Triana and I were sent to the universities to talk about revolution in the campo, to build up a new generation of volunteers, pioneers. The kids were waiting for a lead, and Triana was good with those who'd come to the town from the campo. Told them things like they should own the land because the state could never grow what the country needed. He said he'd seen it at the sugar *centrales*. Triana was seen as someone who had made the Revolution. He wasn't a fancy intellectual or anything, and I think, looking back, that the party perhaps saw him as becoming an official organizer, you know, of mobilizing the masses again. I think they made a bad decision, because anyone could see that Triana could never be tamed. You could never see Triana perform in the Cuban circus. And it was his idea about the yellow. I think he said it was something to do with the sun at dawn."

"Yellow?"

"Yes, you know, the t-shirts, the sheets of paper. It all got forgotten some time ago when the government decided on the 'rectification' and then the crackdowns followed and people got afraid. Wearing yellow could mean three years. But now you're seeing it again."

"What do you mean, again?" I said. "I haven't seen it, so you have a long way to go."

"Oh that's something for later, my friend."

Vladimir was rolling his eyes. "Come on, guys. Get to the point. This isn't about weepy stories of nostalgia for revolution in the campo." Isaac ignored him.

"Felipe, your dad is a legend out in Santiago. Because he got out and was never broken. He showed what a man can do alone."

Vladimir offered Isaac a Marlboro. He took two. Vlado wanted to talk business. "Look, Isaac, Felipe and I have picked up some signs that the rules of the game are changing here. For once in our lives we wanted to do something ourselves before we were told to. And it would feel really good to have what we were not supposed to have."

Isaac smiled. "Well, it should feel good if it works. And it will work one day. I just hope I'm not sitting up on my balcony when it does."

"So how about next week?" asked Vladimir.

"I don't know, my friend. If I knew I wouldn't be listening to some second-rate rock music."

"No one ever called the Beatles second rate." I said. "Maybe I should come back to your balcony, Isaac. You know, when I've done some thinking."

"That would be good, jovencito. Never act before you think. But don't wait too long."

Víctor

The last thing I wanted was a lecture from Contreras. We met in a state guest house in Lagunita; you know, the old estate where the most luxurious mansions ever built in Cuba are scattered around a lake with flamingos. Anyway we Communists know when luxury is needed. And Contreras always said he liked the surroundings.

Contreras spread himself out in an armchair. "The important thing is to keep to the ritual of Moncada. At Moncada the CDRs are supposed to realize what they have achieved for the year. A record attendance; some will sneer at this, but every person has to feel something bigger than themselves."

I enjoyed that. Contreras said he knew the mentality. No one expected to hear anything new. If it was new, that would be like changing the words of José Martí. He died in 1895, so it was a little late to be doing that. It was enough to hear them repeated. A familiar song we knew sung well; that was what mobilization of the masses meant.

Contreras was a big fish. That's why I was privileged to have his phone number. He never invited me to his home, of course. That was private property, and it was a rule here that we should never know what things anyone else had in their homes. That would lead to too many questions, about equality and the rest. So we met on neutral ground.

"Sánchez, you and I go back a long way. Your father was brave when Batista's murderers broke up the meeting in Artemisa. I knew then that your family had exceptional potential, because our comrades in Artemisa only helped conceal young men of outstanding revolutionary potential. Moncada was made by those comrades in Artemisa, and our pueblo will now contribute something more that is special for the Revolution. Sánchez, I am pleased that you have agreed to continue with this little project. It will give the events in Santiago some proper attention. I can't understand why we did away with the military stuff at Moncada. I think the people liked that." Contreras seemed to get angry at the thought. "You know, we did away with the military stuff after the Soviets betrayed us. From then on we were about peace. Cubans united in peace. But it makes Moncada seem pretty limp."

Thank goodness Contreras had a lot else to do. That man could talk. He could eat as well. I'm not sure which he was better at. He said he had a guest for dinner, and a woman was waiting in the lobby when I left.

Contreras would back me. I could tell not so much from what he said but the fact that he saw me. I had done well. Before all this, a lot of people were doing better than me. That was true. Just look at Lagunita or Tarara. My hand in dominoes was okay. I wanted to see if anyone else's was better. That was what you did. Contreras was confident, and he saw a chance of doing something where he could grab a little more power. So it was important that I had a way out with him. That was the difference with today's kids. They'd given up planning; they stopped thinking of the moves their opponents would make. The kids weren't interested in organization, results. Oh yes, I saw them all around the CDR, day and night. All they wanted was to lie around enjoying themselves. A cheap bottle of rum and they were yours. They wanted university life with money to spend. Max, I think, was weary of planning. That comes when you turn seventy, maybe. What's the point anymore? Max, I'm sure, didn't have a fallback. He despised crawling to others. If you are a tobacco farmer there is no fallback to a hurricane. I would follow Max to the end because he might always have some better ideas than me.

Moncada was the first attack, the first blood that was shed. I felt proud that we were about to do some bold things on that sacred day. I had come a long way.

Mateo

I glanced at the papers Fausto had given me. I kept thinking that Fausto was building up to something, but he just continued talking.

"Look, Fausto, you seem a nice guy and a patriotic Cuban. I know the problems that you have had here as a journalist, and you think things are changing. I can't do anything really. It's a choice …"

Then suddenly Fausto dropped his vagueness. "Mateo, you are the only one who could rescue me when the change happens. We know what happened in some countries of Eastern Europe. It all happened with violence, the settling of grudges. Everyone and everything gets swept away. No one would believe what I have told you today. A voice like yours from outside Cuba would tell the truth and perhaps talk of some of these discussions we have had. I have never talked like this before to any non-Cuban."

"I am shocked to hear that you expect some dramatic events. You are in government, and I don't understand why you don't tell the police so that what you fear doesn't happen. Isn't that the obvious thing to do?"

"It's not quite like that," said Fausto, smiling for the first time. "There has been careful preparation. It's not as simple as you say, Mateo. I have not been a supporter, but a member of my family has—let us say—kept me in the picture. Even if my heart was not in it, Mateo, I would say there is a 50 percent chance it may succeed. And the Cuba we know will be gone."

CHAPTER 21

Sunday July 25

Yoel

It was Sunday. My family always came together for Sunday lunch. Revolutions might come, but Sunday lunch was an order. My mother would squirt a small drop of perfume behind her ears, Giorgio Armani I think, that her old aunt from Bradenton had brought down a couple of years ago. My abuelo said it was the only time we saw family, so it was right that we treated ourselves. We tried to get pork, *moros y cristianos*, beer, and sometimes a cake. Abuelo didn't like to talk about where the money came from. Poor Abuelo. His little brother had tried so hard to persuade him to go in 1962. He had even come back once with empty suitcases. Mother still talked about it, but Abel and I were too young, they said. Things would get better after the worst of the Revolution, and it was true that the firing squads were happening less. We had the "foto de familia" on the fireplace. There he was, Tio Lazaro, the man who bought our Sunday lunch, courtesy of a sum sent via Western Union on the last Tuesday of each month. That was always the problem with Felipe. They had no one. Laura, that rich kid, she didn't need Western Union or anything.

I had my kids early, I know, and that made me think differently. Yes, of course I was no role model. I didn't live with their mother, and I had them for a full day every other Sunday so my former wife, Barbara, I should mention her name, could get a break. By the way, I included Barbara in the trip to the nice hotel in Varadero. I thought having kids would change my life, maybe put something back of the ambition I had. Kids want to do things. They see how to make their own toys. Give them a piece of paper and they'll make a plane. They dream and don't see the limits. With kids you have responsibility. You watch them every day. I decided that they were what I had to offer the world, those kids. They were the ones who would ask me later what I did. But one thing I hadn't expected was that they were embarrassed that we had Uncle Lazaro, the man from Yuma. They had heard the conversations every Sunday when Abuelo thought they didn't understand. "How is it we have more money than anyone else? The kids say you are mercenaries, sucking up to the Yanquis. I'd rather be poor like everyone else."

My mother loved the Sunday mornings. She had collected the garlic and prepared the beans, soaking them for hours. Sundays in July she would make mango mousse if there was crema de leche in the stores. It was the buildup, the waiting. Would the pork be as tender as last week?

The meal began with grace. Mother insisted on Catholicism. Every Sunday we prayed for Lazaro's family in Bradenton. She didn't mention the reasons, of course. Then the food and the talk. It meant a day when we spoke about our lives. It was a ritual, but there was a rule that no one would mention government or religion. Baseball was okay. It had to be, I said, because if it wasn't Abel would have nothing to say. But we were supposed to talk about our plans for the week; you know, what we were doing at school. I would usually tell them about the French lessons and what the kids told me about their families, how the foreigners lived in Havana; the bread deliveries and how many times I had used the van or the motorbike. Mama would talk of the piano lessons she had been giving for forty years. Her F sharp on the piano had stopped working, and no one could find a new string in Havana. The piano was valuable. She would sometimes say how much it would be worth. But then the termites might get it first.

Abuelo talked about the past, and usually by four o'clock he had cried. Our kids complained about Sunday. It took away a day of hanging out with their friends.

That Sunday, Abel arrived late and we had already started the salad made with lettuce my mother had grown in the back yard. "Abel, you might show a little more respect. I've spent three hours on that vinaigrette."

Abel knew better than to make baseball excuses. "I'm sorry, Mama. I had to see the kids today; you know, to see them before Moncada. Won't get the time otherwise. They're going to the zoo with their mother." I noticed that Abel had stopped calling his wife Yamelis now to stress that he was separated. In any case he was lying. I knew he had been checking with César in Santa Clara. Abel left nothing to chance.

"And Yoel, how are you juggling your life?" asked mother. "Isn't it time you concentrated on one job? You know, like your father did."

I knew she was trying to provoke me. She hated telling her neighbors that I delivered bread; her son Yoel with a degree in French. "The Varadero trip was great, Mother. You know I have always dreamed of getting to that beach—beyond that house called Xanadu. You feel that you've broken a rule. You're a Cuban who's made it."

"Well, that's good, Yoel," said Mother. "We used to go to Varadero as children. You're right; it's very beautiful. But how did you pay for a good hotel?"

"You know me, Mother. I am the most honest guy in town. It's all those jobs I work that you dislike. The guy from Cameroon, the diplomat whose kids I teach French, said he wanted me to experience what they did. So he paid the hotel to set it up. In any case there were lots of other Cubans there, so the kids were fine. Weren't you guys? But it's overrated, that beach. That was the nice thing. We know now we're not missing anything."

Abel seemed to want to poke me in the eye. He opened his mouth, taking the high ground, which made me boil. "Yoel, what's the point of pretending you can live well off the charity of diplomats? It's a way to cheapen your life. Who cares about fancy hotels with overweight tourists drinking and eating all day? Now the people who gave you this wonderful time in the hotel will know you can be bought for anything. You sell your soul."

"Shit, Abel, what would you know?"

Abuelo was listening carefully. "Yoel, I will not allow such language, especially in front of the children. Whatever you hear in the barrio, we will not stoop to that level. Not at Sunday lunch."

"I'm sorry, Abuelo, but Abel has never been able to stand anyone who does anything for themselves." I couldn't be bothered to say anymore. Next Sunday would be exactly the same.

Felipe

So Papa was a hero. At least he was to his friends, and Mama had wanted me never to meet them. "Don't follow your father's footsteps; he has nothing to pass on to you. I beg that you build your own life." Mama always slept an hour longer on Sunday. It was her little reward to herself, she said, for getting through another week. Even so, she was up at 6:30.

Rafa was bothered by the heat, or maybe the fan that had fused, so he had been up all night. He kept asking me what he could do to win the volleyball finals. I told him the best thing he could do was get some sleep. Without that he would collapse on the court.

Mama came in just as Rafa had finally gone to sleep. She was yawning. "I have to ask Gloria if she has any coffee left. Last week with everyone coming around to pay respects for Pepe, we're out. Those guys upstairs were knocking on walls for hours. They must have found some cement."

"Mama, it's been a bad week, I know. We tried to get away from it yesterday, Laurita and I. The Beatles concert made me feel worse. I feel like my life has been hit by a big wave, when the ocean seemed calm. I need to come up for air."

"Why was the concert so bad, Feli? I thought you liked Lennon."

"I don't know. First it was Laurita. She seemed so down about Miranda; you know, her friend in customs. She just left the concert on her own. Then I met some friends of Papa. Never seen them before."

Mama looked worried. "Feli, I don't like to hear that. People are watching these things. Especially at Moncada. Where did you meet?"

"Oh it was at the Lennon park; you know, in Vedado. A man called Isaac. He was a doctor, I think. Knew Papa—all that went on in Santiago. I had never heard about it before."

"What hadn't you heard?" said Mama sharply.

"Well, all about the escape, the hostage stuff. I was never told. You said Papa had died in jail after he left Pinar; he got sick. That was what it was. But Isaac said Papa died a hero. He escaped from Boniato, and all the people know that Triana never gave in."

Mama covered her face and ran her fingers through her hair. "Oh no, not all that again. Just when we were over Pepe. Just when Rafa wants to win the volleyball. Please let it drop, Feli. What happened with Laura? I can't believe you would let her go. If her friend has left she really needs you. Feli, why are you so bothered with the past? I'm telling you the truth when I say I never knew what Papa did. All I know is that he was never here.

What good is a hero if he's far away from his family in jail? Being a hero doesn't put food on the table. There are a lot of people who'd like to convince you that they were heroes."

Laura

Sunday in Havana, and suddenly a busload of architecture professors from North Carolina did not seem a bad way to spend the day. If only Feli would devote as much time to impressing Carlitos as he did to finding out every detail of why his dad spent most of his life in jail. It's the past here, and everyone is ashamed of it in some way. You can't live your life in regret. But, Feli, he wouldn't let it go.

For the smart guys in Cuba the past is just that; it's old stuff. Bearded guys on tanks. They won. So what? Stories about jail; what is the point? My family treats the world as we find it. We are good at that. My family members do their own things. My stepfather, Papa Two, is smart. I have no idea how he makes his money, but he has at least provided for me. Feli's father; look where he left them.

Papa Two rang just as the architects were getting off at the Bellas Artes. "Laurita, they want to speak to you. Someone has come around here from MININT."

He never rang me at work, and I could tell he was nervous. MININT at our house was a big deal. "It's about someone called Miranda Reyes Colombo. They say you knew her. They say you knew her very well. You need to come around right now."

So it was MININT who had opened the envelope. Even Miranda hadn't known whom she could trust. I called the office and said there was a family illness and took a cab back home. The MININT Lada was outside, and the driver was asleep at the wheel. The officer, sitting in the formal dining room, was smoking and not in uniform. I saw from the tray that she had been through quite a number. She was tall and black with large eyes and crooked teeth, which she flashed in a smile.

"You are Compañera Laura?" I nodded. "I am an officer from investigations in MININT. My job is to look into breaches of state security. We believe that you have recently been in touch with one of our former employees, Compañera Miranda Reyes Colombo. It is my job to find out how much she told you about her recent work."

"I think there must be some mistake. Miranda Reyes was a customs official. I have known her ever since I can remember."

"Compañera Reyes has been guilty of a major breach of security, and we think she may have spoken to you about it."

I am not naïve. I knew about the informers and state security, but I had never met anyone who admitted to working for them. Now I was being told my best friend did just that.

"I'm sorry. I don't understand; she was a normal girl. Loved dancing, Che pictures, boyfriends. We shared everything. No big schemes. I never talked about politics, state security."

"I'm afraid, compañera, that you did not understand that young woman. She worked on some very sensitive matters, and she has abandoned her duties. We have reason to believe she took some papers with her. She wrote you a letter just before she left. And we know that your family here has met with some people smugglers." She spat out the words, paused, and looked intently at me. "Those who trade like that are the worst kind of parasites, the sort the Yanqui imperialists have always tried to encourage."

"If you are surprised by all this, imagine how I feel. I have nothing to do with any of that sort of smuggling. I am an ordinary girl. I make my living with what skills I have."

"And your skills are provided by the state, you should never forget, Compañera Reyes. We are making our investigations, and we will soon be able to decide if the version you have told me is truthful. To assist an enemy of the state is a very serious offence."

She stubbed out her last cigarette and opened her clipboard. She made some hasty notes and left without a word.

Vladimir

Was everyone who wanted some action in Cuba over seventy years of age? What had happened to us? Did those biotech wizards in Siboney find a vaccine in 1959 so we stopped thinking for ourselves? And Felipe had gone and lost the plot again. Felipe and his old men. Even his dad would have realized it's about tomorrow in Cuba. We had to be able to do better than Isaac, with his crazy eyes and yellow t-shirt.

Now Saluki was different; there were some younger guys. Even Istúriz. I would never have believed about that Istúriz at the CBM. But the more I thought about it, the more it made good sense. Like a lot of the biotech people he started in computers and must have been good. I looked at the CBM Web site. His specialty was bioinformatics, fast computers applied to biodata. So Saluki knew their man. I know that Felipe said Istúriz was really smart and that one day he would be super rich from all the stuff he learned about cancer and AIDS. No wonder he wanted to write that stupid article Felipe was so proud of. Get your name out. Good for Istúriz. He sounds like my man.

There were no more e-mails about the meeting in Playa. I didn't know why they met, and that was what worried me. I had to report to the MINTEL controller, so I told him the truth. That may sound unusual, but it was true that the trail had run dry with Saluki. I told them I would continue looking, but my professional judgment was that the thefts were a one-off and the computer losses were by some criminals who would sooner or later make a mistake. First I needed to talk directly to Carlos, and I didn't tell Bertie that.

Mateo

Lunch was always prepared for all the seminary priests and the bishops who were in town on Sunday. I think a lot of them would arrange special trips to Havana because the food was good. It was our way of reminding ourselves that we were together in the church in Cuba. Our cook Clara set herself the challenge that the menu would never be the repeated during a month. She spent hours on her bicycle justifying her boast. I remember that Sunday there was fresh grapefruit from the Isla de Juventud and that the Philippines embassy had kindly sent over some camarones that had "arrived" from the provincia. They were good, but Clara apologized that there were only three each.

The lunch began with comments about the excellent quality of the grapefruit. The bishop had visited the Isla, as I'm sure he'd told us before. "Isla de Juventud; it's the loneliest place I know," said the bishop, who was in philosophical mood. "No wonder they set up a jail there. The people in Havana know nothing about what's happening in the world. The people in Juventud know nothing about what's happening in Cuba."

That was the last remark I remember. There was a knock on the door, and Clara came in and said there was someone to see Padre Mateo. I excused myself and went out to the meeting room. Sitting in the far corner was Haydée, and opposite her was the man I had met as Cubano.

I hugged Haydée and shook Cubano's hand. "Haydée, it's very good to see you. I was worried, you know, when you just disappeared. Silvia, your friend, seemed to think you would know what you were doing. She said she wasn't surprised."

"Oh, Silvia. There's one who talks too wildly, I'm afraid. She used to be better; you know, someone we could count on. Now, well I guess she's like so many here; she's just there to tell stories so the police will keep her in her sewing business."

"I also know this gentleman," I said, turning to Cubano. "I understand you are from Santiago. What brings you back to Havana?"

The man shuffled nervously in his seat and looked at Haydée.

"It was Haydée who brought us here. It's Haydée who really wanted to do this. Padre, is it safe to speak here? I know there are so many people listening."

I looked around and couldn't really believe that what we said in the seminary waiting room would be bugged. But I found myself saying. "Okay, Cubano, let's go into the garden."

I made my excuses to the bishop and we went out to the garden. At the end was a bench under a jacaranda tree. "Padre, you didn't believe me when I came to the church. I said I would have to prove what I said. So here is Haydée, who has been a good friend to me. She is my proof because you trust her. I know that Héctor is someone real to you as well. Well, Héctor is my other brother. You see, Haydée is my sister-in law."

"Well, that makes things a little clearer, and I'm pleased that nothing has happened to Haydée."

Haydée looked down at the floor. The man spoke. "Look, sir, I haven't been honest with you, I know. I did not think it was right for you to know. We have been working over in Santiago for some time, and I will be going back with her today. What we are doing will now happen, and after what you said I am more determined than ever."

That made me worry. What had he thought I said? I didn't encourage any plans. "I don't understand, Cubano, if you still want me to call you that. It is not my business to advise in these things. I am not even a Cuban."

"Padre, we are trying this time not to bring more conflict. This time we need to convince everybody. Everybody can have their say."

"Well, Cubano, it seems to me a good idea to let people speak. Some will choose to listen, but the listener must be willing. They must be sincere."

"I have no doubt, Padre, about our aims. We are sincere. It's just the means that is concerning me."

I turned to Haydée. "What do you think? Do you know these people your brother-in law, Cubano, speaks of?"

"They are with us, Padre Mateo. They are trying something different; it's being done together with others. People who think differently from us, some of them. But we respect each other. I know when we talked on the Pinar trip I wanted to tell you something but I hadn't the courage, not then. I just told you the stuff you expect me to say. I am sorry I have withheld the truth. But that group who came for me; you know, the false dissidents. It made me confident that I was not marked out already as someone to watch. They came to me because they saw me as the innocent wife. That gave me hope, because I had deceived them. But I'm sorry I deceived you as well. That is how we live here. Not even today, not even here with churchmen, can I tell you any more. I want you to know why we have done this. We are doing it for Héctor; of course we are. But you met Sam, didn't you? It's for him as well. We've had our lives. It's our generation that made Cuba. In any case send up a prayer for us, Father Mateo."

They left, and I returned to find all the prawns eaten. Oh well. And Clara came in again. "Padre Mateo, you are in demand today. A man called Contreras called. He said he was in the government, I think. He just said he wanted to leave a message. He said it was about some friend of yours, but he had no idea where the lady was that you asked about."

The bishops looked at each other. Maybe they were shocked. Maybe they were impressed. Who was this woman? "You missed some excellent prawns, Mateo. I hope it was worth it."

I was happy in spite of the prawns. It was good that Contreras had shown himself to be serious. I respected that and was comforted that the government didn't know everything about Haydée.

Yoel

It was a relief to get away from the Sunday afternoon; a Sunday going nowhere apart from more whines from Abel about why our family was to blame for his separation from Yamelis.

Mid-afternoon and Havana was in siesta. I dropped the kids off at a friend's and went to see Chino. Someone somewhere in this city must have been busy, but Chino was passing the time in the kitchen roasting his mani. "Moncada is a great time to sell this stuff. There are lots of us mani people around, Yoel, but I play a little music as well. That goes down well. Last Moncada I made four hundred pesos. Bought me a new a string for the guitar. Oscar here seems to be getting nervous, but I told him to trust you."

Oscar looked better than before. I could see how he was the best at what he did. He stood up, greeted me, looked me in the eyes, and gave me a high-five that nearly took my wrist off. He seemed taller too than I remembered him.

"Well, Mr. Torpedo, I have good news for you. We leave for the cayos late on Monday, you know, after all the Moncada party is over. Most of the police will be drunk. But in any case the bread van has to make deliveries to the new hotels. I've got plenty of stale cardboard we can fill it up with. It will be fine."

Oscar didn't reply but made what seemed like a prepared statement. "Chino told me you are a good man. That pleases me because I am used to careful preparation. Running, lifting, punching regimes. Repetition always. Nothing left to chance. Is the boatman the best at what he does? Is he certain to be there? I have seen these things before where no one is prepared. All they want is the money. We must anticipate all the problems."

"This is one thing I know. I met him personally. He didn't know it was me, so I made extra sure we would not be traced. I am a professional, my friend."

"That is my dream as well," said Oscar firmly. "To be called a professional so I can support my family on what I do best."

"The money is all arranged. That guy in Orlando really wants you. You will be given free lodging for three months, all the trainers you need, and a first fight. Let's hope you win, but the rest is up to you."

Oscar smiled. But then his eyes narrowed and he took a deep breath. "What about the kids? They are all I have. Can they come as well within a few weeks?"

"Oscar, no one has mentioned any kids. This is strictly a no-kids run. They cost just as much and are twice the trouble." I could see he was troubled. "Hey amigo, I have kids too, but just think that these things take time. The first steps are the big ones. It could take time to get them over, but you will have money, and no one is going to tell you how to spend it. Who knows where we'll all be in five years? So amigo, the future is bright. Just be ready when I come to get you. I don't know when there will be another chance."

Chino came out from the kitchen, wiping his hands. "Young men making plans. Oh well, one day you'll both settle down."

Felipe

Fathers who become old men could explain it all themselves, but young men who die leave you to figure it out. So Sunday morning I went for a walk, knowing that Mama hated to have to talk over arguments. She usually would just move to her chair, rock a little more, and forget. I knew when I returned it would be as usual. It was best to give her time.

I had Papa's book with me. It was something real. I could
carry it with me. Apart from my vaccines documents, my wallet,
and my ID it was probably the only thing I owned. I took it on
a walk we had made before Papa was arrested. I realized now
that it was Papa being a father, spending time with me, teaching
me. He wanted to show me Old Havana on foot, he said. I was
strong enough to walk all the way, he said. That made me feel
good. I came to a square outside the Capitanes, and I found
the exact place where we sat and talked. I had never been in
the big building that they said was the residence of the Spanish
governor. Papa took me over to show me close up. He said it was
about where our forefathers had come from, across the ocean to
live in Cuba. I said to him that it seemed like something out of a
Stone Age book, it was so old. That was because we had just done
the Stone Age in school, and I guess I tried to impress Papa. Papa
told me he knew a guard there and he used to go in and chat at
night to drink some rum together. Papa said it was the best place
he had ever seen. Maybe Papa was trying to impress me.

I found the bench we had sat on and opened the book. Papa
was right to have written it, because it was all we had to keep.
The words were sleeping in my head but they woke up that
Sunday morning. After the names of people to count on, Papa
had started on his four pages called simply "my life." "Felipe,
you were my gift from God. I have left something that is a
treasure. I gave love to Mama, which made me proud, but then
I couldn't give anymore. Mama, of course, knows a lot, and she
saw that sadly what I did in my life mattered more than my love
for her. That is the terrible confession you make to your wife
when you are in jail. I was guilty as I was charged. I was guilty
as a man who betrayed his wife for something else. At least I was
guilty for something, not someone. I never loved anyone else but
Mama. But there is something else even worse that I did. I know
I betrayed you and Rafa. And because Rafa never knew me as a
father I betrayed you more than Rafa.

"Today they are taking me to Santiago, to the Boniato. It is for a punishment so I cannot receive more visits. I will not tell you why I am to be punished. I think I have lost all sense of right and wrong. They told me I will be in a truck for fifteen hours with three murderers. That was just to frighten me, I think. But I am not frightened. If they allow me any paper, I will start a new book in Santiago. But this is the end of this book. I think it will open a new chapter."

Vladimir

Carlos and computers and brains. So far, so good. But I wanted to talk to some of them because I knew there were plenty who thought they were good enough to play big boys' games. I needed to find out if they were smarter than the last lot. Computers mean power but need the brains and determination to make them count; people who are ingenious, unemotional, and quick like the machines they control. Now I had knowledge of those who were doing the unexpected. I had a big card to play, so maybe Carlos would be interested to hear that I knew about Saluki.

Of course I didn't know Carlos's phone number or where he lived. But I did know his e-mail account. It was an easy matter to send him an e-mail using the Saluki address. The problem was whether Carlos would be checking his e-mails. So I looked further on the CBM server. There were one or two feeble attempts at security encryption, and the site with the supposed emergency numbers at CBM didn't show anything at all. Who was supposed to be paid as a Web site manager? I must remember to ask Felipe. Maybe these guys were not as smart as they thought they were. But there was a guard's number whom I imagined would be in a hut smoking and watching TV. I called just in case anyone picked up. He did. "I need to contact the director, Carlos Istúriz. It's an emergency. I'm phoning from state security."

"Look, whoever this is, Dr. Istúriz does not like being disturbed. It's the weekend."

"Compañero, I think this decision is a little out of your league to make. If you want to stay in your air-conditioned box I suggest you give me his cell number. His phone belongs to the state. It is against the law to conceal that information."

So it was as easy as that. And Carlos answered quickly. I could hear children laughing in the background, but Carlos wasn't laughing. He said he needed to move away from the crowd. "Who is this speaking?"

"I know about Saluki; that is all I will say. I am not interested in betraying you. I give you my word. But we should talk. Where can we meet?"

There was a long pause. The five-star brain was thinking. "I think it's best near the Club Havana. It's Sunday and there are hundreds around; you know, the baseball field on the corner of Quinta. In an hour."

Víctor

Max stopped on his way back to Santiago. A pretty dumb thing I would say to drive all that way. I'd rather sit back in a plane for a couple of hours. Max would have none of it. "I'd always trust German over Soviet engineering. Think rationally, Víctor. Those planes make it on rubber bands. I wouldn't trust them to carry my dogs." He had an old BMW that he had bought off some German hotel manager, and it still carried some German beer stickers and a German flag on the back windscreen. No one asked Max how he got the authorization.

"Max, that is no car for a Cuban patriot. Anyone would think you were going around picking up sixteen-year-old girls."

"I'll be getting rid of it soon; you know, when all this is done. Víctor, you have to concentrate now. If we keep our nerve, this will be successful. Santiago starts three hours after Havana.

That is now fixed. Once the equipment is in place, it will take a few more hours to deliver."

"Max, fine, fine. But what has everyone got in mind for the day after? This is all great fun, like fighting in Africa, but you knew you could leave from there and come back home. This country is our home. We make our beds; we lie on them."

"Víctor, my friend, you have always listened well and learned. You have played your part in the preparation. I cannot tell you everything about what will happen after all this. We have to keep the discipline." He leaned over and tapped me on the shoulder.

This was the old Max, arrogant—leave me alone; I know best. It was Max being impatient and patronizing. Poor old Víctor. He's loyal to anything he's told about. Let him go back to his CDR and the complaints about leaking roofs, too much dog shit in the park. Max got out the keys to the BMW.

"Okay, I understand, Max. I'm not one of the leaders. Those in the CDRs never have been. Well, just look around you my friend. Don't you think all this could be chaos in a few days? People in the streets, burning shops, destroying food and what little medicines we have. What would I tell Félix, Freddy, and Frank? Oh I'm sorry, boys. I don't believe in one revolution anymore. I used to, but now we need another one. I don't know what I'll do about that, because I chose the letter that begins your names. That's up to you."

Max opened the car and looked angry. It was the low voice of the Pinar guerrilla who distrusted the dumb city folk of Cerro. "Stop all this emotion, Víctor. No one ever made anything worthwhile without upsetting others. Your kids' names? Just the sort of comment I'd expect from a sentimental beer swiller. Forget it. The weak will whine, the strong will triumph, and the rest will follow. I never met a Cuban who wouldn't talk and whine. But when it comes to action there are few of us who count. Cubans are strong when they see the justice of what they do. Oh, and that idiot Manuel, who kept giving you those messages; stay away from him. Or he'll end up like the colonel in Manzanillo."

With that Max bent his gray head and quickly got into the BMW, slammed the door, and left. I never expected an "I'll call you" or a "Don't worry." Max despised all that. He was right.

Mateo

I didn't have a clue what to do. You know, life suddenly gives you a shaft of light that breaks through the mist. Would there be a kingfisher? And what do you do if there wasn't? Do you run fast to see if the mist lifts entirely, or do you sit and wait? Do you ask Clara if there is anything else for lunch? Do you go for a walk? Do you carry on with your packing and check that you have received all your clothes back from the dry cleaners? There was no point in calling Rodrigo again in Santiago. There would be only one day after Moncada to tie it all up.

I got a strong message that what Haydée and Cubano were doing was to use me for guidance. There were things in life that people can't decide by themselves. But once their minds get reassurance then they are able to do anything. This is one thing our Lord's life teaches. And then there is no other path to take. I was taught that the best way of behaving was to pray. You needed some moments of silence. And the way forward would be clear. It would open up and the road would be walked and run with total conviction. There would be no turning back.

I won't embarrass you in this story by writing what I prayed, but I felt satisfied. Should I remain on the sidelines? Or was there something more I should do? I had done what Haydée had asked. I apologized to the bishop for missing the lunch. At least they would be pleased to see me go.

Vladimir

Carlos was a professional. I could see he was determined to show me he was calm. He was sitting on a bench under a caoba, cleaning his glasses and watching a couple of kids throwing an old baseball.

"How did you know who I was? I'm not exactly a rock star."

I thought the guy had some class. He smiled at the thought of comparing himself to a rock star. Felipe had judged him right. Carlos, just the sort of man who would be making plans for himself.

"Well, Compañero Director, let's just say I have a lot of connections. I don't mean I have a lot of friends. But I know where to look when I need to know something."

"We have made some mistakes, I know. But not everyone is as observant as you. The group at Saluki has proved its strength; we have done nothing illegal, and the actions we have planned will go ahead."

"Well, I assume you know my interest in meeting you. It is not to tell the authorities, as I could have done that already."

"Well, amigo, I suppose you will not tell me your real name and that you are asking for some money."

"Wrong, again, Señor Director. No one does important things for money in Cuba. Let's face it; there's not a lot to spend it on! Those who ask usually want some small amounts to survive. In any case I have enough from, let me say, my business activities."

"So what is it? I am curious." He put on his spectacles and looked at me, hoping to learn.

"First, I am curious as well. What makes a brilliant, respected scientist like you get involved in some freelance dealings like this? You have everything here. You have worked your way to the top. You talk with the Council of State. You travel. You have a nice car. You get to decide big issues of science. It's your system, isn't it?"

"Well, since you want some philosophy lessons, I'm happy to talk. I just think that what we have here could be so much better if the ideas we Cubans have were debated. I mean all of us Cubans; you know, the stupid and the dangerous, the naïve and profound. If all of us could talk to foreigners about business in a language they understand. If we could build our lives without the bureaucracy."

I could see he was testing me out. "That doesn't sound a reason to throw away everything."

"We don't have to. But we lose so many ideas. The brightest fish swim away from Cuba. The beautiful birds feel they are in a cage. In the past they had some good ideas." And Istúriz pointed in the vague direction of Revolution Square. "It's obvious that no one has a monopoly on good ideas. The system is safe because it is controlled, but no one wants to stay in a child's crib forever. We all have the right to make mistakes and learn, not just the government."

"I'm getting a little closer to understanding, Director Istúriz. But here if you make a mistake it costs you a lot. It costs you everything."

"Amigo, that's exactly it; we never really experiment. You know, for a scientist we have no laboratory for ideas. We have our brains pounding, but no one listens; not because they are wrong, but because they are afraid. Our experiments are supposed to produce the answer they want, and if they don't they are scrapped. They are afraid to question anything. No one ever got promoted in Cuba for showing flair, the boldness to think."

"Well, this is Sunday, and I'm sure some of your activities are about to happen. The reason I have come to meet you is to make a proposal. I don't want money, but I would like to come in with you. You know, I would like to be part of this plan."

Carlos laughed, and his face seemed to regain some color. He wiped his glasses very quickly. "I met you five minutes ago. You have read a few e-mails from Saluki. I believe you are not from state security. But you could easily come in and steal our ideas, ruin everything. How can you contribute apart from stopping us? The people we have are tried and disciplined. We have been working for months."

"I have worked on computers for over ten years. I know the servers here. I know the MININT trackers, a few young people. All that is valuable. Look, I want to do something, to be part of it. And in any case what's all this about stealing ideas I thought we were supposed to share? You know you are supposed to be building a better Cuba."

"Okay, whatever your name is. I'll come back to you with an answer this evening. How does that sound?"

"I'm impressed with you, Dr. Istúriz. But I will be even more impressed if you keep your word. That really would be exceptional."

CHAPTER 22

Felipe

It wasn't a day for going home. Sunday was usually for Rafa. That was how we started the volleyball. Every Sunday afternoon. He never let me forget. But I had crossed the line. I knew that if I didn't get some things straight now there was never a better chance. I had to see Isaac. This time he was waiting for me.

"I knew you would come back, but not this soon," Isaac said. "This time we can talk. Forget everything you ever knew. Did you know that Isaac means laughter in Hebrew? I can't say everything we did was laughing, but your papa would make us roar until we cried. You know that voice; he could imitate anyone you named—all the speeches of the politicians. He was optimistic about everything. Even the sugar harvests in those days! He was so excited that day you arrived; you know, I was a doctor in the rural clinics. All of us medical people, it was the first time the government had ever bothered to look after the cane cutters. I liked it. Not much supervision, time to chat, pretty girls who loved my tales of the big city, university; life was good. People were so happy to have these clinics, and for them it was like a new circus in town. Everyone loved us, so we were given everything we wanted. I mean everything."

Isaac redirected the fan onto his yellow t-shirt. "You know, Triana would like to be alive today. He would like to feel young again."

Those were the sort of words I needed to hear. Some bright words from an old man who lived liked an animal, even compared to Jalisco; this old man with the wrinkles of optimism, a smile that had confidence, a belief that one day no one would notice the wrinkles anymore.

"I don't know you, Isaac. I know nothing about you. But you spent more time with Papa than I did. You said you were with him the day I was born. How was that?"

"Oh, mi hijo Felipe, my specialty is obstetrics. I was always on call, day and night. It was 3:30 in the morning. Yes, I remember because I was the guy who delivered you. I brought you into this mess. You have a lot to blame me for."

"Isaac, if you were so close twenty-seven years ago, how did we ever lose you? Why did it take a family crisis for you to come back?"

"It wasn't an accident, you know. Triana was not the best friend to have or to be seen with if you wanted a quiet life. Your dad was a magnet for anyone looking for a local leader out in Pinar. He had no education, but he could do everything. He was the best at cutting cane, the best at singing, the best looking, the best company any Cuban could want."

"Do you know that photo of him smiling?"

"Of course I do," said Isaac. "I can remember the joke he told us as it was being taken."

"So why if you liked him so much did all this end?"

"It was a deal I had to make, Felipe. That was how the state worked. They didn't just jail everyone, you know. So they would say to people, 'Stay out of trouble or you'll never be a doctor again.' It was the same with old Chino, you know, the guitar player. He was told to stay away, and I'm not sure what exactly he did. It was sad, but it wasn't long before your dad had his first spell in jail."

"That was in Pinar?"

"Yes. It was a short spell, maybe just a few months. They did that. He overstepped the mark in what he said and because he started organizing. You were just a baby. But Triana was clever in jail. He admitted mistakes and took the reeducation, He was very clever, you know. Not educated like he had passed exams, but he had the instincts of a politician. In reality, he never intended to change.

"But I kept my deal. I'll be honest about that. They sent me to Africa after they had promised me a hospital to run, which was my dream; you know, down in Old Havana. That would have been so satisfying."

"So, Isaac, you played the game, but why didn't that happen? I think sometimes they forgive. That's what my boss at the CBM told me."

"Well, somehow it went wrong for me, Felipe." Isaac walked over to an old cupboard with a bent coat hanger as a lever. "Look, this is what I have in this tin. I'm not trying to get your sympathy. That's it. I am a doctor, but I can't do anything here. I sit here. It's better than jail. I have my buddies, you know, like the ones in the rock band. It's no good just looking back."

I looked at this man with the name meaning laughter. "You said Papa would have been excited today. He would have wanted to be alive. What do you mean?"

"Well, Felipe, I owe it to Triana to tell you something. It's all these years ago since that hostage stuff, and I guess there are times when the state security just get bored with looking at us. We have been off the radar for so long. In any case what is being planned is not a revolution; no tanks, no violence, no firing squads. We are perhaps naïve, but for a doctor a different way is always better if it cures the patient."

"So Vladimir is right."

"I don't think Vladimir has a clue, Felipe. Vladimir is looking for a deal for himself. Fine, but there's been too much of that. He's a bright kid, but he wants to be on the right side when the music stops. He doesn't seem to care which music or which side. Come with me, Felipe. I want to show you something."

"Isaac, I'm sorry it's taken so long. Show me. But I see you have a phone. Could I just call home? My little brother may be expecting me." I called Rafa. The phone was working. He said he was bored. I said I was sorry I was late for volleyball. I said I would try to get back later.

Mateo

I watched TV that Sunday afternoon. There were still a couple of hours before the final Mass. It sounds odd for a priest on a Sunday. But it was the best thing I could think of for my feelings. I wanted to leave, I think, because things were getting difficult. I was ashamed to be watching TV, but it was safe. It wasn't my job to say goodbyes, because that was all about me. The new priest would come in and do the job. He would be fine, and he would be the man who dealt with the spiritual needs of Cubans. I would move on in my career. That was how the bishop liked it. So all I had to do was get through the day.

The baseball game on TV was finishing. I had grown to like some baseball. Maybe that confirmed me as having some Cuban blood. But this was not a close game. The crowds were leaving the stadium, as there was a fourteen run lead. The commentators were talking about what they would be doing for the holiday. It was winding down to the political report entitled "Moncada, Our Inspiration."

I stayed, watching. Grainy black-and-white footage; an enormous barracks and fort. The dead bodies; the attackers and the defenders. Tortured captives; a valiant band outnumbered ten to one. Crashed cars, bullet holes, destruction. The drama of rebels. Trials, prison, and the beginning of something new.

Fast forward to the scene of today in color. Batista had covered up the bullet holes on the barracks, but they were put back to show how the people triumphed.

The official commentator sounded proud. He talked of the writings smuggled from jail, the defiant speeches. July 26 will live forever.

The cameras returned to the studio where there were a number of experts who were to debate the meaning of Moncada for the current generation of Cuban youth. "First we have Compañero Fausto Gómez, deputy editor of *Granma*, and Dr. Carlos Istúriz, director of the Molecular Biology Center. Our final member of the panel is Minister Ricardo Contreras."

I guess you have been in a place too long when you know all the people on the TV panel.

"Minister Contreras, perhaps you would remind us all of the significance of Moncada to today's Cuba. Two-thirds of Cubans were not born at the time of that courageous revolutionary act. What does it mean to them?"

"Well, thank you for the opportunity. I think the young people we have now in Cuba are exceptionally mature. They have seen what has been built through this famous struggle. We have never surrendered to the forces that would destroy us. Young people can see that they should be proud of Moncada even if they think of it as deep in our history. There is much still to do. I would like to describe some of the main tasks that the Revolution has set itself for next year. The first ..."

At that moment my television picture disappeared. I immediately thought it was a power cut. More nostalgia for Havana. Just my luck on my last chance to watch the TV. But there was no kicking in of the generator, and the ceiling fan purred as fast as ever. There was a TV in the main seminary meeting room. I went upstairs and turned it on. Just the same.

I went outside, and I wasn't the first. Havana had no television on a Sunday afternoon. Omar, the gardener of the seminary, was there cursing. I remember his very original expletives. "Hey Padre, you can't even depend on TV anymore. Did you see that big blowup? They'll be racing to put it right by the parade tomorrow. The big guys will be close to blowing up themselves. I bet it's all that Soviet equipment. I tell you we should have got into bed with the Japanese, clever people who can make things. I always said that, Padre."

An Irish nun who lived at the end of the street had come out with the group of kids she had with her. "Mateo, we were watching the cartoons. It was only to fill in a few minutes before the Mass. We're just checking, but I guess we'll sing some songs now."

Laura

It was a signal that Felipe didn't call. It had happened once before, but not on a Sunday. I called his home, but they said he'd gone walking. I talked to Rafa, who seemed very down. At least the Trianas had the phone working.

The architecture professors got a call from the Tropicana. I knew they were on the waiting list for tickets for that evening. One hundred dollars each, but they were ecstatic. A group had fallen sick and couldn't go, so a dozen tickets had come free. I guess they were not only interested in the architecture of buildings. We had done the Capitolio and the museum of the Revolution. We took them to the club in Marianao. Joaquim at the Tropicana would look after them for the rest of the evening.

I called around at Jalisco. Felipe's mother was sitting on her rocking chair at the window. The fan was making so much noise she didn't hear me come in. I went up to her and saw she was dozing. I tapped her on the shoulder.

"Oh my dear. Have you made the wedding dress? It will be such a wonderful day for all the family. Just like we planned. You will be perfect for each other."

I smiled. Felipe told me about her dreams in her rocking chair. "It's okay, Sra. Triana. It's nice to have dreams. Sometimes I do as well. I wanted to catch up with Felipe. He's been a bit down lately. I think he's become kind of distracted by some things."

"I think you're right, chica. I think Felipe is a sensitive boy, Laura. He was always like that. That Rafa in there. He gets on with his life. He's a leader; no one would bully him. He listens to people but makes his own mind up. Felipe, he's always thinking about what is behind everything. But once he makes up his mind he is very stubborn, and you can't do anything, I'm afraid. Like today; there's nothing that will change his plans. We'll just have to wait until he comes back to Jalisco."

She wiped her brow on her t-shirt and came over to a bench near the door. "This place here used to be full of people; you know, Alberto, Pepe, Donna, Luis, Pepe's girlfriends. Even Pepe's girlfriends' husbands. Yes, Alberto's girlfriends as well. That was how we lived. It didn't matter who came. Our kids preferred the space outside, and Felipe never brought friends home. He helped Rafa's friends. But I don't know what it was. Felipe said he preferred the walks on the Malecón. Isn't that where you met him too?"

"Felipe was with Vladimir on the Malecón, I think. They were talking to some girls and pretending to be tourists, not Cubans. I guess they were pretty good at it. Then they tried it on my group of tourists, who were from Malaysia.. They started talking about where they lived. I can't remember where they pretended. They talked about Malaga or something but said they had emigrated to Cuba. They were funny; they appeared like they had done it before. I knew they were Cubans, but they could see I was enjoying the joke. The Malaysians then tried to speak Spanish, and that was funny. Felipe noticed me and winked. Then he winked again. That was it."

"Oh well, he told me it was the Malecón. That was where he met his friends. He talked of the smell as fresh and then as a young boy he started to call it sexy. He thought it was a new cool word. 'Everyone is equal on the Malecón,' he said."

I could see this was going to go on a while. "Obviously Felipe isn't here now. Is he coming home today?"

"Oh, Laurita, if Felipe comes back it won't be the same anyway. I think he has learned too much about his father. It's something I knew he would find out one day. But he's seen through the window now. He will never stay off the subject of his father again. It's like he's trying to understand how it all fits in with his life. For me it was a piece I lost. I knew I would never find it again."

Sra. Triana now had tears, not sweat, on her face.

"Laura, mi amor, I told Felipe that he could do whatever he wanted. But it should be for him. Live time in the present. Always reliving the past, that's bad. You get into trouble with these big thoughts."

I didn't plan on saying anything more. Then I saw that the television was blacked out but the fan was still working. "I'm afraid your TV seems to have a problem. I'm sure you'll want to watch the show on Moncada tomorrow. We have a spare TV in our basement. I'll get someone to drop it over."

"Laura, you are so kind. That would be such a wonderful thing."

Felipe

Isaac was fit and determined. He was walking fast, too fast for me to keep up. "What's the hurry, Isaac? This is Sunday in Havana. Where are we going?"

"Oh, you need to listen and learn. Havana plays by its rules. The camello we need passed twenty minutes ago. I saw the fumes of diesel from the houses across the roofs in Compostela. That was early. They're all coming through early today, because the usual drivers have the day off tomorrow. The camellos are all on parade duty."

Isaac, smiling all the way, turned the corner, and the guagua, one of the last camellos still on the streets, was there with the line of people waiting. "I trust these guys," said Isaac. "That and my own feet. Let's enjoy the company of real Cubans, my friend."

The line doubled before we reached the bus as travelers came out from alleys, behind the street stalls, and from inside doorways. I couldn't stand the camellos, heads forced up for air, bodies battered to cram the last person in. Look after yourself and get the space with the fresh air, because the weakest had to smell the worst.

"A camello? Are you sure, Isaac? I think I'd rather walk."

"No, Felipe, it's time to insist. Today is your last chance to understand some things. It's the education your father wanted you to have. It's time for you to see how we survived, the pride we had, and why at my age I walk so fast. The young today despise us. I know that from hearing the kids in the barrio. They think they know it all with their Chicago Bulls, Boston Red Sox. We're Cuban, Felipe, and this camello is what we built. Revolutionaries need to have muscles as well as brains. Just like doctors."

Tourism in my own city. Being taught about my home by the guy who delivered me into the world. Boarding a camello was an art I knew. You got in just before the animal left. There were usually no doors. The Chiclets stuck to your feet, and with a last shove you could keep a centimeter between you and your sweating companions. Well, this time, maybe with the holiday, cologne seemed as common as sweat. Cubans heading off home, ready for a party, back to their abuelos, the big weekend of whatever you wanted to make it.

I stood next to a tall woman with skin like parchment and white hair. Isaac was the most cunning. He got in, didn't like his position, and then pretended he'd forgotten something. He shouted to the driver to wait, got out, went around the back of the bus, and reentered where there was a gap.

"Another little triumph, Felipe. That makes me feel good. Now we can go."

We got off close to Juan Delgado in La Vibora, a quiet place where the houses were large and old.

"Another reason for you to see where we used to hang out, Triana and me. It was this house here, Felipe," Isaac said. We were opposite a two-story gray concrete house right on the street, which had a staircase alongside which led nowhere. It had two windows on each floor. It looked as if it had been built in a hurry. "We had never used it before. It belonged to someone's aunt, who liked having people around. So we met there. We were naïve, I guess. We had some discussions about who would do what. It wasn't really anything special. There were a lot of groups, but I'd never seen most of them before."

"Groups of what?"

"Oh, they were beginning to be called dissidents. Most of the groups there didn't even have a name. They were a mixture of everyone who would raise their voice in the barrio. Every group you could think of; it was very Cuban. Most of them were from Havana. But the unusual thing was that some of them had come in from outside. Anyway, it should have been exciting. But it was a mess, you know. I began to feel ashamed and wished I'd gone to a bar or something. These people were just talking about themselves, monologues in what was supposed to be a dramatic conversation. They were not politicians, any of them. Yes, they were well-meaning people who wanted to do things. But they all said they had the answer and everyone else should listen. That was one problem. The other was if you want people to do things you need to bring a vision. That you were not just about talking or writing some meaningless documents that no one could be bothered to read. You need to convince everyone that people can count, that they can make a difference."

"So it was a mess. What's new here, Isaac? I could have taken you to my laboratory as well. It's a *fracaso* pretty much all the time."

"Well, it wasn't quite like that, amigo. See that window up there on the left?" I looked up and saw a shutter. "You see, Triana walked over to that window. I could tell he was angry and frustrated. We had been there all night and the dawn was breaking. He just got up in the middle of someone else's monologue about Cuban culture or something. He stood there, with shafts of daylight behind him. His eyes were bright; his voice was strong. And everyone stopped talking."

I thought of the photo of Papa; you know, the one we had at Jalisco that was torn.

"Wait, Isaac. There's a lot I don't know. How was Papa in Havana away from Pinar?"

"It was part of the deal. Your mother was allowed to stay in Jalisco. It used to be her abuelo's place; you knew that. But Triana had to stay in the fields. Came home once every two weeks. It was their way of keeping an eye on him so he was tracked, of course, wherever he went."

"Including to this house?"

"Felipe, you know how it works here. And so did Triana. What he did at that window - he knew it would be seen from outside. I think that's why he walked over. There was quite a group of agents outside. It was a dramatic night. I had a hunch what was going to happen, and sure enough Triana got to the point where he was announcing 'a manifesto.' I looked around the room. Everyone was focused on him. Most of them had never heard of Triana, but I saw Chino beaming with joy. His eyes were sharp and bright. He had lit up a cigar, I guess to maximize his pleasure for that moment."

"What group was Chino in?"

"He hung out with us in Pinar. His friend used to bring some of the collective's bananas in to the university twice a week. So there was usually space on the truck. In any case, Triana enjoyed his company. He liked to see his face."

Isaac took me to the end of the street where there was a derelict shack. "It was from here that the men came out who broke up the meeting. I only knew because one of our friends who was late in arriving saw them leave. It had been a planned ambush. Triana had showed that flash of leadership, you know, the flair, the risk taking. He was getting up and doing something. That was what did it. I'm absolutely sure of that."

"And what happened to Papa?"

"He was dignified. He kept talking for a while as they led him away. Just quietly; then he began talking to the agents. Trying to reason with them, saying things like 'We are all Cubans too.' He went down those back stairs. And as they led him out, he was still talking. And one of the guys who wore a black cap shouted 'mercenary' and clubbed him with what looked like a baseball bat. That was the end of him talking like that."

"That blow. It damaged his brain. He couldn't speak properly. But he could still write. I know that."

"Look, Felipe, I've thought about it a lot. They only allowed me to see him again once. Hell, that was a long trip, and I had to pull a lot of strings through the prison doctor in Boniato. It may have been something that happened in jail. But his speech was slurred and much slower. It wasn't the man who was standing up there in that window all those years ago. But I know he was still writing."

I looked at Isaac and saw that he was looking down at the earth as he spoke. He looked like an old man. I glanced again at the window and saw that the old shutter, which was half closed, was painted yellow.

"Tomorrow, Felipe, we will go to Moncada."

Vladimir

The television was blacked out for over two hours, maybe two hours and twenty minutes. I know from the timing of the e-mail I got about a Lenin high school alumni meeting after Moncada and then being distracted until I replied. The TV had come back on line with some apology that was read quickly. There had been a technical problem that had taken time to resolve. The program with Istúriz and the others discussing Moncada then resumed, but you could see that they had lost the momentum. They wanted to get it over as quickly as possible.

The moderator had orders to wind it up with a message of strength. I could tell that there would be no suggestion of a debate. Contreras took the lead.

"The technical problems have been overcome. The Revolution has shown in this small example another sign of its strength. We never hide our problems. We never hide from a challenge. We throw all our efforts into building a better, more just society. One thing we have learned from more than fifty years is that we can solve anything together. *Conciencia* for the Revolution."

The moderator turned to Istúriz, who looked surprised that he had been asked for a final comment.

"Yes, I agree with Minister Contreras. We will do it together. The Revolution has always drawn in all the talent and ideas it has needed. Tomorrow will show that again."

My phone recorded the time of the call from Istúriz. I was surprised that Istúriz called then. It must have been as soon as he got out of the studio.

"Look, can we meet, my friend? There are some things you may be able to do with us."

Istúriz chose a bar not far from the TV studios they had used in La Rampa. He was sitting and reading the new *Granma* supplement. "I have to say that our friends at *Granma* do a good job on these things. Take a look. That Fausto is a real professional; well you know what I mean."

Istúriz was more relaxed than at the baseball park. "Look, I have something in mind for you, my friend. We don't have a lot of time, but we could certainly use your expertise. Computers are important here, as you know. But we realize that the passwords rather than the machines have the power. If you can get some passwords we do not yet have that could help. We need you to get as many as possible. Your surveillance unit is one that we don't yet have within our plans. So the fact is that meeting you is an opportunity for me. But let me say, what you do is up to you. We will recognize your contribution, but we will not inform you of anything about the rest of the plans. Do we have a deal?"

I knew I had more to offer than passwords. I knew he had more to say about what was going on. "Dr. Istúriz, you seem to forget that I could do you more damage. I am not planning to do that. But the deal does not sound very attractive. First of all, what do the words 'recognize your contribution' mean? And what happened on the TV tonight? Were you involved in that?"

"Well, it is true that you could undermine a lot of things in Cuba by doing something to the TV. It is the center of calm information where everything can be controlled. So we will see. I don't think the authorities believe it was an accident. I'm not sure myself what to make of it. What is going on here in any case is maybe not what you think. If you do damage to me I think you overestimate the effect it will have. They will close Saluki, but that is not the control center. They can ask me what else I know—or do worse to me of course—but I simply don't know. So do we have a deal? I really am quite busy, my friend."

I could see that they had chosen well with Istúriz. I didn't believe even 50 percent of what he said. I was about to leave, thinking of the things that could be done quickly that evening. Then Istúriz pulled out some paper from his jacket.

"Oh there's one thing you might find useful. This code word will give you the opportunity to get into MININT files on all security operations surrounding Moncada. It would give you a few hours to tap into systems we haven't covered. You see, I know many of your MININT colleagues, and no one has done this work beyond their area. Once you're in the files you can use your skills to get some more passwords. That will be extremely useful after the events of tomorrow. By the way, they all say you're good. So I'll take their word for it. We need to show we have some good brains and that we have prepared to the greatest possible extent. And before you go what do you know of this?"

Istúriz produced another scrap of paper. "Have you ever seen a symbol like this?" It was something written on a napkin along with the letters SP with a number seven through it. "I have seen this around in the last few weeks in places where it could be dangerous. I can't find out what it's about. I'll be honest, my friend. It worries me, because you should never enter into a major enterprise with gaps in your knowledge."

CHAPTER 23

Yoel

Santa Clara was to be the assembly point. This time I needed to take the bread van. There was a problem about where to get people together, as the police were watching places in Havana and Cárdenas. So I needed to check on an alternative that César had found.

I called around to see Abel, who was fussing as usual that everything was going wrong. He had lost a candidate from baseball who had been persuaded by his mother to wait even though the money was there. Abel said there might be a clown whom he had met at his kids' birthday party. One of the problems was that the guy turned out to be a doctor as well. There was a guy who dreamed of being a farmer in Florida and couldn't get any land. But then someone gave him twenty hectares over in Holguin and an old tractor that needed doing up. He was happy again for a while. It might not matter. In any case they mostly reapplied, because the money was usually not the issue.

"Abel, I'll check with César. He's said there's been a lot of roundups in Santa Clara, so the boat traffic is picking up. It's all last-minute stuff, but he has five certainties, and there's a married couple from Matanzas. He's a magician and has been promised a job in a Las Vegas casino. Lucky bastard, but I wouldn't bet on him making it." That brother of mine never got any joke. I left him to rearrange his beloved highlighters.

So I had to get Oscar to Santa Clara. I picked him up from Chino's place. He was standing outside with his bag, which wasn't exactly intelligent. "Just remember, Oscar, that you need to use your brains all the time now, not just in the ring. This is the most important round of your life."

The kid was quiet until we got to the carretera. Then suddenly he said out of the blue. "I could never stand Havana; that's why I was waiting outside. Just leaving that place is half the journey. Everyone we met in *boxeo* treated Havana as the center of the universe, you know. Big plazas, big gyms, big statues. We were kids who knew nothing except that we had biceps and we could move. I never wanted to live here.

"I liked the feeling of a rough gym. You know, over in Las Tunas. What we did was brutal, physical, no excuses, real. Same weight, no help. Boxing is honest, you know. Just honest. We got our rewards, but all this stuff of parades, flag waving, millions standing around chanting and clapping—that's for Havana. Thank you, Yoel, for taking me out. And I promise that I will use my brains."

We got to Santa Clara, but Oscar didn't say anymore. I was stopped once by the police near Guanabacoa. César had thought of that. He had given me a permit for bread supplies to the Villa Clara stadium Augusto Sandino.

I saw that Oscar's hands were sticky and his forehead had beads of sweat, which began dripping to the floor. It didn't seem to bother him as he let them drop. César was standing outside a cinema, knowing that there would be crowds milling around. I parked the van opposite, and he saw us straight away. He walked slowly to his motorbike and drove off along Marta Abreu in the direction of the Che Mausoleum. The streets were full of the usual sellers, mani, peanut candy, all ready for the celebrations. César veered off to the left and climbed a hill. At the top of the road was a kids' playground. Behind it was a single-story building with rocking chairs on a small veranda. A large man was sitting on a couch watching the TV.

César didn't introduce us. The man looked seriously angry. "Whole damn TV just went off for two hours. Power was fine. Guess a load of fat cats in Havana will be looking for other employment."

"Oh yeah," said César. "Did you know that, Abel?'

It was good that César was playing along with the Abel thing. I nodded and waved Oscar in.

I was impatient. "Look, César, the TV is okay now; that's what matters. Cuba will be able to survive another day. Let's get this over with. I don't have time to watch that damn box; I have to get back to Havana. Where should Oscar go?"

"Through the back there's a room with no windows, but we put in an AC. They have to stay in there. Tomi here never leaves, and by the way we need your van for an operation tonight."

"Come on, César. How do you mean tonight? I can't just leave a Havana-registered van lying around in some corner of Santa Clara. You have a bike, and I'll bring the van back tomorrow. The date is July 27, right?"

"There's no change to that," said César. "But we need the van. Don't blame me. We just got a message from Sergio that the boat is coming in on another run tonight. It has no people on board, but it's carrying something they want to deliver. So that's part of the deal. They need a van to deliver it, not a lousy motorbike that hasn't seen a proper service since the Russians invaded Czechoslovakia. Take it or leave it, Abel."

It occurred to me that perhaps this was why César had come to us in the first place. I knew how Abel liked to brag about the van we used. Perfect cover, he said. "Okay, César. Hopefully we'll make enough money to buy plenty of bread vans. I love Santa Clara, but it wasn't my idea to spend the night here. I think I could do better things with my life."

"Take my bike if you like, Abel. I guess there will be lots of bikes with strange plates coming into Havana. You'll be fine."

It was too late to start arguing. Abel would be even more gloomy when he realized that there was another operation that could go wrong. He never told me who got him into this whole thing. If I knew, I probably wouldn't be impressed. Bill the American boatman seemed a professional, but he was now in it for more than just a quick trip in and out. Double the risk.

Mateo

Felipe came around to the seminary just as the streets were emptying and people returned to watch the TV. The storm had been dramatic, but the TV blackout had happened before. Felipe looked pretty battered, as though he been through everything without shelter. He was distracted and looked shabby, strange for a man who always cared about his appearance. I didn't see the boredom that I had seen before, and his eyes were darting in different directions.

"I need to walk and talk. Mateo. I've got to keep moving. Look, I'm sorry I called you a non-Cuban, Mateo. Maybe we need to get more ideas from outside. I kind of feel like an outsider myself."

We slipped out of the back door of the seminary to avoid more long farewell conversations, emotional goodbyes. But the gardener Omar was leaving as well. "Hey, boss, have a great Moncada and whatever comes after that. We'll miss you. Buen viaje."

I returned the good wishes, and then Omar pulled me away from Felipe. "Oh Padre, if you are looking to get rid of anything you don't need, I'd be happy to look after it for you. I'm sure you must be very busy with all your plans. Soap, electrics, you know how life is. I'd be happy to pay you, of course. It's just difficult to come by some things."

"Of course, Omar. The day after Moncada my life will change. So you are welcome to have what's left. I will put them in a bag and leave them in the kitchen."

Felipe walked ahead, striding out like an impatient puppy. Usually he was respectful, walking with me, pushing conversation. He was walking ahead now on his own, saying things to no one. I couldn't hear everything, but he said one thing so often he made me listen.

"I've heard so many lies that I don't even know what's true."

We reached the Malecón, and he was ready to talk or rather unload his mind. "You are just like the communists, all of you in the church. You talk mumbo jumbo. You pretend to be special. You say you are the only ones with the truth. You are just like the PC. Either accept everything or you're out. There's no halfway. Tell the people to pray. That will keep them quiet for another week."

"Felipe, I know we're not perfect, but that seems a little hard." Felipe was not done. "Mateo, you're a visitor here. You're coming from somewhere, and you're going on to somewhere. Where *we* come from, where we're going, it's all the same."

The wind had warned us, and the waves confirmed the warning. It was not a day when the Malecón invited visitors. The potholes on the boulevard glistened with water, but Felipe was sure footed, relishing the challenge and splashing through to his objective—standing on the wall. I thought of telling him to be careful but realized it was useless. The police had closed the road and were waving people away. Felipe didn't notice, shouting as he vaulted onto the wall.

"Just tell me one thing, Mateo. Are you like all the rest? Did you know that Papa was a hero? A man who should be known in this country? Known because he sacrificed himself for others?"

He said something else, but a wave crashed over the wall and Felipe didn't see it. Perhaps he didn't feel it either, as he didn't flinch. The water covered him, but his expression didn't change. He swept his hair back and continued to look out to the ocean. "All this behind me is a sham. All this is rotten."

I was surprised that in the story you are reading Felipe never wrote about this visit to the Malecón. It seems he wanted to avoid recording what his true emotions were. Maybe he felt he was betraying something. Maybe he made up his mind. I thought at that hour he probably wanted the water to take him. I called out to him, "Felipe, Have some faith. Have some faith in something."

Felipe fell silent for a while. He continued to look out and was focusing on something on the horizon. "They go out there to die, because they want to live so much." Felipe was quoting from that song, but he had made the sentiment his own. I was happy to think that Felipe was still thinking rationally. "Tomorrow everything starts again. Isaac has said it's a new year, a new beginning."

I thought the wind was playing tricks with his words. "Did you say Isaac? Who is Isaac?"

Yoel

The bike ride back to Havana seemed like the road home when you sense that you are close to things you know. I was worried but calm. I enjoyed the loneliness. I forgot a lot of things. It was just as the daylight was fading that I entered Havana. I remember it because there were mosquitoes hovering all over Abel when I found him. He had jumped because he couldn't face another night. He had jumped from that old balcony, which he said a neighbor claimed belonged to him. But then Abel told me that the neighbor used to rent his e-mail password from the baseball federation. Business was business. Unfortunately Abel had landed in a pothole. It was pretty dark, so maybe his neighbors thought he had been drinking off his marriage disasters. But it wasn't the time to call the police. Not before I had checked the room. Just as well I did. I walked into the top floor. I remembered the heavy wooden boxes he had acquired somewhere—must have been used to store baseball bats. Anyway our kids would play with the rusty locks, banging them to their rhythms. It was a big room that my kids always liked. They used to pull on the branches from the tree outside, the one that overgrew the balcony. And they made toys with the sticks.

You know, there are some moments in life that you can't explain. Why should it be me left to face this after all these years? Abel was supposed to be waiting for me with some more outfielders, which is what he called them; you know, the guys in baseball who were close to the edge and running out of the stadium. I think he despised the outfielders anyway. He had always wanted to play shortstop. In any case he said there were things he wanted to put in the van, just in case. That was why I went around. It never occurred to me that Abel wouldn't be planning and prepared. The travel permits, the first aid kit, bottles of water. Even a special pouch to carry some spare dollars, just in case. Baseball always had plenty of these supplies around, and Abel liked to prepare.

Abel had left two pieces of paper, neatly folded on that box nearest the window. He didn't write a lot. But the one for Yamelis was longer. I thought it was impolite to read that. But I didn't know he really cared that much. Maybe he just couldn't express it. Mine was shorter. It was written in green highlighter.

> My brother Yoel,
> I have made a lot of mistakes. So today I have decided to do the right thing. It is right, but in all honesty there doesn't seem to be any other course. You and me, we are crooks. We are not

trusted by anyone. We were given blood by our parents, but we have decided to make money out of the blood of others. We have stopped working for anything we believe in. I am sad. I have let you down because you are my younger brother. I had a duty to help you find something honorable to do here. I think you believed in something else and not just the money. I am sad to leave you, but I can never believe that we have the right to live our lives selfishly. I am sick of the lies. I guess I should have stuck to baseball.

It is strange what occurs to you at moments like this. I saw Abel when he first went to the elite baseball school, throwing balls at me in his new cap. Man, was he proud! Then it concerned me what he had said about making money out of blood. Abel was trying to justify me but also himself. It was Abel's idea to get into the outfield. He underestimated himself, and that made me think as well.

CHAPTER 24

Monday July 26

Vladimir

I realized that Istúriz was buying me off, buying me with time. He'd given me a code word, something that might be genuine. But he had also made sure I knew he had worked out a lot about me. The conspiracy was happening, and sooner or later I would see whether Istúriz mattered in it at all.

I called Bertie's cell phone and said I was working on a lead related to one of Compedex's clients. I needed to check something in the files. No one called supervisors at 1:00 a.m. on the night before Moncada, and I knew it was a good time to get people making unusual decisions. "If it's not something new about Compedex, it's not a priority for MININT. I have plenty on my plate. You'll have to come in yourself. You know my name. Get them to set up a computer and your e-mail will get you in. It's the MINTEL building on the seventh floor."

On a busy weekend people cut corners. Carlos knew that Moncada would be the best time to cause some distractions because everyone was looking elsewhere.

I got into MINTEL as the new shift was arriving. They were due at 3:00 a.m. , and I knew they stayed until 10:00. My usual ID was okay, and the seventh floor was awash with light. Istúriz's code word got me into the stuff on Saluki, but it turned out they had mostly been sent to me already. The minutes of the board meetings were in a sub-file, code-word protected, and all had been transcribed from a bugging device in the room. Of course Istúriz knew about the bug. Many of the comments were marked "CI." There he was asking all the right leading questions just so the conspirators would commit themselves. Why didn't they just round them all up?

On the last meeting on July 23, there was a note from Dr. Carlos Istúriz: "This must be seen urgently by RC."

So Istúriz had strung me along after all. He was as smart as Felipe said. I had been led to the seventh floor of the MINTEL building in the middle of the night. I wandered to the window. I knew nothing more about Saluki, but Istúriz would get a medal for being the most devious man at Moncada. The masses were quietly assembling below in Revolution Square, a whole nation patiently filling a space, waiting. There were still no colors, no identity. There were lights from cigarettes and the headlights of a few trucks as they deposited their loads. A group started shouting and pointing as the big mural of Che was projected onto the wall opposite the Council of State steps. I opened a window. There was a low buzz of noise, almost of wonder. A few thousand cigarettes turned to see what it was all about.

Felipe

You will know by now that Moncada day started in the calendar at twenty minutes past midnight. It was wrong to call it a day, because the night before was when we first saw the choreography. The Revolution was showing its steps, and the ballet of the masses was about to begin.

I remember Mateo joking when he first arrived in Cuba. He thought it was amusing how so many people would show up for the rallies. "One thing I don't understand. Why do you all go, when you know what will happen?"

I tried to be polite. He didn't understand. "Padre Mateo, why do people go to Mass? Do they expect the priest to drop the incense? Besides, with the rallies, what else is there to do apart from get into trouble?"

Of course Moncada rallies were not the coolest thing to say you'd been to. So I, Felipe the rebel, tried to stay away. I'd been pretty successful. I hadn't been for five years or since the CBM had "suggested" that I should start attending again. I guess Rebecca had been every year since she joined. This time it was different; it was Isaac who said he wanted me to go with him. He said it could be fun.

"We will stay up all night just like I did with Triana. We will be like the Sierra revolutionaries, tough, clever, survivors. Felipe, you will stir yourself like a new revolutionary. You have to show others you are stronger than they are."

In any case Moncada sounded better than going home. I was not thinking of anyone else. I had nothing else to do. Of course you are punished for your selfishness. I have noticed that before, but it came to me in the darkness when Isaac was ahead of me walking. I saw there was an old volleyball net strung between two trees. Rafa would have been looking for me in the crowd at his game. He would now be having the best or worst Moncada ever. And I didn't know. You cannot escape your responsibilities, Felipe.

Groups of pioneers were assembling in the side streets to the square with children practicing shouting and waving flags. No one cared about the noise, even at 4:00 a.m. . There was nothing else going on, and no one had a right to be asleep. We were all walking in the same direction, heading to the same place. Isaac and I picked up our red t-shirts on the corner of Calle 15. Isaac said he was sure they could spare another two. Cuban production targets were always exceeded in revolutionary t-shirts. "There's always a new design, you know, Felipe. Every year there's a new Víctory." Isaac's eyes were bright even in the depth of the night.

Isaac slipped the t-shirt on. "You see, Felipe, I still fit into a medium. I'll make you a bet that in a few years you'll need an extra large. You and that Vladimir, you like the whisky too much."

"Close to old age and still wearing revolutionary t-shirts. It doesn't get more depressing than that, Isaac. I bet you still like all those songs—all the nostalgia of the cane fields, huh?"

The music was coming from the telegraph poles. "Querido comandante," military bands, and Lennon's "Imagine." A black woman was eating and selling bananas she had brought on her truck from Matanzas. "Just get to the square," she said. "There's water and pizza, and the best part is they say they'll illuminate the Che face. You must see it before the day breaks. It's magical. After that, it's not the same. Che is my lover; Che is my life." And she threw another banana skin on the street.

Isaac said he would scratch his nose when he saw any plain-clothes security. We passed a Red Cross van. "That's an old favorite," said Isaac, scratching furiously. He was almost running now.

Mateo

Felipe had gone off into the night. I didn't see him again. I was packing my couple of cases for my Tuesday departure when the phone at the seminary rang. It was Fausto Gómez. "My friend, I have a proposal to make for your last day in Cuba. I would be honored if you would accompany me to Moncada tomorrow. Or rather later today. It would be a fitting farewell event for your stay in our country. I'm afraid it will be an early start. We need to be in place at five. If you are interested, I'll call around for you."

Well, a priest can be flattered as well as anybody. Who would want to spend a last day in Cuba without plans? We all knew what was going to happen, but we still went, Felipe had said. "I'd be pleased to accept, Fausto. I have nothing planned. Early rising is in the blood. If I'd become a monk I would have been up by three every morning."

Yoel

I took Abel's letter and called the police. I knew that Abel would have been careful about the records. They would be buried in some baseball tournament stuff under false names. His death would be put down to one of the suicides that happen when people drink. Oh, and the fights with Yamelis, they all knew about that. The letter to her I did read, I should admit. It said nothing about betrayal and blood. It showed the good husband Abel, and that was nice.

I had to get back to Santa Clara. We would be one short for the ride, but it was always possible that César would have a reserve. The water and first-aid things would have to be found somewhere else. In any case César said he needed me to sort out something.

The roads out of Havana were a dream. Everyone was coming in for the Moncada speech. The trucks, buses, vans, everything was being checked and waved through. I had my baseball ID, and my story was that I was leaving to pick up the van, which had broken down in Santa Clara.

César was good. He had looked after Oscar well. Oscar was fed and jumping to go. Rendezvous was set for 2:00 a.m. on the twenty-seventh. I was due to spend the next day setting up an alibi for why I was out of Havana. The first thing I noticed was that the van was gone. César had moved it into a friend's garage.

"Yoel, we got the equipment. But that's not the end. Someone needs to take it to Santiago."

I said César was good, but this whole thing was becoming too big for him. Someone was pressurizing him. Money talked. There was an enormous crate of stuff in the garage. Okay, it was already in the van, but Santiago was eight hours away. Even with a good run, I wasn't in the mood to add to my tiredness. "César, I'm used to carrying boxers and bread, not carts of I don't know what."

César was tired and didn't want to talk. "Yoel, you have to take it. You can't stay here anyway. There's a cop who lives next door. This is what Bill's boat brought last night, and they won't come back tomorrow until they know it's delivered. That's the deal. These people are not amateurs. Just think about the greenbacks you'll be able to spend. Get some fancy clothes to go with your French accent."

"How did you know about the French?"

"I know plenty about you. I've checked on everything. That stupid stuff about Abel won't wash anymore anyhow. You'll just have to come clean, Yoel. We're in this together. While we're thinking of all the problems here's another. We're one short, by the way. You'd better think. Perhaps you should use that long hair of yours to get in touch with the gods."

There was no time to sleep. I had to be in Santiago by daybreak.

Laura

He was half the age of the rest of the environmentalists. They were all Italians, I think from Modena. He had come along for the trip with his father and said he sang at local opera festivals. I tried to get him to sing, but he laughed. He didn't start talking to me properly until we had a picnic at the Morro. "Don't eat on your own, señorita; we have so much food. *Comunque*, it's not very good. So it's not really generous to offer you some."

"No thank you. I've eaten."

"Then come and talk, my pretty one. These guys are boring, you know. One thing they do know. They know about Cuban girls. They talked about them all the time on the plane coming over. Just like in Modena."

I have always liked Italy. I think it is what a lot of Cubans think of as the best in the world. What we might be. It shouldn't be Spain. There's too much history there. With Russia we were never a match. America, there's the tragedy. But Italy, culture, beauty, sun. No one talks of Italy together with politics. I agree with them.

Flavio was amusing, optimistic, full of stories. It wasn't a day when I was looking for love, but there is only so long you have to decide. "I bet you're tired of Cuba. Let's get a taste of Italy." Flavio knew the Italian restaurant in the Melia hotel. Pizzas at fifteen CUCs; you know, a month's wages for me. But that made me feel better. And he insisted I didn't eat pizza.

"You can have too much pizza. That is one of the problems here. 'Truta con limone' would be good for the taste buds. You will bloom along with what you taste."

"You have been doing your homework, Flavio."

Did I think of Felipe? Well, it helped to be with someone who wasn't Cuban in a restaurant that only foreigners could afford. For most of my life we Cubans couldn't even get in. So I liked the idea of seeing it. It was like a vacation from Cuba, and I felt I deserved it. The waiters even thought I was Italian, and that was cool for once. Felipe was taking time off. And so was I.

Víctor

Okay, it goes with the job. The CDR beauty contest. I passed the test. Forty-four trucks out of forty-nine turned up for the Moncada rally. That was good, more than okay. One had broken down; one had crashed. The driver claimed that a stray dog distracted him. I told him the damn dog should have more respect for a revolutionary truck. A third no one knew about. Hilde loved this night stuff. She said it reminded her of the army. I told her you'd never get a real army guy like Max crawling around the streets at night. He would be hanging out at some military club, where the old guys would be talking about the African girls they knew in Angola. You bet. I never saw these places, but Max had mentioned once that the perks of the military were better than the party. And that was how it should be. No book-reading party pen-pusher would defend the Revolution. So the military clubs were the best. There would be nice beer, even whisky, because that's what the military is here. Always better than the political tramps like me. Real class, that Max. Could move around Cuba, Spain, Florida, making deals. Me, I had Cerro and Lucas and Lucia, and once a year my arse got kicked if things went wrong in Moncada.

Anyway, this was my deal. The poor, simple Víctor with his sons whom everyone knew, except their father. This year I would get to go to Santiago for a good party. I had even been given a plane ticket. Someone on a motorbike delivered it to the CDR. That felt good, even if it was on Max's Soviet airways. I think maybe most of the guys didn't think that Santiago would be much fun. Better to stay in Havana. After the parade in Havana the whole day there was left for drinking. Why bother staying on your best behavior in that armpit of a city, Santiago? In Santiago we would be on display; you know, the big boys up from the capital city.

At the airport I was escorted into the protocol lounge. I knew I wasn't that big, and I soon learned that some were being treated better than the CDRs. In the lounge there was a slick guy travelling who called himself an events organizer. He said he planned to spend a few days after Moncada in the Paradisus, which he said was a new hotel.

"Above my pay grade." With that I said that I needed to take a nap.

"Not sure about these damn Soviet planes. I prefer the Airbus, you know," muttered the events organizer looking out of the window. I pretended to have dozed off. There was nothing more to be done.

Felipe

Right now my image of the square is of road sweepers under driving rain, entering to clear away the debris of the people and their Moncada party. They were arriving to reclaim that massive space. I can see the grayness of the tarmac, the buildings with no color; only the red, blue, and white of the Cuban flag, limp in the rain. The tourism buses parked in rows. The tourists came out slowly, putting up their umbrellas and then scurrying into the vast space to get the best pictures of Martí's statue eighteen meters tall, the Council of State, the image of Che. You never knew when they would illuminate that image, because they liked to save it for special occasions. But most times they didn't bother. I don't know why; maybe it was to save power. The tourists would leave disappointed, staring at their guidebooks. They would complain that they had been promised that the image would be lit.

But that Moncada night in the square all was well. It was magical, just as the banana lady said. That night we were ants in the dark. At the Malecón you feel the scale of nature, of man's wish to create big spaces, spaces where there are no limits. Revolution Square was man's creation, and on that scale what could possibly stop the march of Cuba? Isaac and I turned the corner from Paseo, around the big national theater, and there was the light of Che's face projected over a full wall. That was what they knew would be the star attraction in the Plaza. That was Che, young, serious, idealistic. The light in the darkness.

The teenagers had seen Che long before us; a group of kids I recognized from Jalisco. Pedro used to say that his weed was the freshest in Cerro, so they took him in for rehab or reeducation.

He was there in charge of this group of teenagers who were now called social workers, *trabajadores sociales*. "Hi Pedro, I like the new hairstyle. You used to be coming back from the streets at this time, not starting a day. What happened?"

"This is my job now, Feli. I was a wild kid. So were a lot of us, weren't we? But now I train these kids. You know we're there to build a new social revolution in our barrio, Diez de Octubre."

I looked at him and was about to joke again. But I saw he was deadly serious. "It's good for discipline being here at 5:00 a.m. I know my place here now. It all fits in. I'm happy."

Isaac was bustling forward and didn't want to wait. The children's choir was beginning a sound check on the podium. Pedro's trabajadores were sitting on the ground and handing around cigarettes. But they weren't talking. Pedro was looking around anxiously.

"Look guys, when the TV cameras start, you put those out and get some smiles on your face."

Isaac had turned his back to the podium and was looking at the image of Che.

Vladimir

The first hint of dawn was a lightening above the Martí statue; nature being dramatic. The best lighting effects you could have. The lights didn't go out in the MINTEL building, but then suddenly the plaza was blacked out completely. There was total calm on the ground with a few nervous sniggers as an "apagón" had finally occurred in front of the TV crews. That would give the commentators some chance to show their imagination. A few truck drivers quickly switched on their lights near the national theater.

I returned to the computer, looking at that note from Istúriz. I read further the record of the last meeting of Saluki. Istúriz had highlighted a phrase that had come up: "La prensa oficial va ayudar." Local press involved. This is even more worrying than RC.

That was when the power surged and the computer showed urgent messages to shut down.

Out in the plaza there was a surge of noise. Heads were turning to the wall of the MININT building, and the metal structure of Che's face was now lit up. But now it was different. Instead there were the colors of the Cuban flag and the words "We are all Cubans. Await further messages."

Mateo

Fausto had arranged everything to perfection. We had a seat just to the right of the podium on some raised benches where the children's choir was gathering. Fausto was greeted personally by some of the stewards in red t-shirts. I stumbled on my way up the steps, but Fausto was relaxed and took his place confidently. "The Revolution does not like darkness," joked Fausto. "But you always get more out of light after the darkness. And of course we are like bats. We revolutionaries have special antennae; we don't need natural light to guide us."

We had been sitting for only a few minutes when the mural went out. I noticed that Fausto had been looking at his watch.

"Is that planned? I suppose that's a silly question in Havana."

"It's planned, Mateo," he said with a smile, yet his eyes looked heavier than ever. "Oh it's planned by someone, but unlike the speeches, I'm not sure by whom. We need to wait and see; there are some new ideas here. Just like the words over there."

I was feeling uncomfortable. This man was pulling some strings I couldn't see. I knew he was using me for something as well. He wasn't my friend, and not for the first time I had been taken as very naïve. By getting into the politics, I had been shown to be out of my depth. Fausto's invitation had another purpose than to say goodbye.

The veneer was thin. Fausto's eyes were now alive. His hands were clasped together, but he wasn't smiling. He looked at the podium where the work on fixing the microphone positions had stopped. He stood up and waved to a colonel. "Compañero Colonel, what's going on over there?" he said, pointing at the mural. The colonel scratched his head and seemed to think he should look busy. He rushed off to a control car.

The image then changed. An apple appeared on a head with the words "Guillermo Tell."

"This is all getting beyond me, Fausto. What has Guillermo Tell got to do with Moncada?"

"I know the answer to that, Mateo," said Fausto. "It's a song. I'll tell you about it later. It's about doing things yourself, you know. Not everything should be planned."

Felipe

Isaac didn't want to turn away. He just stood there looking at the mural and didn't say anything. Not everyone had noticed yet, but then the sirens started. The magic of waiting was gone. The wave had come in, crashed against the wall, and was in the past. For a few minutes there was chaos. Isaac was wet eyed and looking at his watch. Pedro's trabajadores were on their feet looking at the podium. Men in uniform started running down the council steps.

"I think we will not have much of a Moncada now," said Isaac, smiling. A military officer started testing a microphone. "Attention comrades. Attention comrades. The Moncada celebrations in Havana are suspended. I repeat: they are suspended. We have to investigate some threats to the homeland. There may have been some mercenary elements that have infiltrated our territory. This threat will be eliminated, and the Revolution will respond with courage and determination. Please seek instructions from your unit leaders, and the square here will be evacuated. The Revolution never panics, so stay calm as always. Viva La Revolución."

Víctor

The sirens were distant at first outside the terminal. They woke me from my nap. Those VIP lounge seats were really comfortable. At first I thought it was normal, maybe some traffic accident. There were a lot of convoys heading out of Havana for the regional celebrations that always happened later in the day. But then the announcement came to clear the protocol room immediately. I knew at that point that events were moving. I asked the protocol lady what was happening. "Change of plans, mi amor. It seems that some of the leaders have decided to go to Santiago instead. I guess they feel like a change of scenery."

My first thought was of course my main concern. "What about my plane? Are they taking it over?"

"I doubt it, compañero. They have their own planes. We know that here. They're always on standby. It will be routine."

Vladimir

I didn't know why, but it was the eighth floor in the MINTEL building that seemed to be attracting most of the attention. There was lots of thumping on the floor above me; banging and shouting with the chasers cornering their prey. It was strange that it was from the floor above me, because I hadn't seen any lights coming from there. The plaza looked calm with some cell phones taking pictures of the images that had been up now for only a few minutes. The power was back, and I switched on the TV in the MINTEL office. It was showing a rerun of the May 1st celebrations and a note that Moncada would continue later. I thought it was time to log off. Whatever I was doing was behind the game, so it was a good idea to leave. I felt excited. I still do.

The police took all the people they wanted from the eighth floor. And on their way down they stopped by on the seventh and took me in. Oh, and there was a gentleman called Carlos Istúriz with them; he knew exactly where to find me.

I can't say I expected Carlos would be so hands-on; you know, coming himself to do the arrests. But that was his style. I have to give him credit. He was accompanied by two bull-nosed heavies who couldn't wait to rough me up. Istúriz was upfront. Then it was just like a performance-appraisal meeting Felipe had told me about at the CBM. He was judging whether I had come up to standard. Carlos looked at me calmly and gave his verdict. "My friend, you made some wrong choices. You will know better next time what to do and when. The Revolution will take into account the tasks you have performed in the past, but disloyalty will always be punished."

I suppose that was how the prosecutor would be instructed to present my case.

Felipe

Of course Isaac knew all about this, and he knew when it was over. He knew when it was time for us to go.

I don't know why, but I was disappointed if that was supposed to keep us going for the next thirty years. I showed my cynicism to Isaac. "Okay, that was fun for two minutes. But is that all until next year? What you told me about Papa seemed a lot more exciting."

Isaac was calm as we walked away. "Felipe, these things start small. There are many sons of William Tell. It's a thinking game we are playing. This move we have here is to show we are thinking too. It needs another step. Just like with the camellos, we need to plan a move ahead. That's what your Papa said too. He did not get to that window without a lot of careful planning." The old man must have been disappointed in me.

We walked back toward the MINTEL building. The projected images had now been extinguished, and the television crews were taking some calm shots for the news bulletins. We took a shortcut across the back of the square, the side that heads off to the baseball stadium. There were several PNR cars parked, and a crowd was gathering with Pedro and his trabajadores at the front. Individuals were being led out of the building by plain-clothes security. Pedro was organizing the chanting of slogans by his group as each one was bundled into the cars.

"Mercenaries, traitors, you will never defeat us."

The police were flashing pictures of everyone standing and watching. It was, I guess, like the Oscars ceremony they used to show on Cuban TV. Everyone there was a celebrity. The pictures would be useful for later analysis. Isaac did not want to be photographed with them. We were turning to leave when Isaac pulled me back. "Isn't that your friend from the Lennon concert? You know Lennon concert/Lenin school. You said he is in computers."

Isaac was right. There was Vlado, and with him there was Carlitos. They appeared to be talking, and Carlitos had his hand on Vlado's shoulder. But as they approached the cars the big guys took over and pushed Vlado's head down. I couldn't stop myself from shouting. "Thanks for the Famous Grouse. Friends don't forget that." Vlado, you will know from the start of this story, kept himself in shape. And the big guys weren't expecting his push. Before getting into the car, he lurched up strongly and pushed them away. He wriggled free, caught my eyes, and made a V sign. Carlitos looked worried. He saw me too, but he said nothing. Isaac was already walking off.

It was obvious that Isaac didn't hear the words he expected from me. I don't think he saw me as bursting with ideas. He expected to see me fired up. "What do we do now?" was all I could manage.

"Think, Felipe. Think for yourself. I'm not telling you anymore. It's time for you to go home, to go back to work, to make up your mind. I enjoyed your company yesterday and today. You know where to find me now on my balcony. In any case there's nothing I can say if you don't believe it." He walked off, stripping off his red shirt to show his fading yellow.

The dawn was breaking, and everyone was figuring out how to spend the rest of the day. We convinced ourselves that we had been doing something by coming to the square. But we were deceiving ourselves. It had been done for us. We had just watched again, but now we had nothing. The show the others had put on was over. I wandered over to the bus terminal off the plaza just as the crowds were gathering in the hope of getting away. It was so long since I had left Havana. Why not get on a bus? No one would make me pay. Not on Moncada. It was something that appealed a lot.

A blue Peugeot pulled up behind the buses near the bus terminal. Carlitos wound down the dark windows. "Going anywhere in particular, Felipe? If not, I can get you on a plane to Santiago. That's where a good party is going to happen."

I looked around, and there were no police. Carlitos was alone. "Wait a minute, Carlitos. I may be a nothing at CBM, but I'm not totally stupid. You were with Vlado when he was arrested. You were the one he wanted to work with, and you betrayed him. There's no way I'm trusting you, Carlitos. Whatever I've done I have my pride. Right now Vlado ... he's no saint, but he doesn't deserve any of that." I started to walk off, trying to look calm.

Carlitos parked the car on the sidewalk and forced his way through the hundreds of people pushing to get on the buses. "Look, Felipe, this is our day. It's a day to make something and remember what we did. I know you. I know you like a son. If anyone has helped you through these last years it's me. Why would I betray you? I could have done that every day for the last five years. I could have kicked you out after Spain. I know you're a rebel, Felipe, but you can't just go on shrugging your shoulders and pretending you're a cool guy. Someone who's going to make a difference when you get around to it. I'll tell you about your friend later."

I sat down on the curb side and looked at Carlitos. He was cleaning his glasses and looking human again. Why was he bothering? I couldn't figure it out, but what else did I have to do? So that was why I got on the plane. Carlitos had a group going along from biotech, so he said it was okay. "You look terrible," said Carlitos. "You look as if you haven't been home for days."

Mateo

Fausto didn't apologize that the show was so short. Someone tried to get the children's choir to start singing. But they were more interested in getting some more pizza. There was going to be a lot of pizza left over. The kids were shouting and running up and down the stairs. No one seemed to be telling them where to go.

Fausto didn't seem to expect me to ask any more questions. "I can drop you back at the seminary, my friend. I have a plane to catch. You know there was always going to be another party in Santiago. All this will make it much bigger. So I need to be there."

I felt deflated and ashamed. I should have been with the kids in the hospital, with the old people who had no visitors. This was froth, bad novel stuff, movies that never stuck in the memory a minute after you left the cinema. All these people were wasting their time coming out to the demonstration, and Fausto knew it would be all over in a minute. It was probably the last time I would see him, but when he mentioned Santiago I thought I might as well satisfy some curiosity. I drew the sign I had seen in Haydée's room. "Since you're going to Santiago, I saw this sign and was wondering if you knew what this meant."

Fausto walked over to an arc light near the podium and looked carefully. "Padre, where did you get this?"

"I first saw it in the apartment belonging to a Cuban friend; you know, an ordinary Cuban, not in the government or anything."

"Mateo, this is not healthy, this sign. It can mean violence and chaos. Cuba has seen enough division and fighting. It has led to families setting brother against sister, separated by oceans, and it all was for nothing."

"I'm sorry. I had no idea. But these people are not violent, Fausto. I know them pretty well."

"Padre, I'm not sure you know them that well. We must never let our country get into the hands of these people. We struggled for peace, and now we don't kill each other anymore. We must never accept that again. Never. Whatever the cost, we must never go down that route."

"Good luck in Santiago, Fausto. I will remember our conversations."

"Cuba owes you a debt, Mateo. I know that your friends in Santiago will as well. Keep us in your prayers." With that he bustled off, still carrying his briefcase.

Yoel

These long hours in the van I never liked. Roads in our island could only go so far, and nothing ever surprised you. The van smelled bad and sticky from too many pieces of stale food, too many sweaty bodies. The air conditioning had never worked. In any case you never discovered anything new on these roads. Most of the road signs were stolen so people could use the materials, so you might as well have been anywhere. Then I was worried about the permits. There's no way the police in the Oriente would buy my story. I was tired. It had been a long time on this deal, and I had lost my brother. My kids were asking why I didn't come home. Now this mess I had got into, driving a van halfway across Cuba during the night.

There was virtually no traffic after Las Tunas. Some kids were piled in a truck heading north. I shouted at them just to hear a voice, "Hey where are you guys going at this hour?"

"Amigo, there's nothing like Playa Uvero at dawn. You should try it. Get out of that bloody van and live a little. Everyone will be at Moncada. We'll have it to ourselves. Just like we always dreamed of."

My life hadn't prepared me for this. You know, this was really big. Before I had always been in small things that made me feel that I was in charge. But now I was a stupid overgrown kid who happened to have his own kids. I missed having Abel to blame. What did I ever do that was serious? I looked back at what I had in the van. Who were these guys who needed this so badly? Santiago, Cuba's hero city, July 26, 1953. I didn't know a soul out there.

I read César's instructions again. The Moncada barracks. Dawn was just breaking as I entered the city. Just half a day since I had found Abel. I hadn't a clue what there was in Santiago apart from the Moncada. Thank goodness they had chosen the railway station to meet. Between the station on Menéndez and the *fábrica de tobaco* there'll be a red Lada with some broken lights. He'll be parked by the roadside. Just slow down and get out of the van to check the tires, and he'll drive out. Follow him. It will be about three kilometers, and then you will meet somewhere to drop off the crate.

CHAPTER 25

Laura

I woke up with Flavio. Of course I felt embarrassed to be in a tourist hotel, the first night I had ever spent away from home. Yes, that is true. Really away from home. That is what I thought of. I wanted to get out of there. Everyone was headed for Moncada, and I wanted to be there too. That was the excuse I had to use to leave. Flavio, of course, found out that Moncada was cancelled or something like that. Everyone in the Melia lobby knew that by the time he had had his full American breakfast. He had three more days on the island, so he didn't even suggest we meet up again. I walked out of the lobby with the security guard's sarcastic comments. "What's the problem, mi amor? Wouldn't he pay for your breakfast as well? Cubans eat beans and rice, don't they? Get back to reality."

Overnight Havana seemed to have changed. I walked out into my town, and it was different. I got a cab. It was all the driver would talk about. "Did you see the stuff up at the plaza? Trust me to miss it. I was working all night. Just imagine seeing that message over Che. I'm scared, compañera, I want to tell you. But excited as well, un poco. Who knows now?"

I went straight out to Miramar. Familiar things you cling to. It was good to see Edy the guard. I told him I had had to

344

stay all night at the airport because some flights were delayed. He seemed to buy it. "Oh, chica, you just missed a call. It was the *novio*; you know, Felipe. He said he was getting a plane to Santiago."

"What? That must be a mistake, Edy. He can't be. He never goes anywhere. What did he say?"

"He just asked where you were and said he missed you. That's it. Oh, he said to tell you he was with someone from the CBM and that it was his phone he was using. He asked me not to forget to tell you."

It was true what I felt. Everything was changing. For once Felipe had done something I didn't understand.

Víctor

Max had never told me what was in the crate. He said the fast boats had never brought things in before and it was important to get it right. This was his brilliant new idea. At first I assumed it was arms, but I knew Max wasn't that dumb. And with his contacts he could get plenty of arms. No, Max was doing something that he had never tried before, and like a good military man, he didn't need to tell me because I didn't need to know. Sitting on that plane to Santiago, of course I thought about it. I knew I would be coming back that day, but I was not sure what we would all find. Max and I, we didn't really agree about anything, but I guess Max was probably the person who I wanted to be with on that morning. Just in case in Santiago.

Besides, there comes a time when you want to be on the side that is going to win. I thought Max was a winner, and he had waited a long time to get out of his dull existence at Pinar. That couldn't ever be what Max wanted. The way he had dealt with our colonel in Manzanillo, well that showed there was more to this man than drying some old leaves for months. But what could Max possibly want that he didn't have? I guess it was the feeling of doing something. And Víctor, they will say, he could

346 MONCADA—A Cuban Story

anticipate, you see, how the wind was blowing. Of course Víctor, that wise old bird, knew all along. And my sons would brag one day that their dad was in on it. You know what it feels like to be smart and inside rather than dumb and outside.

The muchachos in front of the Moncada would be ready for trouble. Santiago would not be a pushover. Max knew what he was up against. But the big thing he knew was that Santiago would be the centerpiece, not just a sideshow. The guy who was supposed to be number one in Santiago was Ricardo Contreras. He'd been wanting to do something like this for a long time; you know, a speech before thousands. Not like mine for volleyball games. Contreras saw this as his big chance. A big shot from Havana. He would be marked out as a talent to be watched, and deep down that's really all he wanted from us. We knew that Moncada was the day to make the impact. Something had to go on after the Havana party collapsed, and there couldn't be a second catastrophe on Moncada day. Santiago was the home of Moncada after all. It was unthinkable to have no TV, no ceremony, no marches, no speeches. That could only be because of some war or at least a hurricane. And any Cuban knows that hurricanes on July 26 are pretty rare. You might as well expect snow.

So my first job in Santiago was to contact Contreras' people. They were everywhere already, because the guy liked the limelight. The ceremony was due at eleven o'clock, and the Santiago people wanted to show off. "Here is the spreadsheet for arrivals, the rice growers, the fishermen, the Slovak solidarity band. That gap over by the parking lot—that's for the cement workers' musicians from El Salvador."

I had to come in and knock heads. The whole scenario had changed. Contreras was now the big item, not just one face on a parade. He would be making the real speech for the whole of Cuba, and these guys from Santiago had to accept that the other speeches from the party secretary, the leader of the pioneers, and the Santiago union of agricultural workers would all be scrapped. Contreras had settled all the timing with the Council of State. The TV commentator was tearing his hair. "Don't worry, you can just let the guys come on and speak. No one really cares if they all say the same thing."

Vladimir

I think those moments when I saw Felipe were what kept me going. It was not just that I saw him. It was because I did so well in that moment I was out of the shadows. I was there saying exactly what I meant to say. I hit that guy. They, or someone, would remember me. It was spontaneous, without fear, and I didn't regret anything.

We were told that the connections you make in Cuba never lose their value. The bonding of the Revolution lasts forever. I was still proud of that, and they always told me the Lenin school has people everywhere, including in jails and in courts. I thought a few phone calls should sort it out. Anyway it was certainly a day for learning. The guards didn't care what I said about my connections. They said that everyone tried that one. The guy on the stool outside our row of cells said he hated everyone from Havana and that they deserved what was coming to them. "Señor Vladimir—he called me señor—you sound from your name like you came from a good communist family. We'll see how good a communist you are now. We'll see how well you live up to your name."

Yoel

I remember that the red Lada looked cheerful and bright even though the sky was heavy as dawn broke. César had chosen well. Nothing on that street stood out as strange. It was dull and dusty in the dawn. The shuffling figures checking for food in the rubbish, the bicycles carrying chickens from the campo, the children kicking a tin can across a derelict railway line. A priest hurried down the track checking his watch, looking late for Mass.

As César had said, there were no words. I got out of the van to check the tires. The driver of the Lada threw a cigarette out of the window and started the engine. I felt that the end of my job was near. Havana seemed a long way away, but the return on the investment would be the best thing that I had ever done. I had thought about Abel's share. I would give some to Yamelis. That was fair and would be okay for the business. There would be no need to tell her where it came from.

There were three guys and a woman in the Lada, and they didn't look around but watched me in their mirror. The station was busy as the train from Havana had just arrived, but I doubted that César had calculated this. Train timetables were something that only existed in Switzerland and not the Caribbean. But the masses of people streaming out made me feel better.

We drove to some assembly depot for trucks and agricultural machinery. I think they just needed some heavy-lifting equipment for the crate. It was down a hillside and opened up onto a basketball court, which was overgrown with weeds. I noticed that there were several crates of the same size and color on the court. The two guys at the back walked across to an old lifting truck and drove it over to the van. "Open up, compañero," they said with no frills. "We'll be done in a minute; then get your arse out of here." They knew what they were doing. They stacked the crate on top of two others. It fitted perfectly.

Felipe

Carlitos seemed keen to apologize. It was as if he was trying to regain some self-respect. He suddenly remembered who he was and who I was. The pilot had just told us to prepare for takeoff. We were number two in line. Carlitos asked for his phone back and switched it off. There were plenty of other high officials doing the same. They enjoyed showing their new models to the rest of us.

"Felipe, I have thought a lot about your best interests since you came to the CBM. I am sure you know that. These are times when we need men of ideas and original thinking. You are part of the new Cuba. We are in a maze now, and we will need some good guides to get out of it. It is important to keep active, not to get side-tracked, and to be vigilant."

"Carlitos, you sound just like you did at our corporate meetings. Are you trying to get me to confess to something, like that I was working with Vladimir? What are you trying to say? I have tried to bring my work to some biological conclusions, but you stole my article, and now someone has stolen my research papers. Everywhere we are stopped by some new barriers. You're right—we live in a maze. One day I guess we'll probably find a way out. But right now I don't think my heart is in it."

"Felipe, you need to leave the CBM and Calle Jalisco. Look around you. You have seen with Vladimir that life is complicated here. He was brave but not very clever. You are better than that, Felipe. You have showed that in spite of everything you can be loyal. I have never doubted your commitment to CBM. Oh, and by the way your papers are safe. I will let you have them next week."

I had my chance. There were no longer any barriers; I was talking to Carlitos as a Cuban. "Carlitos, I don't believe what I am hearing. You are now telling me you stole my papers as well as the article. If this is the new world order you are creating, I think I'll stick with the old. You treat me like some puppet you can play with as you wish. You have betrayed my friend. How can I trust a single word you say? I must have been mad to get on this plane."

Carlitos smiled. "Frustration, Felipe. You feel frustrated, but that is nothing new. Getting on a plane to Santiago shows that you have come to the end of this road. You have nothing else to do. You can now choose again. It's because you feel the pressure, Felipe, that there's no longer the easy way out. In Santiago you can't just wander the streets and hang out in bars. We are there to play a role. That's your first real test, Felipe. All that has come before is nothing in comparison. I will be with you."

Mateo

I had just returned from the plaza. "Is that you, Mateo? This is Haydée."

"Yes, this is Mateo. Haydée, where are you? How can I help you?"

"Look, I'm sorry we've been so much 'molestia' to you these last days. I think this may be the last time we talk. Cubano – you know Héctor's brother who came with me to see you in Havana. Well, he's now made his decision."

"Decided what? Haydée, you sound nervous. I don't think this is wise to be talking on the phone. Not at all wise. I have just returned from the plaza. Odd things are happening here. Everyone is nervous. That is all I can say."

"Mateo, that's okay. It's just so you know we will be involved in what will happen in Santiago. It will not happen like you fear. It will show we have decided to be peaceful. It will show that we forgive. I know you have prayed for us. I hope your prayers will be answered."

"Haydée, I am pleased that you have called. I think Santiago has now become the center of attention. I have no idea what is going on, and I will keep praying. At Moncada you realize how many people must be involved to create a movement, to convince people to think in one way."

Haydée didn't seem to like that. "That's not possible, thinking the same way. Cubano has said that he's broken with his brother. We don't know what they will do. We're different. But we tolerate each other. That's the important thing. You know we …"

"Haydée, what?"

"We will try something for Héctor."

"Yes, I understand. How are things in Santiago right now?"

"It's looking like a beautiful day," said Haydée, recovering her voice.

Yoel

I had come all that way. It was still early in the morning. I needed to rest, so I thought I'd find somewhere to park near the Cuartel de Moncada. You know, I'd never seen it, and I guess every Cuban should. It would be something to tell the kids about. I didn't need to get back to Santa Clara until the evening.

So I found a place near the Santamaria park. I got out and walked to a bench away from the traffic. I didn't care if the police would start asking for the documents. I was tired, and I was sleeping in seconds.

Felipe

Two Moncadas in one day. It was absurd after all these years. Now I was alone in a city I didn't know with a man I had never known other than as a designer of the system that controlled my life. He was saying he wanted me to forget everything he had told me before.

We were met by a convoy of black Mercedes that came to the side of the plane at Santiago. Carlitos said he wanted a car on his own with me, and no one seemed to question that.

We were taken to an official guest house for a "merienda" to keep us going through the morning. The food they had prepared was for the size of an army, and of course they knew there would plenty to take home afterward. We ate and drank for over an hour. Carlitos was in high spirits. "You should have seen those pathetic animals we found in the MINTEL building in the Plaza. I have never seen such a bunch of clowns, thinking they could pull off a trick like that."

He took some more ham and cheese and poured spoons of sugar in his coffee.

A lady in uniform saw me sitting on the side. I was too tired to eat. "Can I get you some coffee, muchacho? You have a long day ahead."

"I've never seen food like this. I'd like to take some home for the kids."

"You have kids already? You are so young."

"No, no, I mean my little brothers, you know."

"Here I'll make sure there's a bag for you to collect. Compañero Istúriz here will come back after the ceremony. It's all going to be short anyway, after that circus in Havana. I think the guys down here are a little nervous. The police have now been called in from all over the Oriente. Whatever happens, don't forget the food."

Víctor

Max came into the gathering crowds looking for his crate. I know he was, but he was talking about other things, trying to look in control. He was using his Veterans of Africa ID to get through security and was soon surrounded by old guys in uniform. Max was spinning his tales. He was talking to a young major who'd just been training some army unit in Mozambique. "Let me tell you, this movie you're about to see is the best ever about the revolutionary struggle to where we've come today! You'll never have to go back to Africa."

Contreras's people were in full flow. This was his big deal. His assistant was a young man with cropped hair who looked as young as my kids. "The minister is a strict timekeeper. He is resting at the moment. He will be starting his speech at exactly 11:00, and the film will start at 11:30. Make sure there are no problems. This is live on national TV, and this is Santiago's

Moncada. Go test the sound system one more time. You need to make sure the backdrop catches those bullet holes in the wall."

Okay, Contreras had received his payoff. Of course he knew that it would only be Santiago that would get the national coverage. He expected everything else to fail, and then he could claim the credit. I don't know why Max trusted Contreras. Maybe there was nothing and no one else and he hoped for some senior job in security after it all. I'm sure he didn't want money. Max wanted to stretch himself. What else can you do when nobody cares about your ideas anymore?

Moncada was in any case just a day when some people like Max tried to get on a platform. It was talk, waving flags, nothing real. Just another mobilization of the masses, but no one thought of it as a way to change anything. Not in our group. We'd done the people-trading stuff, so that was over. It was time to try something else. The Manzanillo colonel was gone, but we knew that the party people were in the mood to trade for something. Sometimes when people with power saw that you had some too they would bring you in and do a deal. That was how it worked. We were now on the ground, and the Revolution needed us.

Laura

That morning we all kind of forgot about the normal things. Your life is only normal, family and friends, when you know what's happening. The expected gets you through a lot, but once you see through the door you realize that everything might become different. More than that, it even should become different. I had never known anything different.

I wasn't going to watch the Moncada TV from Santiago. It might as well have been in a foreign country. But I wanted to see what the foreign news people were saying about Havana. We just had rumors. You know, I was proud of what we did as Cubans in the world. We'd sent doctors to other countries and all that. But what was happening now in Cuba? We would never know until after it was over. There was a doctor I knew, David, who treated my tourist groups for sunstroke. He had his office in Siboney with Internet access, so I stopped by with my five dollars. David said he couldn't stand to go onto the Internet because he was waiting for an e-mail he knew would never be there. He never said what it was. But he was probably involved with some of his tourists, which would make life pretty complicated. David changed his password every day so his clients couldn't use more than their allotment. He was a good businessman and not a bad doctor. He will be running his own private clinic one day.

So were the foreign journalists saying anything different from my taxi driver? This is what I remember. BBC, AFP, and CNN had been told by unnamed diplomatic sources that Cuba was in a state of confusion. Cuban security was not able to explain who was behind the prolonged national TV outage and the messages projected on the Che mural in Havana. A government spokesperson, Minister Ricardo Contreras, interviewed in Santiago de Cuba, said that all the hysteria was generated by the foreign media.

"It is all ridiculous. There are always criminal and antisocial elements in Cuba who want to make a show, but they are there to amuse the rest of us serious people. The Cuban government is totally in control of national security. We are here to reveal the hypocrisy of the neoconservatives who claim to respect human dignity, but their life is a record of selfishness, greed, and individualism. This is the why we fight our continuing revolution."

The BBC said that Minister Contreras would now be the key speaker at the celebrations in Santiago, which had taken on a special significance.

Felipe is in Santiago. That was why he has gone.

Felipe

We walked into the garden of the protocol house. Carlitos was looking at his watch. He wasn't speaking.

"Why have we come here? I assume it's for something pretty important, but I'm sure you've got a return flight to Havana. Tomorrow the CBM opens again. You have lots of plans to travel. You have a car. You eat well."

"I have my own reasons, Felipe, and I hope they are not purely selfish. But we have waited, and not everything we have been promised is happening. In fact, we see the same problems and frustration we had ten, twenty years ago."

"You don't know how things will be, but you have your own reasons. Isn't that selfish, like a kind of vanity? How do you know if anyone at all agrees with you? What if everyone else did the same as you?"

"It's like being in a family but never getting to meet the people who sit at the dinner table. We had a sick leader, but we are not told where he is or what disease he has. Then they call in a Spanish surgeon because we Cubans are not good enough to treat him. After all these years, we are not good enough for that. Medicine and the Revolution. What does that say? We are part of it but just have to accept it. The problem is how we get a place at the dinner table without destroying the family and breaking the furniture in the house."

"Okay, Carlitos, tell me about these wonderful ideas. By the way, did Vlado not agree with you on something? Is that why he's locked up?"

"Vlado has played his part, and if we do what we want he won't regret it. I give you my word."

"So I guess being here with you means I'm not exactly safe either?"

"Come on, Felipe, you can't go through life just wanting to feel safe. I haven't done anything like this before, so I have much more to lose than you do."

Carlitos got a call on his phone. He walked back into the house to take it. He wanted me to be part of his plans but not part of everything.

It was time to head to the square. We used the same cars that had taken us from the airport. Carlitos did not say anything to the driver, who knew where to go.

Yoel

I was awakened by security and asked for my papers. The park had filled up with brown and green uniforms and Cuban TV vans with satellite dishes. It was 10:30.

I checked my van. And then I saw why there were so many police. At the opposite side of Santamaria, a big banner with a strange sign was being torn down. A group of muchachos was face down on the floor. Another group was lined up against a wall. I joined a crowd gathering to watch the process. A tourist with his children seemed to get caught up and had his camera snatched off him by a young guy who wasn't in uniform. In about a minute all the people, men and women, were herded into a convoy of vans with no windows.

I stayed back and said nothing. The place was cleared, and I could hear the noise from across the park, the chanting of crowds and bands playing military music. I heard a sudden fluttering sound behind me as a group of kids was running to the square waving their flags. It was nice; they wanted to go. This was kids making a party.

I was following the kids when I saw a tall black guy come from behind a tree. He asked in a low voice. "Amigo, I can tell you're not G2. Just nod if I am right. Have they all gone? Sometimes they stay to check." I nodded again.

"Why did you trust me?" I asked the guy.

"I saw you sleeping, and they asked for your documents. You are a friend. Am I right?"

"Friend?" I said. "You don't want me as a friend. My own brother has just killed himself in Havana. I am trying to make money out of other people's bad luck. I am the last person to trust with anything."

"So why are you in Santiago? This is a big day for us here."

"Oh, it's a long story. I guess it's best to say I was asked to deliver something and then I'm heading back. So it was nice to meet you. Stay safe; it looks as if those poor guys will not be enjoying the party today or on any other day soon."

"The next hour is important. The police think they have the whole group. That was part of the plan. But they are wrong."

"Look, I don't know your name, and perhaps it's better I don't. I really have nothing to say about plans. I have a job to do here. I did it, and then I have to get back to other things in Santa Clara. So I have a busy day ahead. If you escaped from that lot, I wouldn't push your luck. You should get out as fast as you can."

The man seemed to have no doubt what to say. "We have all done enough escaping. You are Cuban, my friend, maybe even younger than me. I'm staying around, and so should you. You will not regret it."

"This smells like politics, and I'm afraid, my friend, that's not for me. Leave the running of the place to others like we always have. That's okay. Well, it's not okay; I accept that, because I complain a lot. But realistically, why waste your time? Do something for yourself."

"What we have here is being done for ourselves, amigo."

Felipe

The kids seemed happier here than in Havana. Maybe because they hadn't got out of bed so early and they never expected to be waving their flags for the TV. I thought the TV guys seemed grumpy, as they thought they'd have the day off.

The producer came up to Carlitos. "Compañero Director, we need someone to fill in before Contreras. We have been told to broadcast for an hour in total. There's no one else from the Council of State, so you are next in line. Just give us the usual historical stuff; you know, like you were doing in Havana when the TV had its little problem."

Carlitos was surprised and seemed worried. "You really want my face up there. I'm not sure. I think you need something fresh and new." He turned to me and put his hand on my shoulder. "Here is a very smart young member of the CBM. He is one of the Revolution's brightest scientists, and it is his first visit to Santiago. Compañero Felipe Triana. He will give you a new angle. I'm happy to introduce him."

The producer was not amused. I could see that he was impatient and wanted everything settled. He looked at me and rolled his eyes. "Okay, but he looks like shit. Take him off to get him cleaned up. I'll get fired for having some tramp talking to the country. Don't you mad scientists ever sleep? And listen to me, amigo. Don't screw this up. It's important. Mostly for you. Stick to what you know about and say there's plenty of hope for the Revolution, okay?"

So that was how I was given the opportunity to talk to Cuba. Carlitos didn't know about this in advance, I was sure. He was improvising, and so was the Revolution. In any case it would be better than sitting around another hour waiting for Contreras.

An assistant took me to another "protocol house" and offered me a shower, soap, and coffee. I hadn't used a mirror for a while, and I could see that the producer was right. I looked terrible. The Malecón had left my clothes covered with salt and mud. Of course since I spoke I have had time to think what I should have said. But then I only got one shot. Like Papa said about music, you should leave the listeners wanting more.

I was away from the square for the final minutes, so I missed seeing a lot of what was supposed to be happening in Santiago. I think that Carlitos was playing for time. Maybe he thought that nothing in which I was involved would matter. It would all be washed away in the deluge.

Yoel

The man had gone. He wasn't the only thing the police had missed. As I wandered toward the Cuartel, there was a cloth flag or banner that had been blown against a bush. I picked it up and saw that there was a strange symbol with an SP and a number seven through it. I went back to the van and stuffed it in the back. It would be a souvenir of Santiago for the kids. These people were strange here. Imagine getting arrested before a party where there would be free pizza.

Laura

I said I would work on Moncada day; maybe it would clear my head. Alex, my boss, said he could use some help with a group of tour operators at the Riviera who had been trouble from their first day. I headed down, and Alex was despairing that they would ever be on time. He was in the Riviera bar waiting for them to come down for breakfast. Yes, it was 10:30, but tour operators knew how to live, especially when someone else was paying for the hotel. The coffee was good, and I was just pleased I wasn't in the place where Flavio was staying.

The barman was talking to anyone who would listen. "Oh well, it's a shame the excitement's over for another year. Moncada, that stuff. I think of the Che picture; someone put it on Youtube. Cell phone pictures. I can't wait to see it."

"You think they won't block it," said Alex. "Of course you'll never see it. Don't talk about it anymore, amigo, not if you want to keep your job. You think everything is different now. Well, I'm sorry to say it isn't. Just look at the TV."

The barman tried another line, "I wish I was a tourist in this place. I once saw the bedrooms here, you know. I had to take up some room service. I ..."

"Shut up. Just look at that screen," I shouted and put my hand over my mouth in total shock.

"Okay, it's Moncada in Santiago. Didn't you know the country will never miss its chance?"

"Turn up the sound, can't you?" The barman looked shocked and did what he was told.

It was Felipe, wearing a red t-shirt.

"Well, we are here today with a visiting delegation of scientists from Havana. They have come to see the outstanding achievements of the Revolution in the Oriente. One of the best young scientists in Havana is Compañero Felipe Triana, who is described as an expert in animal vaccines."

"Good morning, compañero, and welcome to Santiago."

"Good morning."

Felipe

I was thinking of my papers that Carlitos said he'd return to me. I was thinking of Mama at her window. Why did Papa make her that little chair? And a volleyball game that had happened. That's the truth; that's what I was thinking about. It's not me trying to be clever.

"Compañero Triana, what is it that you see the Revolution has contributed to science?"

"My life has been determined by the Revolution. My mother and father's lives have also been ..."

Víctor

We were waiting inside the Cuartel with a TV screen to watch. The crowd was respectable enough for the camera angle behind Contreras. I could hear the TV producer talking as they zoomed in on the podium. "Yes, sure, that's good enough." Max was in the Cuartel now, but he didn't talk to me. Of course not. The intro was the role of Santiago in the Spanish surrender against freedom fighters in 1898. A close-up of the document they signed.

"Then of course," said the commentary, "in 1902 the U.S. imperialists colonized Cuba again until the process of liberation began here in Santiago in 1953. Santiago has been a center of learning over the decades, and we have shown that we are the driving force in new approaches to agriculture. We are here today with a visiting delegation of scientists from Havana, and they have come to see the outstanding achievements of the Revolution in the Oriente. One of the best young scientists in Havana is Compañero Felipe Triana, who is described as an expert in animal vaccines."

I couldn't believe it. Oh no, the boy from Jalisco. Don't they know about Triana? Who's running this show? Triana could have been a leader; everyone knew that. He was unlucky. The kid always struck me as unlucky as well.

There was no doubt that the boy was confused. And so he talked about nothing but his family in some vague words that meant he wasn't thinking clearly. But it was that remark about the shirts that showed something. That was planted in Santiago. Everyone admired anyone who got out of Boniato. And I think the boy looked good; handsome, you know, like he had his life in front of him, optimistic. But it was overwhelming. He could never do much in three minutes.

Mateo

I didn't see the interview. Of course I've seen it since. But the impact is less because we know what happened. Felipe summoned enough bravery for the moment so that he can look back with pride. That is what I have told him.

Yoel

I didn't realize that Felipe was anywhere near Santiago. I didn't see his interview either. I wandered over to the square and found some pizza and water. It was a beautiful morning by then, and the mist had totally cleared. There was no humidity, and I remember that it felt fresh. Even the pizza was warm.

CHAPTER 26

Felipe

So I started to talk. First there were some questions to answer. "Yes, I have always loved science and the chance to join the polo and the CBM. It was a dream come true. I have used that position to stretch my mind and also to stretch the boundaries of knowledge in Cuba. I owe that to the Revolution. Life is about the discoveries we make. I have learned that from my family. They gave their lives to this Revolution. They believed in it, and they believed that they would discover something more about themselves. But then it changed. No one asked them anymore what they wanted. My mother sits today by a window looking out. She tries to discover what more there is in life. My father was behind bars looking out of a window in a jail not far from here. But he was determined to get out of the window. He wanted to discover something for himself. And do you know something? When he escaped he left nothing more than a yellow shirt. I see some in the crowd today. Moncada is about hope and inspiration in the past. But now we need new discoveries. New ideas. No more bars on windows. This year my generation of Cubans will…"

Víctor

The producer was steaming. "Get this bonehead off of my program! He's a piece of dung. Get Istúriz on; run some of the old Contreras footage—his trip to China; anything. Guantanamera. Get this idiot off right now!"

Felipe

No one seemed sure what to do with me. In any case where would I escape to? It didn't seem to matter much to me anyway. I said a few things and mentioned the yellow because I could see Isaac on his balcony watching that. Carlitos was looking busy with some of Contreras's people and left me alone. So I wandered off. I guess they were afraid of some foreign media filming me being taken away. The action they would take would be later.

Víctor

The producer had too much to worry about right then. Contreras and Max were talking and were not interested in anything about the boy. Max was smoking, which I assumed was nerves. He had told me his doctors would kill him first and then tobacco. He moved off to use his cell phone.

Contreras looked in a mirror. He had chosen to wear a suit rather than a guayabera. He adjusted his tie. "I'll speak for twenty-one minutes, and then the film."

Vladimir

Monday was my first morning in jail, but life had become just one long night. I was worried about who was looking after Kurt. I looked around the walls. Had everyone forgotten me? Felipe had seen me. The banging and obscenities were my entertainment at night. That was my punishment. A lot of people would be pleased not to see me in Playa. They would have already taken away all the laptops.

Felipe

Carlitos escorted Contreras to the podium. They marched to the music as both turned to pick up their wreathes to lay in front of the Cuartel.

The loudspeakers boomed: "Never forget the martyrs of Moncada. Never forget the martyrs of the Revolution."

Contreras was serious. "Today we have witnessed threats by enemy agents in Havana. This sort of sabotage and vandalism we have met before. Santiago and Santiagueros will never submit to attempts to disrupt the Revolution, and today in Santiago we have taken strong action against another group of antisocial elements."

Mateo

Clara was shouting to me in the seminary, "Padre, don't you know this gentleman, Minister Contreras? He is speaking on the television. Come. Come." I saw Contreras already into his speech.

Laura

I caught that look in Felipe's eye when he was confused. But then he revived, looked into the camera, and was confident again. Here was the man who smiled at me with those Malaysians. He was natural; he knew what he wanted to say. But I wondered why Felipe never said anything about what he was going to do. What use is a color?

The bar was filling with some Cuban staff now who were leaving their jobs in the kitchen and the laundry as news spread about what he had said. They wanted to see him, but Felipe had gone. Where would he go now?

Felipe

I don't think the police had been told to target the yellow shirts. I think they had something more in mind. Then I saw that a tall man with swept-back gray hair was handing out more yellow t-shirts from a cart. It looked like a barrow you would use in the tobacco fields. He was smoking a cigar. The yellow shirts were all over the square while Contreras was speaking, and the attention was growing. When he had given out everything he walked off.

Contreras was using his time. "Compañeros, the Revolution will enter a new phase. The Revolution will have new energy. We have shown today that Santiago is true to the spirit of the Cuartel de Moncada."

Mateo

The TV coverage was uninterrupted. I noticed the growing space of yellow shirts in a picture that was supposed to be showing the singing of a group of enthusiastic Santiagueros. It was unmistakable against the official red t-shirts. I figured that they had suddenly appeared during the Contreras speech so that the cameramen would not get instructions to turn it off. The world was watching Santiago.

I remembered the smooth Contreras in his office, giving instructions to Ileana. Here he was with the biggest of rewards, the biggest of tasks anyone could have. He was alone and making decisions for the country.

"Now we will show a dramatic reconstruction of the assault on the Cuartel behind me and new film that will chronicle the achievements of the Revolution. Never forget that this is the same Moncada where Batista's brutal police and army mercenaries oppressed the heroes of the Revolution."

Contreras moved aside, and the lights flashed on the screen. "Fotos de familia. Somos todos cubanos," came on.

Yoel

I knew it was time to head off. But this film was really weird. It was like a family scrapbook, not a Revolutionary propaganda film. I recognized photos of Frank País, Camilo Cienfuegos, Che Guevara.

And then we saw a set of images of old Havana with no violence, the pioneers in the fields, the music, the educators with children. But we also saw the prisons, the firing squads, the students from all countries at the Latin American medical school.

We saw the present. The film included parts of the crowd in front of the Cuartel wearing their yellow, and they responded with jubilation. They were being shown themselves. There was a close-up of the man I had seen in the park before the rally. He looked ecstatic.

Felipe

There were images of Chucho, Linares doing a double play, Juantorena running, even pictures of the CBM and the building of the polo cientifíco, the inside of Boniato, the singing of Silvio, Che at Santa Clara, Celia Cruz, Varela's songs at Karl Marx with the crowds chanting of "Libertad" and the vans of security outside, the final scene of Suite Habana when Lennon has the tear in his eye, the masses leaving in boats at Mariel, the Chevy truck at sea, the pictures of those who died "de ganas de vivir." Elián's mother, who did that; and Elián's father as the returning hero. Ochoa in Angola, headlines of his execution, the twenty-four who died in Grenada, the bodega with eggs at .25 pesos each, and the line that went around the block. Kindelán winning the Olympics. Martí of course. Father Félix Varela and the petition in his name. A café called Versailles in Miami, I think. The *paredones*, innocent walls used by the firing squads.

I had never seen a collection like this. Then they moved to the final sequence of still photos. One face I didn't recognize from the history books. It had the numbers 23 10 01 across his face. He was in prison.

Yoel

Contreras was looking around, wondering what to do. He looked lonely. The spotlights were still on, and he was sweating. No one could decide what was happening. The Revolution looked okay, but there was plenty that was not good for them. It was just that I saw so many other Cubans on the screen and I had never seen them before. I guess that was the idea. All those Cubans who would have never been part of Moncada. The choir didn't seem to be paying attention. But the yellow t-shirts were making a lot of noise.

Then I saw Carlitos; you know, the man at the CBM, where I delivered bread. He was talking to the guy who had had been handing out t-shirts. The cigar smoke formed a cloud above his gray hair.

Víctor

Well, this was pretty much a surprise to me. I hadn't expected Max to be delivering so many things in his famous crate. All that stuff about the colonel from Manzanillo; who knew what Max was really working on? Maybe he simply wanted to make some money and leave for Spain. It was his idea to use the fast boats to bring in his special equipment, and I should have asked him more about that.

Contreras looked threatened. He was slow to respond. It was some local party secretary who pulled the plug. He was on his radio, and the film was stopped just when they got to that image of the prisoner. Then it was back to the studio where the real action began.

I had noticed Max's BMW parked behind the Cuartel.

Felipe

I remembered that Carlitos had promised me my documents back. I think he said next week, but he hadn't mentioned any plan to meet me after this event. Papa had made it on national TV, and so did his color. But then Contreras seemed to realize what had happened. He took the microphone again.

"I am proud to announce that we have today in Santiago foiled another flagrant attempt to stab at the heart of the Revolution. The organization called SP7 has been eliminated, and its leaders will face justice."

With that he tore up a banner with some emblem on it, and the red shirts started cheering. Those in yellow did not attempt to move. Where would they go? They had after all identified themselves and their faces were on TV.

Control was returning because the police, like my food lady had said, had come in from all over the Oriente.

I saw the TV producer, who was walking away. "Well, my friend, when I got up this morning I never expected this. You have made my name, but I think I will wish I still had my old one." With that he hugged me and walked off.

Carlitos had gone. I was a kid from Havana in the Oriente a long way from home, and I didn't know where to go. But then I saw that the lady from the protocol house was looking for me. She had brought the food. The kindness of a Cuban I remember at Moncada.

"I thought you might get forgotten," she said. "You look as though you could eat a lot." And then I saw Yoel. It was almost as if he had delivered the food. But then it didn't seem that surprising after the rest.

Mateo

It was a spectacular film. It lasted just a few minutes. But it was put together so that each time you thought it was becoming political it came back to things every Cuban could accept. Fotos de familia, one family. If you haven't seen it, it sounds maybe cheap and sentimental. But it wasn't, and I couldn't bear for it to end.

When it did end it was hard to believe it happened. Contreras ripping up the banner seemed to restore reality.

That afternoon, I went to see the Trianas. Felipe's mother surprised me. She was angry, not proud. "Of course we saw Felipe. We always watch Moncada. I don't know what has become of that boy. Padre, how has he got in with such a bad crowd? He does not tell his own mother he is going to Santiago. He forgets his brother's volleyball final. He cuts off the best girlfriend he ever had. What for? So he can get himself talking on TV?"

"The image at the end of the film. Did that not have a special meaning for you?"

"Oh, Alberto would have loved that. Of course he always wanted to be on the big screen. He and that Isaac, the doctor, they would all have loved that. Now Felipe has shown he wanted that all along as well. They leave home and we never see them again. For what?"

Felipe

So we, Yoel and I, headed to his van. That was all there was. The police had plenty to deal with, but in any case where would we hide on an island?

Yoel was looking for the black guy in the yellow t-shirt, but he had disappeared. Carlitos's Mercedes was gone as well. So Yoel said I should come back with him. He had to go to Santa Clara, but I could get a ride from there. So Yoel was giving me a ride near the end of this story, just like at the start.

"I wish we knew more about each other's lives," said Yoel. "I think you did something really important today. But I don't understand it. I'm not going to tell you why I'm here. We have time to talk on the road to Santa Clara. But let's only talk of the future."

Víctor

Contreras seemed pleased to see me. I had played my part well—the senior official from Havana with hands-on experience. "Get onto Havana and tell those bastards there has been disruption here but everything is now under control. I am due to have a briefing with the police right away. I know they arrested most of the troublemakers. We need to close the airports. Stop the flights to Jamaica."

"Could we have a quick word?" I said.

"Later," said Contreras, "The Council of State will have our balls. We need to come up with something good."

"I think some people could not be trusted who organized what happened here. We've had this sort of thing before, Minister. In a week's time it'll all be forgotten. So will the yellow shirts." Old Víctor from Cerro. I had made a difference.

Yoel

Felipe was asleep before Cobre. I think it was around Las Tunas that the idea hit me. I could see that Felipe was down. I think it was Carlitos who had pulled one last trick on him. He thought he saw a way forward with Carlitos, and now there was nothing.

Mateo

The phone rang after I had returned from Jalisco. Contreras was speaking loudly.

"Padre, I am having a busy day, as you may know. I wanted to give you an answer to the question you put to me a few days ago. That was the whereabouts of a lady of your acquaintance, Sra. Haydée Sebastiano."

"Haydée, yes. I heard from her, but she did not say where she was."

"Well, I'm sorry to say she has been arrested. She has been involved with a terrorist group, the SP7. You may have heard reference to it."

Felipe

Papa on the screen. Me on the TV. It was looking bad. Was Carlitos really involved in all that? Had he used me on TV to protect himself? He knew about Papa. But he left me on my own with an old bread van.

Yoel was talking a lot about his kids and Abel. I never heard him say so much about family. He kept saying that he didn't understand what I had done. But it made him proud, and he couldn't have done it. And I thought of Papa's book and how he was never in our lives. The book was still there, but Papa wasn't. His photo was there, but he had lost his life. "Hay gente que se muere de ganas de vivir."

Yoel

Get through tonight, and life would be better. This would be the last thing. I would pay something to Yamelis and then go for a vacation to clear my thoughts. My kids needed a father now. I could make more perhaps as a tourist guide; you know, with French and French Canadians.

We reached Santa Clara before I mentioned it to Felipe. "You know we have a boat leaving tonight. It's all set up."

I was surprised at how Felipe replied. "Fine, Yoel. But how will I pay?"

"I can fix it through Miami. I can lie like I always do. I'll guarantee it. We have some others coming from Havana."

There was nothing from Felipe about what he would do at the other end.

Felipe

It seemed the only thing to do. It was a decision. It was better that way. It was better that I knew no one going with me. Make the decision. Jump out of the window; jump off the Malecón. Better never to go back to Havana. Yoel did not give me time to pick up anything. Thank you, kind lady from protocol. The food you had given was enough for two days. Is two days food enough? Two days is not long to watch and wait.

We circled Santa Clara. I think Yoel was checking that no one was following us. He had just enough CUCs for the last fill of diesel.

Yoel

César was waiting at the house in Santa Clara. The evening of Moncada and dark had just fallen. César had lit some candles. There was a power outage. "Maybe they had too good a party over at the Che mausoleum." Oscar was walking around, full of nerves and punching the old settee, which could not take any more. The manager in Orlando would be impressed.

Who would pay for Felipe? I still hadn't thought it out. That is business. The boat guy would know.

César said he had four more passengers from Santa Clara and looked inside the van. He threw in some water, some old t-shirts from the parade, and some rum. He wasn't as thorough as Abel, but I didn't know he would be so kind. "Who's your friend? Is he part of the deal?"

"I think so, but you never know until we get to the cayos."

"Yoel, I've seen this before. It's tough for them. We who stay here keep our different problems. But it's not a paradise over there, so I send them with some love from the family here. Anyway it's perfect weather to fly tonight," he joked, "except that we go by sea."

"I'm sorry for those guys in Santiago. They are saying that the reinforcements are sealing off the town. They've arrested a load of officials trying to fly to Jamaica. Some have already left. It doesn't seem that anything will change, which I guess is good for our business. So let's look on the bright side, Yoel."

Felipe had gone out for a walk. He said he wanted to take in the Cuban air. I saw that César was busy in the kitchen, trying to fix the fridge for one last bucket of ice. "César, I can see that you have a warm heart, amigo. I need to tell you that this new muchacho is a good friend of mine. I don't want you to screw him. Have you any spare money that could go around? This should not just depend on money."

César didn't hesitate. "Sure, Yoel. I understand. I can talk my way around that boatman from Yuma. He thinks we Cubans are stupid. We have some money from the trip in May. I owe you as well, Yoel, for taking the crate. There's nothing to stop us now."

Vladimir

The trial was set quickly. The guards seemed to be looking forward to it and described the details with great care. "You are one of the main plotters in Havana, so it will be high profile. You will have signed a confession, and for that you will be granted a lower-order sentence. You will have access to a defense lawyer, so those clowns from the international press will be impressed. In any case we will do the job properly in Havana. In Santiago they are rounding up hundreds. Don't know how Boniato will cope."

Felipe

I couldn't see anything on my walk that made me want to stay. I had been pulled and pushed around without any ideas of my own. Even the TV stuff was Carlitos's idea. Jalisco? Well, I wished for a lot of things for Jalisco. But do you never wish anything for yourself? I thought of the picture of Papa. I thought of Rafa and Tico growing up without me. I thought of Mama at her window waiting for the footsteps on the stairs. I had my book, but there were no more numbers to call, no more addresses to check. Isaac may be excited, but he would stay watching CNN. Now his entertainment and the yellow shirts were over.

I talked a little to Oscar. He helped me. He was thinking straight. "You fight your next fight. Don't think you'll get hit by the same punches as last time. You always learn in the ring and always think you can conquer. You must never have any doubts."

We picked up another four guys at Cárdenas and then a family at Redondos. Yoel was quiet. I never asked him any questions. The family was frightened, and Oscar knew how to behave. He lifted the kids to the sky. "There's nothing you can't reach." Oscar was a champion.

Yoel

Felipe was calm, but César looked nervous. I liked him now more than on the motorbike. He was smart but human. "What will you do with the money, my friend?"

"Oh, it's stupid to plan. In any case it's far nicer to look at it and count it than to spend it."

Víctor

It was a good job that guy did on the television. He soon got a grip on what was happening. We all returned to the protocol house and checked what had been shown on that ridiculous film. Then of course the filming of the crowd made them look even more stupid. Every wearer of a yellow t-shirt was recorded. And the stall that Max had put up was surrounded by the pioneers and trashed. Max had gone. Lucky for him.

I never really understood before how Contreras had reached where he did at the Council of State. But I had to admit that Contreras was good in the TV press conference. "I pay tribute to the heroic work of our loyal CDRs who responded with great efficiency. We will hunt down the traitors and their accomplices with the determination and valor that the Revolution has always shown."

I was called by the protocol lady to attend to the phone. The police had found a BMW on the road to Manzanillo. Before he got to Pilon, in fact. Yes, you know how dangerous that road is around there with mountains rising steeply on one side and on the other side cliffs plunging from the road straight down into the sea. The driver was an older man with gray hair who looked in good physical shape. He lost control of the car. The police would be checking it for defects.

I called to tell Contreras about the BMW. He simply said, "Good."

I'm pretty sure he hadn't known Max that well. Despite what he had said about military parades, Contreras never liked the military. He never mentioned the veterans of Africa in his speech. I was the one who brought Max in. Maybe Contreras knew I would be there to clean up the mess and he could get what he wanted. He seemed happy as the TV was replaying over and over the moment when he ripped up the banner.

Laura

No news of Felipe. I knew I should have been there to get his call. My phone at home had saved the number that he had used, so I tried it. The call was picked up by a man, and the voice said Felipe was not there. He would not say anything else. But I heard an announcer say something in Spanish about a flight to Kingston, Jamaica.

Felipe, it must be over now in Santiago. You can't go wandering around the streets there forever. Come back now and it will be the same as before.

Felipe

Yoel was looking at his watch. I'd never seen him doing that. It felt strange, but then I wasn't living my life as before. I was afraid, but I was more afraid to go back. I was excited to be in the van and going somewhere new. Laurita, I tried to call you. But you will know how much it means to travel.

I knew we were close to the rendezvous as César had turned off the headlights. I had never been anywhere as remote. In Cuba you are always with people and talking. Now we were sharing a water bottle, but we didn't speak. This time we were there to do one thing together, and then we would never see each other again. The trust we had to have was complete, but now it didn't matter what we said. Who could inform on us anymore because we were leaving?

We didn't stay alone for long. As we approached the cayo we had company. Another van appeared, and then another. They turned on their headlights. I thought César would turn around and try to run. But the kids started screaming, and he seemed confused.

Some men with guns but no uniforms came out of the van. And a small man with wispy hair and bad teeth.

"Hola Felipe. Your papa always asked me to look after you. I think this is not a good idea."

So Chino had left his mani selling and his guitar playing. I noticed as he came close to us that the smell of tobacco and alcohol had gone. He smelled fresh with even a touch of cologne. Oscar the fighter rushed at him, but three of the guys held him and pinned him to the floor.

César stayed calm and tried to reason with them. "Look, why do you want to stop these guys from leaving? It means that there's a dozen less mouths to feed in Cuba. It's their choice. They would pay you a little as well. Just pretend you didn't see us."

One of the guys had been searching the van. He handed something to Chino. "Colonel, look what we found. I think this is serious."

Colonel Chino. Who was he watching all those years at the CBM?

Yoel

Of course it was stupid to leave that damn banner in the van. But you know, what else did I have to show the kids? Who was I to know that the sign was anything special? No one had ever heard of those people. In any case we knew there was to be no money. How did they know about the rendezvous with that American? I still haven't figured that out. Well, it may have been something they found at Abel's. I just wonder. I should have spent more time there. After all he was my brother.

Felipe

We had stepped outside of Cuba, and we were no longer part of anything. We were punished for being alone. Think about it. The police, the courts, the press, the employers; they are all on the same side and not on yours.

Chino came over to me at the holding station. He looked odd in his clean shirt, using his cell phone. He didn't speak to Oscar. Maybe he was afraid of the boxer. "Felipe, I knew you were becoming bitter. It's time for you to be convinced about what we are building here. There's a place for an ugly old man like me. I didn't do this personally. I have good eyes and a passable voice. But I look simple. That's good. I have lived well here and done something I believed in."

"And Papa was wrong about you? But then I wondered why you were never on his list of people who would help me. Maybe Papa did know."

"Oh, Papa, that was a long time ago. I was with him. But I took the deal and he didn't. My new assignment was to watch Istúriz outside the CBM. You may be surprised, but we knew that he was involved in all this."

"So why didn't you stop it?"

"You follow a number of trails before you decide. We can always wait. But Istúriz was right about one thing. Moncada had to go on."

Laura

It was in early August that another letter arrived. This time the envelope was from Miranda. I could tell from her handwriting.

"I have now been reassigned to duties within Cuba. I have relearned some of the ways of the Revolution. I have found out where Felipe will be held so you can arrange to visit him. He is now a criminal of course. But one day he will have a chance again to contribute to the Revolution. He will be held at Boniato."

So Miranda tried but never left. Would she still be loyal to the Revolution or to me?

Mateo

I never heard from Fausto again. I think he left before I did. If I knew where he was I would have asked him to write something of this story. The rest of it was my attempt to show what happened in this strange week.

I write this as Felipe will be released tomorrow after serving his sentence of five years. I was told recently by an American friend that a Cuban scientist was on a chat show talking about some new vaccine discoveries. He looked calm and assured and was cleaning his spectacles.

I visited Felipe once, and he told me that his mother had been to see him. She left with him a small wooden rocking chair, which sits near Felipe's small window. Rafa was at university, and Tico was playing volleyball. I asked Felipe if he knew about Guillermo Tell, and he said he had thrown away the apple.

Haydée and Cubano. I think I agree with what she said. It was a really beautiful day. Contreras may have put in a word for them because he thought I would care. They have more time to serve because of the wilder people in SP7. Héctor should be out at nearly the same time as his sister and brother-in-law. But I worry about whether their strength will be sustained. I pray a lot for them. Peace and persuasion.

Víctor

I don't want to say anymore about this. I liked the boy from Jalisco, actually, and he would be better off now if he had not been misled by that traitor Istúriz. Contreras looked after me as he should have. In fact Contreras was on his way out before Moncada, and that was the reason for what he did. He didn't gain anything in the long term. He just stayed where he was, but he still attends his diplomatic parties. In fact he has surprised me. It has been good for me that Contreras is still there. He knows he should not forget me.

Felipe

Mateo has insisted that I have the last word. Well, probably Víctor did really, because his life did not change much. But Mama likes her yellow t-shirt. She sees a lot of Isaac. They walk Celia, the mestizo, together, and Isaac keeps Rafa and Tico fit. That's nice, and Isaac makes Mama happy.

"At least you are alive, Felipe. Whatever you did, you stayed alive. You have to be alive to do anything in life. Unlike your father."

She likes the Varela songs now as well, especially the "little dreams" that don't really mean much.

Five years has meant a lot of time to think about that week. Rafa is fine with me, and he loves telling the kids in the barrio about my three minutes on TV. Yoel, I know now, is my friend. I know he was prepared to pay for me. He lost his van but not his freedom, because I think he did another deal. He sends me pictures of Quebec he received from the French Canadian tourists he works with. And Vladimir. I am sorry now for not understanding him. We have no friends outside Cuba, but now we know we have friends inside. Laura, let's see. This country can be good for both of us. Mateo changed the names of Víctor and Contreras for this story, but the rest of us didn't. I make my own notes now, and no one wants to steal them. I have forgiven Carlitos for the documents. He taught me far more than some vaccines. Thank you. Thank you, Mateo. My friends are still in Cuba.

One week, one day like that. It doesn't mean that everything is different. But it's just as true that not everything is the same. Moncada in 1953 was a failure as well.